# HAD WE LIVED

## After Captain Scott

YouCaxton Publications
23 High Street, Bishop's Castle, Shropshire, SY9 5BE
www.YouCaxton.co.uk

Cover: Detail from Ninety-Four Degrees in the Shade by Lawrence Alma-Tadema
© The Fitzwilliam Museum, Cambridge.

ISBN 978-0-9571454-5-0

Printed in Great Britain

# HAD WE LIVED

## After Captain Scott

by

# Richard Jopling

*www.richardjopling.com*

# PART ONE

It was during that terrible second winter, when every hour and every day seemed to be the same and the longing was part of the darkness that never seemed to go away, as though Cherry had been plunged into perpetual blankness and the world was intensely cold and bleak and all that really mattered was dead. Then they heard the dogs 'singing', a high-pitched, primeval cry from another world and Cherry's heart leaped for joy in anticipation of the one thing in all the world that would bring back the light of life. They were transfixed and staring at the door. Cherry stood by Debenham and Deb's face was ghastly white. 'My God!' muttered Deb. 'It's them.' There was dread in his voice as though he feared the arrival of the five missing men, who by now could be no more than emaciated and frozen spectres.

Cherry saw the door push open and Scott came through, knocking the ice from his body with his mittens and he looked straight into Cherry's eyes just as if he knew everything. Then came Bill, Bill who could never change no matter what and his blue eyes danced to see them all and he allowed himself a smile of recognition. Then finally Birdie came in, still wearing that ridiculous green hat and he just shook with laughter. Cherry couldn't move, he desperately wanted to rush forward and touch them to feel their life but he couldn't move. They counted three. Taff and Titus were not there but then they never could have made it and, as he thought that, Cherry knew that none of this was real. It seemed so real and brought him such intense happiness but the moment would pass. The dream slipped back into the darkness and the cold light stole back painfully into his brain. They had not lived and neither could he. The door would stay closed and the darkness and the cold would return to claim its own.

Cherry would remain suspended in the thrall of the ice for all time.

# BEFORE CHERRY (BC)
## Balte Spruit 1879

Once there was a great empire. It was the biggest and boldest and best empire ever known to mankind and it bathed a quarter of the earth's surface in a glow of pink-enlightened light. As far as Major Apsley Cherry was concerned it brought the true values of England to uncivilised parts of the world and gave responsibility to Englishmen, in particular, to empower their civilisation across sub-continents and continents, from Cape to Cairo. The major knew that it could have its darker side and he had seen some of that when he had served in India but as he was fond of remarking, 'You can't make an omelette without breaking a few eggs.'

Now with the 'good old' corps, the 90th Light Infantry, he had been in The Eastern Cape for some time and it seemed to him that he had been in the business of breaking eggs for a very long time and he yearned for the green, rural heartland of that great pink empire and for the woods and farmland of his native Surrey. As he looked around him all was browned by the relentless sun. In the Cape summer he saw the swallows dipping and sweeping across the veldt and he longed to send a message with them on their return to England. He thought of the swallows which nested at the back of Lamer and idly wondered if these African swallows could be bred in the very barns he used to play in as a boy and on his visits to the great house. It was strange how often his thoughts wandered to Lamer and away from his duties as a soldier. Lamer was not his home and never would be but his visits there to his aunt had inspired him and it seemed to him now to be a place of dreams. He thought of the old house with its ivy clad walls but more of the garden and grounds. He thought fondly of Hobbs, the head gardener, and the times he had taken the visiting brothers down to the stream and over to the lakes so that the boys could swim in the roach-rich waters. Hobbs had some wonderful stories that he used to tell the boys that gave a very fanciful account of how Lamer and its park had all come about. There was one in particular that made him smile whenever he thought about it that involved some strange old people, the very first English, wading up the stream to the south of Lamer and establishing a colony on the bush-surrounded common.

Africa seemed to him to be an empty world, devoid of all that really mattered, a silent, dried up world as far as the eye could see. It had been some time since his last leave and before that his youth seemed like a distant memory, a memory punctuated by the liquid song of the nightingale as delicate and precise as the goldcrest nest he had once found in a conifer. Whenever he thought of England it was always late spring and filled with a sound as pure as a blackbird but fired with the intensity of a wren:

> *'Oh, to be in England*
> *Now that April's there*
> *And whoever wakes in England*
> *Sees, some morning unaware,*

*That the lowest boughs and the brushwood sheaf,*
*Round the elm-tree bowl are in tiny leaf,*
*While the chaffinch sings on the orchard bough*
*In England - now!'*

There was an intensity to that 'now' as though both the poet and Major Cherry felt the poignancy and urgency of being denied an English spring. Browning was his favourite poet and he kept a copy with him in his kit.

Saltmarshe and he would sometimes talk about poetry after dinner. Saltmarshe was a great giant of a man who stood six foot three inches without boots, a great gentle giant unsuited to soldiering. He combined two great passions in life. His first great passion was the Greeks and he read avidly from Homer, keeping his own copy of *The Odyssey* and marking the pages with the work of translation which he had first begun at school. His other great interest was in natural history, an interest that he shared with Major Cherry and both had collections of birds' eggs back in England. Saltmarshe added assiduously to his collection and claimed specimens of secretary bird, bateleur and lilac-breasted roller. He was keeping them to take home and to add to his collection. This amused Major Cherry, who argued that nothing could be more perfect than the blue of a dunnock's egg.

*'The buttercups, the little children's dower*
*Far brighter than this gaudy melon-flower!'*

He quoted with amusement to Saltmarshe.

Major Cherry enjoyed his evening conversations with Saltmarshe, the easy camaraderie of the camp fire and the sweet taste of the port which they shared after dinner. The light would fade on the veldt but they would talk on in the dark of books and poets, and of all that was left behind in England. The other chaps ribbed them about their enthusiasms and they were careful not to bring down derision on their heads. 'The Mess', even here in this far away place, still had its power and need to display conformity. They had to be careful about being seen too much in each others' company as if they were two lovers who needed to keep their precious associations concealed from the public gaze. Stevens, in particular, seemed to watch out for them and never missed an opportunity to draw the attention of the others to the peculiar friendship of Saltmarshe, the landed gentleman, and the old soldier.

Saltmarshe's mind was somehow not truly with the realities of soldiering but lived more in the abstract. His admiration for the Greeks was tempered by first hand experience of warfare and it puzzled him that the nobility of the Greeks was compromised by the callousness of their deeds. He called it a low form of butchery and likened it to the ugliness of 'squabbling with Xhosa over cattle.'

They had been ordered to clear out a kraal of Tini Macomo's rampaging warriors but when they found the camp the warriors had moved on so they razed the place and stole the livestock. Major Cherry thought it an ugly, distasteful business: the sight of the screaming women, with their hanging breasts and wretched ugliness, the terror of the children, the stench of excrement, the burning and the screaming and barking of curs cut into Major Cherry's memory. He had seen other things like this before, in India, but the sheer meanness and pettiness of that action haunted him.

Saltmarshe, stretching out his ungainly limbs by the camp fire, was even more vocal on the matter.

'Empires,' he said 'are the same. They may be nobly intended but they are in the end only held together by force and brutality. Now in *The Odyssey* all sorts of mean and vile things go on, women raped, people slaughtered for no good reason, the very devil's stuff and yet the people doing it are noble champions, loved by the gods. Even old Odysseus is much the same sort of chap. Take his raid upon the Cicones, for example. There is no reason for it. They are not threatened, the Cicones have done nothing to them and yet they just pitch in there with a sort of blood lust.'

So saying he pulled from his breast pocket his copy of *The Odyssey* and read from his own translation:

*'The same wind that wafted me from Ilium brought me to Ismarus, the city of The Cicones. I sacked this place and destroyed its men folk. The women and the vast plunder that we took from the town we divided so that no one, as far as I could help it, should go short of his proper share. And then I said we must escape with all possible speed. But my fools of men refused. There was plenty of wine, plenty of livestock, and they kept on drinking and butchering sheep and shambling crooked-horned cattle by the shore.'*

'You see what I mean?' he reasoned with Major Cherry. 'Why does the great, ingenious, heroic Odysseus demean himself in this way? How many cattle can a warrior want for God's sake? Now you explain that to me?'

Major Cherry was at a loss. He could never quite understand why Odysseus had two names: sometimes he was named as Odysseus and sometimes as Ulysses. The name Ulysses always seemed more familiar, more English. It put him in mind of Tennyson's poem and a strange picture of Ulysses leading his men to the land of the lotus eaters that hung in the hall of the old family home at Denford. In the end he was inclined to leave the Greeks to their primitive inscrutability. He pondered for a moment or two before taking up Salt's challenge.

'The point is, I suppose, that the Greeks built their empire and indeed their civilisation on mutual distrust and lack of respect. They were for ever at war with each other just as much as with other people. In the end you have to acknowledge that our empire is somehow of a higher order. It is not just bigger than anything the world has seen before, it is also unified in its purpose and aims at more than simple subjugation. I suppose the word, the idea, which is missing from the Greek world, is the notion of service. We serve one monarch and one set of ideals. I suppose if you like, one God. Now the Greeks were loyal to certain champions and appeased many gods but they didn't have the same straightforward view.

You see, their champions were flawed people and things were made even more random by the caprice of flawed gods whom those champions were compelled to obey. So, Ulysses does what he does in a random kind of way.'

Saltmarshe was not so convinced and knocked his pipe out on the heel of his boot.

'I'm not so sure any more, Cherry. Sometimes I look at the mean lowly things we have to do and I see more of the Greeks in us than I would like.'

The evenings were made poignant by the realisation that Saltmarshe was leaving. His uncle had died leaving a landed estate worth a fortune to his nephew. Major Cherry as second brother to the squire of Denford could expect no such future and would have to remain a professional soldier but he didn't resent Saltmarshe's good fortune. Saltmarshe would make a wonderful landed gentleman. Major Cherry teased him about the girl he would have to marry and the many female Saltmarshes they would produce. Saltmarshe would have his own museum in the west wing, where he could retreat from the chorus of giggling girls and be free to write books on the nesting habits of the willow wren.

'Won't you at least allow me one son!' protested Saltmarshe, who was conscious of the need to safeguard the name and honour of the family.

'Very well, but he will be a little, timid, bespectacled chap who will be quite unsuited to soldiering.'

'To hell with soldiering!' retorted Saltmarshe, who had drunk a little too much port and was forgetful of Major Cherry's circumstances. 'I'll not subject him to this butcher's life. No, I will want him to be a classicist and a good, landed gentleman.'

As soon as he said it, he regretted the words and mumbled an apology.

However, it created a break in the warmth of the evening. Major Cherry poured out two full bumpers from the decanter in a decidedly dismissive manner.

'No offence taken, Salt. It looks as though I am stuck with this job for some time to come but I promise you this. I'm not staying for more than a year or two and then I'm out. This is a rum business and no mistake. I can see these damn, squalid wars going on forever and I have done enough of it. No, it's England for me and a new start. I may be fifty and have had the best of life but I'm still fit and game for anything. I want to wake up in England, preferably next to a lovely lady in a house filled with children. So, let's have a toast to England and a new start.'

They solemnly toasted, raising their glasses to the dark veldt. Saltmarshe looked across at the weathered face of the old soldier, caught in the light of the fire, which showed intensity and hope against all the odds of probability. He was amused at the prospect of that imaginary life of domestic bliss so far from any realistic prospect but he felt apologetic for speaking without thinking.

'Look, Cherry, the estates are going to be a hell of a thing for me to administer and sort out and you know that sort of thing isn't my strength at all. The whole business is so complex these days, it's no easy matter as it was for Uncle. Also, I am much more of a thinking sort of chap and, let's face it, I would rather be writing a book than dealing with farms and business and all that sort of thing. So, why don't you buy yourself out and come with me. There's a house there for you and you can fill it with children if you like but more to the point you would be doing me the most amazing favour.'

The evening was marred by the presence of Stevens who came up to them, in his self-important way.

'Saltmarshe, there's a message from Colonel, it seems that you and I are to go out on patrol tomorrow morning, sharp.' The word 'sharp' irritated Major Cherry but worse followed, 'so, go easy on that decanter.'

Major Cherry was damned if he'd have that because he outranked Stevens. 'Are you speaking to me, Stevens?'

'Colonel's orders,' said Stevens.

'Are you telling me that the Colonel ordered you to come out here to tell me when I should or should not take a glass?'

Major Cherry was a respected serving officer and Stevens knew he was out matched. He mumbled something about 'trying to get it right' and made his retreat to audible mutterings from Major Cherry which included the words 'Bloody little Popinjay.'

They finished the decanter but Stevens had soured the mood and Major Cherry went off to bed, reflecting on Saltmarshe's offer and feeling that he had had enough of the petty realities of soldiering.

The action next day took them to Burns Hill. Major Cherry had been sent forward with a patrol and had orders to hold a position north of the hill. He could hear sporadic firing but he had his orders and imagined that Stevens had it all under control. Stevens was one of those fellows who prided himself on having everything under control and was something of a braggart. Major Cherry was not inclined to defy orders only to be lectured by Stevens on the subject. He was always to remember that moment. His attention was taken by a pair of hamerkop, great crude, primitive birds whose bizarre behaviour mirrored the shimmering absurdity of the place. The birds were in a baobab tree, pushing yet more twigs into the great bundle that formed their nest. He was wondering if Saltmarshe had a hamerkop egg in his collection when a rider galloped up in a frenzy of excitement. Stevens and Saltmarshe had been hit and G Company overrun. Colour Sergeant Smith was now in command and requested support.

By the time Major Cherry and his men came on the scene the Xhosa warriors had completed their surprise attack and were pulling back. Major Cherry saw Saltmarshe's great body prone on the field, gashed and bloodied with two assegais thrust and left in his tormented body. Major Cherry's assault had merely hastened the pace of the Xhosas' withdrawal and put them into full flight. One small group of Xhosa was so intent on the fight that they hadn't realised what was happening and suddenly took to their heels. He galloped after the fleeing Africans and rode them down one by one, shooting them in the head with his revolver. One last warrior nearly made his escape. He dropped everything and simply ran for dear life but

Major Cherry caught up with him nearly a mile from the battle scene. The fugitive was spent, exhausted and overwhelmed, the adrenaline of battle sapped from his body. He fell to his knees and raised his hands and face in childlike supplication. For a second Major Cherry hesitated. He knew that he could simply pass by and leave the man to run back to his kraal. But then he thought of Saltmarshe and he pushed the revolver into the man's face and discharged his last shot so that the whole head was split apart in a riot of blood and mess. Even his horse's flanks were splashed in gore. He left the man where he fell and cantered back.

He could not take his eyes off Saltmarshe's body. What had been alive only a few hours ago was gone already. There were several great gashes where the spears had thrust deep inside and then been pulled out leaving the body ragged and bloodied. The great ungainly limbs were cast about in the throes of an agonising death and his face drawn of life and blood grinned in deadly mockery of life itself. There lay the dead body of his 'orders', a bloody reprimand to his conscience which left him with the desperate nagging knowledge that if he had come up more quickly then neither Stevens nor Saltmarshe would be lying there dead. He had the most terrible feeling that he had let them down. While he had been watching those bloody hamerkop and thinking about birds' eggs, the life had been stabbed out of the best man living.

Sergeant Smith came up beside him. 'Will you take some personal effects sir?' Smith knew what to do even now. 'The sort of thing family might want? Best that an officer checks his pockets.'

Major Cherry had to steel himself to the task. The great body of Saltmarshe already buzzed with flies. He saw the cadaver of his friend, but it wasn't the man he knew because the stuff of life had been bled out of him. There was just a hollow cask, a shell and nothing more, with the spirit and soul and essence of the real man gone. It reminded Major Cherry of an insect specimen, impaled on a board with a great pin struck through its body, or the empty shell of a blown egg in Saltmarshe's collection. Smith's voice called him back to his duty. Major Cherry had to unbutton the tunic like an old nursemaid, and his hands trembled while his spirit raged between disgust for the task and anger at the waste. He couldn't look at Saltmarshe's face, the eyes would search his soul and find it wanting, and there was the terrible dread that if he looked into the face he would see not the dead Saltmarshe but the warrior he had just shot and in that face there would be the child's fear. He slid his hand down the side of the dead meat of Saltmarshe's body to the tunic pockets and he thought of Thomas feeling the open wounds of Christ. He knew what he would find there: a note book and pencil, an old pipe with a pouch of sweet briar tobacco and a box of matches, and finally, an old, worn and tatty copy of *The Odyssey.*

After the action they shot the wounded Xhosa, leaving them and the other native dead for the hyenas and vultures. The bodies of the rank and file were buried at the foot of a large fir tree on Burns Hill with makeshift crosses. The Colonel performed the service. Saltmarshe and Stevens were sent back to King William's Town for burial. Major Cherry inherited Saltmarshe's copy of *The Odyssey*. He had marked the pages:

*'At dawn they were on us, thick as the leaves and flowers in spring, and disaster sent by Zeus to make us suffer, overtook my doomed companions and me. They fought a pitched battle by the swift ships and exchanged volleys of bronze spears. Right through the early morning and while the blessed light of day grew stronger we held our ground and kept their greater force at bay, but when the sun began to drop, towards the time the ploughman unyokes his ox, the Cicones gained the upper hand and broke the Archaen ranks. Six of my strong-greaved companions from each ship were killed. The rest of us eluded our fate and got away.'*

Major Cherry felt a stab of guilt and remorse. His decision to follow orders closely and not to return as soon as he heard firing had cost Saltmarshe his life. That passage in *The Odyssey,* and the very existence of the book, would be a constant reminder of Saltmarshe and what could have been. He wanted to be as far away from Africa as possible, far from the heat and smell, far from these terrible memories and the burden of a secret guilt. The Cicones had taken their revenge.

It was a darker, lonelier world after Saltmarshe's death. Endless squabbles with the tribes anticipated darker and greater troubles with the Zulus. If he had ever had a taste for this sort of thing he was losing it fast. His missing of England turned to a longing that not even promotion could gainsay. At last his chance came to retire on half pay to Bedford and he took it with alacrity, leaving poor Saltmarshe to his inheritance of six foot three of the Cape.

Major Cherry had done his bit and seen his last of active service. Bedford was a good place for the newly-appointed Colonel to try to forget and to start again. The leafy hours were spent in an endless cycle of promenades, hat doffing, social soirees and the chatter of Empire. Here he would finish his days in red-faced company, drifting into respectable oblivion. Nobody would ask him anything about the past and he would not need to tell them. But he often thought of Saltmarshe and the thoughts confused his mind. He carried secretly his burden of guilt because he had not responded as soon as he heard the action and the burden was made heavier by his sense of disgust for his vengeful murder of the African. How different things could have been had he ignored orders and gone straight to the action Saltmarshe would have lived and he would have been far away from Bedford He tormented himself with images of the young Englishman, alive and well and in full possession of his rural property. He would be there too as his friend, and agent, sharing the life of English landed gentlemen who had served a great Empire with distinction and had now come home to the source of all that made it what it was. It was not to be, he held his pain as a penance and lived on.

But as the years passed it was as though Zeus accepted the sacrifice and was appeased. The gods in Olympus decided a different destiny for Colonel Cherry. It was as though Saltmarshe's body, buried in the Cape, had been accepted as an offering. Athene's way prevailed. The gods' earthly agent came in the form of a doctor's daughter with a straight back, light brown hair and flashing eyes who, despite being twenty five years his junior, saw something within the gruff exterior of the man worn by the bloodshed of India and Africa:

*'Alcinous' daughter Nausica was the only one to stand firm. Athene put courage into her heart and took the fear from her limbs, and she stood her ground and faced him. Odysseus considered whether he should throw his arms round the beautiful girl's knees and beg for help, or just keep his distance and beg her with courtesy to give him clothing and direct him to the city. He decided that as the lady might take offence if he embraced her knees it would be better to keep his distance and courteously plead his case.'*

The Olympians looked down on warlike Colonel Cherry and of all the Achaeans viewed him with favour. First they engineered his final promotion to general then they gave him Denford, on the sudden death of his childless brother, Charles. Not content with that, they added the most glittering of prizes: Lamer, seat of the Garrards and home of a childless aunt. Then, they added impishly the requirement that his name should be changed to Cherry-Gerrard. Thus it was determined that it was not Charles, nor even poor Saltmarshe, who married the girl and filled the house with children and inherited vast estates but Lieutenant General Apsley Cherry-Garrard.

The gods may give but their true delight is to take suffering for their sacrificial reward. It amused them that General Cherry had lived and they gave him prizes but they also decreed that the remainder of his life would be shadowed and haunted by an African's face which, as it begged to be spared, twisted into the tortured features of Saltmarshe who demanded to know why he had not been chosen to live. The gods also stored their malice for the general's son.

# CHAPTER ONE

## *LADDIE AND LASSIE. THE UNDERWORLD*

### Lamer Park, Surrey 1892

England had once been as lawless and uncivilised as any part of Victoria's empire but over the centuries the warring tribes and factions had given way to the power and authority of overlords. These great beings based their wealth and status on the landed estates and subjugated the people who inhabited them. The overlords took all they wanted from the people including their common land, but in some places where the land quality was poor and not good for profitable farming they let the people keep their commons. When the young queen came to the throne, Lamer Park was probably at the zenith of its power. Lamer was not one of the greatest houses in the land but it was a substantial, comfortable property for an English gentleman. It was rumoured to be on the site of an old castle, which had acted as one of the protective block houses to shield the great city of London.

The visitor entered the house through a great hall which led off to good sized living rooms: the dining room, a sitting room and a bow-fronted library. There was also a study, or smoking room, for the conduct of estate business and a withdrawing room for the ladies. A kitchen wing had been added at a later date. At the rear of the hall two wings went back to the laundry and the dairy and from there to the larder, game larder, butchery, brew house, lamp room and an outside room which was used by the gardener. Over the years a warren of rooms, workshops and stables had spread out at the back. In the attic of the house were the servants' quarters. The servants found their way to the family rooms through a number of stairs and passages which enabled them to scurry to and fro and to appear from unmarked doors. They moved in a twilight world of service, barely recognised as human beings and more like ghosts.

The house looked north toward the capital and was serviced by a carriageway, which swept down from the most profitable northern end of the estate straight up to the front of the house. The carriageway was wide enough for vehicles of all description and lined with linden trees which formed a splendid avenue. Around the house they made their gardens: lawns were laid out and flattened, sun-soaked walled gardens were created to sweeten the house with English fruit and gleaming greenhouses were erected to anglicise the exotic, pools were dug and statues and features added and all was garlanded with shrubs and flowers.

The house and gardens were as a keep in the middle of all that belonged to Lamer. Beyond this safe place a park had been created and beyond the park was the estate. To the east of the house, and down a yew-lined avenue, they built a private chapel on the bank of a small stream that ran away to the south. The chapel was a separate private place for the Garrards to commune with their gods and to bury and record their line. Finally, as an afterthought, they gave Lamer an entrance to the south. This was more modest than the great carriageway from the north and a suitable way for carters and the like to bring up their offerings to the great house. It was a coarser simpler route but with a sense of caprice they planted an apple and a mulberry to mark the southern end of the park and to stand as sentinels to the southern and poorer end of their estate.

Beyond the park, all the farm lands, to north, south, east and west of Lamer Park belonged to the Garrards. All was for the Garrards and their kind: farms, mills, smithies and houses. Upon each substantial building a large floral G was inscribed, a G for Garrard. These houses were inhabited by the substantial tenants, the lesser lived where they could.

To the north, their estate went all the way up to the small town of Redhill. Between Lamer and Redhill was the village of Earlswood. Here the Garrards had built a large church on the site of an older but humbler building. The church of St John's looked down and over their lands and taught the populace the eternal glory and permanence of the Garrards. Later a school was built and attached to the church.

To the east there was good farm land and a rich source of income for the Garrards. This encompassed the village of Nutfield.

To the west the returns were patchy. Some land was good for farming but the rest was only fit for commons. The old marshes had been drained and dammed to create two lakes of equal size to provide a landscaped effect.

The south was a concern for the Garrards because it was never as productive as the rest of their estate. The poor quality of the soil made it difficult to farm and the old bushes, which people believed had been there for centuries, were largely left to flourish. Central to this area was Whitebushes Common, which still retained the feel of being a gap in the dark bushes despite all the changes brought. The common was an open area, spotted with clumps of close-set bushes, which clung fiercely to its old and strange identity. On the common the cottagers kept their livestock and held back the encroachment of the bushes, which grew thickest and hardest to the south. The bushes were as hard as their name and as dark as ebony. In early winter their bark was powdered green and beneath them laid the sodden litter of small dark leaves which shrouded the clay-laden soil. In winter, the bushes bound the snow close to them in their tight-knit, claw-like hands. They grew dark, impenetrable and callous in their sharpness. Old grey thrushes from the cold north came down to feast on the harvest of berries and to chortle to each other. There was always something alive and moving in the undergrowth, even at the worst of times. The bushes defied any path or way to be made through them - in all but one place. For as long as anybody could remember there had been just the one man-wide track which ran to the south of the common, through the impenetrable undergrowth and away to a farm on the edge of Salfords. This track was called the 'Magic Pathway'.

But, no matter how harsh and cold the winter when the spring came there was change in the dark menace of the bushes. The sloe came quickly to the summons of spring and sprinkled flecks of white through the leafless branches, like hope among a crown of thorns. Later the full rush of the hawthorn came to bedeck the gentle green of May and overflow the bushes in cascades of white. Then the bushes filled with sound and song and birds of all sorts came to feed and breed. Best of all the singers was the nightingale which came unseen into the woods and sang through the magic of an English summer night long before there was human ear to hear it.

Whitebushes was a hamlet, its few houses encircling the original common. The housing was generally poorer than on the rest of the estate and only a few buildings proudly displayed a G as an emblem of their substance. The others had been built straight onto the ground and on clay, they were poorer and shoddier and temporary. The people in these houses used the common for their livestock and as a central area. Near to the common was Whitebush Farm. The farmer was at constant war with the commoners, keeping his sleek cattle away from the bare-boned creatures of the common and allowing only his own cattle to drink from the pool of clear, carp-gliding water that was the farm pond. Boys would come at night and tempt the great fish with bread and hook. The small community also had a smithy, a cobblers and a general store. All that could be done was done in the hamlet, vegetables were grown, bread was baked, hair was cut and even babies born with only the aid of local people. The people walked to work in the big house or on the neighbouring farms.

There was also a brook called the Earlsbrook which linked the elements of the estate. It flowed down from the north east of the edge of the park, past the back of the chapel, and away down south and west. Where it crossed the road that led up to the southern entrance of the house they built a bridge of white stone. The brook then ran away to the south west and after a mile or so into the lakes. In due course they built a lodge cottage with the inevitable G. Some said that this lodge was built on the site of what had once been a stone gatehouse. Here generations of a family called Hobbs lived as keepers of the southern lodge and as gardeners to the house. The main lodge lay to the north and guarded the proper entrance but 'Hobbs's House' as it became known kept watch on the southern aspect on what had always been regarded as the rougher end of the estate.

The seasons moved round in an endless cycle of work. Labouring men and women worked on foot at the pace of a cart. They worked long hours through the heat of summer and the chill of winter under the command of their overseers. When the day was done they went back to hovels on foot and in the dark to rest and eat from the a sole fire and to begin again at first light. They saw the great house like a great ship far out in the sea of its park. They knew the names of the people who lived there and saw them from time to time whisked past in carriages, remote, godlike, the providers of it all. Like the old gods they shared space with the mortals, commanded their destinies, sometimes had sex with them but kept their separate Olympian splendour. Although they were mortal and could die, in one respect they kept true to their godlike state and the Garrard name seemed to go on for ever.

The Queen grew older and the great British Empire thrust its dominion over the world and the value of the landed estate declined. It was as though the great cities - and London in particular - sucked the life and people out of the English countryside. The Garrards put less value on their farms and spent their gains in dealings with the great metropolis of London. The farms were still there but they could not alone feed the appetites of the Garrards. The Garrards found farm tenancies to be less profitable and looked to ways to make more money from the estate and other sources. They cut down a section of the dark bushes to establish a brick yard which would turn the yellow London clay into bricks to feed the rapacious demands of the London wen. Not content with this they sold even more of the nearby dark wood to build a hospital remote enough for people suffering from scarlet fever. They sold land to the railway company, which struck a railway line to roar from north to south, racing people and goods from London to Brighton. The railway carved their lands into two and, although it brought wealth in the short term, it cut deep into the heart of their agricultural business. Such profits as there were brought money to the owners of Lamer, which they wasted and speculated away, leaving the estate the poorer.

The coming of the railway hit Whitebushes hardest of all parts of the estate and rendered it even more remote and distinct from the rest. A great embankment was thrown up to establish a permanent perimeter on the west side so that the train could speed headlong over it. The railway passengers, high above on the embankment, could now be taken pell-mell to London and could look down on the Whitebushes common and think no more about it than any other patch of the English countryside. The children working in the fields saw the great trains thundering past and waved to them but the passengers never had the time to see and respond. The embankment split Whitebush farmland in half leaving the farmhouse on the Whitebushes side cut off from its fields in the west. Water poured down the embankment and flooded the farm pond turning the area into sprawling marsh. Three great arches were drilled through the embankment in order to span the road and provide a tunnel and an entrance from the west. The central arch of the Three Arches was like some gigantic entrance hall to the lost lands. A road thrust through the tunnel and round the northern edge of Whitebushes, chopping its way through the dark surrounding bushes and speeding the traveller away to the east and on to Nutfield. They left the rough track through the middle of the common and they left the hovels and houses that ringed the common around. The track went south up to the hospital and then on and away down the old pathway.

The old grey stone of Lamer stood firm through it all and linked to Lamer was the endless line of Garrards. In the chapel at Lamer the Garrard bodies were stockpiled from generation to generation. Yet drawing closer it was possible to see that something had changed. The ivy had bitten a little deeper and the stone was blackened in places from the burning of coal. The century ran to its close and the Garrards, and their way of life, were failing slowly. It was a time of change but Lamer had not altered or adapted. The Garrard family reflected the passing fortunes of their estate. Even their name was dying and the last representative of their line was called Mrs Drake, a strange old lady whose only heir was General Apsley Cherry. It was from Mrs Drake that he inherited the estate, on the condition that he changed his family's name to Cherry-Garrard.

Whitebushes continued to form its own community around the common. There was still a general store and services were still largely carried out by local people, but Whitebush Farm had not prospered after the coming of the railway and became an alehouse known as Nan's. Nan kept a few cattle on what was left of her land but her real income came from the evening trade of drinkers who took their ale in her front parlour. The majority of the inhabitants of Whitebushes worked on the land and now there were people who worked in the brickyard or in other occupations and in the evening most would go to Nan's. Few visited Whitebushes. In winter the redwings returned to feast on the crop of berries and in the spring the nightingale returned to fill the languid nights with liquid sound. The gypsies came and went, their caravans adding a dash of the fearsome and exotic while their horses tugged at the rough grass in the security of this no-man's land. Some stayed on and inter-married with the local people who already had a reputation of being unlike others on the estate. Some said that they were descended from strange people who hid in the sloe bushes, moving silently and unseen, unkempt creatures left over from a savage time. The boys were unlike other boys, being wilder and rougher in appearance and manner and they could never truly be tamed. It was rumoured that they ate hedgehogs rolled in clay, snared rabbits and caught and ate the carp from the pools. They were no respecters of property and were indifferent to rules and even beatings.

The widowed queen had grown old when the old woman of Lamer left her estate to General Cherry-Garrard. Broadly speaking, the people on the estate eagerly anticipated the new family. Old Hobbs, the head gardener and keeper of the southern lodge, came from a long line of servants to the Garrards and despite his loyalty hoped that a new family would be good for Lamer and would bring it back to life. Old Hobbs was a man of some standing who lived in a good stone house with a G proudly stamped above the door. The lodge stood by the White Bridge over the Earlsbrook directly between the great house and the Common. Although he worked for the big house and stood above the rest of the regulars of Nan's, Old Hobbs would walk down to Whitebushes and take his ale in the most civil manner. In due course he brought his son with him and the two of them acquired some status in the proceedings, Old Hobbs for information about the goings on in the big house and Young Hobbs for his easy manner and fine singing voice. Old Hobbs was so esteemed in Nan's that they kept a high-backed oak chair for him just to one side of the fire. If Old Hobbs came into Nan's and there was somebody already in his chair they moved away deferentially. In a frivolous moment Young Hobbs had carved on the back:

*'Hobbs Chair: Sitter Beware!'*

Young Hobbs had his own way of doing things which was not necessarily the same as his father's and at times he was critical of the Garrards and their ways. He danced with the Morris and dressed as the Green Man to the delight of the locals and to the terror of his young son. Old Hobbs was not for the Morris but he had a wonderful gift for telling stories and there was one story in particular that they all loved and never minded how many times it was repeated.

He told it on a night in May 1892 when the locals were huddled in Nan's to speculate about the new arrivals at the great house. Rumour had it that they were arriving the next day and that it was a general, his wife and their children who had inherited. Old Hobbs had known the general as a boy when he and his brother had come to stay at Lamer. He remembered the boys bird-nesting and swimming in the lake. Nan's customers loved to hear him talk about the Old People and how they had come and found the place that they all knew as their own common. If Hobbs told it well Nan herself might pour him a free pint, just for the pleasure of hearing him talk, and his listeners would gather a little closer as they waited for the next bit.

Hobbs recounted that long, long ago all about was forest and bush and the weather was warmer so that all grew in abundance. The very first people to arrive in Whitebushes, whom Hobbs called the Old People, came from the coast where trees and bushes grew right up to the water's edge. They lived by the sea well enough because there was plenty to gather and eat, but then a new people arrived in boats. These new people were a bigger and crueller clan who murdered and harried the Old People. So the Old People decided to leave the coast and to push their way up through dense forest and follow a great river. As they went they found that the river divided and became smaller so they chose the quieter tributaries. The tributary they chose was narrow and quite shallow and by then their nerves were close to exhaustion. Some urged them to give up the quest and to return the way that they had come as quickly as possible and before something terrible and unknown took them. But one was stouter-hearted than the rest. He was not particularly big and was not the best fighter in the group but there was something about him that inspired them as a leader and a true pioneer. He put courage into their hearts and urged them to look for somewhere to make their own so that they could settle away from the forest and away from the possibility of sudden attack and murder. He argued that there was no going back. They buried their fears and pushed on into the dark unknown.

Hobbs paused to take a long pull at his beer. There was silence in Nan's and the customers saw in their minds the small band of fugitives, clutching their few belongings, whispering their fears and struggling through the dense forest, women and children, dressed in rough skins and with wild, unkempt hair.

They were tired, hungry and worn down by fear of the darkness and the things of the forest and dread of murder springing from behind dark bushes and at the hands of people wilder and stranger than themselves. But they had their leader with them and he drew their hopes to him as a light that shines down a dark tunnel of bushes.

They made their way along a narrow river hoping and searching for some safe, open place where they could live. Finally, they came to a feeder stream that is now known as the Earlsbrook and followed it. After a short while, their leader scrambled up the bank and peered above the vegetation and saw a safe place. They left the safety of the water at the very place now known as The White Bridge. When they clambered out of the stream they looked at one another in great joy because they had come to a place where there was open country, ringed around by dark bushes and forest and nobody else knew they were there. They stayed and gathered food and fuel from the woods that were all around them and drank from the waters of the brook. At night they built great fires to further clear the open ground but also to light up the world around them so that they could watch out for dangers. They heard nightingales singing in the bushes and thought them to be kindly spirits that watched over them.

The Old People were happy where they were even if they lived secretive lives feeding on berries and nuts and hunting for meat in the forests. They found the shallow lake and its marshes and swam in the warm water and caught fish. Hobbs said that their world was warmer and lusher and it made the listeners in Nan's think of foreign places where the English army now marched. It was as though there was once something of Africa here in the very heart of England.

But the route up the stream was open to others. Generations later a new people came up the stream route and they were bigger, sharper and crueller. They found that first common and thought it good so they took it for their own. The new comers were fiercer and better organised. They felled and cut and cleared with axes, bringing light to feed their crops and livestock. Their clearings grew and their ambitions swelled and they fought and squabbled for the rights of their cattle, and buried their dead on the edges of the lakes so that their spirits would float away.

The Old People crept into the woods and hid. They still crept back to their common to steal anything left unguarded but more and more open spaces were created, encroaching wider and deeper into the wood. The Old People were pushed further and further back into darkest and most impenetrable and hostile places. Hobbs was sure that their descendants were there still, secretive, hidden, spiteful and resentful. They moved between the remaining dark copses, a secret, hidden people. Some called them outlaws and green people, elves and fairies and the like, but Hobbs said they were the Old People and the only true English and that their first, and maybe last, place was Whitebushes Common. Hobbs also spoke of the pathway which formed a tunnel through the dense bushes, to the south of the common and ran on past the hospital and away to a farm beyond. He said that, if you walked down it on a night in May and then you stood very still, they would watch you through the bushes and that you could hear them whispering to each other.

Hobbs's story always kept his listeners in wrapt attention but on that evening in May 1892, unknown to anybody inside, Alfred Hobbs had followed his father and grandfather out of their house and down to Nan's. That evening at Nan's ended in song. Young Hobbs led off with *The Greenwood's Shady Dell* with Ernie on his fiddle. Outside, young Alfred Hobbs listened while his father and grandfather led the singing to the tight strain of a fiddle:

> '*I was sore and troubled more than I can truly tell*
> *So, I took me a wandering to the Greenwood's shady dell*
> *And there I sat a whistling upon a mossy mound*
> *When I heard a whistle answer from underneath the ground*
> *Now sprang me up and clutched my staff to meet a deadly foe*
> *When from the branches low and green someone fired a bow.*
> *And there appeared in front of me all dressed up in the green,*
> *the finest fist of fighting men that you have ever seen.*
> *Fear not voyager for you have journeyed long*
> *To meet with Robin of the Bush and his merry greenwood throng*
> *But if you have a goodly spirit and true English manliness*
> *We will touch you with the spirit of true English gentillesse.*
> *For we have waited long for you to swell our woodland band*
> *So take us now as brother and shake us by the hand*
> *And then you'll join us now, my lad, and roam the Greenwood free,*
> *to sing and laugh both day and night and live in liberty.*'

Before the music was over, Alfred Hobbs made his way cautiously homeward to the safety and security of his bed in the lodge on the White Bridge but all the while the tune reverberated in his head and he looked about him carefully to make sure that he was not being followed by any Old People.

The next morning the new comers arrived. Ernie and George spotted a horse–drawn carriage as they tended their cattle on the common. The carriage came through the great tunnel of Three Arches and swept round the common. They were surprised to see a carriage coming in from the southern entrance instead of the main entrance to the north of the house, and stopped their work to stare. George pulled off his cap when Ernie nudged him. The carriage crossed the stream at The White Bridge, went past Hobbs's House and up towards the two old trees that stood as sentinels to the grounds. Then it passed out of their sight.

Inside were four people: an upright, sun-weathered man in his late fifties, a young woman in her late twenties who nursed an infant, a young girl and a slightly older boy. The two adults conversed sparingly and the boy looked fixedly out of the window. What he saw was the vast parkland of their new estate. Later in life, he remembered coming through the Arches' tunnel and his father calling out his name so that it echoed round the walls. But then they clattered over a White Bridge by a lodge cottage and for some reason that he always remembered but could never explain there was a boy standing to the side of the bridge who looked closely into his face as they went past and went on looking long after. The boy was a few years older and wore the rough clothes of a working boy but it was the quizzical expression on the boy's face that the boy in the carriage remembered. The carriage clattered up the white track way, passed between two great trees and down the longest drive he had ever experienced. At the end of the drive there was a great mansion. The boy in the carriage remembered the General telling him that one day he would be master of it and would have to take charge but not yet. In the future, whenever he heard the sound of horses' hooves he would recall that moment, the great park, with so many mighty trees the glint of water from the stream and the strange look of the boy.

Old Hobbs saw their approach from his garden room at the back. Their arrival via the southern entrance caused confusion but Hobbs knew the General from boyhood and ushered the newcomers round to the front where the housekeeper and servants were gathered to welcome them. The General knew them all and shook each one by the hand introducing first his wife then his son, Apsley also known as 'Cherry', and then his daughter, Ida. Cherry stared up at them and screwed up his face to discern their features. When Cherry walked into the house behind his parents, he felt uncomfortable in the stiff, new collar and apprehensive that the house was too big and too old to be home. He missed their real home, Denford, and felt that he had deserted it and that the move to Lamer was no more than temporary.

Yet in the days and weeks that followed, the great house shrank as the two children ran through it, opening doors and cupboards and peering round into all the new places. They ventured into the servants' places and because she was a girl Ida was indulged and allowed to go where she liked and talk to whom she liked and was given sweet and warm things in the kitchens and variously indulged so that Cherry learned to keep her close.

They had brought some items from Denford. Cherry recalled his father supervising Hobbs, and another who was known as Young Hobbs, hanging his father's favourite picture in the hall. The great painting showed a hard-muscled, Greek warrior who stood proud and strong in the prow of his boat and pointed to the land. The warrior's firm resolve contrasted with the men beneath him as they pulled on their oars. Some looked towards the land in feverish expectation, others stared at the great waters in terror and others looked up to their leader in devotion, but all pulled on under his command. The strange land to which they were heading was crowded with dark mountains and great rivers and inhabited by ghoulish figures. The picture frightened Cherry even though the image of the warrior was uplifting and he knew that with such a leader all would be well.

'See here,' his father would say, 'Ulysses leads and his men follow,' and sometimes he would proclaim, 'Courage, he cried and pointed towards the land!'

Cherry and Ida went everywhere together and the house became familiar and gradually became home. The servants encouraged and indulged them because after the old lady who had lived there they were new and young and offered hope for the future. The servants taught them 'blind man's buff' and 'what's the time Mr Wolf?' These games caused them to laugh hysterically at the children, and Mother allowed it all because she had a new infant to look after and was pleased that the children were happy. The game they loved best was 'hide and seek'. Cherry thrilled to the freedom of this because he could run to any part of the house, except of course the bedrooms and the General's study, and discover new and wonderful places that were big enough to conceal a small boy. Cherry was the older and a boy so he won and had to win but not every time because this would spoil the game.

The old house became familiar. There was plenty of room for a growing family and the children had their own rooms. Cherry's looked southwards and over the park. From his window he could make out the sparkle of the Earlsbrook and the dense clumps of impenetrable bushes that lay beyond the stream. He planned long and exciting expeditions to these exciting places. Ida's room looked north and was sweeter and neater and much closer to their parents. Once when playing in Ida's room they discovered a loose floor board. Cherry used his pen knife and was able to lift the board clean away to reveal the most perfect hiding place. This was where they kept their most secret treasures. It was their joint hiding place, but it was in Ida's room and remained especially important to her.

The garden was a more male world, presided over by Old Hobbs. If the house was Mother's country then the garden and the park were the General's and Hobbs was the General's man. Step by step the children found their way round the garden and from there they strayed into the grounds. They went down the south entrance like pioneers setting out to find a new world. At the end of the drive and at the entrance to the park were two trees: an old mulberry with low twisting branches, which made it easy to climb and an ancient apple tree. Cherry claimed the mulberry for his own and in a handsome gesture bequeathed the apple to his sister.

But as time went on, the house became more Ida's place, something drew her close to Mother and the ever-present infant girls. Cherry wandered more in the grounds and they became his territory. As he discovered more he showed Ida, but much of the time he was on his own and his instincts took him on further from the house and garden and into the estate. Sometimes Mother arranged for other families to visit with boys of Cherry's age but he found little in common with them. Cherry had to dress in jacket and stiff collar and sat down to tea and cake with similarly clad boys and heavily dressed girls. After tea, the children were sent to the play room but the other boys always seemed better than Cherry at the games and he never enjoyed them. There was a doctor's family from the Isolation Hospital who came to tea on occasion. Elspeth, the eldest girl, was friendly with Ida and they played together easily but Cherry resented her closeness with his sister and despised being part of the games they played.

Cherry preferred to be on his own and to wander the grounds. He spent an increasing amount of time with Old Hobbs, who always found time to talk to the young master. Hobbs knew things that interested the boy and Cherry would often sit with him in his garden room and watch him make a brew on an old stove. The top half of the door was kept open in spring and summer so that the swallows could whisk in and out. They nested on the beams high over Hobbs's head. They never seemed to mind the pair being there and would sit tight on their nest or, later in the season, feed their young who greeted their return with open beaks and flapping wings. Cherry never tired of watching them and found it hard to believe that those same swallows had flown all the way from Africa to nest on the same beam in Hobbs's garden room. Then there was the coal chute that added to Cherry's imaginative meanderings. The chute was positioned adjacent to the base of the half doors and when Cherry got down low he could hear the talk and sounds of the kitchen funnelling up from the depths. When the supply of coal ran low he could see through and it occurred to him that if the coal was all used up then a small boy would be able to crawl down the chute and into the kitchen. This amused Hobbs considerably who advised strongly against putting this theory to the test.

In some ways Hobbs was a frightening character. He was old and dressed roughly, he smelled of old sheds and paint and pipe tobacco, but Cherry grew to like and respect the old man and marvelled at his knowledge. Ida had no difficulty in winning him over, she was fond of the old man but wary of him. Hobbs called Cherry, 'Laddie' and Ida 'Lassie', and the names which seemed to suit them at this age were adopted, intermittently, by the family. Hobbs told them many wonderful things about Lamer and what it has once been. It seemed to Cherry that in his talk of his own father and even of 'Granfer' he merged into an old man of all the old times. Ida did not care for some of Hobbs's talk and found his stories about the Old People very frightening but Cherry thrilled to them and his mind ran wild with the notion of those lost, free people and of a world that was all dark green. In his mind he could see the Old People wading up the Earlsbrook and whispering together in fear of what lay about them in the dark woods. Their leader would have the same bearing and nobility as the man in the painting, which hung in the hall. He pressed the old man for more and more information. What did they look like? What did they wear? What did they eat? Those stories tumbled into his mind and the Old People found expression in many strange ways: in the nightingales which sang on summer evenings in the park and in stories such as *The Elves and the Shoemaker*, *Robin Hood* and all manner of dream-like things.

Cherry loved stories and the evening would always end with a story. Mother read little stories from the *Children's Book of Bedtime Stories* and sometimes she would croon a little song and always she would say a prayer with him. Jesus, she reassured him, was looking down from heaven and smiling on him because he was a special boy. But as he grew older Mother had less time for him individually and the reading petered out. Her first concern was the ever-increasing tribe of girls.

The General also read to him from time to time and his choice of reading was more varied. Cherry loved Richard Jefferies' *Wood Magic*. The stories were filled with the spring light of childhood and the magic of talking animals and special places. The title made him think of the woods round Lamer. At other times the General's reading was more robust. They particularly loved an old volume that the general had owned as a boy, entitled *The Stories of Robin Hood*. Cherry adored Robin Hood. There was something perfectly English about Robin who lived with his group of friends in the wild woods of Sherwood. They were free spirits who lived in secret and were at one with the woods. Robin's merry men had the most amazing adventures that employed all their reckless resourcefulness. Their energies were directed against bad rules and the bad people who tried to impose those rules. Although not the strongest, Robin was the leader. Cherry particularly loved the meeting of Robin and Little John and begged his father to read it over and over again. He thrilled to the great fight on the bridge, the two men driving at each other with the staves they had cut from the trees and making the green wood reverberate to the sound of staff on staff. There was a picture of the moment when Little John knocked Robin over the bridge and sent him spinning into the stream below. Robin's followers looked on from the sides of the wood in dismay at their leader's defeat, but Cherry knew that although overpowered, he was not defeated. Robin sat in the stream and laughed at his pain and invited Little John to join their merry band. Little John, although victorious, saw the strength of Robin's leadership and his inner power and became his most devoted follower.

Every Sunday morning the whole family would go to church. If it was a special occasion a carriage would take them up the driveway and on to the great church of St John which Garrard benevolence had supported for so long along with the school for the children of the estate. St John's was largely attended by the people of the estate and gave everybody the opportunity to appreciate the distinguished General and his family. But the General preferred to go on ordinary Sundays to Lamer's chapel down the little, yew-lined path. Here the Garrards had piled their mortal remains and he always pointed to the tomb of one of the Garrards which had the words, *'Sum Quod Eris'* inscribed on the lid of his boxed remains. The General promised Cherry that he would teach him Latin so that he could understand what this meant.

The General would walk into the Chapel first, standing tall and patriarchal, his presence a confirmation of the durability and permanence of all that was the Garrards: the church, the estate, the county and the empire.

*'Hills of the north rejoice!*
*River and mountain spring!'*

The master of Lamer loved that hymn, with its urgent tune and clarion call to tall parts of the world as if summoning up and drawing up all the clans of the good and strong and binding them together under a British flag. It reminded him of his own father and those happy days at Denford but also of the regiment and Sunday services far from home.

*'Though absent long your lord is nigh*
*He judgement brings and victory.'*

It was as though the General carried a great responsibility and the burden of a man who has been given much and far more than he deserved. Why should God so reward him at so late a stage in his life, he who did not love the Lord with all his heart and doubted sometimes that all of it could be true, he with his many sins - even murder - to his name?

*'Isles of the Southern seas*
*Deep in your coral caves.'*

The General remembered when he had been shipwrecked close to Sumatra and had rowed to an island with his fellows soldiers to live a rough camaraderie for a week before being picked up by a passing ship. Then his thoughts wandered on to the hills of the Eastern Cape and then, uninvited and unwanted, a pair of hamerkop flew into his mind and proceeded to push twigs into their nest. The tone of the organ and the voices around him merged with sounds of battle and gave rise to other thoughts, Saltmarshe's body with those spears thrust in his side and, worst of all, the face of the African seconds before he discharged his revolver. Joy and pain merged together in those memories. He must drive out the bad from his memory and be cleansed by the present. He felt the tears pricking in his eyes as he journeyed home. There was still time left to him and there was hope for the future and there was Cherry.

*'Shout while you journey home*
*Songs be in every mouth.'*

Cherry imagined that all the parts of the world were being summoned to this small corner of England and to the General in particular. The General towered over his small son and female family, he was strong, famous and important. As the Old General sang he knew that his small son was staring up at him and blinking. The light of the chapel window caught them both in a great blur of gaudy colours. Cherry knew that he could never be as good as his father and for all the General's unassuming kindness Cherry felt shy of him. The General was like the leader in the painting which hung in the hall. How would the General feel if he knew that in reality Cherry was fearful of the painted land they rowed to and fearful that when called upon his courage would fail him?

The General seemed to know that Cherry was staring at him, even though he stared straight ahead and sang without reference to the old, leather-bound hymn book in his hand. He gave a wink of recognition and in that wink there was the pleasure of fatherhood but also hope and expectation.

*'City of God the bond is free*
*We come to live and reign in thee.'*

The General took to the duties and obligations expected of a squire with the same clear purpose that had defined his days as a soldier. He was firm with the people of the estate and expected their complete loyalty and subservience but he cared for them in return and took the time to know them and their ways. They were his England and his responsibility and somehow he knew that that was what Saltmarshe would have expected. There was always so much to do and so much more that could be done. Had Saltmarshe lived all would have been so different, they would have been close friends and fellow landowners who would have shared each other's troubles. Now, he had to journey on alone. He looked at his small son and wondered how the boy would fend in the great, challenging world of England and its empire. Sitting alone in his library his mind would wander to those days on the veldt and the dark things that he had seen. Then he might pour himself a whisky from the cut glass decanter and turn the pages of old Salt's copy of *The Odyssey* and let his mind drift. At those times he could hear Saltmashe's voice,

'It is easy for the gods in heaven to glorify or debase a man.'

The General liked to have some moments of calm, away from the domestic world of the house and the unending worries of the estate, which struggled to pay its way. So many people and so much now depended on him. The farms were all complaining about the depression and blaming the markets and the weather and even the railway. In his moments alone he heard the dry shuffle of boots as they marched across the veldt and he smelled Africa, the distinctive, dense scent of rotten fruit, human bodies, pounded mealie meal and open fires. Saltmarshe was often in his dreams, his long legs draped over a camp chair, but then the General saw the African's face leering into his and he had to force his mind away to other thoughts. He thought of Evelyn and the children and his great fortune in finding her and having them. He must and would make the very best of things.

The General had decreed that he would introduce his son to Latin and other essential skills before he went away to preparatory school. Each morning, Cherry would go to his father's study and the General would show him how to add, to take away and to multiply. He taught him to write on a slate and to ponder the maps of the world, great and pink and glorious. Here was India where the General had been a soldier and here was Lucknow where he had fought a great battle.

Cherry wrote: '*Agricola puellam amat*' and his father was pleased.

Cherry pressed him for an explanation of '*Sum Quod Eris*'.

'Ah, for that you need to know both the present and future tenses of the verb 'to be'.'

Cherry looked puzzled.

'*Sum* is in the present tense and means 'I am',' explained the General, '*Eris*, is in the future and means 'You will be.' *Quod* links the two and means 'What.' So, if you put that together you have, 'I am what you will be.'

Cherry thought hard about this but couldn't decipher the meaning and needed more explanation.

'It means that we are all mortal and that at some time we too must die.' Cherry looked quite horrified at the prospect, which amused the General. 'But not just yet, dear boy, not just yet. There is a lot of living to do first and an awful lot to be done, and that living should combine duty and honour and some pleasure as well. '

Cherry loved that time he had alone with the General in his study: the book-lined walls, the small fire burning on the grate and his father's most prized photographs. There was a photograph of the General and his House in his last year at school. He looked out from the frame with the youthful authority of a senior boy. Then there was a group of undergraduates, lounging in front of their college. They looked so assured as if they alone understood the secrets of the adult world but cared not a straw. On the desk, in a smaller frame, there was a picture of the General and Saltmarshe in uniform holding rifles. On the ground in front of them were the buck they had shot. It was in every sense a man's room and Cherry sensed the privilege and distinction of sharing it alone with his father.

Sometimes Cherry walked with the General, who told him things that he loved to hear. He loved to hear about the life of a soldier and far away strange places with black people and endless sunshine. He heard about battles and knew that one day he too would have to fight in battle and that excited him but it also made him scared. The General said that the greatest soldiers were often scared and that being scared was therefore good. In the end battles had to be won but it was the fear of not winning the battle that worried Cherry most.

Cherry loved the General's stories. His favourite was the story of the General being shipwrecked and living a wild, free life on a lost tropical island. He and his fellows hunted like savages round the island and built a hut for survival. Cherry played this game many times with Ida acting the part of a fellow soldier, their attempts at lighting a fire and cooking some eggs that they stolen form the chicken run were doomed to failure and resulted in a severe reprimand from Mother.

He could go where he chose on the estate but he knew to avoid the south and not to cross over White Bridge into Whitebushes because it had a bad reputation. The fact that this was strongly discouraged attracted his attention and aroused his curiosity. He talked about it often with Ida and planned various pioneering expeditions but she was not so eager and found a number of ways to divert his attention but he always came back to it. He would climb up in the old mulberry to a height that alarmed Ida but was no more than eight feet above the ground. From this vantage point he could look down the path and could see Hobbs's House and White Bridge and something of the lands beyond. As he grew older he felt the slight on his character for delaying his expedition.

He learnt from the General and from Hobbs the names of the birds and butterflies and kept a nature log where he drew the birds or any insects that he found. He showed them to Mother who had to guess the name of the bird he had drawn. He had his own special places that nobody knew about but him: bushes he could hide in and far away corners of old buildings where he made dens. One favourite place was behind the chapel where there was a reasonably safe descent to the stream. He decided that this would be the starting point of his expedition and persuaded Ida to go with him. He had been reflecting on Hobbs's story of The Old People and how they had first come here by wading down the stream that ran past the back of the chapel. Their expedition would join the stream from behind the chapel and would follow it down to the White Bridge where they could climb out, just as The Old People had done. Ida eventually agreed to the enterprise.

They met behind the chapel. She had managed to acquire some bread and some cake. He had secured a tin of golden syrup in a green can with a picture of a dead lion and buzzing flies on it. Cherry put these into his knapsack before heading to the bank of the stream. But from here matters started to go down hill. It was not as easy to enter the stream as he had planned and the banks were quite steep. In sliding down the young explorer was stung several times on the backs of his legs by unseen stinging nettles and his left hand was bloodied by briar. The water was deeper than expected and his wellington boots were not tall enough to prevent an inevitable soaking. He stood up in the stream, feeling decidedly insecure and looked for Ida on the bank above him. He remembered seeing her anxious face and was wondering about the wisdom of proceeding when he became aware of her sliding down the bank after him. He tried to steady her entry into the water but he couldn't prevent the inevitable bootfulls that followed. They steadied each other in the stream and looked about anxiously. There was no obvious way back up the steep bank, but when they started to wade down the stream it soon became apparent their progress on the unsteady bed of the stream, and in waterlogged wellingtons, was not going to be easy. Each step was weighed down by the pressure of water both in and outside of the wellingtons and then there was the unevenness of the stream bed to contend with. Ida fell first and stood up soaked from head to foot. She was cold, wet and scared but determined not to show it and Cherry saw this in her face and admired her for it. When Cherry fell over himself he felt the full weight of his failed responsibilities. They waded on but seemed no nearer to White Bridge than when they had started and they became increasingly scared. They thought about abandoning the project but didn't know how to. Cherry remembered that in Hobbs's story of the Old People, the real leader scrambled up the bank to look out over the top for a safe place. He tried to scramble out of the stream but found the banks were too steep so that he was not able to get a foothold in the wet grass and fell back. He tried to cheer them up by taking the supplies from his knapsack but found that they were all sodden and that he had no way of opening the tin of syrup. After several more attempts to climb out he was overwhelmed by the sense of his own failure and began to weep. Ida stood wet and impassive at the edge of the stream not knowing whether to go back or forward or to attempt to comfort her brother. It must have been the best part of an hour later before Young Hobbs found them. Cherry remembered the sense of relief when Young Hobbs's cheery face appeared above them and his strong right hand pulled them up the bank to safety. But he also remembered the sense of mortification he felt in being rescued in such an abject state and with so little achieved. It added to his sense of humiliation that Young Hobbs's son, Alfred, stood behind his father and witnessed the whole thing. Mother was very cross and lectured him about looking after his sister but worse still was the General's silence on the whole matter.

When Cherry looked back on those pre-school days they were to be a time of dreams and unreality, all was childish and therefore forgivable. The General felt that his son should move on from childish ways and bought him a little pony. Young Hobbs showed him how to saddle and manage the wayward creature. When he had enough confidence he trotted round the estate and the people called him 'sir' and touched their caps although the boys and children ignored him because he was not of their world but his own. He would go to the edges of the park and called in regularly at Hobbs's house where Hobbs's wife treated him to milk and biscuits. But the presence of Hobbs's grandson, Alfred disquieted him. The boy had looked at him in a way which Cherry found both insolent and unsettling.

There were concerns and worries that could be sorted with age. However there was always the brooding concern that he could not see very well. The General would point to a bush and say, 'There do you see it?' but Cherry saw nothing, just the bush and not the special bird. It made the General cross, he wanted his son to be more observant. Perhaps he would grow out of it and there might be some special training to improve the eyes? Despite the limitations of Cherry's sight there were moments when he came close enough to catch glimpses of unexpected, English richness: the jewel-like blue of a dunnock egg, the delicate lemon of the first primrose and an exotic flash from a male stickleback in full breeding colour as it swam through his fingers in the brook. These glimpses made him long to see more.

Beyond the focus point there were dreams and hopes, marching armies, cheering men, ribbons, braid and doting ladies. Men marched onward at his command, while he rode ahead on a great white horse and defied the swirling dust and overpowering heat. Then men looked to him to command. They saw in his face the resolution, the power, the godlike qualities of the champion and they were reassured by his presence. He trotted through the park on his pony and raised himself high in the saddle so that his men could see his strong features and know that they had a leader who was more than mortal and would make all well. He slashed his way with his stick, cutting and carving through the very thick of battle. The swarthy enemy screamed and cried and ran away from this great champion. He went higher and higher up the hill, driving all before him until he reached the summit and beheld all that he had conquered. Then he stood tall, raised his great sword above his head and heard his army cheer and roar back,

'Cherry-Garrard, greatest of all our leaders, stay and be our King. Rule with the gods here for ever!'

But for all that, when he marched with his armies, swinging his stick, or rode his pony fast and charged the enemy lines, the doubt he had experienced that time in the stream kept him company.

# CHAPTER TWO

*Sunday 3<sup>rd</sup> November 1894*
*The Grange*

*Dear Sister*
*Everything is fine here at School and I am doing a bit better at things now. I am doing better at Latin and Mr Hussey gave me 8 out of 10 for my last prep which is my best yet. I quite like Latin because it makes me think of Caesar and Pompey and great battles.*

*We are going to have a bonfire to celebrate Guy Fawkes and some of the older chaps have been helping to build it. It is already quite tall.*

*Do write if you can and tell me all about Lamer.*
*Love*
*Apsley*

## The Grange Preparatory School, Folkestone, 1894

In the weak sunshine of a Victorian September morning, Master Cherry went away to School to become 'Cherry-Garrard'. Mother, assisted by Ida, began the great business of packing a trunk and his tuck box. This was a special task which Mother supervised personally and caused much coming and going for the servants and some tears from Mother. Cherry tried to take an interest but the whole thing filled him with dread. He wanted to stay at Lamer, to stay with Mother and all the things which were the surety of life. Everybody told him that he would soon be back for the 'hols', that it would all be fun, that he would make ever so many friends, but it seemed to Cherry that he was shutting the door on childhood, losing the soft feminine swish and touch of life. He knew instinctively that from the day he left nothing would ever be the same. He went to see Hobbs for the last time. Hobbs seemed to accept it all as the right and inevitable thing. In Hobbs's garden room all seemed as before. The old stove, the old stories, the new season's swallows whirling and whispering and gathering on the high beams were just the same. Hobbs said that if you listened very closely you could hear the swallows chattering of great sand filled deserts, wild jungles and the lure of Africa. Hobbs said that they knew that it was departure time for them and for the young master of Lamer but that there would be return in another spring.

Before he left he went to visit all the old places with Ida. They took up the old floor board in their most secret of places and hid away an envelope containing certain treasures such as a pressed four leaf clover and a very old coin that they had found in the garden. They wrote, as low down to the floor and as carefully as possible so that it would be hard to detect, '*Laddie and Lassie. The Underworld.*' Then they lowered back the floor board and to ensure absolute privacy pushed a small cupboard in front of the writing and over the board. Cherry said that their 'Underworld' would be absolutely their secret hiding place and that nobody must ever know of its existence.

He went to the two trees and did not say anything to Ida because he wanted to be alone. He climbed up into the lower branches of his tree as he had done so many times before but this time he made himself climb higher than before. As he went up he found himself shaking and a terrible sense of his own vulnerability took hold of him. What if a branch should break or his hands no longer held the branch but slipped away? All below him was getting further away and smaller and more remote. Would he ever be able to get down? He longed for the security of the ground and its utter predictability. He was somewhere near the top when he decided that he would climb no further if he made himself lie out on a thick branch and look across at the open land. Pushing off with his feet from the trunk of the tree he carefully and slowly stretched himself along a branch. Lying horizontally along the branch he felt the void on both sides of his narrowly balanced body. He lay for some time with eyes tightly shut while his mind focussed on balancing. At last he made himself open his eyes and there was the park that he knew so well and beyond it Hobbs's house and then the White Bridge. Beyond that there was the common of Whitebushes and the tethered animals. He could see them but they could not see him and he felt the comfort of it but it was now time to come down. As he edged himself back to the trunk all his insecurities returned. He knew that as his back was to the trunk of the tree he must turn himself around. He leaned round and hugged the bole of the tree as firmly as possible before he scrambled and scraped his knees onto the branch. Now he could drop his right knee down and could hold the tree in a lover's secure embrace, the rest was easy.

Back on the ground, he lay on his back and looked up at the old mulberry tree and was at one with the earth. He closed his eyes and it seemed to him that he was at the very centre of the whole world and that everything else moved and swam and rustled all around. Were he to stay still and lie like this for long enough then the grass and the ivy and foliage would grow over him and slowly suck him down into the centre of the earth and claim him as their own. Then, almost on impulse and to avoid being taken down, he opened his eyes and saw the leaves of the tree moving and slapping like great green hands and the sun light shone through them as though the tree was waving and saying goodbye to him. When he eventually stood up, he folded his arms round the trunk and tearfully whispered his love for them all.

The General took him away in the carriage and he looked down the tree-lined avenue to where Mother, the girls and Ida were waving. Ida waved frantically as though the harder she waved the better it would be for him, even though she knew that things would never be the same again. His heart was so full he wanted to cry but he gulped hard on the bile in his mouth and the General gently touched his arm to reassure him. He never forgot that kindness of that moment.

When Cherry looked back to his early days at the Grange they were filled with noise and confusion. There was the bustle of boys, talking, asking questions, laughing and feeble treble singing set against the strident notes of the piano:

*'Lord receive us with thy blessing: Once again assembled here'.*

Sometimes the voices droned:

*'Dominus, Domine, Dominum, Domini, Domini: Domino.'*

The ringing of bells and the scraping of chairs intruded harshly into his world. There were strange smells of new uniforms, floor polish, bleach, latrines and the press of boys in number. There was the taste of drab overcooked food and the sweet delights of the tuck box, which brought back the loss of home and warmth and something feminine and caring. There was the chill of dormitories and the stiff, unyielding coldness of an unknown bed and sheets and the terrible sense of utter loneliness in the midst of fellow human bodies. Finally, at night, there was the hum and mumble of prayer and hope of respite in sleep.

All these things swam in his head and blurred images of a bigger, faster, pushing and scraping world where everybody except him knew where to go and what to do. After the initial interest, other boys chose to leave him alone. There was something about this quiet, short-sighted and uncompetitive boy that didn't interest them. He was allowed to be alone again in their midst, neither feted nor bullied, neither clever nor stupid, just alone.

Slowly he began to find his way through the agonies of a day and then a week. Hour by hour school became less strange and terrible. There was comfort in books. Each classroom had its own set of books and the boys had to choose two a term to read. Time in the day was set aside for reading and this was the time that Cherry liked best. He read avidly the school's copy of *The Adventures of Odysseus, A story for boys*. It drew him in closer to the world of the imagination, a world which was on one level very foreign to his own and yet on another strangely familiar. There was 'the wise' Telemachus, a son who could not match up to his father and yet was his father's son. In his father's enforced absence young Telemachus aspired to keep his father's house safe and planned to protect his mother and all from the ravages of the suitors and their new world. The wise Telemachus was befriended by the gods, his nobility clearly recognisable in him. When the time came, Telemarchus stood, side by side with the 'godlike' Odysseus and drove the suitors from the hall.

Cherry was also captivated by *Bevis: the story of a boy*. It reminded him of the General reading *Wood Magic* and brought him closer to home. Bevis had become a boy and was regardless of the adult world to the point of recklessness. Bevis's world reminded Cherry of the outside freedom he enjoyed at Lamer and yet it was different. He loved to hold the book in his hands and to feel the weight of it and he was captivated by the pictures. There were Bevis and Mark in the brown-grey of their hut and in their hands they held the gun they were making, while Pan the Spaniel looked on. Then there were the captions:

*'Bevis put barrel in the stock and began twisting the copper wire round to fasten it.'*

Cherry thrilled to the picture of Bevis and Mark out hunting in the woods. The illustration was washed in dark blue for night and the moonlight of a mad midsummer eve flooded down the ride and illuminated the two boys who ran free and unfettered through the woods. Mark carried a spear and craned forward into the gloom. Bevis pulled back the string of a great bow. Best of all both boys were utterly naked in their savagery. There was something of the elfin spirit about the naked boys, something primeval and wonderful. Cherry thought of Hobbs's stories about the Old People and he tingled with joy. His spirits roamed the dark woods with Bevis and Mark.

Afternoons were given over to sport. Cherry held his own in the classroom but he hated sports. In winter the ball was sodden and heavy and smacked into unsuspecting boys and all was running, shouting, confusion and cold, wet misery.

On Sundays there was a change of routine. After breakfast the boys would dress in full school uniform and were marched down to the church. They took their caps off at the entrance and filed into the side pews. During the endless drone and intermittent standing and kneeling Cherry thought of Lamer and how his family were doing much the same. When they were commanded to pray he talked in his prayers to Ida and told her his innermost thoughts and hoped that she heard his prayers.

On Sunday afternoons they had to write home and the boys knew that their letters were vetted and so they erred on the side of caution. Cherry was careful to include nothing of his thoughts or feelings in his letters for fear of being discovered as wanting.

This was a time of loneliness when hours were huge blocks of drear time. Cherry stood apart from the others, although wanting to be part of their jostling and ragging, wanting the freedom to rag and fight. He longed for the fraternity and power of a special friend, a Mark to his Bevis, and was denied it.

He also had other wants, which somehow set him apart from the other boys. He wanted home and missed all the old familiar things and he longed for the General, Hobbs, Mother, the girls and Ida most of all. He could say nothing of this in his letters. Alone at night and under the secret confidence of his blankets, he sang softly and as if in Mother's voice:

*'Jesus bids us shine in a pure, clear light*
*Like a little candle burning in the night*
*He looks down from heaven to see us shine*
*You in your small corner and me in mine.'*

The term crept on slowly, each week becoming colder and more dismal. The hope of Christmas and the holidays shone through the night with promise. But when the holidays eventually came all was not as it had been before but was disappointingly remote. He was no longer truly a part of it all but a visitor. He could see it but not feel it, as though he was feeling something warm and precious through a gloved hand.

Slowly each experience became less intense: the going away, the returning home. The summer term brought a new experience and summer sports were less miserable, although in summer the ball was hard and uncompromising and it was all too quick. He would wait endlessly to bat but when, eventually and by default, it was his turn to bat he took his place with great reluctance. His only chance was to go forward with his bat just a soon as the boy at the other end had let fly. He would stab into the thin air, hoping against hope that he would feel the contact and knowing that there was little chance.

Nobody wanted Cherry-Garrard in their team. His appointment to a team was greeted by muffled groans. Yet at night in the dormitories and under the cover of the bedclothes he imagined a different world. 'It's a damned close run thing. There are eight to make and only three men left to bat. Cherry-Gerrard comes out to bat for England. There is polite applause from the pavilion but all the world holds its breath. The Umpire gives him 'Middle Leg'. Cherry-Garrard strikes the crease and stands tall to survey the fielders. The bowler comes down fast from the other end but Cherry-Garrard sweeps the ball away for a magnificent four runs. The General sees and nods to his companion, '76 to go.' The second ball is nicked through for two runs but the fielder is quick and retrieves at pace. Bravo Cherry-Garrard is in!'

Under the covers, the runs neatly tallied, Cherry stayed awake to the end.

In English they read Newbolt's poem and had to learn it by heart, each boy mechanically recited the words in a dreary voice:

*'There's a breathless hush in the Close tonight -*
*Ten to make and the match to win -*
*A bumping pitch and a blinding light,*
*An hour to play and the last man in.*
*And it's not for the sake of a ribboned coat,*
*Or the selfish hope of a season's fame,*
*But his Captain's hand on his shoulder smote*
*"Play up! play up! And play the game!'*

Cherry found the words uplifting and was pleased to somehow own them. He was learning to survive. He learned about declensions and acquired a confusion of ever-changing verbs. He read the poetry of Newbolt and Tennyson and Browning. He had calculated the most improbable sums but more than anything else he learned to live apart from Lamer.

There were Sunday afternoon walks when Mr Hussey took his form out in a long crocodile. They walked along the sea shore and saw the fishing boats drawn up on the beach and breathed the invigorating coastal air but they were never allowed to go near the water's edge. The older boys were made to plunge into the sea as a fine manly pursuit but the first years were spared. Cherry, who could not swim, dreaded the prospect and feared that this would be another area where he let the side down.

Lamer missed him when he went away to school, and when he came back for Christmas and Easter holidays it was all too brief and painful. He felt that at each return to school he left something more of himself behind at Lamer: a small piece of *Woodland Magic*, something that he longed to discover again on his return. He also felt a growing desire, a compulsion, to prove himself.

It was a May holiday time, all the bushes were soaked in white blossom. Cherry stood on the lower branches of the old mulberry and rocked himself forward and backwards, his eyes fixed on the lane and the White Bridge beyond. Ida was sitting by her apple tree, watching him. Cherry was attracted by the sun on the whiteness, the dirty white of the lane, the White Bridge and beyond it the pure white of bushes. He had to go. He swung down to the ground and started off down the lane, calling to Ida over his shoulder and telling her to stay. But she ran down the lane after him and caught him up long before he reached the White Bridge. Cherry heard her running and turned to catch sight of a young girl running well and strongly, her hair blown back and framing an intent face. He urged her to go back but he knew that she wouldn't and he was pleased with her company. They walked together all the way down the white path to Hobbs's house. All the adults were away at work but young Alfred Hobbs was there working in the garden. As they approached the White Bridge he stopped working to lean on his spade in the manner of his father, and to stare at them. They were passing over the bridge when he called to them.

'Where are you going? You shouldn't go down there.'

It reminded Cherry, too uncomfortably, of the time that they had been found by Young Hobbs in the brook. It was as though Alfred Hobbs was watching them and found them wanting. Cherry answered that he would go where he pleased. Alfred went back to his digging and let the two children to pass out of their world and into the unknown world of Whitebushes.

At first it was all simple enough, the two children walked on to the common. There were the white bushes in the full glory of May, the air was laden with their heavy, unfragrant perfume and from the top of a great bush a song thrush belted out his old, repetitive song. There was a variety of animals tethered on the common, goats wrapped themselves round their chains and bleated in protest at their confinement and an old cow looked up at them as they passed but didn't stop chewing. Further down the path a small flock of geese obstructed their progress and bent their necks low to the ground to hiss at them. Both children found this unnerving and were quite pleased when a group of boys with sticks pushed the geese aside. The three boys seemed very dark and unclean to the children. Their clothes were old and shabby and their heavy boots were too big for them and clearly second hand. Cherry and Ida were pleased to be clear of the geese but the boys' manner was unsettling because they came right up to them with no show of respect and looked hard in their faces. One of the boys put his hand on Cherry's jacket and looked closely at the material. 'What do you want for that coat?' he demanded. Cherry was confused and didn't know how to reply. 'I'll trade you,' said the boy and from his pocket he produced a very old and shabby pocket knife.

'This is a good knife,' added the boy as he rolled the small knife in the palm of his hand. 'It could cut a throat.'

Here was a poorer, nastier world that was pleased to show its lack of respect. Cherry found the boys dark, foreign, menacing and reckless.

'No thank you, 'he stammered. 'We must go home now,' and taking Ida by the hand they started to retrace their steps back up the path. The boys followed behind them calling out, 'Trade for the knife! No thank you, no thank you,' and laughed raucously. The two children started to run but the boys ran behind them calling to them over and over again in the same mocking voices. 'No thank you, no thank you!'

The boys could run faster than the two children and easily kept pace, sometimes darting in front of them to pull ugly faces and to shout out their refrain but as they neared the Hobbs's house the boys dropped further behind so that by the time the children crossed The White Bridge the boys had already turned back. Cherry heard them singing, in hard taunting voices, and he knew what they were singing because he had heard Young Hobbs whistle it and he knew the tune of *The Greenwood's Shady Dell.*

Worst was the knowledge that Alfred Hobbs had seen them. Cherry couldn't see him but somehow knew that he was watching and taking it all in. The incident upset Ida but Cherry felt it more deeply. He insisted that they should never tell and that they would keep it as their secret.

The summer holidays came at last and Cherry breathed again something of the world of childhood and went with Ida to 'their' trees. He told her about his time at The Grange. In her mind Cherry had grown immensely older and wiser as though his journey to prep school was an expedition to a foreign land. He told her about some of the boys and one of the boys in particular called Carpenter whom he greatly admired and secretly hoped to befriend. He also told her about the sea and his fear of the water. He meant to sound strong and positive but she sensed his loneliness and isolation. They liked to sit and chatter with the outside staff and Hobbs, in particular, and then there were the expeditions. They made a good combination because her sight was good. She could spot the birds and butterflies in flight and tell him where to look and he could run in pursuit. His discoveries delighted her and he delighted in pleasing. She would direct him where to find things and he would always bring his catches back to her.

Hobbs had time for them because Young Hobbs took on more of his real workload. Hobbs showed them how to mount the butterflies. Their first was an orange tip and Ida's heart nearly burst as she saw it fluttering to death in the chloroform. Cherry winced at the sight but he told his sister and himself that it was important to do it for their natural history collection, but the butterfly took a terribly long time to die. Hobbs showed him how to lay the corpse on a board and to pin back the wings so that its powdery, veined delicacy was resurrected. They loved the hunting but hated the killing despite reassurances that there were plenty. Their butterfly collection increased one by one: red admiral, tortoiseshell, meadow brown, wall, speckled wood and some skippers. Hobbs also showed them how to blow eggs, but laid an injunction on Cherry never to take more than one. Chaffinch, dunnock and robin joined the egg collection and best of all, there was the red-backed shrike or butcher bird, which impaled small creatures on blackthorn and kept its own larder. Ida spotted the birds going to and fro from a high, dense hedge of hawthorn and Cherry inspected the place but then had to climb and work his way through the hard thorns, tearing his flesh as he climbed up into the narrow branches and clawed hands of the tree. His face hands and arms were cut and scratched but he managed to push his fingers into the nest and extract one, small, warm egg which he carried to the earth in his mouth. When they went to blow it the egg had already started to incubate and despite all his care with the needle and gentle blowing the shell crumbled slightly. They were desperately disappointed but Ida was not deterred. She set the egg carefully in its bed of cotton wool so that nobody could tell.

At the end of that first summer term, the General called Cherry into his study to discuss the lad's school report. There was little here to thrill the heart of a father. The boy was a duffer at games although his academic progress gave reason for qualified hope.

'Cherry-Garrard has made reasonable progress this year but his mind does tend to wander and there is an air of dreaminess about him,' wrote Mr Hussey in his assessment of a year's Latin.

The General read the words aloud to his son. 'Something we must watch,' the General commented. 'Dreaming is not altogether a bad thing but a little goes a long way.'

The General's role as a teacher was redundant but he still watched the boy carefully, hoping for signs of manliness. He realised that Cherry's poor sight would handicap him in team games and decided that he would teach him to swim, which was a fine, manly pursuit. The General ordered Young Hobbs to clear an area of the lake and when it was ready father and son set forth. Old Hobbs saw them leave in a trap, the old man wearing angler's waders and the small boy, wearing his trunks under his trousers, carried his towel under his arm. The General waded in first and stood in the water which came up to the top of his waders. Cherry was ordered to follow. The mud of the lake floor squeezed between his toes as he edged forward into the tepid water but the General's voice was even and uncompromising, so he waded on up his waist and stood a short distance from the General with his arms folded round his white body.

'Push off my boy and float to me,' commanded the General.

Cherry felt the rush of the cold water as he slid forward. There was a moment of chill abandon before the General's strong hands caught and gripped his and lifted him up, effortlessly and clear of the water. His father was pleased, Cherry felt the strong hands and glimpsed the General's face as he rose from the water to stand in the lake.

The exercise was repeated with the General standing first six inches and then a foot further away. Cherry was told to kick his feet and paddle with his arms to assist the forward motion. That night Cherry dreamt that he was down in the lake and swimming round and round, his arms working a breast stroke entirely unassisted. He told the Old General about the dream and the General seemed much amused.

'Of course you can swim,' he said. 'You just have to believe it.'

At the second session the General stood some twelve feet away and further than could possibly be attributed to simple push and glide. When this was accomplished, the General announced that Cherry could swim and so saying waded from the lake to the bank where he proceeded to sit down and light a cigar.

'Go on then. Just swim round as you please. Dreams always tell us something.'

It seemed to Cherry at that point that his father believed in him and that the Old General's display of nonchalance was to prove the point. Cherry pushed forward as he had done before but this time he kicked firmly with his legs and worked his arms and to his immense joy he felt himself making forward motion through the water and incredibly he was swimming. He heard the General chuckling and his heart filled with joy.

That first year passed and it was in a stronger frame of mind that Cherry went back for a second year to the Grange. The second year was much better than the first, even though there was no improvement in Cherry's sporting prowess he had gained in both age and confidence and no longer felt so strange in his world. The Grange prided itself on its healthy sea air and on Sunday afternoons the boys marched down to the beach to swim in the English Channel. Most of the boys dreaded this but to his surprise Cherry found the whole experience not unpleasant, the cold did not seem to bother him so much and his vision was not a handicap. Best of all he found that he could swim better than the other boys.

A boy called Carpenter was particularly impressed and lent Cherry a copy of *Boys Own Paper*. One story was entitled *The Thrilling Tale of Captain Matthew Webb* and the picture showed a muscular Webb swimming gallantly in the violent sea. The story went on: 'Every English boy worth his salt would be proud to be like Captain Webb who defied the great challenge and swam the English Channel. They told him that it was impossible but the captain was not a man to stop at that which is merely possible. Webb defied the tides, jellyfish and dolphins to be the first man ever to set off from the English coast and to put his foot down on French soil some thirty six hours later.' It added, 'The young Webb first learned to swim in his native Shropshire and as a young lad saved his brother from drowning in the river Severn.'

Something changed with the gift of that paper. Cherry became known as 'Cherry' to the boys and the 'Garrard' element was lost. The loan of the paper, combined with his name change, signalled that he was accepted. He threw himself into swimming and Carpenter and he achieved some notice as 'a couple of rum 'uns' but not soft.' Their emerging friendship was desperately important to Cherry. Keeping Carpenter's esteem was crucial so Cherry swam furiously no matter how cold or rough the sea might be.

On the face of it, it was an unlikely friendship. Carpenter's people were not from the land-owning classes and he would not be able to go on to one of the great public schools but would have to attend a day school nearer to home. He may have been untypical but he was a tough character and was not bullied. Carpenter, like Cherry, was something of an outsider and in his own way needed Cherry's social respectability as the son of a General and an heir to estates. By the end of that second summer the two were friends and drew one or two other boys to the fringes of their friendship.

Holidays at Lamer were a time of growing affection between father and son. The General would take Cherry shooting and Cherry marked the hits in a leather-bound notebook and was instructed to watch and learn. He wanted to hold the gun himself and be a hunter like Bevis, but the General said that this must wait a while.

The General also taught him the basics of fishing. He bought him a reel and a bamboo rod and walked with him to the pools on the estate and to the lakes. There they fished with float and worm and caught roach and perch and sometimes carp. Cherry fished the pools of the local farms and the tenants indulged him and sometimes brought out mugs of tea while he was fishing. He was content to sit for hours, mesmerised by the float. When it bobbed, he knew it was a small perch or roach, but when it slid beneath the water, his heart raced in anticipation, and on striking he hoped to feel the firm pull of a carp. Sometimes Ida went with him on his expeditions and divided her time between chatting with the farmer's wife and gathering wild flowers, and sometimes she would sit beside him and watch the painted float but its movements never held much charm for her.

Then there were red letter days when the General would boom out to the children, 'We're off to the lakes, make haste for the lakes, make haste!'

This cry sent the children into a flurry of excitement, even though the whole event had been carefully stage-managed by their parents. Full of laughter and fun the family clambered aboard the carriage, the younger girls squealing in delight and not being corrected. Mother and cook had already prepared the picnic. When all was ready, Hobbs led off his animated wagon load of laughing, chattering people and they made their way to the lakes. On arrival the first thing that had to be established was the pitching of the tent. This fell to Young Hobbs who was directed by the General and assisted by Cherry. Cherry focussed hard on driving the pegs into the ground and trying but not succeeding in making his strokes as easy and hard as Young Hobbs. Bit by bit the flapping canvas began to acquire status of a tent and there was that moment of intense excitement as it rose from its sprawled state on the ground to the living form of a tent. Mother then ordered the dressing of the tent, while the General, aglow with delight at it all, played excitedly with the little ones giving then piggy back rides and generally over-exciting them to such an extent that even Mother had to protest. When finally prepared, the great tent embraced the sky over Cherry's head in canvas.

But sometimes when the General lay on his back in the tent, and looked up at the taut canvas, his thoughts drifted to his tent on the veldt and those days with Saltmarshe. Then he had to shut his eyes tight and focus on the sounds of the children, grasping the here and now and the warmth all around him, and shutting out the memories. For young Cherry those long days of childhood were utterly joyful, the warm canvas smell of the brown tent as it gently flapped in the breeze, the squeal of the girls as they ran about playing games with the General and Mother, and the rush of muddy, carpey water as Cherry swam in the lake. They played and ate and laughed and swam until Young Hobbs returned with the carriage to take them home. Cherry longed to hold on to the moment until the very last and to seal it safe in his soul for all time.

There were also times, which Cherry treasured more than any other, when the General took him fishing on the lakes. It was a time of quiet pleasure too for the General who recalled with affection the times that he and his brother, George, had spent on the same lakes. When Cherry was older the General took him winter fishing for pike on the upper lake. A boat was kept ready for these special occasions. The General taught him to row so that he could take charge of the boat. They would row out to the middle and drop anchor. The General showed Cherry the technique of paying out the heavy line and dropping it into folds at the bottom of the boat. The end of the line was weighted with a heavy spoon and could be cast quite easily out into the lake. The angler wound the reel to bring the flashing spoon to the side of the boat so that the exercise of casting and retrieving could be repeated. The lake was fairly shallow and full of weed and the progress of the spoon was often halted by the weed. Cherry had to persevere but he was determined to catch a fish and when he caught his first pike, a four pounder, he was delighted. The General was visibly pleased and shook him by the hand, a glorious moment for Cherry and one he treasured all his life.

Those short years rolled by summer by summer as Cherry eased into the routine of terms and 'hols' that brought him to the time for his Common Entrance examination, which he passed gaining a place at Winchester, while for Carpenter the local grammar school awaited. It was decided that Winchester would harness Cherry's intellect and make him less dreamy. The General thought that a boy must grow to be a man and play his part in the world, and if this was not to be in the army then it would be as a scholar and a landed gentleman. The Cherry-Garrard estates must be maintained and passed on to Cherry and his heirs, a man could not be too vigilant in this regard.

That last summer holiday Carpenter came to stay for a week. The visit was not a great success. Carpenter seemed overawed and did not fit comfortably into life at Lamer. The discomfort was most acute over dinner. Now that Cherry and Ida were old enough they dined, most evenings, with their parents and during his stay Carpenter was included. The younger girls still had nursery tea and only dined with their parents on special occasions. Carpenter looked uncomfortable in his new grammar school uniform and the conversation was stilted. On one occasion they were dining on fish when Carpenter set up a terrible choking noise, followed by a good deal of coughing and spluttering, from which it was gathered that he had a bone stuck in his throat. Everybody expressed concern which only made matters worse. Cherry was detailed to take Carpenter to the kitchen and to see what could be done. In the kitchen the unfortunate Carpenter gargled and spluttered under the tap until it was decided that the bone and he had parted company. Their return to the dining table was warmly welcomed and the fish course dispensed with as a gesture of solidarity but Carpenter remained in total silence for the rest of the meal.

Because Cherry was to be a 'public school man' the General allowed him to swim on his own in the lakes. Carpenter could not ride so the boys cycled there most days. At the lake they were more at ease and enjoyed each others' company but on the final occasion they arrived at the lake to find that Alfred Hobbs and two older youths, who Cherry identified as sons of Ernie and of George, had defied convention and taken noisy possession of the water. Carpenter was surprised that this seemed to annoy Cherry so much. He stood on the bank with his arms folded and stared at the swimmers. They saw him but made no effort to leave the water. To make matters worse they pretended not to see the new arrivals and whistled a tune which was only too familiar to the heir of Lamer, followed by a good deal of shouting and laughing. Cherry was very put out and insisted that he and Carpenter return to the house immediately to report the matter to Hobbs. Hobbs apologised and said that the matter would be dealt with, but Carpenter was confused and couldn't see what all the fuss was about. It was a hot day and there was space enough for them all. Cherry was put into an unusually bad mood by the whole affair and avoided the lake thereafter. It seemed strange to Carpenter that if Cherry was so upset by this incident he should say nothing of it to the General. It became clear to both boys that their friendship was doomed.

Cherry spent the rest of the summer in his own way at Lamer and he added many specimens to his natural history collection. These included a white admiral and a silver-washed fritillary. Ida came with him on some of his walks and on one occasion felt sure that she had seen a purple emperor, which they chased along a wood for some time before accepting that it was gone. There were several expeditions to hunt for a purple emperor but they never saw one again.

Ida was not always with her brother. Because there were now four girls, Mother needed her in the house. She had her own friends, including Elspeth from the hospital. Cherry was growing to accept Elspeth's presence more and more. Elspeth didn't want to come on their expeditions and indeed Cherry did not want to share them with her because these were very much private ventures, but Elspeth was welcome enough in the house and she had a good sense of humour and made them both laugh - although there were matters and places that Cherry and Ida kept separate and secret from Elspeth and everybody else.

The long summer ran to another close. It was a time of ending and beginning and Cherry prepared to end childhood and to begin young manhood. This time there would be no leave taking of the mulberry. He remembered that occasion with embarrassment and was glad that there had been nobody there to see him. He was nervous of Winchester but determined to put a good face on it and acquit himself well and in a way that would please the Old General. He would never shine but he was determined to make a good fist of it. He could never be Odysseus but he could aspire to being Telemachus.

# CHAPTER THREE

<u>3rd November 1899</u>
*Culver House*
*Winchester*

*Dear Ida*
  *Culver House is really very nice. The men all refer to it as*
*'Kenny's.' Every morning starts with a cold tub and all the other men*
*make a big fuss about it but I know how Father would be if I funked it*
*so I show them that I am strong enough for it. They call me 'Penguin'*
*because I am not afraid of cold water. If there's going to be swimming*
*at Gunner's Hole then I'll show them, just as I did at the Grange.*
  *You would laugh if you saw me because I now have to wear a straw*
*boater and a funny short jacket. There is a boy here called Matthews*
*who has a hobby egg in his collection at home and sometimes we talk*
*about natural history. Matthews is my 'Pater' and shows me how to*
*do my duties as a fag. I have to fag for a chap called Preston. I am*
*lucky to have Preston as he is not a great fellow for beatings. I am*
*going to have to be a 'Peal Caller' and wake up all the men in the*
*galleries for Chapel on Sunday. The bells are rung for fifteen before*
*Chapel on Sundays and for five minutes on week days. 'Bells go*
*rotten' for the first five minutes on Sunday, when at regular intervals*
*a single bell is tolled three times. 'Bells go double' for the second*
*five minutes, when six bells are used. 'Bells go single' for the last*
*five minutes and 'Bells go down' when they stop. I do hope that I*
*remember all this.*
  *After the Grange it is all so much bigger and more challenging*
*but I will do my best to make a good fist of it, for Father's sake if not*
*mine. One really good thing about this place is that they are far more*
*relaxed about letters home and certainly Preston isn't too bothered*
*about censoring letters home so we can write much as we please.*
*When I write to you I want you to know and understand how I feel.*
*Let's have our very own, special pact in this respect.*
  *From your brother*
  *Apsley*

## Winchester, 1899

Winchester: ancient, stony-hard, forbidding seemed to Cherry to be infused with darkness. The future heir of Lamer had to take his place as a new boy again. It was as though Fortune's wheel had taken him to its apex, at The Grange, only to cast him down as the lowest and newest and least significant of all boys. He owed deference to all as though he was a mere native in the glorious empire of Winchester. Here the great boys ruled and kept their order by the swish of the cane, but they were admired too for their athleticism and strength and for the great power that they wielded and the rough justice they administered. Above them were the ancient rules of Winchester and the unpredictable, unfathomable and unchallenged laws of the gods. Yet through all this a fag must do what was asked of him and hope to be favoured by the gods. If so, he might become a champion one day and rule as he had been ruled. The gentler, female world grew further and further into the deep recesses of a fading past.

In his new House, familiarly known as Kenny's, there were new rules, new places and even a new language. Cherry took to his surrogate 'native' duties without complaint and as dutifully as he could. He retreated into himself but found that he could survive the worst brutalities of man on boy by grinding at the classics where he could achieve better than most and he avoided the worst brutalities of boy on boy by showing the same 'guts' he had shown at The Grange.

The daily routine in Kenny's started in the same way. The duty 'dorm prefect' strode into the dormitory:

'Hands off cocks and onto socks!'

A cold tub followed, which even the biggest and toughest of the boys hated but Cherry feigned indifference and earned respect. This was followed by dressing and when he was old enough, fagging duties. All had to be performed at the greatest speed possible before the boys clattered through breakfast. Morning Prayer and school followed.

There was still the challenge of games but no reputation had preceded him from The Grange and there was no expectation and no bitter disappointment to overcome. He accepted his insignificance in these things and winter sports had become tolerable in that his rotten vision could be compensated, in part, by sheer bluster and intent. When the ball came into his vision he hacked at it fiercely and he developed a determination in his tackling that earned him some admiration. At all costs the notion to avoid was 'funk.' A man who 'funked' was the lowest thing, just not being good at something was tolerable.

A new century, rich in British opportunity and wealth, was about to dawn but the old century ran to a troubled close. Something was wrong in Southern Africa and the word 'Boer' was spat out with contempt. New words such as 'Kimberley' and 'Ladysmith' troubled the mind. Worse was to come in the form of 'Colenso'. Somehow it had to end in the empire's favour, it couldn't last the year but still the Boers came on and it wasn't over in a year.

Down in Whitebushes, in Nan's, they were used to talking about wars as they chewed their cherry wood pipes and drank pints of flat beer. The cycle of wars rolled through their lives and the brown-stained wall of the alehouse stored anecdotes of desert, plain and veldt. Some of them carried the scars of war in mind and body. But this was a different war, a war against Europeans and not against natives, and those Boers knew how to fight. Young Hobbs was past the age when he could be expected to enlist and his son, Alfred, was far too young to go. But even had he been the right age Young Hobbs would not have wanted to go, he wanted other things and didn't share his father's inner content. In Nan's there was confusion about the war. Hobbs was not pleased but there were those who said that it was nothing to do with them. In spite of this, Ernie's lad had gone and George's boy had gone with him. They had wanted the adventure and dreamed of the excitements beyond the confines of the estate. Those two young men had been the backbone of the Morris side and this added to Young Hobbs's negative attitude to estate life. No matter what Hobbs said or felt, something of the old ways slipped away with the dying of the old century.

Back in his study, the General took it all badly and fretted over his copy of *The Times*, looking over the names of the dead and remembering their fathers and brothers. He thought about Saltmarshe and wondered what he would have made of it all. No doubt he would have cited Greeks fighting Greeks as further evidence of a disintegrating world order. The General also missed his son and worried about him.

Winthrope, the Kenny's House Captain, planned to join up at the end of the year. The House buzzed with phrases such as: 'Now those Boers better watch out. Old Kruger is in for a terrible brocking,' or 'it'll all be over before he gets there, damn shame!'

Winchester formed its own corps and drilled with intensity. The new thing was the khaki uniform, brown and dusty as the veldt. Old boys came back to the school in their new uniforms, confident of imminent victory but victory became less certain and the confidence of empire wavered. The impossible could just be possible and all the breeding and training and making ready of bodies and minds could fall to some mounted barbarians on the plains of Africa. This was a war that had to be fought and won.

Cherry had to join the Corps and be drilled in army discipline. The boys were issued with ill-fitting uniforms and had to parade on the playing ground, striking their heavy boots on the hard surface. For the senior boys it was an opportunity to learn the place of the NCO, barking orders, demanding endless marching and revelling in their power over the juniors. To his disappointment Cherry found he had no aptitude for it and the Friday afternoons dedicated to corps were a trial.

A red-faced sixteen-year-old in a forage cap thrust his face in front of Cherry's and bellowed. 'If your pater is a bloody general why can't you bleeding well march!'

Cherry hated that boy with intensity but he hated himself more.

Between Cherry and his father there grew to be an understanding that Cherry would never be right for the army, his poor sight was not the only barrier to this ambition. But there were other things a man could do to make a mark. Young Cherry was to be fitted for spectacles. The ugly, pebble thick glasses hurt his pride but there was the compensation of seeing. He couldn't use them for football but he could for cricket and his game marginally improved and, most excitingly of all, he could wear them on his walks. He saw the dipping green and scarlet head of the woodpecker, marvelled at the flash of kingfisher blue and could identify all the butterflies on the wing. He no longer needed Ida's eyes and could see what he had always imagined to be there, but he never saw again an elusive purple emperor.

His academic work improved and he showed promise in Greek. There was a thrill to reading words that he loved in their original but he was always too quick to rush to translation and hurry on the story line. He learned the trick of using one of the many annotated copies of the original that abounded in the school and simply memorised translated passages from *The Odyssey: 'But before we were out of earshot, I shouted out derisive words at Polyphemus. Cyclops! So he was such a weakling after all, the man whose friends you meant to overpower and eat in the hollow of your cave! And your crimes were bound to catch up with you, you brute, who did not shrink from devouring your guests. Now Zeus and all the other gods have paid you out.'*

*My words so enraged the Cyclops that he tore the top off a great pinnacle of rock and hurled it at us. The rock fell just ahead of our blue-painted bows. As it plunged in, the water surged up and the backwash, like the swell of the open sea, swept us landward and nearly drove us up the beach'.*

Cherry pondered the situation. Odysseus had just saved himself and his men through his cunning and ingenuity but now indulged in unreasonable passion and pride, provoking the Cyclops, for no purpose or gain. Poseiden was so enraged that the crews of both ships would eventually be lost with the sole exception of Odysseus himself. He translated further than the set passage:

*At this the Cyclops lifted up his hands to the starry heavens and prayed to Lord Poseidon: 'Hear me, Poseidon, Sustainer of the Earth, god of the sable locks. If I am yours indeed and you claim me as your son, grant that Odysseus, sacker of cities and son of Laertes, may never reach his home in Ithaca. But if he is destined to see his friends again, to come once more to his own house and reach his native land, let him come late, in wretched plight, having lost all his comrades, in a foreign ship, and let him find trouble in his home.*

'The empire is on the offensive - now watch out Kruger!' The school was full of it. In his mind Cherry saw Winthrope as a Greek hero in khaki, driving the Boer before him on the plains of Africa. But the great empire choked and spluttered, like the new motor car which had come down from London to Lamer. Both were meant to be part of the new, modern age and yet neither one lived up to expectation.

The language was triumphant, the euphemistic 'Relief of Ladysmith' and then 'Spion Kop', but brothers and cousins were being killed. The Warden read out the names of the fallen at Chapel and Winthrope was among them. Winthrope, so tall and manly, a lion at Winchester football, feared as a prefect of Hall who dealt out rough justice with his cane but in the end knew the difference between the genuinely good and the bad, was now dead and not yet twenty. It was as though a single sniper's shot had penetrated the head of over five hundred years of Winchester tradition. The Warden spoke in chapel in honour of the fallen. He spoke of the greatness of empire and the malice and evil of those who sought to overturn it:

'Europe is full of envy of us and would like a slice of our great empire. So we must all be ready to protect her. The time may well come when every man is called upon to be ready and to do his duty and I know that you men before me now will keep that sacred trust and will be ready when the time comes to lead and inspire and to do your duty to God and the King.'

Cherry knew that he must take his place in the ranks of life and make his own individual contribution. He must make his mark. It was not enough to be a country gentleman, more was expected. The General's words, 'Some work of noble nature,' rang in the rattle of football studs on the entrance to the changing rooms and reverberated in the chatter of voices in the cloisters and echoed back in ringing tones under the Three Arches on Lamer estate. Duty and obligation were his inheritance, along with Denford, Lamer and all the Cherry-Garrard holdings. The figure in the picture, which Hobbs and Young Hobbs had hung in the hall at Lamer, was a leader who did not shirk his duty. Cherry knew that he must be like that hero and must not let the true values of empire down no matter how high a price was demanded.

Then at the darkest point a ray of light: Mafeking was relieved! The school went wild with delight. Perhaps now order would be returned and all made right? The chapel bell rang in celebration and the corps finished drill with three cheers for good old Baden-Powell and the chaps at Mafeking!

But the war didn't end and neither did the dying. The Boer was defeated in battle but fought on in a new way. The tide had turned but the flotsam was left on the sands.

In Whitebushes all looked much the same, livestock still grazed the rough grass and there were still wild boys with an air of the old times about them. Nan's was still there and of an evening the men from the estate would gather round the fire to hear Old Hobbs's story, even though he had told it many times before and was growing old. Young Hobbs had little interest in the old ways and no interest in the General's world. He had a particular skill with machinery and learned to drive the motorcar and took the General and his family about in it. Others at Nan's were less fortunate. Ernie's lad had stayed over in Africa and George's lad had been killed. The clientele of Nan's had become older and reduced in number as men departed the land or died in foreign graves that could never be visited. England had lost some of its self belief and swung through the seasons less confidently. The flycatchers came back season after season to nest in the ivy below Cherry's window, the nightingales still sang in the dark woods and always the swallows returned to Hobbs's garden room but there was a frailty in this new world and concern as to how things would work out.

The General suffered distress from the war. He knew the nature of war and the loss of men from the estate took its toll on his health. Now he no longer saw the finer quality and aspirations of it all, the drab, mud-coloured khaki of the new uniforms reflected the nature of this war. He wanted the Tories to win the election but he disliked their low tactics and the claim that a vote for the Liberals was a vote for the Boers depressed him. There were contradictions which troubled him, the Tories and Lord Salisbury had seized control but there were two Labour representatives in Parliament and there were other troubles which would not go away. People no longer just accepted things as they were - they asked for more and went on strike. The estate struggled and even though he wanted to keep things as they were he could no longer do so. He was obliged to sell some of the holdings he had acquired from his dead brother.

Then, as if to sum up the mood of change, the old queen died. The General appeared philosophical about it and there was much to be positive about with the promise of a new baby and an invitation to take up the position of High Sheriff but for all this there was a sense of time passing too quickly and matters not being the same. The good news was no more than a sudden spell of brightness before the sun sank below the horizon.

Even after victory, news trickled through of disturbing things. The boys at Winchester couldn't understand what the Boer was up to. They were beaten but wouldn't give up. There was talk of a thing called guerrilla fighting. Apparently the Boer didn't attempt to fight in pitched battles but struck where and when he wanted and then galloped away. The boys were outraged but as time went on a feeling of admiration developed for the sheer pluck of the Boer and his indomitable spirit. The names of the Boer leaders began to be sounded with a degree of admiration and acquired a cult-like status. One of the Boer leaders, a chap called De Wet, particularly caught their imagination. Time and again he eluded capture and was able to ride away in the nick of time. The younger boys swapped stories of De Wet. There were pictures of him, a debonair buccaneer with a broad rimmed hat and a rakish moustache. Cherry could not but help finding something of Robin Hood in this character, as he dipped and bobbed across the Orange River and mocked the rule of the Sheriff. It troubled Cherry that he should admire De Wet and yet not be comfortable with his values. Some had pictures of De Wet, and the guerrilla leaders, and swapped them like contraband. There was a song with a haunting refrain of 'De Wet, De Wet, De Wet'. The boys whispered it to each other, a secret communication in restrained defiance of something they felt but could not explain or justify. It put Cherry in mind of that tune that some on the estate liked to whistle.

The General had been irritated and saddened by developments in South Africa. He was relieved when peace came but criticism of the conduct of the war grieved him. Stories were being circulated of Boer women and children dying in the camps that he had been set up for their protection. When Cherry was away at school the General brooded in his library and sometimes he was alone there with Saltmarshe. He heard Saltmarshe's voice asking, 'Why should the Greeks do that?' and saw his honest, bewildered, open face across the fire on the veldt. But if he thought too long about Africa it always ended in the face of the pleading African, which transformed into Saltmarshe's dead face and his mind became so crowded with terrible images that he had to leave the library and seek out the girls and the bright, white, innocence of their world. The birth of yet another girl, Edith, that July aroused mixed feelings in the old man. When he held the baby in his arms there was the same incredulity at the wonder of it all but there was also a sense of terrible responsibility for bringing something so small and vulnerable into such a troubled world. Cherry noted the change in his father and worried about these things. One day, all too soon, these worries would be his and then he would be found wanting.

The General decided that it was time for Cherry to play a part in the affairs of the estate and that when home for holidays he should attend the weekly meetings with Mr Hampton, the Land Agent. On Monday mornings Cherry went with Hampton into the General's study. The study put Cherry in mind of those days before he went to school when the General has helped him with Latin, and he remembered with affection the time that he had written, *'Agricola puellam amat'* and how pleased his father had been. Nothing in the study had changed, there was the great, oak desk, and there were the General's pictures of College and days out on the veldt with his friend, but the man in the pictures had changed. He was much older but more than this, he had lost confidence and zest for life. The General could be querulous and little that Hampton said pleased him. He kept a tight grip on the affairs of the estate, and his knowledge of the detail was impressive, but something was slipping away. Those meetings left Cherry less secure about the future and it worried him that if the General could not help the gentle slide of their affairs then how would he cope when he was in charge? But the Old General was adamant that there were fluctuations in these matters and that the slide would soon halt and better days lay ahead. There was peace with the Boer and Lord Salisbury was back at the helm and England would always be England and at the heart of it were the great estates such as Lamer.

The time had come for Cherry to leave Winchester and to be a man in a man's world. He would not miss Winchester and Kenny's other than as a marker in life that had passed all too quickly. His time there had been inglorious and he determined to make more of Oxford, the work of 'Noble Nature' remained longed for but unfulfilled. There was one more holiday before he went up to Oxford, one more holiday for the things he loved so well but the Old General was less present to be part of them and the girls, especially Ida, were more independent and more obviously young ladies. Ida and Elspeth spent much time together, talking of things that only interested young ladies.

In that last summer holiday Reggie Smith began to have an influence in Cherry's life. Cousin Reggie was older and something of a man of the world. He was a publisher and his contact with some of the current literary greats was impressive. Reggie owned a cottage in the Highlands, called Burnside, where they had regular visits from the interesting people of the day and where walk and talk was on the daytime menu and talk and food on the evening. Cherry was delighted to be invited to spend some time at Burnside. He saw it as recognition of emerging manhood. On the first visit Cherry felt terribly young and gauche, his only claim to being there at all was his relationship with Reggie but the free conversation of Reggie's friends showed him a new world of ideas and possibilities which offered something different to both Winchester and Lamer. He was excited by the prospect of Oxford where importance and prowess were not based on the narrow set of standards set by public school but by new, open possibilities.

After Cherry's return from Burnside the General chose to speak directly to him. Cherry had many conversations with his father but this one was to stay with him for the rest of his life. He was invited by to take a stroll and to have, as the General put it, a bit of a 'confab' about the estate. The General walked badly and was more than usually distracted. When they came to the old Chapel, he stopped and pointed with his cane at some tall hawthorn which was growing close the place that years ago he and Ida had pretended to be Old People. A pair of magpies made a terrible fuss over a great ugly nest.

'I expect that you have a magpie egg in your collection?' the General said.

Cherry was surprised by the question because the General was well acquainted with his collection but he reassured him on this point.

'They remind me rather of the hamerkop,' the General went on. 'They are such loud, outrageous birds, prone to building the most improbable nests from the most improbable of materials. There was this chap in the Cape called Saltmarshe who had the most wonderful collection of eggs. Poor old Saltmarshe, the Xhosa did for him I'm afraid. Damn waste! I could have been there in support, you know and who knows, if I had, he might be alive today but I stuck to orders and that was that.'

'I'm sure that you did everything you reasonably could,' said Cherry.

'Yes, but what is reasonable in an unreasonable state of affairs? There are times when you just have to trust to your instincts and for friendship's sake put all other considerations behind you. If you don't, you run the risk of spending the rest of your life in regret.'

Cherry was less sure. 'Surely, we have to live by orders and in that way keep the balance of our society? If every man picked and chose, the outcome would be chaos.'

'Perhaps, but in the end I can't help but recall that I let poor Saltmarshe down. His life had so much potential for good and we are all the poorer for the lack of him. Had he lived I could have turned to him for support when I most needed it. We would have been together on the journey. Anyway, what is done can't be undone. I have something of his that I want you to keep. Here, you take this.'

The General drove his hand into his deep coat pockets and took out an old and worn volume of *The Odyssey*.

'It was Saltmarshe's,' he explained, 'and as you are going up to the House to read Classics it is quite appropriate. You can see his notes here. He was for ever quoting from the thing.'

Cherry took the volume and there were Saltmarshe's notes scribbled in the margins.

'You will inherit many things from me in the years to come,' said the General, 'houses, estates and lands, but this book means more to me than any of it. All I inherited by the chance deaths of people I cared about. It has been as though the gods decided to favour me. But, remember this, what the gods can give they can also take away.'

Cherry was at a loss to know how to respond. In the end it seemed easier to accept the gift and to try and move the General's thoughts away to less philosophically gloomy topics. Were not two magpies a source of joy rather than sorrow? New horizons called to him that summer. It was a time of transition when questions could be put aside in preference for the imperative of young manhood. The future was Christ Church, the General's old college, and undergraduate life.

# CHAPTER FOUR

*23ʳᵈ November 1904*
*Christ Church College*
*Oxford*

*Dear Ida*

*Here I am sitting in my rooms at 'the House' and looking out on the same quad that Father knows so well. I can't help wondering what he thought all those years ago and how he planned his future. I don't suppose that he could have predicted all the exciting and wonderful adventures that befell such as being shipwrecked on an island, then going on to be a hero at the Battle of Lucknow? He couldn't have dreamed any of that, let alone that he would inherit Denford, Lamer and all the rest. I wonder what he was thinking when he looked out on the old quad when he was just my age and before all those things happened. I know that I will never be as able as he was, nor have such a purposeful and eventful life, but I will try to. We all owe him so much and I will make him proud of me, for all that he has given us and I will try to prove myself worthy.*

*I am now quite settled in and not so much the 'Freshman' of a month ago. The atmosphere is so much freer than Winchester and I feel very much a part of the House already. There are two chaps in particular who I have chummed up with although you will be surprised when I describe them to you as they are so different.*

*There's a chap on my landing called Stretfield. He's a tall, angular fellow and no sportsman, who narrowly escapes the accusation of being a tedious radical through the force of his personality. Stretfield describes himself as a 'Christian Socialist.' I can just imagine what Father would make of that! But I find him a very interesting chap and certainly somebody who it is good to talk to and to kick ideas around. We sit up at night in my room and talk about these matters. I'm fascinated by the way he conducts himself, he never takes anything stronger than tea and eats no more than he needs but is an avid pipe smoker. Most mornings he is up well before breakfast, just as soon as the gates are open, and takes long hikes down on the river. He's hugely knowledgeable about birds and says that in nature he's closer to God. More challenging to me are his political views, not that he forces the issue but he frames his political views within Christian reference. If Stretfield had his way we would all be living together in one great Christian family. I try to tell him that life on a rural estate can never be like that and that there will always be those who have to lead and make decisions and those that have to follow. But in fairness it is more than talk with Stretfield and he spends all the time he can spare in the House Mission where they try to give boys from the East*

*End a better framework for their lives. He hopes to get me to spend some time there this vacation, which I might very well do just for the curiosity of it all. There is a force to Stretfield's arguments which I find beguiling, the love and care of God to man, and man to man, finding expression in the purity and simplicity of nature. I find all this fascinating especially when I compare it with others in the House.*

*Quite the opposite to Stretfield is a man called Chatteris, or 'Chatters' as all the fellows call him. Chatters has rooms below me and there are always a crowd of fellows down there laughing and talking and generally making free with Chatters's port. While Stretfield keeps his own company Chatters and his chums are always up to some sky larking or other japes. They invaded my rooms the other day when I was out and filled it with pink flowers, pink ribbons, and pink fabric. I had a real shock when I came back but I had to laugh even if my scout was not amused. There are frequent rags when men race and wrestle and delight in making a terrible din until the porters come and check them and Chatters has already had his name taken twice but he doesn't seem to mind a bit. They are all very friendly and there is no malice in them at all. They are terribly keen on rowing and have taken me along to the river. I will amaze you by telling you that they actually think that I am rather good at it. They say that if I really sweat away at it I could make the College third boat for this summer's 'Bumps.' If I do make the cut you must come along and watch. Apparently it is the most wonderful spectacle and lots of the chaps ask their sisters to come up for this event. You must come to a summer ball as it would be marvellous if you were able to come up for this and perhaps bring Elspeth too. Chatters says that the House summer ball is just the biggest jolly ever and even old Stretfield might be persuaded to come and show his paces. All in all there will be plenty of chaps ready to be dancing companions and I am sure that you would both love it.*

*I am getting on with the work and keeping my head above water but I am not so sure now about classics. Chatters certainly advises against it and says that all classicists are 'grey men' and that if I switch to modern history at the end of the year it is less of a grind. He also points out that such a change would give me another year at Oxford. As for old Stretfield he is all for modern history as he claims that our history shows us how we came to this point in time and indicates how things will go on. Any way I will think about it. What do you think?*

*I'm sorry to hear that Old Hobbs has been unwell and I do so hope that he gets better soon. I can't imagine Lamer without him and somehow he seems to be so much a part of our childhood memories. Do you remember him frightening us both with his story about 'Old People' and then the two of us going on an expedition and wading up*

*the stream? I think that Hobbs was more upset than us about getting
into such terrible trouble. Dear Hobbs, do wish him all the best from
me but keep my love for you.*
 *Ever*
 *Apsley*

## Oxford, 1904

Cherry's transition from the Grange to Winchester had been difficult but
his entry into Oxford proved easy. Each difficult stage in his life became
progressively easier and made leaving Lamer less painful. Now he packed
his own trunk and knew what he wanted and didn't want. Oxford was
a little strange at first but he was learning to cope with strangeness and
with new people. He had devised his own strategies for dealing with these
things and affected a reserved and somewhat academic bearing which was
commonplace enough not to warrant comment. The Bloods swaggered
through the cloisters and across the quad and there were the Aesthetes,
affecting the outrageous by walking arm in arm together. There were also
the new 'Liberals' who made themselves angry with stories of camps during
the Boer War where women and children had starved, and quoted a Mrs
Fawcett as an authority on the matter.

Cherry had no wish to be part of any group. It was enough to be left alone
and tolerated. He loved the evenings in the Junior Common Room and the
friendly banter and silliness of it all. From time to time there were events
known as 'Smokers' when all the men gathered together for home grown
entertainment. There would be songs, sometimes good but often silly and
even risqué. Some men read their own poetry which differed in standard and
was received by the JCR accordingly. Various sketches and interludes were
acted out which parodied and mocked the foibles and follies of men in the
House. Cherry escaped the worst of it but Stretfield was a frequent butt of the
House's humour. He was portrayed by some up and coming actor in typical
pose, pipe in hand, searching some remote wood for a sighting of a 'Lesser
Spotted Gooley Bird' while calling on his fellow workers to help him to find
the elusive creature. When it came to the scene where the workers found the
bird but then proceeded to cook it up and eat it, the JCR's hoots and howls
of laughter were heard as far away as the Senior Common Room

Cherry found himself losing that outsider aspect of his personality which
had marked his Winchester years. He was drawn more and more into the
life and pulse of the House. Old Cherry was a good chap to have around
and there was no side to him, the sort of chap who never instigated a rag but
always enjoyed it when it happened. As the year wore on he rose before his
scout and rode his bicycle down to the river in the dark. He learned to love
those early mornings and the quiet, sturdy companionship of the other eight
men as they shouldered the teetering boat and lowered it gently into the
misty, early-morning water. He thrilled to the surge of the boat as the men
swung into life, driving through the cold dark waters, breaking the silence

with the creak of oars and the striking of the blades into the water. There was the unspoken companionship in body and mind of all the eight. Cherry was at one with them, bounded and bonded by the narrow confines of the boat and locked in unity of purpose. His efforts at rowing were noted and he was tipped for the second boat. He toiled at classics but lost interest in them as life surged and awakened around him. But he still loved the idea of heroic adventure and treasured old Saltmarshe's copy of *The Odyssey*, it was the stories that captivated him and the parallels that he saw between his world and theirs, not the academic pedantry of language and tedium of imposed labour. He was in love with life and youth and arranged to swap to modern history and so gained an extra year at the university.

His gradual acceptance into the undergraduate world delighted him and he discovered unsavoured pleasures: the caprice of youth, the warm bond of masculine friendship which found expression in the sports, rags and japes of the House. It didn't seem to matter to be silly and immature and all of them delighted in escape from the heavy and serious responsibilities that awaited them when they put behind them the dreaming spires and took on the mantle of responsibility in the world outside. They had to capture the moment, life had to be lived, and delving at books must take second place.

*'Gaudeamus, igitur, iuvenes dum sumus!'*

They roared from the tower after the Boat Club dinner:

*'Post iucandum juventutem*
*Post molestam senectutem*
*Nos habebit humus.'*

In matters of the Boat Club Cherry looked to Chatteris who distinguished himself both as a rower and as something of a 'blood.' Chatteris had the advantage of coming from a rowing school and his good looks and easy humour naturally endeared. Cherry had to sweat at the techniques of rowing and although he came from the right sort of family and background he had little of Chatteris's confidence and charm. Cherry was conscious that his unprepossessing physical appearance and glasses were a handicap which had to be tolerated.

Chatteris and some chums used to take afternoon tea in The Copper Kettle. One of the waitresses was regarded as an absolute stunner and Chatters fancied his chances. Cherry was taken along on one occasion to admire the girl in question. He thought her to be good looking and she clearly enjoyed the attentions of the undergraduates, responding to their banter, but he thought the thing to be in rather bad taste. His embarrassment and confusion amused Chatteris and his friends hugely.

There were two distinct aspects of Cherry's personality which fused into one in the House. On one level he was as sociable and silly as any other, delighting in the physical aspects of manhood and the joyful mirth of the rags and yet he combined this with a more thoughtful streak which was best identified in his continuing friendship with Stretfield. It was through Stretfield that Cherry first heard about the *Discovery* expedition and indeed the whole House was excited by the story. Stretfield was one of the first to buy a copy of *The Voyage of the Discovery* and insisted on lending it to Cherry. They were both thrilled by the notion of the adventure and the challenge of that great, white, unknown continent. The House buzzed with talk of Scott and his expedition to Antarctica. Here was something pure and untainted which challenged every Englishman. Cherry was fascinated by the account of the three men, Scott, Wilson and Shackleton, and their Farthest South journey. He saw in their exploits, and their endurance of terrible hardships, the characteristics of a modern odyssey. It was rumoured that Shackleton, who had so nearly died of scurvy in the *Discovery* expedition, planned his own expedition south and Cherry dreamed of being with them but knew that it could never be.

Cherry and Stretfield talked about the book long into the night. Stretfield was more measured in his view of Antarctic exploration and reminded Cherry of the death of Charles Bonner, a young sailor who had become over excited at the ship's departure from Port Chalmers, in New Zealand. One evening, in Cherry's rooms, Stretfield read from his copy of the book:

*'And now, whilst our hearts were full of this leave-taking, whilst with our glasses we could still discern the forms of our friends in the receding vessels, there happened one of those tragedies that awaken one to the grim reality of life. Amongst our enthusiastic ship's company who had crowded into the rigging to wave their farewells, was one young seaman, named Charles Bonner who, more venturesome than the rest, had climbed above the crow's nest to the top of the mainmast. There, seated on a truck, he had remained cheering with the rest, until in a moment of madness he raised himself into a standing position, supported only by the slender wind vane which capped the mast. Precisely what happened can never be known, possibly the first sea swell caused him to lose his balance, we below only knew that, arrested by a wild cry, we turned to see a figure hurtling through the air, still grasping the wind vane from the masthead. He fell head foremost on the corner of an iron deckhouse, and death was instantaneous'.*

This incident caught Cherry's imagination, the pointlessness of Bonner's death, the ignominious nature of it so early in the expedition and the wretchedness of his family who may have been there waving goodbye at the moment he fell. Cherry was haunted by a picture of Bonner's terror as he hurtled to the ground, the feeble weather vane gripped tightly in his hand. It brought to mind the figure of Elpenor, who survived the terror of Circe's House only to die an ignominious death. He wanted to share these thoughts with Stretfield and dug out the General's old copy of *The Odyssey* to read out the translation Saltmarshe had begun and that Cherry had worked on at Winchester:

*'There was one called Elpenor, the youngest of the party, not much of a fighting man and not very clever. This young man had got drunk, and longing for fresh air had left his friends and gone to sleep on the roof of*

*Circe's enchanted palace. Roused in the morning by the bustle and din of departure, he leapt up suddenly, and forgetting to go to the long ladder and take the proper way down, he toppled headlong from the roof. He broke his neck and his soul went to Hades.'*

Cherry's enthusiasm for the expedition was tempered by his fear of the physical menace of the place. It wasn't just the farce of Bonner's death it was also the chilling reality of the proximity of death, a reality which was repeated in the death of Vince in the Antarctic who slid past his fellows and was swallowed up by an unseen chasm below. Death stalked them, waiting for its opportunity, whether farcical or heroic, to snatch them by their heels and fling them into the abyss.

But Stretfield saw other meaning in it. 'In the end we all have to remember that we are mortal and that we are in God's hands.'

Cherry looked across Stretfield's simply furnished and unpretentious room and saw the sincerity in the man, it was a conversation that he would recall again in the future.

'The way that Bonner and Vince died was sad but they died in an honourable endeavour. How much better to die doing your bit in a good cause which can only be positive and useful to mankind? Just think of all those young men killed in the brutal and pointless wars of the last century, and more recently than that if you include those who were killed or died of disease in the wars against the Boers. Remember that Scott was setting out to discover and to create and not to sack cities nor to grasp material rewards and in so doing kill people. You can draw too strongly from the Greeks who spent life in a brutal way with no clear view of any other purpose than gratifying their own notion of heroism.'

Cherry was less than convinced by Stretfield's anti war arguments. There was something about them that rubbed. 'I quite agree with you about the heroism of Scott and his party and I think that the achievement of those three, Scott, Wilson and Shackleton, in their Farthest South record is a great triumph for British endeavour but you have to acknowledge that soldiers who have gone through the greatest trials in the farthest flung parts of the Empire were in themselves noble.'

There was a hint of hurt in Cherry's voice, which led Stretfield to adjust his arguments. 'Soldiers like your father have done great things to create our Empire but the time has now come to make it more than it currently is. There is a time for soldiering and a time for peace. Men of action should look to putting their values into peaceful but no less challenging ventures, such as the *Discovery* expedition.'

Cherry was to think again and again of that conversation held in the comfort of Stretfield's rooms, in the warm glow of Oxford days. Could peace time activities ever achieve the nobility and heroism of war time struggles or was there something self indulgent and less worthy about self-imposed challenges? Stretfield had no doubts, but then he had a God to call upon to justify his views.

The General decided that as the war was over it was now beholden on him to make a gesture of faith and to bring together all the things that he valued most: his family, Lamer and the empire. He decided that the estate would make a proper celebration of Empire Day. The villagers would all be invited to Lamer to enjoy a fete and festivities in the park. The centre piece was to be a parade of great heroes from the British and classical empires with prizes for the best costumes. It would be a coming together of all the community, all ranks and classes in celebration of the greatest empire that the world had ever known, greater even than that of the classical world but unlike the classical world bringing order and wise governance to all.

Lamer was decked out in its summer best and in that summer of 1906 the gods favoured the occasion and the sun shone in the full glory of May. Cherry chose the costume of Dr Livingstone the great explorer while Ida was Boadicea. Elspeth came as Florence Nightingale and Cherry noted how well she fitted the occasion and how attached both Ida and Mother were to her. The General and Mother did not dress up but the General did wear full military uniform in honour of the occasion. The sun shone on Lamer and all the many Cherry-Garrards who seemed the spearhead of all that was good in the state of England.

The villagers were told to assemble on their own commons and then to join with the other village groups on Earlswood Common prior to a grand final procession down the Linden Avenue and into the Hall. The Whitebushes contingent was led by Young Hobbs and their Morris side and behind them came the assorted children and musicians who intended to join the main procession. Old Hobbs was ill in bed and not able to join them but as they passed over the White Bridge the Whitebushes contingent halted by Hobbs's house and played the tune of *The Greenwood's Shady Dell* to him and he waved to them from the window. As they resumed their march up the white lane they could hear the gathering of the other villagers ahead of them, so they skirted round the Hall and joined the throng on Earlswood Common at the entrance to the park on the north side. Much banter and good humour followed but in the end Hampton, in his role as estate manager, managed to organise them into something resembling a procession and made them ready to descend on the Hall.

A great beat from a bass drum struck up and then with a cry of 'Remember, Remember Empire Day, the 24th May!' the straggling procession set off. Soon they could be seen marching down the Linden Avenue. First came two older boys who were holding high their Union Jacks and behind them came a motley band of fifes and drums and various instruments. Behind them came the children who were entering the fancy dress completion. Here was a General Wolfe, a St George, a Clive of India, a Gordon of Khartoum, a Nelson, a John Bull, a Robin Hood and Maid Marion. Behind them came the Morris men, their faces blackened in the time-honoured way that ensured anonymity to their employers. They wore great straw hats which were decked in Mayflowers and as they strode up the drive with their sticks in hand the bells on their legs tinkled. Among the Morris Men there leapt and whirled the rather disquieting figure of Young Hobbs who delighted in the role of the Green Man, the essence of England and May. Alfred Hobbs was there but he kept apart and did not dance with the Morris. Finally came the men and women in their Sunday best and all were laughing and smiling, free for a day from the constraints of work and petty village rivalries and united in the purpose of enjoying a holiday.

When they came to the front of the Hall the procession halted on the beats of the great bass drum and the boys who had been carrying the Union Jacks unfurled them. The General stepped forward to give a short address.

'You are welcome!' he began and as he stood there on the steps of Lamer, Cherry felt a glow of admiration for the man who had seen so much and yet condescended to give his time and attention to such simple pleasures.

'Today is Empire Day, the 24th May, and it is right that we remember with pride and gratitude the courage and sacrifice of so many who found and fashioned this empire so that it is the greatest empire ever known to man. It is great not simply in size but in spirit. We have brought order and peace to so many parts of the world and from us they have learned the true values of decency and fairness that have enabled them to live in peace and friendship with their neighbours and encouraged them to be hardworking and dutiful so that they and their families can live in safety and security. But where is the heart of this empire?' Here the General peered forward into the crowd as if expecting an answer but, of course, receiving none. 'Why it is here. Here in the heart of England. Here with you now and in Lamer! So, the Empire says back to you, 'Thank you and God Bless you,' and may there always be Lamer and England and our British Empire!'

Everybody cheered and the band struck up *Jerusalem*.

Cherry sang as lustily as the others and yet the familiar words, which he had sung and known from childhood, seemed, for the first time, strange almost surreal. His thoughts were fired by images of ancient feet, green mountains, shields and bows of burning gold and it seemed to him as though there was a link here with those old Greeks and their forgotten empire, a once great empire which was now no more than deserted stones and ancient writings. It was a glimpse of transience. Cherry knew that one day the Old General would be gone and he would have to take up the reins of responsibility and this made him choke. The singing came to an end and the Old General ordered the assembly to disperse and enjoy themselves. The festivity of the occasion took over with Morris dancing and side shows and good things to eat and the judging of the fancy dress and a good deal of English nonsense that in its own way made such sense. Cherry felt the delight of it all but also sensed its fragility. Elspeth noticed that something was affecting him and took his arm and insisted that he should take her to the coconut shy. In the May sun with Elspeth by his side, smiling and laughing and full of womanly grace and charm, the darker thoughts rolled away and left him giddy with delight in life.

Cherry went back to Oxford for the brief flourish of summer that ended the university year. He had rowed well in the college second boat and it was generally thought that with two more years ahead of him he might well achieve a place in the first boat in the fullness of time.

Ida came up with Elspeth for the second House ball. Ida was as assured and full of fun as ever but Elspeth proved to be something of a surprise, she had acquired a new elegance and ease. Cherry had seen her in various phases of her life but never before as this delightful creature. He was awkward at first, the House was such a male reserve that the presence of two young ladies for whom he was responsible was unsettling. As the evening wore on, he had to acknowledge that the existence of a sister was not an impediment but an asset. Ida, easy and warm in the company of young men, found plenty of partners, including Stretfield who plodded his way through several waltzes. Cherry was forced to dance with several young ladies, who had been variously acquired for the evening, and by no means disgraced himself but he could not help watching Elspeth, who was transformed from the girl he knew before. He noticed that Chatteris was also very attentive. After the ball the House was restored as a male preserve yet, for all that, the figure of Elspeth stole, ball-gowned, slim-waisted and youthful, into his reflections more and more.

That summer had one last, dark trick to play. At the very the end of the term, Ida wrote to him from Lamer with the news that Old Hobbs had died. It seemed to Cherry that, while the very heart of life beat so fast in his Oxford world, something at Lamer had slipped away and would never be quite the same, a peg, a link, with the past gone. He saw the old 'garden room' deserted, the old stove cold, the chair empty. He wondered if the swallows would come back each year to that same place now that Hobbs had gone.

Old Hobbs was laid to rest in the churchyard of St John's. The Hobbs family was represented by Young Hobbs, his wife and their son, Alfred. Young Hobbs had been expected to occupy his father's role in Lamer but his father's duties did not sit comfortably on his shoulders. Alfred was a sturdy, confident fellow who had no intention of following in the family footsteps and had his heart set on a new life and new opportunities in the colonies. The General and Mother and many members of the Cherry-Garrard household were there to pay their respects. Cherry was shocked to see how Hobbs's death had affected his father. The sight of the old man, breathing hard and showing his age was worrying. But undergraduate life was calling him back and he had to answer to its call in the same way that the swallow needs to fly to Africa.

Lamer was still essential to Cherry. While it was safe he could live in the present and leave all the responsibilities Lamer entailed for the future. There was still a special bond between Cherry and Ida, the 'Laddie and Lassie' of old but life was calling to him and he could not resist the call. He had other options for the vacations, chaps from the House encouraged him to visit them and there were new places to be discovered and new experiences to be savoured. He closed his mind to Lamer and Mother and the General and lived for the present. In this way he could keep them perfectly preserved and waiting for when he was prepared to look at them again, like the butterfly specimens which he and Ida had collected and which were carefully stored in a black display case. From now on he would only spend part of his vacation at Lamer. Ida was still part of Lamer, but she was also part of the new world and he corresponded with her to keep the link. His correspondence had grown stronger and deeper because he found a means of expressing his inner thoughts and feelings through her as his muse and with Lamer as the backdrop.

During the summer vacation Cherry went to stay with Cousin Reggie in Scotland. One of Reggie's companions was the celebrated Antarctic traveller, Dr Edward Wilson. Cherry knew about Wilson from the account of the *Discovery* expedition but no amount of reading could have prepared him for the real man. Wilson impressed with his capacity to listen and to understand intuitively and he showed genuine consideration for people and creatures. Wilson avoided talking about himself and Cherry had to get most of his information from Reggie. Wilson had been to Caius, in Cambridge, and studied medicine. On qualifying he worked as a doctor in Battersea but had filled all his time working for the Caius mission. As a consequence of over work and poor living conditions he had contracted tuberculosis and nearly died. He was sent to convalesce in Switzerland and Norway but such was the nature of the man that he refused to rest and walked, climbed, drew and studied wildlife. The exercise improved his health and also provided him with knowledge of alpine matters. This was the background to him joining the *Discovery* expedition, where he acquitted himself with distinction and proved invaluable to Captain Scott.

Wilson and Cherry formed an easy bond and delighted in all things to do with the natural world. Wilson was a scientist but he brought to science an artist's power of observation. Cherry loved to watch him sketching and went out with him in the highlands and kept him company while he worked. They talked of birds and animals and life at university. Cherry was eager to know more about the *Discovery* expedition and Wilson was amused to know that Cherry and Stretfield found so much to discuss about it. Cherry pressed him about the deaths of Bonner and Vince.

'You wonder if their deaths can be justified?' Wilson asked.

'I have thought about it a lot,' confessed Cherry. 'I know that the whole expedition was just the best and finest thing but those deaths, and particularly that of Bonner, seem such a terrible price to pay.'

'What does your friend say on the matter?'

'Stretfield finds in it the hand of God, but it seems to me harsh that men should suffer while trying to do good.'

Wilson looked closely at the younger man. 'It's a price we all pay in the end. We all have to pay for living. It isn't so much how we die that matters but how we lived. Had both men lived longer in the world they would not have achieved more. They died quickly and relatively painlessly doing what they most wanted to do in life. The tragedy belongs not so much to them as to those who are left behind.'

'I suppose that you are right there, but to be truthful, I am more afraid of the pain of dying than the idea of death itself.'

Wilson nodded. 'That's an honest statement and one which most men would share. But you needn't worry too much about it just now. I am sure that you will enjoy more than your threescore years and ten and there is much to be done in the meantime. You will forgive me for noting that your journey is in the early phase and I am sure that it will go on to be a remarkable expedition. When the end of the journey comes you will be ready.'

Cherry found comfort in these words. The idea of life being a journey fascinated him and he drew hope and comfort from Wilson's words.

# CHAPTER FIVE

## *POSTED FROM THE CAPE*

*June 27, 1910*

*My Dear Ida*

*I think that it was Captain Scott, or maybe Nansen, who said that the worst part of any journey is in the preparation. Anyway, it is certainly true that we are glad to have those months of preparation and anxiety over and to be on our way. I have that old book of Father's with me that Saltmarshe gave him all those years ago. I had it with me all through Oxford and Stretfield and I would discuss its meaning and relevance to us. It's like having a piece of Father with me and I am sure that it will bring us all luck. Last night I read this passage which I must share with you:*

*'The men cast the hawsers off, climbed in and took their places at their oars. And now out of the west, Athene of the flashing eyes called up for them a steady following wind and sent it singing over the wine dark sea. Telemachus shouted to the crew to rig the ship and they leapt to his orders. They hauled up the pine mast, placed it in its hollow box, made it fast with stays, and hoisted the white sail with plaited ox hide ropes. The sail billowed out in the wind, and a dark wave hissed loudly round her keel, as the vessel gathered way and sped on her course through the seas.'*

*When I saw you waving frantically, on the quay at Cardiff, just one shrinking dot amongst all those people, I thought that my heart would burst. I could have leaped over board and swum back. It may seem strange to you but at that moment it reminded me so strongly of the first time I went away to prep school and saw you and Mother waving to me from the rear of the carriage window. Then, strangely, I thought of poor Bonner on the Discovery and I understood the seriousness of it all.*

*There is no time for melancholy or regret. It is the most amazing luck to have been selected for this great enterprise. I thought of Father and how pleased he would have been, and the sadness of being parted from you all and from dear old England didn't seem so bad. The other chaps here are such a wonderful crowd of fellows that just having them around lifts the spirits. If a chap is at all downcast then the other fellows rib and josh him so that he can't stop himself laughing. Not that things can't get jolly tricky at times but with chaps like these you are never truly alone.*

*The first few days were very hard because the old Terra Nova rolls like a barrel in the sea and I was very sick. It is altogether a vastly different experience to life on an ocean liner, my previous experiences of being on salt water. We have two doctors on board: one is an old naval man called Atkinson but everybody refers to him as 'Aitch' and the other is Ted Wilson but everybody calls him Bill or Uncle Bill. Aitch is a strange old bird and I can't quite make him. He was helpful when I was ill but Bill was so unrelentingly good to me during that ghastly period that I just had to get over it. Bill is the very finest of men that ever lived. In some ways he reminds me a bit of Father, except that he is younger, but like Father he seems to understand a fellow without you having to say a word. Bill can seem a bit reserved at first, as though he is weighing you up, but when you get to know him he is such a brick. At times I can hardly believe that I am officially 'assistant' to such a wonderful man. Bill has been telling me about his plans to obtain some emperor penguin eggs when we are in the south. The emperor is probably the oldest and weirdest bird in the world and their eggs could explain some of the mysteries of evolution (if you all believe in that!) Wouldn't it be marvellous to have an emperor penguin egg in your collection at Lamer? I will try to get one to bring back for you. Can you imagine the great egg nestled up against our shrike's egg?*

*Talking of birds, I must also tell you about Birdie. Birdie is a comical looking fellow. He is short with a great beak of a nose and a shock of red hair, but he is somebody who I admire tremendously. If Uncle Bill is my governor and mentor then Birdie is my great pal. Old Birdie is the toughest and most hard-working of fellows that you could ever meet. 'Come on young Cherry' he says to me, in a broad Scots accent, how's about we set to with some coal shovelling?' You would laugh if you could see us shovelling coal for all we are worth and as dark as a couple of blacks with sweat rolling down our backs. Birdie is just one of those fellows you want to have around and be around, he is always planning and making things happen and there is never a dull moment with him on board.*

*There is also a chap called Captain Lawrence Oates, but everybody knows him as 'Titus.' While many of the chaps are Royal Navy, Titus is the only one present who represents the army. He saw service during the Boer War and rumour has it that he suffered a gunshot wound in the thigh but he doesn't talk about it much, although Birdie knows all about it and tells me that Titus was amazingly brave and despite being wounded and surrounded refused to surrender. The Boers thought his position hopeless and invited him to surrender but he shouted back at them that he would 'rather be d----ed than surrender to his country's enemy.' I mentioned Father to him and he became very interested and knew all about what happened at Lucknow and the Kaffir Wars. He is quite a military historian but not the sort of person it is easy to engage in conversation. However, for all his gruffness there is something about him that appeals. He can be quite rude to people and doesn't seem to give a damn for anybody or anything. Whilst the ship is full of naval chaps and run on naval lines, Titus goes his own way and can be quite rude about the navy types and calls them 'Wet Bobs.' I'm never quite sure whether it's just joshing or not but no-one seems to mind and they have dubbed him 'Soldier'.*

*How marvellous to think that we have drawn together so many fellows from all parts of Britain and the Empire: Birdie from Scotland, Crean from Ireland, Evans from Wales, Silas from Canada and the fellows from Australia who will join us. We are all together and of one purpose and are now heart and soul for the team. In the end I just love this life but most of all the people who share it with me. It's like a great adventure with the best of possible chums and everything else, discomfort, cold, terrible heat, even sickness, can't prevent the fun and laughter just welling up inside and taking over. We can all be silly and no better than a crowd of prep school lads. In the evening we play some ridiculous games and it becomes hilariously funny. There is one called, 'The Parson's Hat' which Teddy Evans introduced to us. Teddy is Second Officer for the expedition but as Scott doesn't join us until we reach Australia, Teddy is in command. Teddy is a great man for a lark and his laughter is infectious. By the end of the game we are howling with laughter, like a pack of hyenas. It really is so silly but irresistible. In the morning it only takes somebody to say 'Good Morning Parson' to set me off again.*

*The other night the game ended in the most terrible rumpus, which developed into a scrum which then became a great wrestle in the ward room. Bill, Birdie and I defended the 'Nursery' door against all comers and try as they might they just couldn't get through. Eventually they gave up but only after the Chief protested about damage to his ship. All in all it was a great lark. Uncle Bill said afterwards that we made a winning team. Birdie and I really appreciated this.*

*July 27*

*We crossed the bar amid all sorts of larks. I have crossed the line before and therefore escaped being 'shaved' and dunked in all manner of rubbish before being presented to Neptune and his helpers but others were not so fortunate. Most of the chaps took it in good part except for Gran, our Norwegian ski instructor, who found British skylarking and humour not to his taste and tossed the 'Barber' into the sail of water.*

*How's this for an adventure? We stopped off at an island called South Trinidad, which is remote and very few people have ever visited. Birdie is the man for an escapade and Uncle Bill was determined to go ashore and collect specimens but the island resisted landing. We went out in a boat and probed for a suitable landing place but there was a terrible swell and the best we could find was a low rocky promontory which was little better than a balcony.*

*Uncle Bill has some kind of inner knowledge, as though he knows me better than I know myself, because as we approached the island he called out,*

*'Courage!' he said and pointed towards the land,*

*'This mounting wave will roll us shoreward soon.'*

*Everybody laughed but when he said it he looked at me as if he knew. I caught sight of his blue eyes and they were definitely telling me something and then he just smiled.*

*We managed to land without too much problem but it was a rotten place and covered by horrible land crabs. Bill and I found some birds but by the time we were ready to go back to the ship the sea was running frighteningly fast, and spray and swell had turned our landing place into a boiling cauldron of water. I will admit to being rather put out but Birdie busied himself with ropes and lines and all manner of things. Meanwhile Old Bill just sat down on a rock, as cool as you like, and started to nibble at a ship's biscuit just as if we were all out on a jolly picnic. When I saw that I just knew we were going to be all right. How strange it is but I couldn't help thinking of Father and the time he left me to swim on my own in the lake. I can picture him now, sitting on the bank in his waders and smoking a cigar. We fixed a line from the support boat to the narrow rock ledge and from our slippery base launched each man through and over the angry waters. When it came to my turn, I fixed the picture of Father in my mind's eye and put my trust in providence. We all had a terrible dousing and one of the sailors had a really rough time of it and I thought that we were going to lose him but somehow he pulled through. I can tell you that we were all delighted to get back to the Terra Nova and leave the island far behind.*

*<u>August 15</u>*

*You will be pleased to know it's not all adventures. We have met some ripping young ladies here in The Cape and I had to play endless doubles at tennis. I didn't realise that being an explorer would carry with it an obligation to partner every young lady at tennis. Now, for all his strange looks and ways old Birdie can be quite a charmer and has the knack of putting everybody at ease. When I get back to Lamer I must introduce you all to him. I can just see you making a terrible fuss of him.*

*We have enjoyed our sojourn in the Cape and I have found it exhilarating. This is a striking country. In many ways it brings to mind ancient Greece with the sun beating down on rock and where two great seas meet. There is a fine clarity to the light, both warm and intensely clear, which bathes this city as it does Athens. Plutarch compared the quality of this light to spun-silk. Table Mountain rises above the city and draws the eye in the same way as does the Acropolis. I don't know why it is but I keep thinking of Father and how strange it was that he and I would have been to the very same places and looked upon exactly the same sights. No wonder Father and Saltmarshe were reminded of Greece and all things Grecian, including Odysseus, when they were out here.*

*I think that old Titus shares some of my feelings about the Cape. The other day I told him about Father and his friendship with Saltmarshe and how he had inherited the book from Saltmarshe. It turns out that Titus knew Saltmarshe's cousin during the final stages of the war. How strange to think that this land connects us! Do you think that the swallows which nest in Hobbs's garden room fly here to the Cape? It would be really strange to think that when Father was here there could have been swallows from Lamer just overhead. Your swallows will be departing soon for their journey south and I remember Old Hobbs telling me that if you listen carefully to their chattering you can hear them talking of Africa. Tell them from me that all is warm and ready for their arrival.*

*On a darker note, this landscape reminds me of Saltmarshe's death and the wars that followed. I also think of all those chaps at Winchester who died in those terrible wars. What an irony that such beauty and fullness of life should be contrasted with the meanness of those deaths. I considered going to visit Saltmarshe's grave in King William's town but it is a long journey and we must now get on and prepare for our eastward adventures.*

*Your Loving Brother,*
*Apsley*

### Oxford, 1906

The early years at Oxford were over. They gave way to the even pace of Cherry's mid-time there. The river, the warm-hearted companionship of the House, and the rugged joys of Oxford, dominated his time. Academic work, and his evenings with Stretfield, slipped down his list of priorities. He tried to ignore the problems of Lamer and world issues and to focus on the moment. Change was in the air, but for the young man in Christ Church political changes and worries took second place to life itself, which was moving upward and into the light.

The war in South Africa was settled and the troops had come home victorious. But the victory had an ugliness about it that made for a hollow triumph, a victory achieved at too great a price. An election was called and a new government was anticipated. The good mood and conviviality of the House were intruded upon by this general election. Some of the fellows in the House joined in the discussion with enthusiasm and while most young men were Tory some, like Stretfield, talked of change, common justice, and a better place bred from suffering. In Oxford the Liberals and radicals were vociferous and, although vastly outnumbered, their arguments found favour among some of the intellectuals who feigned to be more aware of the world outside. The prevailing demob atmosphere was at odds with the cloistered and privileged world of Oxford. A group of men from the House were chased down the Turl by an angry crowd of townies and there was a fist fight which could have ended badly if the Lincoln porters hadn't taken in the college men.

The election results caused despondency in the House and at Lamer and the Liberals swept to power on a ticket of 'Change' in the Khaki election. The General found it especially hard to accept the outcome and viewed Campbell Bannerman as an opportunist, hell bent on his own selfish agenda. Worse was the growing power and organisation of the Labour Party which now had twenty-nine MPs. The more radical elements talked of land reform and a tax on landowners. Cherry was caught between intellectual questioning and the safety of old values.

After the election, Cherry went down to Lamer for one of his visits and observed the deterioration in the General's health. He still walked as tall and straight as ever but now he carried a cane and seemed more anxious about the future. When he saw his son his thoughts drifted to Saltmarshe and those conversations out on the veldt. He wondered more and more about what could have been if Saltmarshe had lived and they had continued their friendship as two occupants of English landed estates and the heads of their own families. Would Saltmarshe have helped him now and kept an eye on his son when he was no longer able to do so? He fretted about Cherry and what would become of him. Cherry was too intense for a young man and too easily hurt. There was a vulnerability about him that didn't sit comfortably in a complex and difficult world. Cherry reminded the General of Saltmarshe. They both had lively imaginations and a passion for the countryside. Cherry had recently become stronger and more confident, due in no small part, to his time at The House, but there was still a weakness there that needed the love and support of a stronger man and the General knew that he could not keep watch on Cherry much longer.

The General and Cherry grew closer during this time. The General's increasing frailty was counterbalanced by the growth in his son's strength. Cherry knew that the estates would fall to him some day but there was still something more he wanted to do, to achieve in his own right and to show that he was worthy of such an inheritance. 'Some work of noble note' was wanted before he could be content to return as keeper of his father's hall and to fulfil this duty with 'slow prudence'. He wanted to talk to the General about it but the time was never right.

The focus of Cherry's dreams was rowing in the House First Eight during 'Bumps'. It became apparent that the number six position would prove to be a choice between Cherry and Chatteris. Chatteris had rowed for a season in the House first boat but he wasn't dedicated to training. Cherry, on the other hand, never missed a training session and put in extra work on weights and fitness. He was first to rise in the House and became a familiar, bespectacled figure braving all weathers in singlet and shorts. He had never taken to running at Winchester and disliked enforced athleticism, but now he was his own master and forced himself on against the pain in his body. As he ran he devised a rhythm, beat out in the slap of his plimsolled feet, that began with counting steps and developed into a primitive chant.

'Got it, Got it,

Got it in the neck.'

He ran and thought of Lamer and all the people connected with it. He also thought of Elspeth and brought to mind her face as though she was watching him. Cherry's dedication to training was admired in the House but he made no attempt to curry favour with the other men who were intent on being popular and gaining admission to the more select dining clubs. Chatteris was in several clubs and had set his sights on further nominations, but Cherry was steadfast in training and loyal to his friends and earned respect.

Even Chatteris couldn't begrudge Cherry's selection for the first boat. Cherry's delight was tempered by disquiet at causing Chatteris to be dropped but the easy grace of the latter put his mind at rest. Cherry hoped the General would be well enough to come and see him in Eights Week. When Cherry was at Winchester his father had attended the requisite sporting events dutifully, but there had been little enough that involved his son and in which he could take personal pride. Now Cherry was in the House first eight it was an achievement that the old man could take pride in. But it was not to be and despite all Cherry's hopes the General was too ill to be present. However, he did send a telegram with the simple inscription:

'Give it your all! Bravo the House!'

At the start of Eights' Week, Balliol's boat was 'Head of the River' with Trinity in second position. The House boat was positioned third on the river and had the challenge of taking poll position by bumping both Trinity and Balliol within the four days of the races. There was much talk and speculation amongst the undergraduates and the whole college was fired with anticipation.

Before the first race Cherry couldn't eat or rest or find anything to divert him. It worried him that he would miss his stroke or dig too deep or in some other way let the boat down. They hoped to catch Trinity but there was every prospect that Lincoln would catch them from behind and bump them. The first race reflected the tenseness that they were all experiencing. Despite the best supporting efforts of the undergraduates on the bank their boat only managed a passable performance, managing to keep ahead of Lincoln and making modest gains against Trinity. They retained the same positions for the second day of the races.

Stretfield came to see Cherry the night before the second race. He was amused at the sight of Cherry who was pale and ill with anxiety.

'Come, on, old chap, it can't be that bad,' he said.

In Cherry's reckoning it was as bad as it could be. 'In that last race, I was so worked up I rowed like a weakling. I know the other chaps think they should have picked Chatters rather than me. He wouldn't have let them all down.'

'Nobody's thinking anything of the sort. You did your bit and rowed as well as any of them. If you hadn't you would have been caught by Lincoln. Don't be so hard on yourself.'

Cherry would not be so easily appeased. 'The truth is I'm just a fraud and I'm not really up to all of this. I work damned hard at it and give it my all but I am just not good enough, not good enough to be in the first boat and not good enough even to be my father's son. I feel that if I fell off this carousel I would never get back on.'

'Then don't fall!' said Stretfield sharply. 'We all have moments of self doubt and I know that you carry great responsibilities on your shoulders but you're not alone you know. Those of us who know you well appreciate your value. Take Edward Wilson, do you think a man like that would bother with anybody not worth his salt? Focus on rowing with the others and forget yourself and your doubts and dreams.'

Cherry promised to stop being so defeatist and felt more composed. Stretfield's kindness and trust helped to roll back the dark clouds just enough for him to glimpse the light beyond.

He always recalled waiting in the boat with the other men before that second race, all of them poised and ready for the gun. He recalled terror and the most appalling sickness but the easy presence of the others and their steely resolve bled into him the courage to stay fast and to focus on the moment. The gun exploded and released their collective energy. There was a blur of flying, shouting figures on the bank, which he knew included Ida. The supporters careered after the boat in a whirl of excitement. As the boat surged through the water the sun blazed in his eyes and there was a desperate pain across his chest and into his innermost body. He didn't even have time to reflect on their position in the race but he sensed that they were gaining on Trinity and when they made the bump the joy of that moment was indescribable, a joy that was shared with his crew and the supporters on the bank and the river seemed to bask in its glory. If only the General had seen it.

The next day they took second place behind Balliol and although they rowed well and kept well ahead of Trinity they gained only a few yards on Balliol. There was one more race left, one last chance to take the full glory of bumping Balliol and going 'Head of the River'. Cherry had spent the last days in an agony of anticipation but for that last race he was as composed as he could have been. Both Chatters and Stretfield came to see him the night before to wish him well. Chatters was particularly generous to his erstwhile rival and insisted on shaking him by the hand and wishing him all the luck in the world. But theirs was not to be either luck or glory. Balliol lifted their performance and rowed out the comfortable winners. The House boat had to be content with second place, a bitter blow to the hopes of the exhausted crew. They passed the finish and sank at their oars and let the boat float down river. They had missed a golden opportunity once and for all and there would be no second chance. When the Cox called for three cheers for Balliol they dug deep in their hearts and their voices seemed to echo back from the bleak wall of their disappointment.

Eights' Week was the pinnacle of Cherry's time at Oxford, a feast of wonderful images to collect and treasure in his mind. The agony of training and the frenzy of the races produced a riot of emotion. Now that the races were over he had to steady himself emotionally and unwind enough to think of Elspeth and enjoy the summer ball. He decided that this year he would pay particular attention to Elspeth.

That summer ball was the last one for both Chatteris and Stretfield but Cherry had one more year ahead of him. Elspeth entranced him that night. When they danced he felt the slenderness of her body and smelt the fragrance of her perfume. He held her waist and his hand shook with tenderness. Her auburn hair was framed in light and her face was aglow with pleasure. After several dances together Cherry invited her to come and take punch in the Master's garden. The others were busy dancing and it was a glorious evening in early June and the day's light clung to the garden, despite the lateness of the clock, and filled it with English magic. But Elspeth had lost much of the girlishness that had at first attracted him and alone with him she was less animated. She held the glass of punch in front of her, almost defensively. There was something about her which made Cherry feel awkward.

'It's a lovely College,' she said, 'but don't you think it a pity that there are no women here to enjoy it as well?'

'There are rules about ladies in college after Gates but for the rest of the time we have plenty of visitors,' Cherry said. 'Mark you none of us can go into the Master's garden without special permission.'

She seemed irritated. 'No, I mean why can't women study here on the same terms as the male undergraduates?'

'Well, I suppose because it's a men's college. There are colleges for ladies.'

'Yes but there are so few places compared with men and women can't even be admitted to take university degrees. It seems so unfair. What do you think about votes for women?'

Cherry had thought very little about it, it wasn't something that he and Stretfield had ever discussed. Like most young men in the House he disapproved of the antics of the suffragettes but he had not thought about the arguments sufficiently to form a view. In the Master's garden it seemed to be inappropriate and an intrusion from a world outside that had no place there. He stammered an attempt at an answer and was relieved when Chatteris came to find them to claim his dance with Elspeth. Elspeth seemed as relieved as he did by Chatters' intervention and as he watched them walking and laughing together he felt old, as if he was from another time.

That last vacation was different to the rest. Cherry knew that on his return to Oxford there would be just three terms left before it would all be over and the time would have come to take the reins of responsibility. Stretfield would be leaving shortly to go to India where a mission needed him. Chatteris would join his father in his London business. Cherry stayed with Reggie in Burnside but there were few visitors and, disappointingly, no Ted Wilson. He decided that he shouldn't stay away from Lamer too long because the General needed him and increasingly the responsibilities of the estate fell to him.

Lamer did not respond easily to Cherry's authority and he found little support in Young Hobbs. The epithet 'Young' was now entirely inappropriate because John Hobbs was not young but middle-aged and a father himself and Cherry found it strange to refer to him simply as 'Hobbs'. Cherry felt that the way Hobbs looked at him was inappropriate and that there was something approaching a sneer in his expression as though Hobbs knew him and his failings only too well. Hobbs was proud of his son, Alfred, and often spoke of his adventures in the colonies and took pride in the boy's enterprise and courage. Cherry imagined that Hobbs was critical of Cherry's privileged position in the old world and saw Alfred as a better man. Although Hobbs kept possession of the garden room he didn't spend much time there and it was used mainly to store tools for the car. The swallows kept alive the memory of how the garden room had once been and that summer they continued to raise their young on the high beams.

Problems in the country were reflected in the estate. There were any number of petty quarrels and issues to be sorted out. Some days the General was not well enough to go to the office and Cherry had to meet with Hampton on his own. According to Hampton, men back from the war had a new perspective and were critical of the old ways and their attitude was infectious. Hampton reported on a conversation that he had had with Hobbs who talked of opening a garage on the Brighton Road, near Salfords. Hobbs had little regard for the old house on the White Bridge and didn't feel obliged to maintain the tenancy. New times were coming and there was good money to be made from cars. The move would take him away from Whitebushes entirely and his new local would be the Nag's Head, which was a proper public house and far superior to Nan's. It was symptomatic of the changing times that the popularity of Nan's had waned and there was little singing and nobody wanted the old stories. Hampton was worried that if Hobbs left it would stimulate discontent amongst others on the estate and he wanted Cherry to talk to his father about it when he felt that it was a good time to talk with the General.

Cherry's chance came a few days later when one morning, quite by surprise, the General came into his study. He was using two sticks and breathing heavily but seemed in reasonable spirits. The General's desk was still there in pride of place and Cherry was working at a second desk which had been moved into a side position when they first shared the office. The

General said nothing at first but heaved himself into his chair and started to look through the drawers of his desk. After a while he spoke. 'I wonder what happened to that old copy of *The Odyssey*? You know the one that came from old Saltmarshe.'

Cherry explained that the General had given it to him some years previously.

'Oh yes, of course, quite right. I was getting a little muddled. Tell me, my boy, did you find it interesting?'

'Yes, Stretfield and I often talk about it. There are so many parallels in our modern world. I love the adventure and uncertainty of it all and Odysseus, to my mind, is a flawed hero but a very human one for all that.'

The General was amused. 'Saltmarshe would have agreed with you about that but I don't think that he cared too much for the modern world, even if Saltmarshe's modern world was decades older than yours and before we had a war with the Boer. How is your modern world affecting the estate?'

Cherry repeated Hampton's concerns and explained about Hobbs.

'Well, well,' said the General. 'It won't be the same without a Hobbs about the place. There's been a Hobbs at Lamer for as long as there are records. But you're right about changing times. We must do the best we can and the gods may favour us yet. I hear these radicals are calling for a tax on land. Let them spout on about it as much as they like, there is no way that it will be implemented, the Lords will see to that! This would be one change too many. We must be prepared to sit it out and hope some level of sanity returns. I tell you this, a house is just bricks and mortar and land is mud and grass. It's people that matter. Saltmarshe and I were happy enough when we didn't even own the tent we slept in on the dry ground of Africa. In the end we are all just tenants in life. Let Young Hobbs go his way and we will find a new Eumaeus.'

Hobbs did leave and a new tenant was found for his old house. The new head gardener was a bachelor who kept himself to himself and who never went to Nan's or had anything to do with Whitebushes.

The vacation was enlivened by the presence of Ida and by occasional visits from Chatteris. Chatters was pleased enough with his Third and joked that he was delighted that he had escaped a Fourth. Stretfield had just missed a First and had to be content with a good Second but then, as Chatteris put it, none of them *needed* their degrees, having been at Oxford was enough. Sometimes Elspeth came over to Lamer and the four young people played lawn tennis or took a boat out on the lake but Cherry knew that Elspeth was not for him and for all of her talk about votes for women at the summer ball he couldn't help but notice that she expressed none of these views to Chatteris. It was all laughter and jollity whenever Chatteris was around.

Ida's company was invaluable. They still went to the old mulberry and apple trees and talked with all the honesty of old. In the late summer sun they liked to sit together and to look due south. The birds had fallen silent but the meadow browns danced before them as free unbound spirits of summer's end. One day, Cherry began a conversation that Ida was to remember all her life. He was looking south down the familiar track with Hobbs's house in full view and the common away in the distance.

'You remember that time we went on an expedition to Whitebushes?'

She laughed, it was so long ago and their fears seemed so ill-fitting and yet there was still something not quite right down there, something troubling and not secure.

'I remember Old Hobbs's stories and how he put the wind into us with his talk of Old People and the like,' she said.

'Yes, we were a couple of daisies, but I feel something the same now, the same as on that day I climbed out of the tree and set off over the White Bridge. I have to get away and see something of this world. Do you remember Housman?

*'Wide is the world, to rest and roam.*

*And early 'tis for turning home'.*

'You know, Elspeth wasn't right for you,' said Ida. 'You mustn't let what happened there influence anything.'

Cherry shifted position and dug in the corner of his jacket for his briar. 'It's all right,' he said 'I know I'm not much of a ladies' man and probably never will be but there are other things in life, as dear old Stretfield was so fond of reminding me. Obviously, the first thing is to go back to the House for my final year but the truth is that I am not looking forward to it in the way I used to. So many of the fellows have left and their places taken by new chaps that it won't be the same. However, it will all be over soon enough. After that I suppose that I shall travel, that sort of thing. Don't worry old girl, I'll come back to Lamer all right but not until I have seen something of the world and, who knows, perhaps made a bit of a mark.'

Ida looked at him closely. 'You don't have to prove anything to anybody, you know, not to me, not to Father or Mother, nor even Elspeth. There are plenty of challenges already, you don't have to go looking for them.'

'Maybe you're right,' he answered but he was thinking of the picture in the hall.

# CHAPTER SIX

## *POSTED FROM NEW ZEALAND*

<u>*September 16, 1910*</u>

*Dear Ida*

*Well here I am back on board the old Terra Nova but matters have changed since the letter I posted to you from the Cape. Captain Scott, or 'the Owner' as the naval chaps like to call him, has joined the expedition and taken charge of the ship. Matters are better ordered but less fun than when Teddy was in command. We all want to show that we are up to the mark and people are speculating as to who will be in the southern party. We still have rags and everybody is pulling together really well but Captain Scott can be changeable and I am not sure that Teddy likes playing second fiddle.*

*I get on really well with everybody on board but it isn't quite the same. Bill and Birdie are the same as ever but the feel of the ship is more naval than before and a little more constrained and Old Titus has become more morose. There can be an atmosphere between him and Teddy, which is a pity as Teddy is a great chap for skylarking. The strange thing is that Bill and Birdie seem to have earned Titus's respect and he is a great friend of Aitch's and I must say that I quite like the old soldier for all his ways. In the end we are both from landed estates and, although everybody is too polite to mention it, we are the only two to have contributed financially to the expedition. Not that that makes any difference to how we feel about being here and we both want to pitch in and do what we can.*

*It was wonderful to receive your letter and to have all the news of life at Lamer. You seem to be getting on fine without me, although Mother worries in her correspondence. Be a dear and look out for her. There really is no need to worry about me as I am having the time of my life.*

*You tell me that the English summer is fading fast and that there are already signs of autumn. It still strikes me as strange that in this half of the world our seasons are the very opposite of yours. Here spring is on the march and there will be a hot summer to follow. I expect that your apple and my old mulberry will be turning in colour and then the leaves will fall. But the redwings and the fieldfares will soon be with you to bring you cheer from the cold north. Strange to think of all those links and loves that bind us across the world but centre on Lamer.*

<u>*October 15*</u>

*Land again and more social activities. Birdie and I have discovered some of the attractions of Australia and the charms* of the young ladies. I think that even old Birdie was taken with one particular lady but then we have other matters on our minds and great challenges to deal with so this sort of thing is of no real consequence.

We have been joined on board by several Australians and one of them is a really interesting fellow, called Frank Debenham, or 'Deb'. He is as tough as old hickory but has ease and charm in a typically Australian manner. He is also a good physicist and will be a real asset when we get to the great white south. I think that I will make good pals with Deb, he is one of those people whom you like straight off and know that you can depend on.

_October 17_

I have come from a meeting in the ward room. We have been told that Amundsen plans to go south! This is a real shock to us all. Apparently he sent a telegram to Captain Scott telling him he was going south, no apology or explanation given at all. He must have been planning this all the time. Everybody is most terribly put out about it as his objective can only be the Pole while we are on a science based expedition and have a whole range of objectives. Some of the fellows say that if we are going to have any chance of getting to the Pole before the Norskies we should trim our plans accordingly. Teddy is particularly voluble on this topic and a number of the others join him, but Uncle Bill is not of this persuasion and had a long talk with Captain Scott on his own. The end result is that Captain Scott insists we keep to our plans and don't let the Norskies dictate terms.

It's a pity but there can be something of an atmosphere between Teddy and Captain Scott. This business with Amundsen seems to have upset our usual harmony. Even old Titus had his say, muttering that he didn't see that Amundsen has behaved badly and that he is entitled to have a go at the Pole same as anybody. I must say that I can see his point here and wish that we would let it all lie and get back to normal. Then there is this strange business of the wives. We have been joined in Australia by Mrs Wilson, Mrs Teddy Evans and Mrs Scott. Of course, Bill's Oriana is a wonderful lady and Mrs Evans is all very well but nobody in the crew cares too much for Mrs Scott. You should hear old Titus on the subject! I have to say that I find her a rather imperious lady. It is as though she thinks that she is the leader of the expedition. The problem is that the wives keep popping up and getting in the way. Titus has some terrible story about a falling out between the wives but I am sure that he exaggerates. I agree with Titus, it will be good to get away from land and get on with the job.

_November 2_

We are all really impressed by the kindness and friendship extended to us by people in New Zealand. Bill is enthralled by the birds which thrive on these two islands. He explained to me that the birds were here for centuries before the arrival of man and any real predators.

As a result there is a wonderful range and diversity of species and many are flightless because they had no need to escape predation. Unfortunately, since the arrival of man, rats and other predators this situation is changing. Bill hopes that the wildlife here will not be too affected. We must make sure that we leave no dogs or rats in Antarctica when we depart.

We have assembled the most extraordinary collection of stores and items, a chaotic assembly of boxes, containing everything from packets of mustard to ropes and crampons. There are three motor sledges and even two prefabricated huts. Birdie is in his element, rushing hither and thither and sorting it all out. He has the most extraordinary energy and enthusiasm and his knowledge of where everything is and where it is to go is wonderful. We also have a collection of animals which makes us look like a travelling circus. Tied amongst the stores are thirty three ferocious sledge dogs which are more like wolves than dogs. They are enormous beasts and quite wild and very difficult to handle. If they had half a chance they would devour the stores and kill anything they could find. Meares and a Russian sledge boy called Dimitri brought them here from Siberia and I can't see how they are going to be tamed enough to be of any real use. There are also nineteen Manchurian ponies but Titus is not impressed with the quality of these and there were strong words between him and Teddy. He said they were 'a set of rotten old crocks and only fit for the knacker's yard.' They were bought by Captain Scott's brother–in–law and therefore you have to be careful not to offend, not that this bothers the old soldier one jot. I try to stay out of it. I stick close to Birdie and Bill and do what I can and whatever is asked of me.

### November 28

There has been a terrible row over Petty Officer Evans. He was in trouble several times during our time on land but worst was in Port Chalmers where the wretched man became drunk and embarrassed the whole ship's company by falling into the sea when coming back on board. Teddy Evans was livid about it and discharged him on the spot but Captain Scott is very attached to Evans, who was with him on Discovery, and has allowed him to rejoin the ship. This does not please Teddy at all who says that his authority has been undermined. This incident has rocked the harmony of the officers on board. Several take Teddy's part and I know that Titus feels strongly that to go back on a decision of this nature is a sign of weakness. He says that we are going to a place where each man, irrespective of rank, has to count on the other with his life. He insists that there can be no place for favouritism or compromise. Everybody has sought Bill's opinion. Bill doesn't care for Evans any more than the rest of us but he has a good understanding of Captain Scott and feels that we ought to let this one go. He confirms that Evans did stalwart work on Discovery and that, while he is a poor landsman, he is a good sailor and is very loyal to Scott. Bill and Teddy had a long discussion about it all after which there was a meeting with Captain Scott and we have been told to put the matter to rest. I think that everybody has accepted this with the exception of Titus, who now refers to Evans as the 'Weak Link' and mutters negatively about Scott's judgement.

Thankfully, we sail for the south tomorrow and will leave all our land troubles behind us. It will be better once we are away from wives and telegrams and can concentrate on the job in hand. I know that Captain Scott thinks well of me and the work that I have done so far because Uncle Bill told me that depending on how I shape up to sledging he may use me on the ice. Keep your fingers crossed, I could be one of those chosen to go to the Pole!

I can post this letter from here but once we are at sea it's going to be much more difficult. The Terra Nova will bring letters back for posting in New Zealand when she returns from leaving us in our winter quarters. We will be left marooned in Antarctica until the old tub returns. I will then write to you, when and where I can, and will bundle my writings together in separate letters. These can be dispatched to you on the returning ship. I will number each bundle of letters so that you can read them in the order I wrote them. You can make a collection of your very own, special 'Letters from Antarctica' by the celebrated traveller and intrepid polar explorer Apsley Cherry-Garrard.

Just think, the next time I put pen to paper I will be in the Antarctic regions. After all this time I find the prospect exciting and terrifying. What challenges await us there and how will we all respond to them? Will we all return safe and sound? On Captain Scott's last expedition both Bonner and Vince lost their lives in ways that nobody could have foretold. But please don't worry about me personally; I know that with the likes of Uncle Bill and Birdie close to me, I will make it through just fine.

Say nothing of this to Mother. I will write to her, of course, and to the other girls, but there are matters I want to convey to you alone. After all, we have shared so many adventures in the past and will share this one. It will be as though I have you here with me to guide and comfort me and be part of my life journey.

Love to you, dear girl, and all at dear old Lamer,
Apsley

## Lamer Park, 1907

Cherry's predictions were well founded. Oxford that autumn was a poorer place without his friends and the General's ill health overshadowed his return to the House. But he did not anticipate the news in November that the General had died. A terrible darkness swept over them all. Lamer would never be the same. They buried the General with full military honours on a grey November day. Soldiers from his old regiment were pall bearers and the coffin was covered with a Union Jack on which was laid his plumed helmet and sword. Cherry carried the General's medals and walked behind the coffin. Mother and the girls walked behind him. The following procession of villagers was headed by all the servants and tenants. On the General's expressed wish they buried him in the churchyard of St John's and not in the Garrard chapel. Cherry assumed that the General's choice indicated that he did not wish to be left with all those Garrards of the past.

Cherry was not ready to be left alone with the responsibilities of it all. He was now required to make frequent visits to Lamer and decided to pull out of rowing altogether. Oxford was a duller place and he felt awkward among so many new faces. The House had the capacity to regenerate and was quick to forget those who passed through. As he walked through the cloisters he could hear the new gentlemen of the House laughing and talking together, crowding round the team notice boards or planning new escapades, and he knew that somehow he had passed out of their world.

As he neared finals he needed to focus on his studies and deliver that last burst that would push him up to a respectable second. It was enough for the likes of Chatteris to accept a third or even a fourth with a shrug and a sneer to 'the grey men' and the comforting parlance of 'a gentleman's degree' but Cherry had been tipped for better things. The General had hoped for more but would have accepted a second and he wanted to honour his father's memory.

The news came to him in his room in the House. A list had been posted in the cloisters listing him with a third, a stab in his heart that no amount of bluster could conceal. The last few weeks in Oxford should have been a time of delight of fooling on the cricket field or larking on the river, freed even from the courteous restraint of the porters. Instead he was cast down in gloom and kept himself away from the throb of undergraduate life for fear of revealing his inner torments.

It was a relief when the time came to depart and quit his room. He packed his old trunk, the same that had served him from his earliest time at the Grange. It was stored in the attic above his room. He obtained the key from the Porters' Lodge and climbed the winding, dusty stairs up to the very old and shabby door that was only opened once a term. The key fitted well enough and the door opened easily to reveal the attic with its wooden floor boards and clutter of uncollected trunks. It surprised and momentarily startled him to hear wild scrabbling on the cobweb-stained window that provided the source of light. He looked again and saw that it was a young swallow desperate to find its way through the grimy glass to the summer world beyond. Cherry went forward and took the bird in his hand. The window had a latch which, quite remarkably, still worked and he was able to creak it open. He paused for a moment, reflecting on the fragility of the small scrap of feather locked in his hand before flinging it into the open space above the quad. The bird caught flight on the instant and soared away into the open air. Cherry remained, framed in the old window and staring into the sky for a few moments before closing the window and returning to the job in hand.

Oxford days were over, the General was dead and Lamer was his by default. Cherry felt unworthy of it. As head of the household, he acquired the sole right to his father's study and desk. Mother insisted on this since he had to have somewhere to work and run Lamer and the family's affairs. She assumed that she and the girls would stay at Lamer until Cherry found a wife. When that time came she and the girls would return to Denford.

On the first morning Cherry sat miserably at his father's desk. It was all as he had left it, even down to the pictures of the House and the picture of the General and Saltmarshe in Africa. These pictures would not change, but he did put up the picture of the House Eight 1907. He thought that the General would approve of that, and he put the copy of Saltmarshe's *Odyssey* in the top drawer of the desk.

'*Agricola puellam amat,*' he thought to himself.

Hampton came into the study on Monday mornings. He brought news that the Liberals continued to make trouble and that the affairs of the estate were difficult. Cherry felt deeply tired and drained of all energy and enthusiasm. He let himself be guided by Hampton, acquiescing with little contradiction. He drifted about the estate in a half-alive fashion.

Chapel on a Sunday morning was clouded by the General's absence. They couldn't sing and Cherry had the small organ taken away and a plaque put on the wall.

*In memory of Major General Apsley Cherry-Garrard: 1833-1907*
*A great soldier and a gentleman.*
*A beloved husband and father.*
*Shout while you journey home!*

Cherry saw the General singing in full heart and summoning his empire to him. 'If Father could see me now,' he thought to himself miserably, 'what would he make of his son?'

It was as though he had been left behind to rust unburnished. Friends from the House had gone their separate ways and sought their own adventures, Chatteris had become orientated towards London and a new set of people and Ida, through Elspeth, knew more about him than Cherry. Stretfield was established in a mission in India and corresponded with Cherry and was keen for him to come out. He also wrote to Ida, and Cherry wondered about the two of them being more than correspondents, but Ida would not be drawn on the content of these letters or on her true feelings about Stretfield.

Ida's company was as dear to him as ever. She saw him as he was and accepted him without undue expectation and without criticism. Whereas he found it incumbent to match up to Mother's expectations and be head of the family, a view shared by the younger girls. But even Ida, so near and dear, could not be kept forever as his stalwart ally. Stretfield was not the only person to notice Ida and there was particular interest from a Nutfield curate who hoped to come into a living in the near future. Cherry thought of the swallow he had found in the college attic, Ida would and should fly when the time was right. He resolved on taking some time out to travel. He would catch up with Stretfield in India and do something worthwhile before settling down to the duties of the estate.

'Some work of noble note?' Ida teased.

'Well, all right, yes,' he said. 'I need to do something other than just run the estates. Think of Father, he ran the estates perfectly but then he had an exciting and distinguished career to look back on. I haven't even made a start.'

'I think that you have been terrific in picking up after Father's death and running Denford and dear old Lamer,' said Ida, 'not to mention all the rest of it. You forget how many people and their lives depend on you.'

'Yes, but I can't help but feel that there must be something more. You're right to tease me about *Ulysses*. Even old Telemachus had his adventures before settling to serve his 'rugged people'. I'll be twenty-three in January, I want to feel I have played a bigger part in life.'

'I'm worried that if you go away you'll never come back,' she said.

'I could never leave Lamer for more than a year at the very longest. I can't see me being a particularly good missionary, but I need to test myself and see and do things I will never have a chance to do in later life. When I come back we'll have adventures and be so fit that we can run down purple emperors and we'll find every bird's nest in Lamer. What do you say?'

She looked at his earnest face, so full of hope and courage and dreams. Ida knew in her heart that her world was breaking up and she wanted desperately to trap and hold it for just a little longer but she knew that holding on tight was not an option.

'I say are you Telemachus or Ulysses?' she said.

Cherry's travels brought him little comfort. The work was grubby and little to his inclination. His relations with Stretfield became strained because he could not commit to the missionary nature of the work and felt himself no more than a rich tourist indulging in discomfort while not being able to do anything substantial to improve the lot of the people they encountered. He spent some of his money in support of the work but tired of the endless demands for more. The whole business served to increase his sense of inadequacy. There was nothing else for it but to return to Lamer.

Reggie Smith looked out for his young cousin and invited him to stay in Scotland. He had also invited his good friend Ted Wilson to be one of the house guests. Reggie knew that Cherry admired Ted and was confident that Ted would advise him well. Ted rose to the occasion. He didn't lecture Cherry or tell him how to conduct himself. He listened and Cherry valued this highly. Reggie and Ted were full of the news of Shackleton's *Nimrod* expedition. Shackleton and three companions had established a new Furthest

South record and had turned back just one hundred miles north of the Pole. They had left Scott and Wilson's previous record far behind them and had pushed on over the Barrier ice, pioneered a way through the mountains, by a glacier they named after Beardmore, and journeyed on across the summit. It was a great blow for the British Empire. It showed that the Pole could be achieved and it was right and proper that it be claimed by a British team. Peary may have taken the North Pole but Britain would claim the far more challenging South Pole. Reggie was dismissive of Shackleton's expedition, arguing that it had been a fast trick to pull and that the second attempt at the Pole should have been left to Scott. Ted was more generously disposed to Shackleton:

'I was with Shackleton on *Discovery* and when we went on our Farthest South attempt, and in those situations you really get to know the inner quality of a man.'

'What's Shackleton like?' asked Cherry, eager for every morsel of information. 'He may have done well on *Nimrod* but when he was with you on *Discovery* didn't he go down and have to be invalided home?'

Ted Wilson was unusually sharp. 'That's an easy judgement to make by this fireside and after a good dinner. Unless you've been out there and experienced the terrible reality of physical and mental exhaustion, combined with near starvation, you can't imagine what it's like. It can bring down the strongest and we are all human. On our Farthest South attempt, Scott was exemplary and we both needed his example to keep us going. Sometimes the force of nature is just too great. Shackleton was a marvel of courage and endurance but he was hit by scurvy, which is a terrible disease. No man can withstand its physical ravages. No, I claim no superiority over Shackleton. He's a fine fellow with an irrepressible sense of humour and a great spirit that is second to none.'

'I believe he has a high opinion of you too,' said Reggie. 'Didn't he ask you to go with him on *Nimrod*?'

'Quite right, Reggie, I'm not such a great hero after all. I'm a married man and a scientist first and foremost. The Pole in itself means nothing to me, it is just a strange challenge which can beset a man's imagination. In the end it's nothing more than a theoretical position on a map. Now, when they were going for the *North Pole* there were all sorts of mad ideas about there being a warm polar sea or something special at the Pole but the truth is far more mundane. There's nothing at either pole but utter lifelessness, bleakness, desolation of utmost cold and driving winds. What right have we to risk our lives and those of our comrades for that?'

'I hear tell that Scott is planning another expedition,' said Reggie 'and has asked you to go with him. Will you go?'

'I will go but only if it's a proper scientific expedition and that, apart from anything else, I'm given a promise that I can focus on my work with the emperor penguins. They are the key to so many scientific truths that I can't resist having a closer inspection and the best way to do that is to set up our base in Cape Crozier where they breed.'

'It seems to me,' said Reggie 'that you've already made your decision.'

Wilson's words were balm to Cherry's sadness. Here was some work of 'noble note' that a man might aspire to. He admired Ted Wilson enormously and aspired to his aesthetic and spiritual example even though he knew that it was beyond him personally.

'I would love to be with you in the south more than anything in the whole world,' he said, before he had time to think about it. Wilson heard and saw Cherry's youthful, serious face which was so pained and lonely.

'In that case,' said Wilson, 'I will see what I can do.'

Wilson was as good as his word but Scott had far more volunteers than he needed and had no place for a non-specialist amateur with faulty eye sight and nothing other than enthusiasm to recommend him. What Scott needed was funds, not manpower. Wilson came to see Cherry in Lamer and explained the situation as tactfully as possible. Mother and Ida were pleased with Scott's decision but Cherry was dreadfully disappointed. He wondered what the General would have done.

He was standing in the hall and looking vacantly at the picture of Ulysses riding the storm to the land of the Lotus Eaters when the answer came to him. The painting unsettled him, as it had in childhood, but as he looked at it he recalled the General's voice,

*'COURAGE! he said, and pointed towards the land*
*This mounting wave will roll us shoreward soon'.*

Cherry decided that the expedition had to take place with him or without him and that the honourable thing was to contribute to the funding. He sent a covering note and a cheque for a thousand pounds towards the funds of the British Antarctic Expedition. Scott was so impressed with what he described in his acknowledgement note as, 'the act of an English Gentleman' that he offered Cherry the position of Assistant Zoologist on the expedition. He should be ready to join the *Terra Nova* which was due to leave Cardiff on the 15th June 1910. Scott added the words:

'Congratulations, you have made the cut.'

## THE LAND OF DREAMS: 1913-1957

Journeying, travelling, questing, searching, the old Chevalier encountered strange and ghastly things but nothing troubled him so much as the perpetual cold. Bleak and omnipresent it crept into his very soul. He came to the margins of a vast and terrible forest. The track led him into a dark wood and petered out into nothing so there was no way of knowing which way to go. He and his horse stumbled on, picking a way between the trees and bushes as best they could. Behind the dark bushes he thought he saw strange, shadowy people who stared at him and then darted away into the darkness.

'Trade for the knife! No thank you, no thank you,' they whispered from the cover of the bushes.

He was searching for it, but no matter how hard he looked it could not be found and the longer and more ardently he searched the more confused he became. At times he was not even sure of the object of his search.

At last, burdened and fatigued to the core of his being, he came to a clearing in the forest. A mound rose suddenly from the ground. On the top of the mound grew an ancient mulberry tree and all about was covered in feathery green fern. From the mound's core a stream spouted and the water ran clear and fast, down and away into the dark forest. He bent down and drank and water soaked into his dry body. He lay down on the green fern of the mound and felt as though the undergrowth was taking him down into itself. Then he fell into a deep sleep.

Cherry dreamed in the dark, dreamed through that long second winter and the dream went on long after, as though, the real Cherry was asleep in the dark and all he could see and do was in dreams. He dreamed of shadows on the wall but if he looked carefully through the dark shadows there was something real behind them. He saw men marching to war and dragging back sledges on which there were the bodies of the fallen. He saw Aitch drowning and holding his hands out to him, before he slipped below the water. Deb's brother, Herbert, was killed in the madness of Gallipoli. Reggie Smith could take no more of the madness and flung himself out of a fourth floor window. Cherry saw him flying through the night sky in his pyjamas, clutching a weather vane in his hand. Reggie looked into his eyes as he sped past and mouthed, 'Please Cherry, don't.'

Big and bold in his dreams was the house at Lamer but the house seemed to grow old and was less bright. There were more wars and more terrible things: burning buildings, airplanes and bombs. Deb's elder boy, Barry, spun down to earth in a burning plane. Cherry watched him from the steps at Lamer and there was nothing he could do.

Time passed and people grew older: Ida a mother, Mother dead, Deb a stiff-backed, elderly gentleman. Years can be counted in memories, Cherry counted them in dreams, dreams which at times felt real and then not so real. Dreams danced and swayed in his mind, most of them dark and menacing but some of them shone with a glow that was almost light. There was a special dream of Angela, who came into his world like her name and held the dark dreams back. Cherry, vulnerable, prostrate, needed that touch from the mortal world. But even Angela could not dispel the dreams entirely and the dreamer could not be woken entirely because his whole body and mind were exhausted from journeying.

Cherry felt the dream's meaning, even though he could not see clearly. 'Cheery Cherry' Captain Scott had dubbed him but what would Scott make of him now and how would the others regard him? Birdie would be like Angela, positive and never grumbling, but what of Uncle Bill? Bill set such high standards for all. Bill's blue eyes found him and pierced his heart. Again and again the thought tormented him - if only they had lived. Sleep was the most difficult. He couldn't stop the images piling up one on the other: the General, Bill, Captain Scott, they gathered in the dark to compound his sense of failure and guilt. He would wake beside the sleeping Angela, guilty about ignoring her, guilty about being awake and causing anxiety. Broken dreams filled the few hours of broken slumber. Often they were about Lamer, he would be walking up from Whitebushes Common on the southern track to the house. Sometimes he was no more than a boy, sometimes an old man. He would pass the White Bridge and Hobbs's house. Somebody was watching from the upstairs window of Hobbs's house but he couldn't be sure who it was. He came to the two trees but as he passed under them, they seemed to whisper something he could not properly hear. He was at the back of Lamer and it was as he recalled it, the stables and barns and Hobbs's garden room, but all were empty. He stopped by the coal chute to listen to the sounds of the kitchen but could hear nothing. He turned on the gravel and walked round to the front of the house. The front was just as it had always been and there was the Old General dressed in full military uniform, as he had been on that Empire day long ago. He stood, clear, defiant and tall, as though waiting for the procession to approach the house. Cherry was filled with joy to see him and ran forward but the General slipped behind the front door. The front of the house was no more than a façade. Inside there was nothing, it was all gone. He couldn't bear it. This dream was one of many concerning Lamer, the General, Hobbs and sometimes Ida.

There were other terrible dreams. He lay in the snow with a terrible blizzard roaring all about him but he was in his bag and despite the weather he was warm and comfortable. Then Bill thrust his face in front of him. It wasn't the Bill he knew and loved but an older man with something of Bill and the Old General with an angry face. He cupped his hands so that he could be heard above the storm and shouted close to Cherry's ear.

'You let us down Cherry,' he said. 'You let all of us down, you who could have let us live. What price is there for comfort? Yes, you were comfortable in the hut and you are comfortable now in your luxury apartment, but how much has that comfort cost, what is the price of failure?'

Even worse was that dreaded dream:

*It was during that terrible second winter, when every hour and every day seemed to be the same and the longing was part of the darkness that never seemed to go away, as though Cherry had been plunged into perpetual blankness and the world was intensely cold and bleak and all that really mattered was dead. Then they heard the dogs 'singing,' a high-pitched, primeval cry from another world and Cherry's heart leaped for joy in anticipation of the one thing in all the world that would bring back the light of life. They were transfixed and staring at the door. Cherry stood by Debenham and Deb's face was ghastly white. 'My God!' muttered Deb. 'It's them.' There was dread in his voice as though he feared the arrival of the five missing men, who by now could be no more than emaciated and frozen spectres.*

*Cherry saw the door push open and Scott came through, knocking the ice from his body with his mittens and he looked straight into Cherry's eyes just as if he knew everything. Then came Bill, Bill who could never change no matter what and his blue eyes danced to see them all, and he allowed himself a smile of recognition. Then finally Birdie came in, still wearing that ridiculous green hat and he just shook with laughter. Cherry couldn't move. He desperately wanted to rush forward and touch them to feel their life but he couldn't move. They counted three. Taff and Titus were not there but then they never could have made it, and, as he thought that, Cherry knew that none of this was real. It seemed so real and brought him such intense happiness but the moment would pass. The dream slipped back into the darkness and the cold light stole back painfully into his brain. They had not lived and neither could he. The door would stay closed and the darkness and the cold would return to claim its own.*

*Cherry would remain suspended in the thrall of the ice for all time.*

This dream scared him more than all the others. It made him shout out in fear. Angela woke and struggled to make him realise that he was dreaming. The effects on him were alarmingly severe and weakened him for days. Angela decided that they would seek a definitive treatment.

'Treatment' meant more long corridors and small, lightless rooms with cheery old men who peered and asked all manner of questions. Always questions and more questions, white coats and a strange smell like ether but hanging in the smell of ether was the fear of death and mortality. Cherry wandered the corridor of referral and leading off the corridor were more dimly lit rooms. White-coated, peering men sat in the rooms and offered diagnoses which changed back to questions.

'They think that it's in my mind,' Cherry grumbled to Angela. 'They think I'm an insane fool who's lost the power to control his own body.'

'Oh, really Cherry,' said Angela. 'They just think that you have suffered a lot and maybe they're right. Antarctica was terrible for you, you were so young. It is understandable to assume that those experiences have taken their toll on your body.'

'Nonsense!' he snapped. 'Why should my experiences have been any worse than those poor devils who went through the Western Front and survived it? Even in the last war the most terrible things happened, but not to me. I sat them out with a cushy number and a damned illness that defied description. Every time I see a man with his legs shot away or with his face mutilated I envy him. I envy him, yes I envy his physical wounds and the simplicity of justifying himself in achieving nothing in doing nothing but simply continuing to live.'

'I don't see that at all. You were young and so sensitive, it's all together different.' Her voice was low and choked. He could see that she was crying but trying to hide it. He couldn't bear to see her cry, still less be the cause of it. He changed tack.

'All right, maybe I'm just a grumpy old fellow. You think that I should try this electrical thingumabob? After all, I've tried everything else.'

'Oh, yes, please do. It's had the most encouraging results and they really do think it will help to, well, bring you back.'

'Do you really want me back so much? Do you really think I can still do something good?'

'I know you can,' she said. 'You have so much to offer. You will be like Ulysses setting off on an adventure.'

'Ulysses grew old you know.'

'I know, but he did have one last adventure.'

Wars had been fought and won and all awoke to a new world and a new time. But old memories of old wars clung in the atmosphere like the smell of camphor. Grandfathers pottered around in old sheds keeping their stories close and grandmothers kept pictures of lost boys in silver frames, adorned with poppies. Theirs was the first war, the one that they called 'The Great War.' Yet, it was still near enough for them to remember and feel the pain of it all.

There had been a second and more recent war. Fathers had tales of hot places that could be found in maps. They smoked woodbine cigarettes and hung old army belts on dusty nails in attics. They went to work on the bus or rode bicycles that were made in England. Some went up on the train to London, in smoke-filled carriages and wearing bowler hats. Commuters spilled into London to rush for the Underground which took them to noisy offices. They went to work all day and came home late in the evening for meals that were cooked by their wives. Mothers cared for the children and looked after the homes. They walked to the bus stop and came back burdened with great bags of shopping. They washed with boards on Monday, cooked 'Toad in the 'Ole', queued for orange juice and turned Home Guard helmets upside down to be used as hanging baskets. They too remembered the recent war and talked about bombs and things you couldn't have.

The world was moving on and changing. The motor car replaced the horse, television was coming into homes, you could fly in an airplane all the way to Africa. Empire Day was abandoned. The maps at school were still pink but it was the pink of commonwealth, not empire, although the idea of a special responsibility endured. Wolf Cubs were read to from *The Jungle Book* and Rikki Tikki Tavi danced round the old tortoise stove that warmed the hut and hypnotised the great snake Kaa. India was gone but Mowgli lived on. The Scouts drilled with staves and marched behind the trek cart - be smart, be helpful, be prepared. They read about old BP and how we had the better of the Boer at Mafeking and learned from that triumph the values that make a true Englishman. They recited:

'A scout is a friend to all and a brother to every other scout no matter to what country, class or creed the other may belong.'

The old world was balanced on the cusp of the new. National Service was to be abandoned and the older boys would be spared the humiliation of two years of shorn hair and being drilled by screaming corporals. No longer would two years be spent cutting the grass with scissors or painting the coal white. Not everybody was convinced of the value of all these changes. Surely National Service was better than hanging around on street corners wearing winkle pickers and swept back hair, like those Teddy Boys with their flick knives? They had no discipline, no values and no respect. Where would it all end? They should trust Mr Macmillan of Eton and Oxford in his pin-striped suit, who knew what was best.

Lamer Park was dead and only its skeleton remained. Long past was the day when General Cherry-Garrard stood on the stone steps and welcomed the joyful villagers to Empire Day. The villagers and their descendants had been marched away to wars to fight for that same empire. Others had departed the safe shores of England for new lives and greater prosperity in the colonies. Those who remained had slowly freed themselves from the servitude of the estate, and worked for new employers in a new world order that tried hard to forget about an empire and think of a commonwealth.

All that now stood now was the shell of the house. The ravages of age were scrawled across its features. The brickwork was crumbling and many of the leaded windows were broken and unsecured. The garden was in the process of claiming back its own. The old house had been sold and sold again and left stripped of all assets to the developers' pity. The great house braced itself for the onset of the heavy machinery that would pulverise it into submission.

The estate had been carved up and sold off until Lamer and its grounds were no more than a sinking island in the midst of a changing sea. The farms had long ago claimed their independence and only a few of them remained devoted to agriculture, the rest had been developed into roads and housing and small factories. Everywhere there was building and concrete for the new post war generation.

To the north, the town of Redhill had grown, aided by the railway, so that its fringes touched the edges of the great growing wen of London. There was more housing around the village of Earlswood and a group of shops clustered around the railway station. The great church of St John's was still there and so was the school but the school had expanded and it now had an infant section and separate schooling for primary boys and primary girls. The approach to Lamer through the parkland had changed beyond recognition. The main, northerly approach to the house was no more than a track and the linden trees had been cut down. A public golf course swept down from the heights of Earlswood and passed within a spit of the house.

In the east the estate farms were now owner-occupied but the area was still mostly farmland and rural. In the west there had been radical changes. The commons were incorporated into a golf course and other community facilities. The lakes, where Cherry had learned to swim, had become communal pleasure facilities. The upper lake was used for boating and the lower lake for fishing and swimming.

There was more building and a sense of moving on. London gorged on the nearby towns and brought the sloppy tongue of Estuary to Redhill but the villages clung to some independence and the network of commons around Redhill survived.The south of Lamer was the most unchanged. Ida's apple tree and Cherry's old mulberry stood on guard facing south. They looked down the old southern lane to the White Bridge and Hobbs's House. The house looked deserted and decayed but was recognisable. Beyond the house was Whitebushes, not in its original state but clearly identifiable. Houses ringed the common and to the west the three great arches stood firm. The trains, mounted high on the embankment, rattled on. The track from the White Bridge ran down and crossed over Three Arches road before pushing through the heart of the common. From here it became a lane and meandered southward and up to the great gates of a hospital. The hospital didn't treat scarlet fever any more because that illness was no longer a concern in the new age. Instead it had been converted to provide for patients with a new disease which had come with the waves of immigrants from the old empire. The hospital kept its sense of remoteness because access was either from the lane across the common or from the road that ran under the Three Arches, circumnavigated the common and stopped at the hospital. Around and beyond the hospital, the bushes grew just as dark and impenetrable as ever. From the gates of the hospital the lane narrowed to little more than a path and pushed on through the bushes to a farm beyond. The narrow path was still known as the Magic Pathway but in the last war they had built a pill box at the entrance, a hard-faced, angular reminder of the world of men. The bushes enfolded the pill box in their secret embrace and in the rush of early summer emblazoned it in victorious laurels of white.

# HAD WE LIVED

## After Captain Scott

# PART TWO

# CHAPTER SEVEN

## *ANTARCTIC LETTER NUMBER ONE*

*December 6, 1910*
**THE TERRA NOVA**

*Dear Ida*
*Well, we really are on our way to the south. New Zealand and civilisation are far behind us. We have had our ups and downs since my last letter and I have written to Mother about it at some length but I must tell you that the storm we encountered on leaving New Zealand was really terrible and I thought that my last moment had come. We hit the most terrifying waves and I learned afterwards that some of them were as high as thirty-six feet tall. They smashed down on the poor old tub. Water mixed with fine coal and oil from the engines formed balls of grease which clogged the pumps. Eventually the engines choked and had to be put out for fear of fire. We drifted in a helpless state and were battered by the weather. Waves swept over the decks hurling the dogs, still tied to their chains, into the sea. One was swept overboard, breaking its collar, and we assumed that it was lost but the next wave swept the poor creature back on deck. Another dog was swept away and never seen again. The ponies suffered terribly and, despite Titus's best efforts, we lost one.*
*Worst of all were the sacks of coal that had been tied up on deck. These were rendered into battering rams by the action of the sea and we had to cut most of them free and swing them into the open water. If I hadn't had the chaps with me, especially Uncle Bill and Birdie, I don't think that I could have made it and would have funked it all. They were magnificent, with their energy, confidence and unflagging good spirits, and their example steadied my nerves. They knew better than me what a tight corner we were in but they showed no fear. If only I could be like that!*
*As there were no steam pumps and the hand pumps were choked, the ship was awash with water. I thought that we would fill and sink to the bottom of the Antarctic Ocean. You will think me strange, it was as though we had unleashed Poseidon's rage and he would claim us for our audacity in entering his kingdom. Uncle Bill and Birdie put us in line and buckets were handed from one man to the next in a race against death by drowning. We were all utterly sodden but we worked in a mad frenzy and didn't feel the cold. I made myself think of that old picture of Ulysses in the hall. I saw that terrible sea thundering around the boat and the men pulling on the oars for their very lives. It reminded me of Lamer and home and comforted me. I kept myself going for you all at Lamer. Our struggles went on and we became*

*more and more exhausted and dehydrated from lack of fresh water. At one point, Birdie handed me a mug and I downed the contents in one and felt better. It was the best water I have ever drunk. Later, Birdie explained that it was pure navy rum because no drinking water was to be had. It was a race against death with every man working for himself and his shipmates to save the vessel from sinking. Somebody struck up with a sea shanty and we gathered the rhythm and sang as though our hearts would break. As we sang, one song after another, we gained heart and determination. We sang everything and anything we could think of. I led off with:*

*'Hills of The North rejoice!'*

*The first line was enough, their voices swelled and rose in defiance of the din of the ocean. As the hymn gathered momentum I swear I heard Father's voice. You will think this really strange, and I couldn't tell anybody this but you, I just knew that he was there with us. When we came to the line:*

*'Shout while you journey home!'*

*I imagined we were shouting our defiance into Poseidon's face, into the very teeth of the storm. What will surprise you, dear Ida, is that I felt then no fear and almost a mad sense of joy.*

*Our bailing efforts would not have been enough on their own but the Chief and Birdie managed to clear the pumps and get the engines working again in the nick of time. God knows how, but we came through it all, and although we lost some stores and some dogs and ponies, the game is still afoot.*

*December 10*

*We have crossed the Antarctic Circle and have arrived. Now the adventure begins!*

*It was a wonderful relief to see my first iceberg. Nothing that we have seen around Lamer could have prepared me for the great, white, mountain that loomed over our little ship. I am becoming more accustomed to this scenery which ranges from the spectacular to the terrifying.*

*December 28*

*How was Christmas at Lamer? The ship was stuck in the ice for Christmas Day so there was no shortage of snow. We didn't have time to build a snowman but we had the most terrific Christmas feast with roast penguin as well as beef and plum pudding and mince pies and every sort of wine and liqueur. After dinner there were presents and crazy games. Captain Scott didn't join in but Birdie and Deb, and even Uncle Bill, had a whale of a time with much ragging and good humour all round. At one point I thought to myself, 'What if Ida and the girls could see us now, a fine set of manly explorers behaving like a bunch of school lads?' You would have laughed to see us enjoying ourselves so much and your big brother, who is normally so grave and responsible, just as bad as the worst of them. Even old Titus picked up on the mood and sang an extraordinary song that he had learned in the Inniskillings. I couldn't help but catch Bill's eye and he was clearly bursting with laughter at the sight of the old soldier in full voice. Then I heard a loud snigger from Birdie that sent the whole pack of us off and we howled with laughter. This sent old Titus into a new dimension and he yelled, 'Top Gallants All!' The ward room erupted into a frenzy of men, all intent on ripping the shirt off the back of any chap in reach. It was wonderful madness, and I can't remember having such fun! How quickly a little fun, with the best of possible fellows, drives away the shadows of doubt and fear and makes Poseidon's wrath no more than a storm?*

*The ice that held us is at last breaking up and we are able to pursue our journey south. Deb says that we are through the pack ice and will push our way into the Ross Sea. This will please Captain Scott who has been fretting about the time we have been in the ice and fears it will delay the work that can be done before the winter sets in. It's all a great race against time and the dread grip of the Antarctic winter. Not that you should see this as a cold, lonely journey, quite the reverse. Uncle Bill has been teaching me about the natural history of this region. There are plenty of seabirds including skua gulls and albatrosses. There are seals as well and I now know the characteristics of each breed. There are also killer whales, which hunt the poor seals in the ice floes. They come to the surface to eye us with malicious intent. Bill sees them as part of a great food chain which starts at the lowest form of life. I can't regard them as anything other than evil itself.*

*So, all is well, dear girl, and we are pushing on with our odyssey in the south.*

*I will seal this letter now and it can be the first of the Antarctic epistles to Lassie of Lamer.*

*Your Loving Brother,*
*Apsley*

**A New Year, 1958**

The Whitebushes of 1958 had its own carless community. It had one shop but no other facilities and Nan's had gone. The men now walked across the common, through the arches and a mile on to the plastic modern Nag's Head pub. In 'The Nag' were a one arm bandit and a juke box that promised the latest in popular entertainment. A small metal tap released fizzy keg beer, which ran sparkling clean and devoid of flavour. Nobody sang and the old songs were becoming forgotten. People walked or cycled to Earlswoood village, a mere two miles walk, for the butcher, baker and general store. They carried home their daily shopping in old string bags. For the more adventurous there was a walk to the Nag's Head, a long wait for the green double-decker bus and a rumbling ride up to Earlswood and on to distant Redhill.

In Whitebushes, people knew exactly who lived in each of the houses. They knew each beast on the common, whether tethered or allowed to wander unfettered. Things were changing but some things remained the same. Goldie, the common keeper, in full uniform, pedalled his bike along the footpaths, guarding the golf course and the archipelago of commons that formed his empire. His authoritative command - 'Oi, come back 'ere!' – was ignored by generations of boys. His special care was Earlswood Lakes, set like a muddied, freshwater pearl in Earlswood common, but his secret paramour was Mrs B, who ran the Whitebushes' shop.

A gang of boys patrolled and roamed the commons. They varied in numbers and age from eleven to the youngest a mere eight. Their base was a deserted outhouse in the grounds of the Hospital and their home territory was Whitebushes Common. They waged guerrilla war with Goldie in the sprawling empire of commons, thwarting his attempts to pursue them on his aged and civic bicycle, and waged open war on any other gangs that considered entering their homeland. Sometimes they would march north from their common, cross the stream at the White Bridge and go up to the great house at Lamer. They did not like to get too close because sometimes a watchman with an alsatian kept a close guard. The boys contented themselves by crawling as close to the house as they could, sometimes throwing stones to smash a window before running away. The boys in the gang knew all the families around their common and spent time chatting in doorways, denying accusations and knocking to ask for 'bob a job'.

The Hobbs family lived to the south of the common and at the end of the lane which wound up to the hospital. Grandpa Hobbs grew tobacco in his back garden and cured the leaves in his greenhouse. He drilled holes in the children's tortoise shells so that they could be staked to a chain but no matter how strong the chain the tortoise always broke it. When he worked he liked to whistle a certain tune and he taught his grandson, Ivan, to whistle it too. The boys knew that when Grandpa Hobbs had been a boy he had lived at the old empty Southern Lodge, which was then known as Hobbs's house, and that his family had worked at Lamer for generations. He had left to find his fortune in Canada but it was said that he didn't find it. When the Great War broke out he gave up on Canada and hitched a ride on a friendly ship to join up in England. He had experience with motor engines and came through the war well enough. After the war he came back and bought his own house in Whitebushes. Grandpa Hobbs had wonderful stories that the boys loved to hear, but he never talked about Canada or the Great War - it was as though he wanted to forget them both. He told the boys stories about Lamer and the people who lived there, how it had been a great estate with farms and servants and Grandpa Hobbs's grandfather had been head gardener and had grown apricots and all manner of fruit and vegetables for the great house. When Grandpa Hobbs was a boy, a general had lived at Lamer. Later, a famous Antarctic explorer lived there. Grandpa Hobbs also told them some scary stories about the Old People who lived hidden away in the bushes round about.

Mr Hobbs, his son and Ivan's Dad, had been in the recent war and knew the Canadians who came to Whitebushes and built a road to link with an airfield. The road was still there but wasn't allowed to be used and had grown over with weeds. The boys marched down it, pretending to be Canadian, tough, rugged outback men who were straight and honest and sort of British.

Granny Ford, Keith's grandma, kept the old house that had once been Whitebush Farm, and then Nan's ale house. The story was that when the railway came it had cut the few acres they held in half, rendered their farming unprofitable and choked their carp pool with duckweed. The great carp lived on despite it all but you could never see them or fish for them because of the dense green duckweed that covered the water's surface. In summer the gang cast out drag nets to try and catch the carp and in the winter they brought their toboggans so that they could race down the embankment and career across the ice. Granny Ford showed them her damp beer cellars where the boys found newts, living still and silent under old crates. The cellars had supplied the bar above. Granny Ford told them how the men would gather in the evening after work, to drink beer, tell stories and sing songs. There was an old, broken chair in the cellar which had an inscription on it:

*Hobbs chair: Sitter beware!*

It had to be something to do with Grandpa Hobbs but the boys could make no sense of it.

Old Ma Batton kept the village store and supplied basic groceries. She had one son, called Laurie. The gang went to the store to buy comics: *The Eagle*, with *Dan Dare* and *Luck of the Legion* was more thrilling reading than the more juvenile *Swift* and towered over the diminutive *Robin*. Dan Dare, heroically British and aided by his chubby friend Digby, pitted his wits against the futuristic Mekon. Green and emaciated, the Mekon floated on his flying bowl epitomising evil. Less approved by parents and therefore even more desirable to the boys were the *Beano* and *Dandy*. These featured *Desperate Dan,* the massive cow pie gobbling cowboy, and *The Bash Street Kids* for ever being chased and flogged by a master in full gown and mortar board.

Rationing was over and jars of delights crowded the shelves of Ma Batton's store: great yellow pineapple chunks, palate-skinning globules of colour in pear shapes, striped humbugs and winter-warming mixtures tasting of chemicals. They were sold by the ounce, tuppence for two ounces. Or there were the individual sweets: Duncan's Walnut Whip, great, teeth-rotting gobstoppers a penny or ha'pence each according to size, sherbet dabs and chews at a penny for four or a farthing each. All these delights could be washed down in an orange-fizzy stream of Tizer.

There were also disapproved things that tempted a boy to distraction: Domino fags five to the packet and temptingly in the range of pocket money, stink bombs ('the biggest stink since Hitler!') which the gang bought in profusion and then ground under their heels in doorways and schoolrooms and finally in the shop itself. The boys paid for all in coins: great penny coins some of which still had Queen Victoria wearing a bun, farthing coins with their diminutive wrens and octagonal threepenny bits.

One other house was of particular significance to the gang. Along the way from the Hobbs were the Cloughs. Old Clough was a policeman who kept himself to himself and pedalled away early to work in Redhill. He had an oversized daughter whom he ignored entirely and allowed to do as she liked.

The common's populace was swelled by the settled gypsies who had given up the roaming life to settle and live on the common. The Chaplans lived by the common with a whole host of children named after Old-Testament characters and the Ports kept a scrap heap away to the east of Whitebushes. Old Man Port swore and whipped his horse when it pulled his trap up the Brighton Road.

It was a modern world, yet something ancient was trapped there. It was still there in the changes of the season, the white wonder of the bushes and the comings and goings of visitors. In summer the mysterious nightingale sang unseen from the dark bushes and the swallows dipped in salute as they flew over the common and on their way up to what had been the old garden room at the back of Lamer. In autumn the swallows left and the fieldfares and redwings arrived from the distant north to strip the bushes of their red treasure. In winter the robin whistled wistfully from the edge of the bushes. Human visitors also came and went in their own time. Gypsies arrived without warning and tethered their skewbald ponies alongside the commoners' livestock. They lit wood fires in dank places and then left in smoky mystery.

No matter how tightly it might cling to its past, even Whitebushes couldn't escape development. The scarlet fever isolation hospital had been empty for many years but now there were new patients with new illnesses and the hospital was convenient in its isolation to deal with these modern problems. The buildings and grounds were split and developed to create appropriate facilities for twenty four long-term residential patients. What had been the former nurses' quarters were also developed to establish a house for the doctor and his family. In due course a suitable doctor was found and he, his wife, mother-in-law, and four children, moved in to the doctor's house and made it their home.

One holiday morning, a stench woke the family in the doctor's house at the hospital. The stench sought them out in their beds and filtered into their dreams like some unidentified illness. It took time to identify it as 'The Chicken Pot'.

'Oh, God!' shouted Jack from his bedroom. 'It's the chicken pot again.'

'Turn it off!' yelled Tom, in a desperate bid for release from the nauseous fumes.

In the kitchen, singing tunelessly, Mum heard the shouts with amusement and utter indifference. The kitchen was her place, the great engine room of her food industry, where she alone laboured to feed her menagerie of adults, children and animals. The kitchen was a dark and forbidding place with great deep sinks and heavy, spiked taps. A chipped cream-painted door led from the kitchen to a walk-in larder. The floor was laid with heavy flagstones, cold in summer and colder in winter, it guaranteed to smash any object falling from the tall, rickety table. Above the table Mum had erected her own chaotic shelving which was crowded with pots and pans of every size and variety. These blackened, and often handle-less objects, were piled high on top of each other beyond the reach of ordinary mortals. To remove one, she would poke the pile with a stick until the required pot, and many others, rained down. To return any partially washed pots they had to be flung from ground level until such time as they found their own resting place. Terrible culinary crimes were committed here but most dreadful was the heating of the chicken pot. The great metal cauldron burbled and gurgled, occasionally vomiting up morsels. The contents were a mixture of food scraps from the hospital and house combined with mash and an unknown diabolical ingredient (Jack insisted that he had once seen a bandage floating in it). When it had produced a sufficiency of evil smelling fumes, to compare with the lair of Gollum, and had roused the family for yet another morning, it was deemed to be cooked. Mum would wrestle it to the floor and drag it across the flagstones to the outside door. From there it was heaved into a wheelbarrow and wheeled down the path to the chicken run.

Mum was dressed in an old beige mackintosh, which had been badged on many previous runs by escaped slops, and she wore wellingtons. She drove the teetering pot before her while the wheelbarrow creaked and squealed its protests against the drunken journey down the bumpy path. The barrow's progress was supervised by a mad woman, who sang strange, discordant snatches from long-forgotten songs. Her long hair, usually tied up and out of the way, escaped from its restraining pins and bits dangled down in celebration of their liberty. Skellum, the wire-haired fox terrier, padded behind not so much out of loyalty but in order to give those chickens a damned good eyeing.

In spite of criticism Mum continued to feed her chickens. She justified her diabolical handiwork with such indisputable statements as, 'After all dears, it's free.' She dumbfounded her critics with such shrewd observation as, 'Chickens must eat' and finally foiled them altogether with the riposte, 'In the war we were glad enough for the eggs'.

Pip pulled the blankets over his head. If he stayed in bed long enough the pot would be removed, taken on its crazed journey and the smell would subside. He liked his bed and room and was in no hurry to depart. When he was young, and impressionable, Miriam had teased him with the story of Mr Watch who lived under the bed and whose sole diversion in life was grabbing of small boys' heels. Once having grabbed a boy, Mr Watch, (avoid his salutation at your peril!) would drag him under the bed and into his lair. Any prudent boy, who wished to avoid this fate, must take a flying leap onto the bed. Once actually on the bed, or in the bed, Pip was safe. Boys in pyjamas were particularly vulnerable because the ankle-grabbing Mr Watch had a penchant for naked ankles. Miriam had many imaginary characters. These included such terrifying creatures as the Old People, denizens of the copse at the far end of the garden. Miriam so terrified herself with the blood curdling nature of their shrieking enterprises that she had to create the New People to make war on them and drive them away. Also, on the balance side, was Miss Plimkin, whose simpering sweetness tended towards the irritating. Miss Plimkin doled out the odd sweet but her remarkable resemblance to Miriam herself, not fully concealed by the ingenious devices of Mum's head scarf and high-heeled shoes, strained credulity.

Pip no longer believed such stuff although he remained reluctant to look under the bed. Other things took his mind away from childish imaginings. His tropical aquarium had been given to him by a fond uncle. The aquarium was his box of delights and to open it he had to find the light switch and turn it on. At once a wonderful pageant unfolded. Plucky little guppies wriggled through the water and eternally pregnant swordtails glided past. There were serene angel fish whose whiskered sophistication was only spoilt by the fin-nibbling tendencies of the smaller inhabitants of the aquarium. Best of all, if he watched long enough he glimpsed the catfish, *Corydoras aeneus*, as he burbled his way across the sun-drenched gravel and back into the obscurity of the weed.

Pip also had a small vivarium which he had set up with turf and moss from the garden. An old toad, *Bufo bufo*, lived under a concave piece of bark and somewhere there was a slow-worm that Pip had found and captured. Neither of them appeared very often, the former quite happy in his hiding place and the latter ingeniously wriggling down the sides of the glass and under the turf. Near the vivarium were various wooden boxes which contained, among other things: a tortoise shell (the long-dead occupant having rotted away), some fox's bones that a boy from school had given to him and a piece of flint that Pip insisted had been a caveman's hand axe. One box held his father's birds' eggs and some which Pip had added. A willow-wren's egg was the pride of the collection.

Sunday was a home day, a family day. It wasn't like a Saturday when the gang was allowed to come round but at least it was not a school day. On Sundays the children spent time with the animals or played with the soldiers, and did anything useful so long as they kept occupied and didn't disturb Dad. Dad was writing a book which he believed would make him famous. He spent most of the day in his study tap, tap, tapping on his type writer. It had to do with the skull that was on top of his desk and the silver cups that were on the top shelf of his bookshelf. Journals were piled up all around him which held a terror of their own. The children dared each other to go and open them at the most terrible pages. They showed foreign looking people whose naked forms and prominent hands revealed the most hideous disfigurements. Ghoulish things had happened to their faces, arms or hands. The vile distortions could reduce the most swaggering of boys to a gibbering wreck. There were the close-ups showing distorted bellies, or bulbous hands. These pictures were strictly forbidden and could only be indulged in by those who knew no better.

It was better and more rewarding to play soldiers. The soldiers lived in a great wooden chest and play was by strict rules. One of the brothers would tip them on the floor and then all three would select themselves an army from the assorted pile of horses, wagons and men. One popular choice, despite the outrageousness of their costumes, was the Highlanders. They were kilted, busbied and ready for war and were good except for the preponderance of bagpipe players who lacked credibility in hand to hand fighting. A reasonably popular choice were the Redcoats who stood a little too woodenly, with their rifles thin and bent by the rigours of war. The Cowboys and Indians had a whole code of conduct acquired from the black and white television, which sat in pride of place in the lounge. The cowboys had glamour and fired from their revolvers in endless volleys before galloping away from danger. They could be 'patched up by the doc,' should anybody claim to have hit them. Less popular choices included Robin Hood and his outlaws whose mode of fighting was undeniably primitive, but there was an essential appeal in the raw, green, English manliness of Little John as he wielded his staff high above his head. Knights in armour were also less popular and the notion that their armour could deflect bullets was hotly debated. Legionnaires were reasonably popular but the Arabs were a less obvious choice. Their colourful, flowing robes and savage looks made them exotic but their merits consisted in sneaking around at the back and savagely cutting the throats of the unsuspecting. Always popular and in high demand were the modern infantry with their massive guns and wicked bayonets.

The Infantry spanned the two world wars in green-coated, steel-helmeted confidence. Unconquerable, they leaped out of the pages of the comics and into the boys' imaginations as deliverers of bullet-spitting justice. The men were battle-scarred and robbed of their paint. They had individual names such as 'Snitch' 'Tripper,' 'Ryan' and 'Smith'. Some carried signs of torture, with amputations cauterised in the burning flame of a candle. The hand to hand fighting was so intense that their features had become blurred by the cruelties of war. Each soldier had a distinctive character, a place and even a voice. Their exploits were legendary and the brothers knew their history which was framed in fighting. The sole representative of the fair sex was Maid Marion and she did not enjoy a happy existence. Along with a legless horse and a couple of Chuck Wagons, with missing wheels, she was left in the box and took no part in the fighting. Rumour had it that when the battle-weary men were piled into the box at the end of the day they 'had their way with her'. What this meant was never explained.

Once the brothers had chosen their armies they had to set them ready for battle. The three armies had to be standing, perfectly positioned and ready for action before the signal for the commencement of battle. A typical battle started with the emergence of a wagon loaded with burning cotton wool and was followed by the artillery barrage, as cannons fired matches into the standing armies and siege slings lobbed various items. As the battle grew more intense the armies converged, firing at each other and finally coming to hand to hand fighting. There were rules to war and to life. You had to fight but you could only fight for that which was right. The English stood for courage, toughness and resourcefulness and were ready for any challenge but they also stood for comradeship and protection of the weak.

The children, Mum and Granny ate most of their meals in a small room adjacent to the kitchen, known inappropriately as the Nursery. When Dad was home main meals were taken in the dining room. Sunday always finished with high tea in the Nursery and Dad dignified the occasion with his presence. High tea offered something hot followed by sweeter delights and tea. Cakes celebrated special occasions: chocolate or coffee for birthdays, heavy fruit cake for Christmas, simnel cake for Easter with the apostles represented in marzipan. The seasons impacted on mealtimes: sweet corn (mealies) in late summer, nuts in the autumn and winter, roes to celebrate The Boat Race, pancakes for Shrove Tuesday, hot cross buns for Good Friday and eggs for Easter. Fruit dominated the summer, especially strawberries and raspberries. At the height of it, the children were told to go outside and to pick their own desserts according to the season. Plums, apples and pears appeared in autumn and were stored for winter or hoarded in great kilner jars for later in the year. Fruit was also thickened into jam to sweeten winter teas. So the seasons of childhood rolled round in a rolling English way as if it would all last forever.

After high tea Dad would often hold forth. The Battle of Stalingrad was a favourite topic, the plucky Russians represented by the salt cellar and the encircling Germans by serviette rings. The Germans had reduced Stalingrad to rubble but the Russians fought on from cellars, man and woman, for the common good and the wonderful soviet system. They were reduced to eating rats but they would not surrender. Oil and vinegar pots encircled the serviette rings and the encirclers became the encircled and the Germans were made captive. The glorious Russians now drove the emaciated and frost-bitten Germans west, freeing the rejoicing people as they went, all the way to Berlin. Then Hitler was a rat in his bunker, cornered and doomed while jubilant peoples of east Europe raised the red flag of freedom. Mum was heard in the kitchen banging pots and muttering about good old 'Winnie' and our brave boys, the Desert Rats.

Jack was taken with the notion of the frost-bitten men, starving and emaciated in the snow and ice. It made him think of the film *Scott of the Antarctic* which he saw at school and he wondered if the British expedition could have won through.

Dad pondered before answering. 'Well, my boy you have to understand the mind-set of the time,' he said. 'Scott was upstaged by a rival Norwegian expedition under Amundsen. Amundsen had intended to go for the North Pole but as that had already been conquered he sailed south rather than north. The first Scott heard of it was when he received a telegraph in Australia. It must have been a bit of a shocker for old Scott. He thought that he had all the time in the world and then to find that Amundsen was up for the same prize.'

'It wasn't fair,' said Jack, 'Amundsen cheated.'

'Hardly cheated. He knew polar work better than Scott and ran the race better.'

'But why did he win?' asked Pip. 'How could the British could be so easily beaten?'

'Dogs,' answered Dad. 'Amundsen was a professional. He knew all about sledges, skis and dogs.'

'With all that snow and ice up there it would be surprising if he didn't,' said Mum.

'That aside,' continued Dad. 'Amundsen had the dogs and moved more quickly and easily than the British. He loaded his supplies on to the sledges and dashed off. Scott's lot were reduced to man-hauling their sledges over the ice.'

'They had tractors and horses, didn't they?' said Jack. 'They showed us the film at school. The tractors broke down and then they only had the horses and then the horses started to drop with exhaustion so they shot the horses and ate them.'

'Did they really eat the dead horses?' asked Miriam. 'How could they possibly do that?'

'In the ice, a dead horse is no more than meat for dogs and men,' said Dad. 'If a man is hungry enough he will eat almost anything. Think of Amundsen, and his men, as the sledge loads became lighter, they ate their dogs.'

The dog-eating Norwegians became even less popular victors. 'In Stalingrad,' continued Dad, 'the populace was reduced to eating rats. There wasn't a rat left alive by the end of it all.'

'In the Antarctic they had depots of food,' said Jack, pleased to turn the topic back to something British and away from the interminable, rat-eating Russians.

'What's a depot?' asked Pip, who was still optimistic that eating of dogs and horses could somehow be avoided.

'If we take the olive oil jar to be the South Pole,' said Dad, 'then the vinegar can be their starting point, Ross Island. From Ross Island to here is the Great Barrier (a line of superfluous cutlery). They had to go over the barrier, then up through mountains and on to the Polar Plateau. The whole scheme depended on setting up depots of food and essential equipment during the previous summer. In particular 'One Ton Depot' was intended to provide a sufficiency of essential supplies, including fuel oil to turn ice into drinking water. The returning parties would need plenty of supplies to bring them back to an old hut on Ross Island and from there to the safety of their base hut and Cape Evans. They had to journey a total of 1,800 miles, most of it slogged out on foot while hauling sledges, but in that first summer of laying depots they didn't set the depots far enough towards the Pole and they had to establish One Ton depot here.' The serviette ring descended with a click.

'Why, wasn't it far enough?' asked Tom.

'It needed to be much closer to the Pole because everything from One Ton onwards had to be taken on the second summer's expedition,' said Dad. 'As it turned out the distance proved to be just too great. They made it to the Pole only to find that the Norwegians had beaten them. On the way back, Petty Officer Evans died here (a cob nut was reverentially placed) and Captain Oates died here (a walnut honoured his deathbed). Oates suffered terribly from lameness and slowed the remaining four but is remembered for his heroism in going out into the blizzard to die and in so doing giving his companions a chance to reach One Ton Depot. Unfortunately, it wasn't enough. The other three made it to here, only eleven miles south of One Ton Depot but no further. (A plastic green salt pot marked the place).

'Why didn't they go on to the big depot? Why give up?' Pip asked.

'They couldn't, it was too late in the year and they were exhausted, starving and suffering from scurvy. They were confined to their tent in a roaring blizzard with no food or fuel left. They just had to stay in their sleeping bags and wait to die.'

'Was there nothing anybody could do?' asked Miriam.

'No, by then it was all too late and nobody knew where they were,' said Dad. 'If they had known, then perhaps somebody could have got out to them with a team of dogs or whatever, but the men at the base camp had no way of knowing. In those conditions you could pass by a few yards from a tent and never know it was there. Now here's something that will interest you. Mr Cherry-Garrard, who used to live up at the big house tried to go out and find them, but it proved too difficult. I believe that he went with a dog team to One Ton Depot to look for them but they weren't there. He couldn't go on to look for them because he had no dog food. He waited several days before he went back without them. He couldn't have known it but while he waited his friends were struggling across the ice barrier in a desperate attempt to reach One Ton. He, and the men at the base camp, assumed that the Pole party had fallen down a crevasse in the mountains and must be dead. They waited until the following summer and then went to see if they could find any evidence of what had happened. They must have been very surprised to find the tent only eleven miles from One Ton. I expect that Mr Cherry-Garrard felt very bad about not having pushed on to find them. Scott, Wilson and Bowers were dead inside the tent, Oates and Evans missing. They collapsed the tent and put a cairn on top of the bodies.'

'How did the search party know what had happened?' asked Tom.

'Scott kept a diary, which was in his pocket when he died,' said Dad.

'But the three could have made it back?' insisted the film-wise Jack. 'They wasted time on their return and gathered all sorts of stones and things which they then had to carry on the sledge. They wasted time burying Evans, one day's good march would have been enough to get them to One Ton and then there would have been enough supplies for the final push to the hut.'

'Where are their bodies now?' asked Tom. 'With all that snow and ice they would be preserved.'

'Evans died first,' said Dad, 'and is buried in the mountains. He must still be there, but the others died on the Barrier, which is sea ice, and always moving. Their bodies would have drifted away and may be anywhere. In due course they will reach more temperate waters and will sink to the bottom of the sea.'

The table fell silent as all of the children grappled to take it all in. Mum was displeased at the telling of such a grim tale and brought out a basket of fruit to distract the children from 'that horrible cold place'.

The story filled the children's imagination. For months to come, 'the men' struggled to the Pole and died vainly in their bids to return. Sometimes they would find an extra day and live out the cold, cold winter at One Ton Camp, melting ice into snow and eating the harsh supplies before crawling in to Base Camp alive, if emaciated, but undaunted. Only three could return in this fashion. Jack was emphatic on this point. If it was to happen at all, it could only happen without the other two.

# CHAPTER EIGHT

## *ANTARCTIC LETTER NUMBER TWO*

*January 20, 1911*

*Dear Ida*

*I promised that I would write to you again when I was really in Antarctica. Well here I am in our hut at Cape Evans.*

*My first sight of land was awe inspiring. Deb was the first man to see it and everybody rushed to see our homeland for the next two years. At first I thought that it was just more icebergs further on but then I glimpsed the white-topped mountains of Antarctica. I was seeing something that few men before me had ever beheld. It was like looking into the hidden land of the gods! I thought of old Ross, the first man to come this far south, and how he must have felt after being held in the pack ice and then finding that he was free again and able to penetrate even further south. Every mile must have seemed more improbable than the last and for all he knew he might have been able to sail through a clear polar sea and round the earth. Then, like us, he saw land.*

*We pushed on to Ross Island in search of our winter base. Although we were through the pack ice and in better sailing water, there were still icebergs everywhere and there was a general air of uncertainty about what we would find nearer land and whether or not we would be able to get close enough in to unload the stores. My first clear landmark was Mount Erebus and, I can tell you, I was really glad to see it as I found it a comforting sight. Erebus is named after one of Franklin's ships and Cape Crozier is named after a lieutenant who went with Franklin on his fateful expedition to find the North-West Passage. Given his ultimate end, this is not a happy reflection and is one I do not care to dwell on too much. The fate of Franklin's men haunts me. I close my eyes and see them stumbling across the Arctic darkness.*

*Uncle Bill was anxious that we should push on to Cape Crozier and make that our permanent base because it is the nesting site of the emperor penguins and Bill is desperately eager to make a special study of their nesting habits. Bill believes that they must incubate their eggs in the middle of the Antarctic winter! Can you imagine it Ida, they must huddle together for protection against the cold and, presumably, they move constantly so that no bird is on the edge of the flock and in the worst of the cold for any length of time. Bill thinks that they balance a single egg on their feet and under special flap of skin but as nobody has seen any of this nobody really knows.*

*You would have to see what they call the 'Barrier' to understand the problems which we faced in trying to land. It's like approaching the great cliffs of Dover from the sea, and there is no beach and no real landing site. We sailed along the coast, looking for a suitable landing place. A whaler was launched and Captain Scott went off with Teddy and Uncle Bill to investigate landing. I went out in a back-up boat. They chose me because I have experience in the college first boat, but I have to admit that I wasn't best suited to the rowing conditions and made an awful mess of it. There was a terrible swell and everywhere there were floating blocks of ice which threatened to smash into us. When we came close to the cliffs of ice that form the Barrier it was evident that chunks were breaking off. Bill spotted two emperors standing on a dirty ice shelf no more than six feet above us. One was a parent bird but the other must have been the very last of the season's chicks because it was still in down. It was a tantalising moment, Bill was desperate to have a go for it, but we could hear the crack of falling ice and Captain Scott ordered us back. That old picture came back to me and I found myself thinking of old Ulysses being rowed to the strange lands. I'm afraid the reality was rather different.*

*'For God's sake, have you never been in a skiff before?' Captain Scott snapped. It was because he was tense and worried. We could find nowhere to land, which left Uncle Bill untypically 'down'. However, there may be another way that Bill can study the emperors. I overheard Bill and Captain Scott chatting and it was agreed that Bill will make a special expedition to the colony. It will mean a winter march, which nobody has ever done before this far south. I hope he takes his assistant with him when he goes!*

*We found a landing place along the coast at a place known to the Discovery men as the 'Squarry'. Captain Scott has renamed it 'Cape Evans' after our second in command. Our selected site is close to Mount Erebus. Erebus is active and has permanent smoke on the summit. It is not threatening and there is something warm, almost friendly, about this low lying mountain with its ever-present stream of volcanic smoke. It rather put me in mind of an old chap, lying on his back and puffing pipe smoke into the air. There is another side to Erebus. Not only is it named after one of Franklin's doomed ships, but it also signifies the underworld. In our case it will be our landmark forward to the polar journey and so I will make a point of keeping the pipe-smoking gentleman in mind.*

*We set about unloading all the stores and taking them across the ice. The spot that Captain Scott chose to build the hut is a full mile inshore from the nearest point we could get the old Terra Nova in, but it has the great advantage of being on the land of Ross Island and is therefore not vulnerable to the vagaries of sea ice. Every job has to be thought about and undertaken carefully. Unloading all our* cargo on to the ice, which included dogs and ponies as well as the motor sledges and the timber for the hut, was a challenge. We landed two of the motor sledges without much trouble but then the third one was swung onto what must have been softer ice and before we could do anything to prevent it, it broke through the ice and is now at the bottom of the sea. Captain Scott is most terribly put out about it but there is nothing anybody can do. I hope this accident doesn't affect the plans for the southern party.

I was assigned to transport and have had my first experiences of man-hauling. I have seen pictures of men hauling sledges and it all looks easy enough, rather like pulling along a toboggan on a winter's day but the reality is very different. First you have the heavy weight of a fully laden sledge and then you have the unpredictable and uncertain surface of the ice. It can take four men, in full harness, several bursts of full force effort just to get the sledge out of the grip of the ice and into motion. I find being in the harnesses the most physically demanding exercise I can imagine and far harder than rowing in an eight. We have used the ponies but must be careful not to over exercise them, as they are in a wretched condition after the miseries of the sea journey and we will need them later on. The motor sledges help after a fashion but the key thing is to do what I can to help and to show Uncle Bill and Captain Scott that I am up to the mark.

We have an excellent carpenter here and several of the chaps pitched in and the hut went up in no time. Even so, and especially after the loss of the motor sledges, nobody was taking any chances. We all worked day and night (the night here not being much different to the day) and made the hut habitable as quickly as possible.

We are now as snug as we could possibly be. We have a hut that is three layers thick, insulated with sea weed and heated by a stove. Each of us has his own bunk bed and locker. It rather puts me in mind of The Grange. I have some excellent fellows near me. Above, good old Birdie keeps me going with an endless stream of chatter and good humour. He drums his foot on the end of the bed and calls out,

'Are you there down below?'

I tap back in morse. Birdie says he is training me up to be a real naval officer.

You will be surprised to learn that the person in the opposite bunk is none other than the old soldier, Titus Oates. At first I wasn't too pleased with this arrangement, but as time goes on I find myself becoming quite fond of him. He has a bit of banter with the navy chaps and tries to get me to join in.

'Don't listen to that Scots fraud!' he shouts to me and Birdie. 'The British army is the only place for a real man.'

Between the two of them it's quite droll, Birdie with his ever present *stream of chatter and Titus with his dry asides. It is all in the best of spirits. We have some wonderful conversations and great banter, they rib me about being 'The Lord of the Manor' but it's all in good part.*

*Titus can be quite sensitive, almost lyrical. We had an excellent conversation the other day about lakes. There is a lake on his family estate, which he loves. He learned to swim there, just as I did on Lamer Lake, and like me he loves fishing. He told me about a carp he once caught which was over twenty pounds in weight. I try to draw out old Titus about the Boers. Now, you would imagine that a chap like Titus would hate the Boers. I asked what he thought of De Wet and he just said, 'Damned clever fellow that!' and turned over to go to sleep. He seems to admire them and hasn't a good opinion of the war. He takes the view that it is wrong for Europeans to wage war on themselves. This may be one of the reasons why he left the army and came here, but I mustn't ask too much. Titus is not a chap to take a lot of quizzing and you have to pick your moments.*

*There is activity all day long. People come and go and do a thousand little errands in the name of science, the expedition or just good camp management. The dogs are forever barking or howling and the ponies, penguins and skuas kick up a terrible racket. It really is a crazy sort of menagerie but very thrilling and wonderful!*

*There is plenty of planning and organising to do for the depot trip. We must get away before the brief Antarctic summer fades and time is short. The plan is to take a good quantity of supplies as far as we can on to the great ice barrier and leave it there as a depot for the Pole party, who will need it desperately on their return from the Pole. We will be using the old hut that Captain Scott and Uncle Bill established on the Discovery expedition. This lies across the sea ice from here and is on our route south so it will be very useful staging post. It is not built very well and hardly compares with our comfortable base quarters at Cape Evans but it will serve our purposes. We have ponies and dogs and even motor sledges all ready for the trip and I will be on it as Captain Scott is pleased with the way that I have taken to sledging.*

*So, here I am, in the base hut at Cape Evans and waiting to be off on the depot journey. The ship is about to leave to take Lieutenant Campbell and his party of five men along the coast to carry out exploratory and geological work east of here. They are going to build their own hut and be quite separate to all our labours at Cape Evans. After dropping off Campbell, the ship will to return to New Zealand and will take my letters, including this one. You will not receive my future letters for a full year, until the ship has returned with more supplies and your own precious letter. I will continue to write when I find time and will keep all my letters in order just as if they were being sent by post. That way you will know how I felt at the time of writing, even though you will receive my letters in a bundle.*

*Dear Ida, there is so much to tell. I'll try to remember every detail and when we are back in Lamer we'll find that purple emperor that has eluded us for so long. Think of me in the hut with all these fine fellows. Looking over us, and blowing his smoke onto us, is dear old Erebus.*

*Ever,*

*Apsley*

### Early spring 1958

Sometimes Angela's kindness and concern could grate. He couldn't help but be aware of all that she had done to make the transition from Lamer as painless as possible. She reminded him how much nicer it was to be in their own place with no concerns about upkeep. It was snug and warm. She had made sure to take all that he could possibly want: his favourite books, the picture of Ulysses, Uncle Bill's paintings, even the emperor penguin in its glass case, which she set in prime position. She made every effort to be bright, never blaming him or complaining. In some ways her kindness made it worse and seemed to emphasise his failings. He tried to explain how he felt but she was hurt by it and became quite cross.

'You can't blame yourself for everything. You did your best and here you are. Bill thought the world of you and didn't judge you.'

Cherry looked ahead and tried to fix on a point of light. 'If you fall in a chasm,' Birdie once told him, 'don't look down or to the side of you. You must go up, so look up. If you allow yourself to think too much you will lose your nerve.'

Titus had echoed the sentiment when they came back from the bird-nesting expedition. 'Always look into the light young Cherry.' He said. At the time he wondered why he said that.

Maybe he had lost his nerve and that was all that there was to it. He must remember to look up and away from the chasm to the light beyond. If you must look back, it must be deep back to a time when there were no chasms for a man to fall into. So many people had gone from his life. Ida was still important to him although long married to an older vicar who was now an old man. She had brought up his children and they were now married. Her life revolved around the parish and the grand-children but they corresponded from time to time. The other girls had variously married and gone their ways and there were any number of nephews and nieces. Angela knew all about them and remembered their birthdays and special occasions but Cherry found it difficult to build any real relationships with them. He felt guilty for the loss of Lamer and other assets even though they did not hold any of this against him. He had long lost contact with Stretfield because he declined to go back to events at the House. He knew from Ida that Chatteris and Elspeth had gone to live in Southern Rhodesia and by all accounts were doing very well. He missed Reggie and all the happy memories of Burnside. Reggie's suicide warned Cherry that depression must be overcome or it will overwhelm you.

After his treatment, Cherry put much of this behind him and felt better. Angela was convinced that it had been a dark time but now the spring was coming back and he would bounce back with it. At first, it all had to be taken very slowly and carefully. Angela strolled with him in the park. She was full of optimism and chattered happily. He listened and kept his doubts to himself. They enjoyed tea out and they would sit over pots of tea and warm scones, as in the days of their courtship.

He experienced renewed awareness of the world around him and the people in it. He had long chats with Deb on the telephone and spoke of visiting Ida and hearing about the progress of her grand-children. He was reading again and visiting book shops, browsing happily in the antiquarian sections and sometimes coming home with a prize under his arm. Angela was happy and as her confidence grew she left him more space and didn't watch him too closely and let him wander far from Gloucester Place.

He liked the parks where he found, in some part, the countryside he had lost. The parks were shards of light that beat through the dark cauldron of London. They were tamed places but if he wandered far enough he could escape the sound of human voices. There were birds, in the summer swallows would dip and flicker over the lake as they had done over Lamer Lake but the nightingales were long gone from the city parks and it saddened him to think that he might never again hear their song. He wondered if they still sang in Whitebushes' woods and this put him in mind of Hobbs's stories of the Old People making their way up the brook and looking for somewhere open and wild that they could make their own.

'Maybe,' he thought, 'when their leader climbed up the bank and saw the open common, the nightingales watched him too.' These reflections cheered him and let him hope that some part of the deep past endured.

Cherry liked the club. At the club he didn't have to think about Lamer or anything else in the recent past. Here people knew who and what he was and didn't require him to explain or justify anything. It reminded him of his early years in Oxford, before all those things happened, starting with the Old General's death. Reminiscing in the club, Cherry could be back in college dining by candlelight with the other fellows, rowing on the river in the early summer light, dipping his strong, young body to each stroke. Sometimes he was in the hut ragging with Deb and Birdie or pouring over some skins with Uncle Bill. At the club his memory was selective and time suspended. The club members were comfortable with their past and their pasts must have been acceptable otherwise they would not belong. Each man had his store of pain to forget, whether that be war or personal tragedy or both, but it wasn't the done thing to go on about it. He spent many afternoons there, reading and taking tea or just chatting to other members.

Cherry liked it best when old Antarcticians were about. Deb, in particular, was always a welcome sight. Deb knew Cherry's story because he had been there in the hut that final winter and had visited Lamer many times, motoring over from Cambridge to talk to Cherry about his work and the progress of the Scott Polar Research Institute. Deb had overcome his Antarctic experiences well and had established himself as Cambridge's first professor of geography and a fellow of Bill's old college. His scientific work was well received and his crowning achievement had been in setting up the Institute. Deb tried to bury painful elements of his past. His son was killed in action in the recent war and although Cherry never would have a son of his own, he grieved for his friend. Deb appeared to cope and buried his pain in family and work but preferred the anonymity of the present. He was a sharp observer of the world and shrewdly predicted Eden's downfall.

'That's the end of all that Empire stuff. Damn those bloody Yanks,' he muttered when the British troops trailed back, humbled by an Arab and forsaken by the Americans. Deb was an Australian and a scientist and saw things in a sharper more modern way than Cherry.

There was safety in the present, but the deep past was safer. Behind his copy of *The Times* Cherry thought about his childhood at Lamer. It was always sunshine and deep lanes filled with butterflies, bird song and a thousand distractions. They could mutilate Lamer, pull it down, rip up the old walks and ways but they could never erase it from his memory. It was a point of clear bright light in the darkness. The light had grown dim in recent years but after his treatment it had lit up again.

On occasion, he would extend his walk back from the club to the apartment. London was busier, black faces now merged with the white, trilbies with bowlers. Long-legged girls with no hats or gloves jostled with confident young men in off-the-peg suits and all were purposefully occupied, hurrying on. This suited him because it emphasised his own anonymity.

He liked the old familiar places, particularly the Natural History Museum. It pleased him that it hadn't changed. It was old and blackened with the smoke and smog of a century but still solid, permanent and a link with his Victorian past. Even the exhibits were familiar and reassuring. The great dinosaur still stood guard at the entrance and the rooms, packed with specimens, were redolent of Uncle Bill. He chuckled to himself when he came to the room where they had made him wait with the emperor-penguin eggs from the winter's journey. At the time he had been infuriated by the callous disinterest of the museum's management and had raised merry hell with the whole pack of them. Birdie would have applauded his display of emotion but Bill would have been quietly disapproving.

Going back to the apartment could be difficult. London was a place you visited but then you went back home. Now home was a luxury apartment in Gloucester Place. He was better, there was no denying that. The long tedium of treatment was over, but he somehow knew that it was more of a reprieve than a cure. The black-bat clouds and doubts would return as surely as Antarctic night follows an Antarctic summer. He knew that he had to grasp the opportunity that early spring brought. He would never be young again, never feel as he did when he was a boy at Lamer or even in those early days in Antarctica, but he had to try to make the best of things, for Angela's sake if not his own.

'*Post iucandum juventutem,*' he thought to himself.

In the early evening Angela would cook delicious little suppers and they would dine together on the oak side table that they had brought with them from Lamer. Later in the evening they would play music or listen to the wireless. They both liked comedy and *Hancock's Half Hour* was a particular favourite. They had a television but Cherry could not get on with it and preferred the old pursuits. Angela was happy. There need be no anxiety over a great house, with no duties or responsibilities to anybody but themselves. They could look forward to the future and the cruise that she was planning. She adored cruising, remembering how they had first met, and how happy they both were on the shifting transient world of the ship. Cherry relished the freedom it offered, rekindling some of his adventurous spirit. She wasn't much given to poetry, not in the way that Cherry was, but a line crept into her head:

'*Now down at the port the ships' crew are calling and the gunnels are ready*'.

Sometimes Angela's thoughts wandered to the past and what might have been. In odd moments, when dusting or pottering around the apartment, the thought slipped into her mind of how it would have been if they had seized the moment in the early years of their marriage and been blessed with a child? Would Cherry have tried harder to save Lamer if they had had a son to inherit the house? She paused in her dusting and thought of how it would be if they had had a boy who could have shared Cherry's enthusiasm for birds and butterflies and who would have looked up to him and respected him. In that moment of reflection she saw the two of them together in the park at Lamer, laughing in sunshine, running after purple emperors and chasing their dreams. The moment ended and she resumed her dusting. They must not look back. Lamer was gone and that was an end to it. After the war there was so much that needed to be done to make a new and better world and she would do her best to make Cherry a part of it all so that he could enjoy the present. She would leave Lamer in their past and let it get on with its own present without them.

Some things at Lamer stayed the same. The school was in its original position to the north of Lamer and Earlswood and behind the great, grim building of St. John's church. The school had expanded to meet the requirements of the post war generation and there were now two primary schools and an infant school. Along a lane from the church and up a steep slope, which in winter became iced-up and almost impossible to mount, was the infant school and adjacent to it was the girls' primary school. Further along the lane, and separate to the others, was the boys' primary school. All three were built a long time ago with small high windows which restricted the light and prevented the children looking out. In winter the outside toilets froze and the smell of urine permeated the bricks and never entirely left the building. There were no catering facilities at the boys' primary and each lunch-time the boys marched across the common and into Earlswood where they dined in the parochial hall or 'Pokey Hall' as it was affectionately known.

Around the schools was the great common at Earlswood and in better weather the boys from the primary school were allowed out on the common to play where they roared around in gangs, relishing the freedom and the space. All three schools were known under the collective name of 'Old John's' because it had long been planned to close them down. A new, mixed, low, glass-and-light-filled building had been constructed several miles away from the parent church. The new school also called itself 'St John's' and was known colloquially as 'New John's.' But the education authority's calculations were adrift and a post war boom in children required Old John's to stay open and continue to serve the children of south Redhill, Earlswood and Whitebushes.

'If you have to fight a gang, get your back to a wall and hit out hard at the nearest.'

This was Tom's advice to Pip on starting school and it was the most sagacious piece of information ever imparted to him in those early years of his schooling. Tom had been new at the school when they first came to Surrey. He and Jack had stuck out as strange and different to the rest of the boys. Firstly, they arrived in a taxi because it was too far to travel by foot to the school and they were too young to cycle. Secondly they had appeared in a school uniform because Mum had been told the requirements of uniform without also being made aware that nobody actually wore it. Finally they talked 'funny'. The combination of these crimes against the ancient and hallowed traditions of the scholars of Old John's, was enough to send even the most liberal-minded of its proud denizens into an ugly mood. Tom and Jack were able to count on each other and spent many of their breaks with their backs to the grey-black, brick school wall that penned in the pupils. One watched to left and front and the other to right and front. Short-trousered tormentors danced in and out of their range. Blows were seldom landed. It was enough for the followers of a warlord to perform his bidding and to make noises and shout insults without actually doing anything. In time the brothers became respected and gathered about them the boys from Whitebushes who formed the core of their own gang. The gang stuck together for self-protection. They could escape the severe limitations of the playground by going out to the sandy wastes of the open common where they could be themselves.

In those days Pip was too young to go to school and had stayed at home with Mum and Granny. He wandered where he pleased and talked to whom he liked. Among his companions was the old man at the cottage, down the lane from the entrance gates, who kept things in tins and walked every day the two miles to buy tobacco and a few odds and ends from Earlswood and then walked back again. Also, there was Farnham, the gardener, who kept all kinds of strange forks and tools in a linseed-scented room and wore white wellington boots (you must never touch those boots or you could get a terrible disease). If all else failed he could go and find Granny in the garden. She was always in the garden and out of the way of Mum who ruled the house.

Granny and Mum would came together every morning for coffee and to discuss the day's affairs. Pip would join them for orange juice and a biscuit and for 'Listen with Mother' on the wireless.

*'When I was just a little boy, I asked my mother what would I be? Would I be handsome, would I be rich? Here's what she said to me....'*

The voice warbled from the wireless and Pip's mind wandered to a time when he would be handsome and rich, achieving great things for Britain, famous throughout the land. There was one particular game that Granny and Mum would like to play to tease Pip. One of them started it by setting up a whine that Pip didn't love her. Pip countered this by running to the woman concerned and sitting on her knee. Then the other would respond by complaining even louder that the heartless boy didn't love *her* and so Pip would jump down and run to the other. The former whined hideously and burst in to mock tears so that Pip rushed to comfort her. Eventually the game ended with the two women shrieking with laughter and physically pulling and stretching the boy between them each proclaiming that, as they couldn't have all of him, they would at least claim a bit. The game caused the two women huge enjoyment but caused Pip not a little distress.

When the time came to go to school Pip did not want to desert the two women in his life, Skellum the dog, and all his pleasant associations. Being handsome and rich might have its merits but he preferred to defer it for the ease and familiarity of staying at home. The education authority did not share this view. When the dread day arrived he attempted a final bolt for freedom, and hid in the wood, but Jack came to find him. By a mixture of persuasion and dragging they ensured that he was confined in the taxi and conveyed to Old John's.

Within a short time of his arrival at that seat of learning he had to put into effect Tom's wise counsel, but without a supporting brother to watch the other side. He formed an alliance with another misfit and together they had kept their tormentors at bay. His days at infant school were spent chanting, singing, whispering, wrestling and being smacked. He scribbled strange signs on slates and stabbed paper with a pencil. He ate boiled cabbage and swede from a vast plate that demanded to be emptied and heard that there were other children not as lucky as him. He wondered at the success of the little girls, whom he secretly and unrequitedly adored, and never fully understood the mystery of it all. He did not understand how the girls adorned their names, on the great chart that hung in the schoolroom, with silver and gold stars while his own name remained barren of all such honours. Mother became strangely upset by it all and lectured him. She knew he had brains so why didn't he use them? When he went to the 'Big Boys' he would have to buck up his ideas.

But at the 'Big Boys' his ideas refused to buck. Smackings turned to whackings and pencil gave way to nibs and pots of sky blue ink that ran in watery rivulets over the paper to form indelible pools. The swede and cabbage remained but the pink-legged girls, who skipped through his dreams, were gone to the girls' primary school. From now on his schooling would be with boys so that they could learn boyish things and become men, without the distraction of girls.

Life was viewed in terms of challenge. The challenges of boyhood rolled into one great endless challenge. Banger Maynard could hold a banger in his hand longer than anybody. Darkie Green walked along the parapet of the Three Arches, his arms wide open as if in anticipation of crucifixion from the London to Brighton express, hurtling south. The boys challenged each other to jump higher, swim further, hold an electric fence, shoot arrows straighter or fight better.

The greatest and darkest challenge of childhood was the eleven plus. There was now a grammar school for girls as well as the boys' grammar school. Smart girls in green berets enjoyed the same opportunities as boys. Getting into the grammar schools represented a huge challenge to both boys and girls. The eleven plus found out all their weaknesses and failings. Children, who didn't work hard at school, stared vacantly at the walls, listened to the sounds and voices outside and didn't understand fell into the crevasse of failure forever. Behind the red lights of Christmas was the icy desolation of January and deep below the ice lurked the great mid-winter challenge of the eleven plus, like a killer whale.

Miriam had been tested some years back. It ended in floods of tears and the promise of a nice girls' private school, which bandaged and bound the wound. Otherwise it would have been the secondary modern, where some aspired to skilled trades but many smoked and shouted their time away before surrender to the factory gates. The eleven plus divided and bound the young for ever into their sections of society.

The teachers at Old John's knew only too well about the dangers of boys wasting their time. Every morning Mr Rose came into Pip's classroom carrying his cane in his Park-Drive yellowed fingers. Mr Rose was very old and it was rumoured that he had been in the old war. Mr Hagan had also been in the Old War. His hands shook so much that he could scarcely wield a cane but he could be driven into the most terrible rages. The younger teachers would talk about the recent war but with the old war men there was a pact of silence.

'Good morning boys,' chanted Mr Rose.

'Good morning Mr Rose,' the boys echoed back.

Mr Rose would set his cane to the side of the blackboard and begin the lesson. Should a boy be slow, sleepy, stupid or sullen Mr Rose's cane came hissing to liberate him from his torpor. Mr Rose was seldom random in punishing and preferred all rights to be properly observed. The offending boy was summoned to the front of the class and the cane was removed from its resting place. The boy was then told the nature of his misdemeanour, before putting out his hand, palm turned upwards and the skin stretched smooth and tight (Mr Rose would tap the knuckle side until the hand was the requisite height from the ground). All this was a prelude to the cane coming rushing down, but the boy had one final chance, if he could elude the blow three times, execution was deemed to have been carried out and he could return to his seat unscathed. The class would watch and wait in terrified anticipation. First one slash, but the cane hit air to the right of the hand. Then the second came, but hit only air on the left. The final blow came sharp and fast and scored the palm in searing pain.

Mr Rose dictated the pace and the nature of the class, sometimes arithmetic, sometimes writing, sometimes they were taken to the playground and made to pass bean-bags in relays. Best of all, Mr Rose would tell them stories, reworking a medley of tales from *The Arabian Nights* and *The Canterbury Tales* with dexterity.

The academic world of Old John's swung round. The previous autumn, the Russians had launched a sputnik, reasserting the dark, frozen supremacy of the Russian Empire. The sputnik soared into outer space and ripped into the boys' imaginations. Some thought it was a lie, a manifestation of Russian spite and propaganda. Mr Rose was reassuring. The Americans were better prepared and would pull ahead in the space race.

'What about the British?' asked the boys. 'Do we have our own spaceship?'

Mr Rose's reassurance that the British were working with the Americans, did not satisfy the boys. They thought it wrong that the British were no more than the junior partners of the Americans.

In January Tom and the older members of the gang faced the terrors of the eleven plus. The school was closed for the day and the dreary building swallowed up the final-year boys to challenge and sift them. Pip and Jack had to stay away and wait their turn. They spent the day in sullen and solitary pursuits. After the examination the boys returned to school for the rest of the year, but something happened that day to change the older boys' view of the world and created a distance between them and childhood. The eleven plus determined something which would affect their lives for ever. Tom was to be separated from the rest of the boys of the same age and taken away to the grammar school. This would take place in September, but in the meantime life returned to something resembling its former state.

# CHAPTER NINE

## *ANTACTIC LETTER THREE*

*Cape Evans, January 23, 1911*

*Dear Ida*
*Tomorrow we go out on the depot journeys. The point of these journeys is to establish a number of depots before the winter sets in and makes travel impossible. It is so important that we leave depots for the southern party, next summer, as far out on the Barrier as possible. The nearer we can be to the Pole the better chance it will give the returning southern party. Titus feels that it should be as far out on the Barrier as possible and no less than two hundred and fifty miles from the Discovery hut. This is quite a tall order but we will be using eight ponies and the rest can be done by man-hauling. Sledging is the hardest work possible but it does have its compensations, with sledging companions such a Birdie, Bill and Deb. In pulling a man has all the companionship he could want and, when things get bad, a word or a joke can pick a man up so that it doesn't seem all that bad. It's a bit like rowing in an eight. You feel the others around you, even when nobody says a word. You pull together and gain strength from each other. The success of the unit depends on the collective will of all the men. Sometimes it doesn't work so well and the team isn't right. None of us like pulling with Teddy Evans and the feeling of most of the chaps is against him even though he is second in command. Captain Scott, on the other hand, is another matter and pushes himself as hard as he pushes us. He can be a bit strange sometimes and that's when old Uncle Bill comes into his own. Bill knows and understands him better than any.*
  *Discovery Hut, January 26*
*We have crossed the sea ice between Cape Evans and here with some difficulty. The ship is still able to get within a few miles of us and we have taken our temporary farewell of her as she will take Campbell and his five men east to establish their own base for scientific exploration. They have the materials to build their own hut and two ponies to help them with their work. The ship will collect them in March and will return them to Cape Evans before leaving us at the end of the season.*
  *Safety Camp, January 30*
*This is camp three for us and we have named it 'Safety Camp.' We are now well out onto the permanent ice of the Barrier and away from the uncertainty of the sea ice. The ponies are not pulling as we had hoped and they are showing signs of fatigue already. Part of the problem is that their hooves are too narrow to work well on the*

Barrier surface and they tend to sink down too deep and then flounder in the ice. We have patented snow shoes for them but not enough sets were brought out for our eight ponies. Uncle Bill will go back with the dog team, to Cape Evans, to pick up more, but all of this takes time and will make it less likely that we can get out as far as we would have wished.

### Corner Camp, February 5

We have now experienced the reality of blizzards on the Barrier. Outside there was a mighty wind that drove the loose snow and turned all into raging chaos. In these conditions it is impossible to leave the tent because any exposure of face and hands would result in instant frostbite. We have been forced to stay put in our tents for three days and will lose more valuable time.

The ponies are a real cause of concern. Several are very weak indeed and all in all they have proved to be a mixed blessing. They work as best they can but they don't travel well on the ice and they vary individually in quality and nature. Titus says that they are a poor bunch of crocks, but they work so hard and endure such difficulties that you cannot but pity them. The wind on the Barrier adds to their problems. We try to travel by night to let them rest in the day when it's warmer. We also build a snow wall around them so that when they rest they are protected from the worst of the wind. Captain Scott is concerned that we save as many as possible as he is counting on them for the southern journey next season. Let's hope that we can push deep into the Barrier, set up our big depot and return with all ponies alive.

We have called this place Corner Camp because we have rounded White Island and from here our route straightens, all the way to the Beardmore Glacier.

### Bluff Depot, February 10

There has been the most terrible row about the ponies. Captain Scott has decided to send back three of the weaker ones. These are called Blucher, Blossom and Jimmy Pig. He wants to get them back into condition for next season. Titus insists that they are as good as dead already and argues that it is better to conserve men's lives than horses. Titus contends that we must make the final, main depot as far out as possible and that we can still make it to at least two hundred miles out if we drive the weaker ponies on and shoot them when they can go no more. The dead ponies could then be cut up and stored as meat for the returning parties. Captain Scott was distressed by this proposal and said that we should send the weaker ponies back so that they can be fed up and used again next season. Titus was really angry and said things which I would not like to write in a letter. This display of anger surprised me. I find it hard to see how Titus can, on the one hand, give so much care and even tenderness, towards the ponies at *the same time as advocating shooting them for meat. I hate discord but there is little I can do to keep the peace. Thankfully Bill managed to pull things round and it has been agreed that Teddy Evans and two seamen will take back the three ponies tomorrow.*

*February 14*

*We have had a shocking experience. One pony, called 'Weary Willie', has been suffering badly and getting weaker. Today he went down and a dog team went for him with the clear purpose of killing him. We had to use our whips indiscriminately but it was some time before we could get the dogs off and the poor beast is most savagely bitten. Wearie Willie is no more than a passenger now and we have only four good ponies left.*

*One Ton Camp, February 17*

*Well here we are at our furthest point south for the time being, but we have had one heck of a job to get here. We have only come this far by dint of much hard labour for men, ponies and dogs.*

*We have managed to set up several depots from the Discovery hut well out on the Barrier but it taken us much longer than we planned. Our final depot, which we call 'One Ton Depot', is only some 150 miles on the way to the Pole. Titus is not happy and grumbles that it is not far enough. He says that it has to be a good two hundred miles or it is next to useless but Captain Scott will not change his mind and insists that it is far enough by his calculations - and that we have to conserve the ponies.*

*We need to get back to the Discovery hut as quickly as we can and save as many ponies and dogs as we can so that they can be used next seasons for the real challenge.*

*Camp, February 21*

*You have to admire Captain Scott. We had a whole team of ten dogs go down in a crevasse and would have lost them and the sledge if we hadn't managed to anchor the sledge before it too went down. It was a stunning sight with the dogs harnessed together, dangling on their traces and howling. We managed to haul eight out but two had gone right down, through a crack and out of sight. Captain Scott harnessed himself up and went down into the depths after them and we pulled him and a dog out one by one until they were all rescued. Ida, you won't believe what happened next. As soon as the dog team was all back together they celebrated by attacking the other team and we had to separate them with whips. I tell you, these dogs are savage beasts and the devil to drive in a team. We tend to think that we will be better off without them when it comes to the big southern journey next spring.*

*Safety Camp, February, 22*

*We have caught up with Teddy and his party. Two of the ponies he was trying to save are dead so maybe Titus was right all along!*

*February 26*

*I'm back on sea ice and working the remaining ponies with Birdie.
One more has died of exhaustion and we have also lost some dogs,
but we continue to move stores as best we can.*

*March 1*

*We have had a few set-backs and Captain Scott has had some lows.
Despite all our efforts we have lost Wearie Willie. In the end he just
sank in the ice and laid there till he died. Worse was to come and we
have lost three more good ponies in the most terrible of ways. Birdie
and I along with a really tough Irishman called Tom Crean were
detailed to take four ponies and two sledges over the sea ice from
Safety Camp. All went well to begin with but then we saw clear signs
that the sea ice was breaking up further out to sea. Crean, who was
on the Discovery expedition and knows the location well, didn't like
the look of it and Birdie decided to head back towards Safety Camp
and to go in closer towards the Barrier. After a few miles the ice
looked good and permanent so we decided to make camp and to take
a fresh view after sleep. We built walls for the ponies, made hoosh,
and settled in for some much needed rest.*

*I was asleep and the first I knew was when Birdie shoved his head
in the tent to tell us we were floating on a berg and going out to sea.
When I looked out, I just couldn't believe my eyes - what had last
night seemed so secure was broken into pieces and floating. We were
adrift together on an island of ice heading north towards the open
sea. We still had three ponies and our sledges but one poor pony,
called Guts, must have drifted off on a separate berg. I stood there
gaping like a fool but Birdie harnessed the ponies and called to get
the sledges and what gear we could and to make ready to use a sledge
as a bridge to cross to the next nearest berg. Crean saw what needed
to be done and we all worked frantically in a bid to make ready so
that we could move from berg to berg until we could reach solid ice.
It happened very fast and I didn't have time to think. I just followed
Birdie and did whatever he said. We made some progress and the
ponies were working well when we became conscious of snorting
from the killer whales which were cruising in the brash and feasting
on seals. At one point a great brute thrust its head out of the water
and stared at us with its horrid little eyes, as if urging us to attempt
to leap into the water and swim to safety. This made us all too aware
of the dangers of losing our footing on the ice. Birdie and Crean
between them did all the real thinking and work but none of us could
relax. At any moment a wind could have blown up to take us out to
sea and certain death. Somehow or other we came close to solid ice
but the final distance between our floating bergs and the solid ice still
eluded us because it was broken into small fragments. Birdie decided
that one man, unimpeded by gear, could leap from berg to berg in a*

westward direction until he reached solid ice and once on solid ice he could get help from the main party. I volunteered to go but I must say that I was relieved when Birdie chose Crean. We watched anxiously as that marvellous man leapt deftly from berg to berg until we saw in the distance that he had made it. He waved his hand at us and was off.

Birdie and I were left alone on the ice. Birdie decided to pitch the tent so as to make our presence more visible. Then we waited. Birdie's company calmed me and made me ready for whatever happened next. When I looked at Birdie's face he seemed to be enjoying himself.

'You're a good man for a tight corner,' he said.

I was heartened by the thoughtfulness and kindness of this statement more than I can ever possibly explain. We were both relieved when Captain Scott and Bill arrived with ropes to get us off but there remained one final flurry of bad luck. We were able to save ourselves and some of our gear but only one pony, old Nobby. The other two took the last leap badly and slid back into the water. No matter how hard we tried we could not get them onto the solid ice and the intense cold was killing them. In the end Birdie insisted on shooting them before the killer whales took them. At the time the relief of getting to safety was so intense that I could think of nothing else but Captain Scott is quite down about it. Our best chance of beating Amundsen has probably gone to the killer whales. We will return with two ponies only out of the eight that we started with, but Bill says that we can still get to the Pole and we are determined to persevere.

<u>Discovery Hut, March 5</u>

We have had some extraordinary news. The ship is back and so are Campbell and his party. It seems that Campbell didn't land as planned because they found Amundsen in the Bay of Whales just around Ross Island from us. They saw a ship moored on the ice and on closer inspection realised that it was Nansen's old ship, Fram. They spoke with Amundsen and his men and have found out some very unpalatable facts: the Norskies' base is considerably nearer the Pole than ours and they have a much smaller team of specialist polar men. They are here for no other purpose than reaching the Pole ahead of us and have brought over a hundred dogs with them to make sure this happens. By all reports Amundsen is a pretty rough sort of chap and he has an even rougher crew with him and they are all highly experienced. We are going to be up against it but we will give him a run for his money. He may travel earlier and faster than us but he has to do the whole trip there and back and I am reminded of the hare and the tortoise.

Some of the fellows were ready to go on over there and have it out with him as he has no right to be in our section of Antarctica. Amundsen has behaved like a cad and in a way that is against all true *rules of conduct. Captain Scott was livid but Bill says that we are still in with a chance and mustn't descend to Amundsen's low standards. It has been a bit awkward with Gran, our Norwegian ski expert, but Bill was pretty clear about this and nobody holds it against poor Gran who is just as put out as we are. Bill points out that Antarctica is not like the north and there is no guarantee that Amundsen's dogs will go well on the Barrier. The mountains at the end of the Barrier, which you have to get up before reaching the polar plateau, present even more of a challenge for dogs. The Norskies' quarters are no more than an ice house built on sea ice. One surprise thaw, such as we experienced on the depot journey, could dash all their hopes. We have to get on with it and stick to our plans come what may. We are also determined to complete all the scientific and exploratory work and will not be distracted from our real purposes.*

*Our depot laying has not been as easy and as successful as we hoped. We all wish now that One Ton Depot had been further out on the Barrier, and I now have to admit that Titus was right in that we could have pushed on another fifty miles and then left the two or three weakest ponies as fresh meat and as part of One Ton's supplies. Instead of that we have left dead ponies all along the route and nowhere that they can be found and used by hungry men coming back from the Pole. It is sad to record that out of the eight ponies which we took out depot laying only two are still alive and fit for work. However, good old Campbell had given us the two which he planned to use on his travels east. He says that our needs are greater than his. How's that for a true English gentleman!*

*Campbell and Captain Scott have now reviewed the situation and have decided that Campbell's party will now go north and that it will change its name to that of the 'northern party.' We have been feeding them up and toasting their safe return. How wonderful it will be when we next see them safe and well - and when the Pole has been taken by our British expedition!*

*For the time being, we are stuck here at the old Discovery hut because all the ice is out and there is no way that we can return to Cape Evans until it has iced up enough for us to cross safely. There is no other viable route because Ross Island is too mountainous to cross by land. This hut is draughty and poorly heated and not really comfortable at all but we can stick it as long as we need to. When we get to Cape Evans we will have comparative luxury and will stay there for the winter. Spring will be a time of great adventures and summer will find us away on our quest for the Pole! Strange to think that our seasons are inverted and that while we are gripped by dark, cold days and nights of winter here you will be enjoying an English summer. I know that you will all miss me as indeed I miss you and dear Lamer but this is such an adventure that I would not miss it for the world and I know that there will be other English springs and summers when we can be together.*

*The ship will leave very soon to avoid being caught in the ice, and will take Campbell and his party to their northern landing before heading for New Zealand. Campbell and his fellows will overwinter there and undertake scientific work in that region. The Terra Nova will pick them up in the late spring and take them to a new location for further exploration and study. Despite Amundsen's unwelcome competition, you can see that we are pushing on with both exploration and scientific work as we always intended.*

*I must make haste now as Pennell is anxious to be gone and I want him to take back all my correspondence, including these three 'Antarctic Letters' which I have written for you only. Please be assured that they come with my love for you all back at Lamer and rest content to know that never was a man happier than in this fine company. Rejoice with me that I have found something worth the doing.*

*Your loving brother,*
*Apsley*

## Late Spring 1958

Pip was never confident in the underground. It was too tempting to stand close to the yellow lines and peer down into the black void that seemed to call him to his death, because if you fell on to those rails you would be fried in a flash to nothing. You had to wait until the very last minute, until you were summoned to step back, and then the great beast would rumble and trundle in its cavern and finally burst out in a mad rush of light and fabric-warm air. Mum gave it out that it was fine, it was the easiest and most marvellous way to travel. After all it had all been built by the Victorians and those Victorians knew a thing or two. Yet for all her outward expressions of confidence and her undoubted knowledge of all those triumphant names, way above ground, something in her manner suggested insecurity. Maybe it was the press of people and the bustle and the strange smell of it all. Maybe it was simply being alone with one child rather than surrounded by her family in the fortress of home? Although she had known London before the war, it had become strange and detached from her world. The endless seething mass of people looked different with each new visit. There were scruffy-looking people who played musical instruments on the street corners and drunks and most recently there were black-faced West Indians who stepped out of cubby holes, clutching assorted brooms or demanding tickets. They seemed out of place in the grey English weather.

'Poor dears,' Mum muttered as she bustled her way down the crowded twisted tunnels that led ever onward into the labyrinth of subterranean London, 'how they must miss the bright sunshine.'

Pip liked escalators. You could glide down them with grace and speed or defy them and try to run upwards against the cascade. But, you must remember to leap those last few steps, or be caught and squashed into the metal at the end of the roller. It put him uncomfortably in mind of Mr Watch of ankle-grabbing fame. They were pleased to walk out at South Kensington and into the light. The bustle and clamour of London struck Pip like a blow in the face. Vehicles of all descriptions vied with each other: great red beasts of buses, stumpy Dor-beetle-black taxis, angry motor cars and weaving motor bikes. The litter-free pavements were metallic hard, dulled and stained by the morning drizzle and crowded with mackintoshed people who scurried on their ceaseless missions. Pip noticed a newspaper stand, unattended with nobody to guard its produce or its money. He noticed the white-barked trees that lined the pavement and kept guard, watching over the blackened buildings that towered above them and crowded the sky. There was life here too, chequered pigeons slummed it with cockney sparrows and robber starlings to forage on the forest floor of London. Then they saw it in front of them. Its blackened whiteness stood out in gothic splendour, stamped its authority and permanence and proclaimed itself profoundly British.

'There!' said Mum, 'the Natural History Museum. Old Albert may have been a Gerry but he certainly knew a thing or two.'

They mounted the great flight of stone steps and entered the mausoleum of the natural world.

'I remember,' said Mum, 'when Jack first came in here, he could have only been about four or five, he ran straight in on his little fat legs - but when he saw the dinosaurs he ran straight out again! I had to chase after him down these steps before we lost him altogether.'

Pip was half prepared for the huge, muffled chamber and the dwarfing skeletons. His own collection at home was paltry, a few old bones and some blown eggs in a glass-fronted box. Here was real splendour. He stood, head tilted backwards, and gazed in awe at the mighty specimens in the great light-filled room.

'Where do you want to start?' said Mum.

'The birds' eggs, please,' he replied, choosing the sweetest pleasure in a mansion of delights.

They consulted obscure diagrams, clattered up stairs and along galleries until they eventually found the right location. Pip was not ready for the scale of it, the number of cases and drawers and eggs. There were vast sea-bird eggs speckled like the pebbles from the beach and tiny warblers' eggs set in clouds of cotton wool. They peered into tray after tray. Pip was the fascinated by each tray of eggs and Mum was delighted by his pleasure. Inevitably, it was Mother who flagged first and wandered off to find the Ladies, leaving him absorbed with a tray of penguins' eggs. He didn't notice the old man who came up quietly from behind and peered over his shoulder. Pip knew that the old man was there and that he was looking with him at the eggs and sharing his thoughts.

'The emperor penguin,' said the old man, 'is the strangest of birds. It's almost primeval. Did you know, each pair of birds lays a single egg and then incubates it through the Antarctic Winter?'

'How do they keep the egg warm?' asked Pip.

'That's the wonder of it. They stand in a great huddle to shield each other from blizzards. They take it in turns to move to the edge of the huddle so that no one bird is over exposed to extreme weather. The whole colony is constantly moving and shifting and to keep the egg warm each bird keeps its egg tucked up on its feet.'

In his mind Pip saw the emperors, standing against the great blasts of cold, shifting and balancing their lone eggs in a strange shuffling dance that was called by none but co-ordinated by the will of all. 'How did they get them here in the museum?' he asked.

'That's a good question. I would imagine they were brought back by one of the many expeditions that now go to Antarctica.'

Mum hurried towards them and looked anxious. The man moved away.

'Who was that?' she asked.

'We were talking about penguin eggs. It was really interesting.'

Later, they saw the old man in the refreshment room and because he was looking for somewhere to sit, and the room crowded, Mum, very decidedly, asked him to join them at their table. The old gentleman inclined his head and held out his hand in a somewhat shy, but very courteous, manner.

'Cherry-Garrard,' he said.

Mum's manner altered and she melted into her most charming mode. Pip found it difficult to understand why his new acquaintance should at first be greeted with caution, almost bordering on hostility, followed by the manner Mum normally reserved for important people. Cherry spoke in a flat distant voice, as if proceedings were detached from his real thoughts. Mum, on the other hand, provided a mass of information on Pip's enthusiasm for all things living and Pip pressed for further information about penguins and the wildlife of Antarctica.

'I think that he was on the Scott thing,' Mum whispered in one of her all too audible whispers.

'Yes, I was with Captain Scott's expedition,' said Cherry. 'I had the opportunity to visit the emperor penguins at their only known breeding colony at Cape Crozier.' He gave a dry little chuckle, 'You could say that it was the strangest bird-nesting expedition ever taken.'

'But you couldn't take any of the eggs,' said Pip who recalled their earlier conversation, 'because each pair only lays the one egg.'

'Ah, indeed,' muttered Cherry. 'The existing code of honour of all egg collectors, to only take one at a time, can hardly apply when the pair has a solitary egg. Yes, I'm sorry to have to say we had to abandon our scruples in the name of science. It was a scientific trip to establish the evolutionary link between dinosaurs and birds.'

'And did it?' asked Pip, thinking of the incongruity in sizes between penguins and the massive dinosaur bones assembled in the foyer of the museum.

'I'm not so sure about that. Science is a hard task-master and is not easily satisfied.'

'I believe that we used to be near neighbours at one time,' said Mum. 'You were at Lamer Park and we live just the other side of Whitebushes. My husband is the doctor at the new hospital there, the one which used to be for scarlet fever patients.'

Cherry started. Elspeth, forever young and full of vital charm, smiled into his youthful face as she slipped her arm into his when they were standing on the steps at Lamer for the Empire Day celebrations. Like a stab from a sharp thorn of an old sloe bush, 'what do you think about votes for women?' she said and danced away leaving him on an ice floe with Birdie, staring at smashed and broken ice.

'Yes, I remember Whitebushes very well,' he said. 'Ah tea. We must drink it while it's hot. Shall I pour?'

Mum understood people and could handle conversation well when the situation warranted and she did not surrender her sovereignty of the tea pot easily. Pip was not so easily distracted and continued to press for information, his mind wildly excited by it all but Mum gave him one of those adult nudges that tell one to leave well alone. There followed chatter about London and houses and some people called 'teddy boys' who caused Cherry irritation but it all passed off pleasantly enough. Then, quite abruptly Cherry stood up to take his leave.

'Do come and call on us if you are coming up to Town any time. My wife, Angela, and I would be delighted. Take my card and just give us a telephone call to let us know you're coming. We live in an apartment now, very comfortable and convenient, but I miss the old place.'

Mum took his card and scrabbled in her handbag. 'Yes, now, I must give you our number.' The only paper she could find was torn from the inside of a Craven-A packet. She took still more time to find a pen while Pip felt more and more embarrassed at her fumbled incompetence compared with the sophistication of the card.

Yet, strangely it was Cherry who seemed ill at ease to the point of embarrassment. 'Always welcome, goodbye then.' he said before moving deftly and quite swiftly away. He departed as mysteriously as he had arrived, melting into the mass of people.

His card read: 'Mr Apsley Cherry-Garrard, Dorset House, Gloucester Place, London.' A telephone number followed the address.

Pip was full of questions about the man they had met and Mum, not the best one to recall facts, was rather hazy about it all. Mum knew about the Cherry-Garrard family, they had lived at Lamer Park and had sold the house just before she and the family came to the Doctor's House and therefore she had not met them. Mum was concerned that the house had declined and fallen into disrepair and it was difficult for Pip to get her back on the subject of Antarctic exploration. She could confirm that Mr Cherry-Garrard had been with Scott and that he hadn't died. He had written a book about it which was quite famous but she had not read it. There was also a film about the expedition which showed that Antarctica was very cold and the British had shown lots of pluck to be there at all and some of them, including Scott, had died. Pip began to put the pieces together in his mind. He remembered something Dad had said about a rescue attempt, but Mum could not supply any more information and for the time being he had to content himself with what she told him.

Their trip to London would not be complete without visits to Tatchbrook Tropicals in Vauxhall and the pet shop in Camden Town. In the former there was a faint hum and the distinctive smell of warm water as a hundred glass-fronted boxes displayed their jewelled occupants. Pip came away with a water-filled polythene bag containing three fish destined for his aquarium back home. In the latter the choice was more difficult. Here the smell was pungent, urine on sawdust, and the state of the animals was distressing. In one corner a cage of flamingos waved their long necks in the constricted air or drooled their bills in a tin bowl of water. In the end Pip chose a green lizard which was as much as his pocket money would allow. The stumpy middle aged woman who served him had stained hands and a gravelley voice, thickened with a cockney accent and Capstan cigarettes. She reminded Pip of the gypsy women who camped near his home and who came with the travelling fairground. The woman stuffed a smaller second lizard into the bag with a broad wink and the words 'here Ducks take this 'un as well.' Pip was rendered speechless by such undeserved kindness.

At Victoria station Mum was in a fluster not to miss the train and yet she was conscious of the fact that they had not eaten since tea in the Natural History Museum. She rushed up to a stall and bought a wedge of New Zealand cheese and a bar of chocolate before heading off down the platforms with a flapping assortment of bags and containers. They sat in the corner of the compartment surrounded by their bags and Mother broke off hunks of cheese that they ate with relish.

'I suppose,' said Pip, 'if you were in Antarctica you would eat food like this. You know with your hands and all and it would have been absolutely delicious.'

Mum saw the men huddled in their tent and breaking into their supplies of food. She shivered. 'Those poor dears, it must have been so cold and awful.'

'But don't you think that it would be exciting too?' said Pip. 'They were alone together surrounded by hundreds of miles of emptiness, sharing their food with friends. It must have been brilliant.'

The train flung them southward and homeward, rattling through the darkness. They passed through the lighted districts of outer London with row upon row of cramped houses thrust together. Pip saw the wet roofs in the lamplight and smoke from the chimneys and wondered what the people living in them were doing at that moment. All was constriction and hardness, with so little space for the things that really mattered, but he knew that the fish were safe in their polythene bag and that the lizards were curled in a bag by his hand and was reassured that his world was safe.

# CHAPTER TEN

## *ANTARCTIC LETTER FOUR*

*Discovery Hut, March 21 1911*

*Dear Ida*

*We are settling down to a curious type of camping life here at the old Discovery hut, which is very different to our comfortable life at Cape Evans. This hut was never intended for residential living, only for storage. On the Discovery expedition, Captain Scott, Bill and all the others lived aboard ship and only used the hut occasionally during the summer months. As a consequence, we have been pretty cold here and winter is drawing in and both the insulation and heating are poor. We have had to put up with the most terrible blizzards. We have to stay here for the time being because there is no safe way back to Cape Evans until the sea ice is sufficiently thick to afford safe passage. I wonder how old Campbell and his crew are getting on in their makeshift hut.*

*We have organised a blubber stove to keep off the worst of the cold and there are plenty of seals and penguins so we have both meat and fuel for the stove. The only draw-back is that the smoke from the stove has blackened us and all our kit. You would be appalled to see the savages we have become.*

*March 30*

*Bill and some of the others went out to test the ice but it is still not safe. A great piece of the Glacier Tongue has just broken off, which goes to show how unpredictable things can be.*

*April 16*

*Easter Day was celebrated with the usual service. The light is going fast but I went for a walk with Bill and poor old Vince's Cross is still just visible. How long ago it all seems now when I was in Burnside with Cousin Reggie and talking about Vince's death. Strange to think that back then I thought so much about the Greeks and Odysseus. I still see our purpose out here as noble but in poor Vince's death, and our ordeal on the broken ice, I am reminded of the fragility of life. It will be good to leave in a few days and join the others in Cape Evans.*

*April 21*

*We have struggled back over the ice and are back at Cape Evans. All is well and we must now settle down into the dark winter.*

*April 27*

*My first winter and I am enjoying myself. This life definitely suits me and I am going to use my time to improve myself as much as possible and to make myself indispensable. Birdie has been teaching me navigation and a more kindly and diligent tutor a man could not wish for. Captain Scott is at pains to ensure that we are all engaged in meaningful activity so that the dark days and nights are made bearable. He has asked me to edit the South Polar Times, which is a great honour. Apparently, there is a tradition down here of producing a magazine and eliciting secret contributions. All are eligible to contribute but nobody must reveal their identity.*

*I have taken lessons in dog handling. Meares is teaching me, but he hasn't Birdie's patience and the dogs are anything but obliging. They seem to want to fight and squabble and to tear into any living thing. It's a rough and confusing business and nothing like you would imagine. These are not dogs as we know them but more feral creatures crossed with wolves. They really only respond to the whip and this goes against the grain. First endeavours have been pretty disastrous with dogs and sledges going in competing directions. One time out the dogs had a whiff of a penguin and took off like crazed creatures. There was nothing I could do to stop them. I took a purler and nearly broke my neck and it took several hours to get the sledge back. I have to wonder if the polar party can risk loaded sledges to such unpredictable creatures. Maybe Bill is right and the Norskies won't be able to manage the dogs in the mountains as well as they plan?*

*Meares is a bit of a mystery. He is a good man with dogs but they say that it is partly his fault that the ponies are such a collection of old relics, because he and Captain Scott's brother-in-law share responsibility for their purchase. Titus made the observation that a dog man should not have been sent to buy ponies and Meares was given no advice or instructions other than to buy white ponies because Shackleton believed that white ponies performed better in the south. Titus and Meares get on well together and spend a lot of time outside the Hut with the animals. Titus is such a fellow for the animals that Birdie has christened him 'Farmer Hayseed'. They have dubbed me 'Cheery Cherry' which I quite like and shall do my best to live up to.*

<u>*May 16*</u>

*Uncle Bill says that we can go for a trip to Cape Crozier in the Antarctic winter. He looks like taking Birdie with him and maybe me. That would be a bird-nesting trip I would love to be on and I will see if I can bring you back an egg for your collection. How would an emperor-penguin egg look nestled up to shrike's egg? I can't promise anything as I am not sure that I will be chosen and there is no guarantee that the chosen party will get there and back. It means setting off in the pitch black in the middle of the Antarctic winter. We will have to travel over one hundred miles in conditions that could be as much as forty degrees below and drag enough kit to keep us supplied for up to two weeks. It will be the strangest bird-nesting trip ever undertaken. I hope to go but I wonder if I am up to it? One day these splendid chaps around me may stop and realise that I am not worth a straw compared to them in points of courage and manliness.*

*May 24*

*I am reminded that today is Empire Day. I am sure that there will be celebrations up and down the country. How well I recall that day at Lamer when there was the procession and all the fun and entertainments. If I close my eyes I can see Father, in full uniform, waiting on the steps. We had fun here too. Ponting put on a special slide show and we all sang Jerusalem. You will wonder if I thought about Elspeth. Perhaps I did, but my real thoughts were of you all at Lamer.*

*June 6*

*We had a particularly good dinner tonight in honour of Captain Scott's birthday.*

*After the meal Uncle Bill came up to me and, would you believe it, has invited me to be the third man on his bird-nesting trip. The other man will be Birdie.*

*There is much to be done before we depart. We plan to build an ice house/hut at Cape Crozier so that we can stay there for some time and study the nesting penguins. I am to be responsible for this and will have to put in time practising and perfecting the art.*

*June 22*

*We have celebrated mid-winter in style. We had the most wonderful dinner and afterwards there were toasts and speeches of all kinds. Birdie improvised an extraordinary Christmas tree made from a ski stick, skua and penguin feathers and coloured paper, and there were gifts for everybody. One of our crew is a Russian, called Dimitri, who is a dog handler along with Meares. He is a strange little chap and normally keeps to himself and the dogs, but on this occasion he announced that he would entertain us with a Cossack dance. Titus followed his lead and the two of them leaped about in the most extraordinary set of capers. Dimitri was highly accomplished but good old Titus made us all roar with laughter as he failed miserably to come up to Dimitri's high standard and was reduced to rolling about the floor utterly exhausted.*

*In a quieter mode, this was also the occasion for the launch of my first edition of the SPT. I am delighted that it has been received so well.*

*I must now give my thoughts and energies to our preparations for the great bird-nesting trip because we plan to leave in a few days. There is so much to do. I will not write again but, as soon as we are back, I will continue this letter and tell you all about it.*

*August 17, 1911*

*I have tried to write to Mother and to tell her about our winter march to Cape Crozier and our bird-nesting trip but I am not able to express to her and the girls what it was really like. I need to tell you because I know that you will understand and you will appreciate what a burden it has placed on my nerves and will deduce how much I owe to Birdie and Uncle Bill.*

*The journey to Cape Crozier was like a trip into the underworld. We loaded the sledges with so much oil and equipment that they proved impossible to pull in that bleak black terrain. In the end we had to relay them which meant going forward with one and then going back for the second. I cannot tell you how that terrible labour wore down my spirit, and the cruel weather and the darkness, drove me to the edge of my endurance. My glasses could not be used and as, you know, I see little without them even under the best of circumstances.*

*It was a terrible game of blind man's buff. I just staggered on behind the shape of Birdie. If he stopped or stumbled I would jolt into him. All that I had previously known and understood no longer had any value. Erebus had opened up and drawn me in and I was gripped in the darkness. I was held in painful limbo betwixt life and death. I was a stumbling somnambulist experiencing the strangest dream-like thoughts that seemed so real. Through the dreams this refrain kept hammering in my head:*

*'You've got it in the neck,*
*Stick it, stick it.*
*You've got it in the neck,*
*Stick it, stick it.'*

*Round and round it went and my mind with it. Sometimes I was running in Oxford but never coming nearer to anywhere that I recognised. I thought of Elspeth, in the ballroom dancing, dancing on her own. No matter how I tried she was not aware that I was there. I thought of Old Hobbs, and he was coming up the Earlsbrook with a wild assortment of outlandish figures. You were there too. We were running together, running down the southern avenue, past our trees and on to the lane. We could see the White Bridge and Hobbs's house in the distance, but we could not seem to get there.*

*When Bill called a halt the wakeful dreams would stop. We pitched our tent in the dark and then began the labour of getting the stove going and heating up hoosh. The cold and the wind were so intense that recorded temperatures were a mass of negative numbers. We got into our rigid, frozen bags and slept fitfully. Even in my bag my teeth chattered all night. Dear old Birdie took pity on me and insisted on lending me the inside of his own bag. I refused at first but then he reassured me so strongly that he was fine without it that I weakened and took it. I have never been so grateful to anybody in my whole life. The process of getting up was no better than going to sleep and it could take us an hour to get into the harness.*

*At last we heard the great emperors in the darkness and knew that we were above them. It seemed to me that that eerie noise in this dread place was like the call of the damned, calling us to our destruction. The summons could not be ignored and we would have to go to it.*

*Bill found a spot to build an ice cave, on the lea side of the wind. We hacked and scraped away some of the ice to create a primitive grotto in the side of the cliff. I dragged stones to fortify it and we dug the tent in as deeply as we possibly could. Here we set up camp.*

*We tried to get down to the emperors but it proved more difficult than any of us had expected. The cliff would have presented a difficult climb even in the best of weather but in the dark, with a howling wind, it was a tense and undignified scramble, and I fell several times and had to be hauled back by my companions. When we managed to get down, the emperors stood like soldiers, a great sea of living beings facing down the weather. I will never forget the smell and sound of it. We took the two eggs each from a total of six birds. We killed two birds for food and fuel. I didn't say anything, but I felt the strangeness of coming so far in dreadful conditions to do murder upon the innocent in the name of science.*

*Each man carefully packed what eggs he could and we dragged the heavy birds behind us on a rope. The climb back was even worse then the climb down. I fell so often that there was no way that I could preserve my eggs. Birdie and Bill managed to get some eggs back unbroken. After all that I have had to endure it seems that I must break my promise to you in the same way that I clumsily broke my penguin eggs.*

*That night was the worst night of my life. We had the fiercest storm that I have ever experienced, even in this part of the world. It was as though the gods were punishing us for our ravages against nature. The din of the wind was dreadful and finally the tent roof of our improvised hut was ripped away and we had no option but to bury ourselves in the snow and wait for the storm to blow itself out. I was sure that we were done for. I tried to think what to do next and how Father would have dealt with it. Bill crawled over to me and he put his hands to his mouth to shout in my ear,*

*'Please, Cherry, keep still!'*

*There was pleading in his voice that I had never heard before. I lay in the snow and let it entomb me so that it made a monument of my body. We lay there for hours and time became meaningless. I can recall Birdie pulling me out from my tomb of ice and snow and beating me with his hands to clear the snow off and to try to* warm my cold body. When he had finished this to his satisfaction, he said, 'Cherry get something warm inside you, I'm going to find the tent.' Just like that, as though he were going to pick up the football from over somebody's fence. I actually laughed. How could anyone possibly find a tent that had been ripped away like a straw before the full might of the storm and sent flying out across the Antarctic sea? He stood more chance of finding it in New Zealand!

Bill said nothing. He had managed to cobble together the stove and was intent on getting it to work and to get something for us to drink. It was the same man who had sat on the rock on South Trinidad, but this time the face was haggard and drawn, as though he could not find that same confidence and serenity, and his movements were pained and deliberate.

Birdie came back with the tent and dropped it down, like a gun dog with a dead pheasant, as if nothing had happened. What chance that it should have shot up vertically for about a mile and then come down within yards of the same spot, virtually unscathed? He brought us back the chance of life and we just nodded and got on with eating hoosh. Three men sitting in the iron rags that were our clothes quietly eating hoosh with our 'pleases' and 'thank yous' intact and with all the inward civilisation that mocked our outward circumstances. We still had the prospect of a terrible journey back but now we sensed the possibility of life. I tell you this, although it pains me to do so. I couldn't stop the tears and, although I was sitting there and willing myself not to, they just rolled down my face. Bill and Birdie saw me weeping but they were too kind to say anything, or let it be known that they had seen, and that kindness and courtesy made it worse so that the tears rolled freely. What did Odysseus see in the land of the dead that frightened him most? Was it his own shadow? One thing is sure: he would not have wept for himself.

Birdie said something about one more go at the emperors as soon as the weather cleared enough, but Bill wouldn't have it. 'No,' he said, 'I have risked things too far and we must get back alive.'

I inwardly rejoiced at those words because I knew that if Bill and Birdie were for staying then I would be honour bound to stay, but Ida, how I longed for the hut and peaches and syrup and all the warmth of that good company! Beyond the hut was Lamer and you and Mother and the memory of Father. I wanted the chance to live again and to bring Bill and Birdie to Lamer. I wanted to show Bill all those special places, where we saw the purple emperor butterfly and where we found the shrike's nest. I imagined the girls with Birdie and how they would fuss over him and how dear old Birdie would laugh in his shy way, and how pleased he would be to share it all. Then perhaps you too will get to know and love these men as I do?

*Before we could even start the journey back we had to wait for the weather to clear. One night while working on the blubber stove, some burning fat shot into Bill's eye, leaving him in the most terrible pain. Birdie and I did what we could. It was terrible to see him suffer so much, he could scarcely disguise his heart-rending groans. I thought the eye was lost but Bill was more worried about how this would affect the journey back. He joked about only having three good eyes between the three of us. Yet he never complained and it seemed to harden his resolve to get us back alive.*

*When we did leave the cave, Bill was out of pain but could see nothing in one eye. The journey back was terrible but easier than the journey out because our sledges were lighter. Bill's pain was easing and we had a clear objective - get back alive. Ida, at times I felt that I was marching with three men and not two. There were four of us hauling the sledge and the fourth man, silently at my side, was Father. It was Father's voice that whispered in my ear:*

*'You've got it in the neck -*
*Stick it! Stick it!*
*You've got it in the neck.'*

*As we pushed on it felt as though I was not there at all. I was up in the old mulberry tree, watching four figures, bent into the wind dragging their sledge. Then, as I watched on, the figures seemed to be wading up the stream until they found a safe exit point. They clambered up and out of my sight.*

*We fought our way inch by inch, foot by foot, over the hundred miles of hell until the terrain became more familiar. Bill ordered the last camp before we reached the old Discovery hut and at that point we knew that we had made it and survived. Bill spoke to us in his quiet way and I will never forget his words,*

*'I must thank you,' he said, 'for coming with me on this trip. I do not believe that I could have had two finer companions, nor two men whom I could value more. Thank you from the bottom of my heart.' It was so simple and so sincere, Birdie and I were rendered speechless and I couldn't trust myself to try to speak.*

*Later that night, Birdie quizzed Bill on the selection for the polar party. Bill would have to be one of the final four, of course, but Captain Scott would be mad not to take Birdie too. Bill wasn't to be drawn. It was Scott's decision and nobody else's. As for me, I feel that this trip has shown me not to be truly worthy but I still hope. Bill and Birdie saw me weep but they are too generous to pass this on to Captain Scott.*

*In the security of the hut I am warm and comforted by the presence of all the chaps. Old Birdie is just above me in the bunk and all is well. I have been in a very dark place and the memories linger. I have stared into the abyss and seen things that I shudder to tell, but writing it down for you helps me to put it in perspective.*

*You know, I think old Titus knows something of this. That first night back, on turning in, he said to me, for no reason at all:*

*'Always look into the light, young Cherry.'*

*Indeed, I must look into the light because you are there, along with Mother, the girls and all these dear fellows. This expedition has made it clear to me how dear you all are.*

*God bless you all and good night,*

*Apsley*

## Early summer 1958

Froglets exploded on the common and there were birds' nests in the hedges on the way home from school. Schooldays were rendered happiest by the time that the boys were not at school but with the gang in the cold and damp of Sunflower Cottage. Long ago the cottage had been a wash room or laundry for the old hospital but now it had become the gang's meeting place and headquarters. Tom had written on the door, in black paint:

'Trespassers will be persecuted.'

Sunflower Cottage had a particular coldness that clings to empty, single-stoned buildings. An old green carpet that had been acquired from somewhere and thrown down on the flagstone floor made no difference. Even in spring and early summer the building clung to its coldness. Early summer was untypically cold and wet. The boys tried to light paper fires in the great iron grid that had once been a fireplace. These attempts simply resulted in the acrid smell of smoke being mingled with the mildew.

On Saturdays, the boys from around Whitebushes gathered. They leaned their bikes against the wall of the cottage and sprawled in jeans, old coats and wellingtons, in a number of broken down armchairs. There were six regulars: Tom was fractionally the eldest, and the leader, Pip was the youngest and only allowed there because he was brother to Tom and Jack. If there was a challenger to Tom it was Keith whose country skills dignified him above the rest but for all Keith's sturdiness and resourcefulness he could not match Tom in 'wrestling', despite frequent attempts. Ivan and Laurie were quieter spirits and easier foot soldiers, pleased to follow in this microcosm of a militaristic world. Others swelled the ranks of the gang from time to time including Chris, a public-school boy who joined the gang in the school holidays when he stayed with his mother in a caravan down by the Nag's Head. Chris's estranged father paid the school fees and his mother battled to make a home on a small, residential caravan site. There was also Dick, a gypsy boy who travelled with the fair that took place from time to time on Earlswood Common. Skellum, a grubby wired-haired terrier, was usually where the gang was but his independent nature meant that this could never be taken for granted. He might be behind an armchair or under one of the old iron-framed beds that lurked in a corner, or he might have sauntered off to be about his own affairs.

Tom was leader but this was a fledging democracy. 'Well,' said Tom, 'what do we want to do today?'

'Go on an expedition,' suggested one voice.

'Fight a battle!' called another.

'Build a camp,' said Keith.

'All right,' said Tom. 'There are German paratroopers in Top Wood. We capture that and then go on to the tree camp and check out the rope swing.' It was as though he had planned the expedition in advance.

Each boy had his own distinctive uniform: a stick carved and whittled to a unique design, a feather stuck here or there, the top of a Wellington boot turned down. All wore helmets salvaged from the Home Guard or Civil Defence, painted in lurid colours. Pip's helmet was riddled with holes and had done supplementary service as a hanging basket. In their van they carried a flag, an old white pillow case, with the gang's motto painted in black. They sang as they marched:

*'Onward, Christian so-o-oldiers*
*Marchin as to war.....'*

When the mood was upon them they sang:
*' 'Itler, 'e only 'ad one ball!*
*The uver was two but very small!*
*'Imlar was somewhat simlar!*
*But poor old Goballs 'ad no balls at all!'*

Shocking though this was to any would-be adult listener, all would approve of the disrespect it showed Hitler and his kind. The combination of vulgarity and character assassination delighted the boys. Pip usually brought up the rear of the platoon and Skellum was usually somewhere in the vicinity of Pip.

They marched southwards in good order, heading for the farmland that bordered one side of their kingdom. The fields had been cut into the dark bushes that had once been ancient woodland. The bushes lingered on the margins of the fields as thick, impenetrable hedges. The fields were mostly pasture, which provided the boys with open access and enabled them to move long distances. But these lands were guarded by enemies in the form of strange adults who on occasion watched over the land and were collectively known as 'the farmer'. If they came across 'the farmer,' he would invariably shout, gesticulate and emit his cry:

'Oi! Get back here!'

As soon as they heard the cry the boys would scurry to the edge of the field and dive into the concealment of the bushes. From there they could crawl away to reunite elsewhere. Pip was a nuisance on such occasions. His legs being shorter and his responses less finely tuned, he had to be bundled along by one of the older boys. Skellum was another problem. He could never be entirely trusted to retreat, his nature being for attack. The farmer showed little enthusiasm for pursuit and the boys always managed to get away. They never discovered why the farmer requested their return.

The boys climbed to the top of the great fence that marked the end of the hospital grounds and leapt into the open field, rolling like parachutists. Pip did the same and tried to make it seem smooth and effortless so as not to be ordered to crawl under the fence, as was his way in childhood. Only Skellum had to use that route to the farmer's lands. Pip hit the ground with the low thud of wellington boots and rolled, his helmet shot away from him and his stick somehow became entangled with his legs. When he regained his composure and dignity the other boys were already advancing on the enemy position. A wave of Tom's hand told him to keep down. The gang crawled forward, their sticks, now rifles, in forward position. The objective was a thick, sinister copse, home to rattling pigeons and, allegedly, the foxes that persecuted Mum's chicken house. They went forward on their bellies, the wet grass soaked their clothing but did not dampen their ardour for the attack. Silence was of the utmost importance because surprise was the essence of any good attack.

'Come on!' hissed Keith. 'Let's go.'

Tom waved him down. They must be nearer yet. You must almost wait until you can see the whites of their eyeballs.

'Now!' went up the cry. The platoon sprang to its feet and surged forward. The Germans were taken by surprise, they had probably been sitting around fires and eating sausages and muttering strange guttural things. The English burst into the wood firing with all their guns.

'Achtung! Achtung!' yelled the Germans, snatching up their Bren guns and firing into the oncoming rush of young English manhood. Nothing could stop that gallant charge. Soon all were at hand to hand fighting, leaping, bayoneting, howling in martial rage, until every last sausage-munching monster was rightfully dead.

Free from the fit of battle, the boys lay on their backs and looked up through the canopy of trees. Their jeans were torn, their knees muddy and their faces and hands scratched by brambles. They lay for some time in silence, each locked in his thoughts after the heat of battle. They knew that they would never fight the Germans, not like their fathers and grandfathers, but, being British, fighting noble wars was in their nature. Generation after generation had experienced war: Granny talked of the Boers with contempt, Nelson lay on his deck, Wolfe died in glory at Quebec. It was all like that in what was left of the Empire, some native somewhere wanted more than he should, skirmishing, bombing, rioting. There would never be peace

Keith's voice brought them back to the here and now, 'I can smell foxes.'

'A fox smells his own 'ole!'

'No, really, they're here.'

They crawled their way round the copse, locating various gaps and undulations in the damp layers of the floor. Sometimes it seemed hard to define just what a hole should be. At last, Keith hit on a spot and declared it a den and if it wasn't a fox den then it was definitely a rabbit hole.

'Let's snare it,' he said.

The prospect was delightful, man the hunter, surviving by ingenuity.

'After we've caught it we'll skin it and cook it over a fire,' said Ivan.

'Yes, and skewer it with green sticks,' said Jack. 'It has to be green sticks, otherwise they burn.'

Keith produced a long double twist of wire, looped at either end. They sharpened short sticks with their pen knives and thrust them into the ground to act as pegs. Slowly the mechanism began to evolve in Pip's mind: the animal creeping forth from its hole and the noose slipping silently over its head, the holding fast, the tightening with each movement, the choking struggle and the blind terrible fear. These images blocked out the joy of the hunt.

'Isn't it all a bit cruel?' he asked.

'Na,' said Keith. 'They're vermin. Sometimes if they get caught by a paw they chew it off and limp away. It's just nature.'

The others didn't see his logic and shared some of Pip's scruples. Still, it seemed a shame to dismantle their handiwork and perhaps the trap would catch nothing at all.

'Come on,' said Tom. 'Let's head for the tree camp. Best not to stay too long in case the farmer heard the battle.'

They went through fields, over ditches, under hedges and wire, always southward. The going was hard and Pip found it hard to keep up, especially as his wellingtons had been inherited and slopped and drew against him on the rough terrain. They came to the river, dark and sick with water and overgrown with brambles and shrubby plants, more of a stream than a river. It marked the southernmost boundary of what they regarded as their territory. Beyond the river were houses and people with their dogs. There were also the gypsies, strange lawless people and denizens of an old and hidden world, who had a regular camp no more than a mile on.

The boys followed the stream eastward to the tree camp. Somebody had been there before. The planks that they had nailed in the branches of the old oak tree had been prized up and flung to the ground and the rope, which they had managed to secure to a branch so that you could swing across the stream, had been cut with a sharp knife. There were other claimants to these border regions. The boys felt uncomfortable and their morale sank.

'Time to move on. We'll go on to the Fox and Dog Bridge,' said Tom.

They shuffled along the briar-strewn edge of the stream until they came to the old redbrick bridge that carried the cars, vans and even the horse carts, which the gypsies so loved, from one sprawling village to the other. The bridge earned its name from a famous incident in the gang's lore. They had marched along the road and stopped on the bridge to look down into the swirling, muddied waters of the Mole and there in a frothing eddy they caught sight of an old hessian sack, tied with rope and floating in the water. The boys scrambled down the steep sides of the bank and hooked the sack in with a stick. Somebody produced a penknife; they cut the rope and peered in. Inside were the terrifying relics of a dead dog and a dead fox, locked together in death, their wet matted fur stained with old blood. In that instant the boys had seen enough. They retied the rope and pushed the sack out into the stream so that the current took it again. It floated, bloatedly, downstream, like some funereal Viking ship.

They scrambled up the bank and stood on the bridge peering over.

'That's where it was,' said Jack, 'just over there.'

'Yeah, and when we cut it open they were both dead, dead and stinkin.' This was for Pip's benefit because he had not been there at the time. He had been kept at home by Mum, who insisted on buttoning him up into a coat and wellies, while the older boys took the opportunity to slip away.

'Why were they there?' asked Pip, who wanted to savour the full horror of the story while being secretly glad that he had missed the gruesome sight. The older boys could not present a credible explanation. The sack with its terrible secret flowed down the stream into Pip's imagination.

One of the boys took something from his pocket. It was a small tube of cardboard with a blue paper end, something like the twist of salt in crisp packets. Other boys produced their own, some bigger than others but all with the bold writing, 'NOT TO BE HELD IN HAND'. They rooted around on the banks with their sticks until they found some clay, which they squeezed onto the bases of their bangers. The fuses were lit one by one, the blue paper glowed then burst into fizzing life. The bangers were dropped into mid-stream where they sank, angrily, out of sight into the muddied waters. Bubbles rose rapidly to the surface and to everybody's delight a vortex of water bubbles powered to the surface as the bangers exploded like depth charges.

All too soon all the bangers, both penny and tupenny, were spent and there was nothing left for it but to begin the long trek home. They went back the shortest way cutting across fields and hurrying because it was getting on to lunch time and they were expected back. Pip's wellingtons contrived to drag him back with every squelching step. The others urged him on. Skellum reappeared, running effortlessly over the muddied ground with his four legs and light body weight. Pip, dizzy with hunger, was too proud and too determined to ask for any help.

They came to a pathway with dense thorn bushes on both sides. It was dark and narrow through infrequent use and they could only walk, not march, in single file through its sharp-fingered sides. It was ancient and frightening in its agelessness, and yet reassuring. It led straight back to the entrance gates of the hospital. They called it the Magic Pathway. Ivan said that it was magic because in the old days it had been used by strange people. You had to keep the magic off, and pass safely through by whistling a tune. They had learnt the tune and although they believed none of Ivan's stuff, they whistled it through several times as they went. At the end of the Magic Pathway they came to the concrete pill box. Once there it was safe to stop whistling.

Across the fields, as if searching them out, they heard the rattle of the gong. It was in fact a metal shell case and Mum used a poker to rattle it from the inside. The distinctive noise could be heard over several fields. It was Mum's means of summoning the brothers to return to home and the signal that the others must mount their bicycles and depart for their own homes in the village. It was all over for the week.

Later that afternoon Tom slipped away. Pip saw him go and said nothing but waited out for his return. When Tom came back Pip saw that something was secreted in his pocket. The wire from the fox/rabbit trap had been wrenched up by Tom to prevent it working. Next time the gang went to look they wouldn't find a fox or rabbit trapped and ready to be skinned and cooked. They would find nothing and would blame the gypsies.

# CHAPTER ELEVEN

## *ANTARCTIC LETTER FIVE*

<u>*August 26, 1911*</u>
*The Hut*
*Antarctica*

*Dear Ida*
   *The light is back. Unfortunately we are yet to properly appreciate it as we have been confined to the hut through a terrible blizzard. In spite of this, Captain Scott insisted on champagne all round to toast the return of the light.*

   *We are able to spend much more time outside. One of my tasks is to work with my pony so that I can handle him on the southern journey. We go for walks together, at first no further than up to the Ramp and back, to build up his stamina and help his coat. There is enough light for this but it is still terribly cold. We must build up the ponies' strength and general condition in readiness for warmer weather and the southern journey.*

   *The glory of our bird-nesting journey has now well and truly worn off. At first we were treated with all the awe and delicacy which befits people who have been to hell and back, but in a matter of a few weeks we have returned to being the rough and tumble mortals that we really are.*

   *The winter has been so dark and, although we have tried to keep busy, there has been a lot of time to sleep and dream. The scientists, like Deb and Silas, have kept particularly busy as there are always measurements to be taken and recorded, even in the worst conditions. The rest of us kept busy so as not to drop into some kind of torpor. Captain Scott can be quite sharp on a man who spends too long in his bunk. I think that he fears that the dark could drive a man out of his mind and it is true that lethargy begets more lethargy. If I allow myself I am in danger of drifting. I keep busy with work on the final winter edition of the South Polar Times. I intend it to be the best ever. I wonder where we will all be next winter and whether or not I will still be editing the SPT then. The chaps are very keen for this latest volume and there is some great fun about making contributions. There is a box for submitting articles and ideas. Submissions are anonymous so there are great larks about people submitting their work and some of the chaps go to ridiculous length to write their material in secret and then get it into the box undetected. Even old Titus has been suspected of some late night antics! The only person, apart from me, who is perfectly above board about their contributions, is Uncle Bill. He is the sole artist and illustrator for each edition and he has produced some wonderful material both serious and comic.*

*We have lectures in the evenings on all sorts of topics. Many of them are of a scientific nature and, while I try to take an interest, I cannot profess to share Captain Scott's enthusiasm. Ponting's lectures are particularly popular because he illustrates them with slides taken on his travels. There is something both incongruous and yet marvellous to hear and see of his travels in Japan whilst sitting in a hut in the middle of the Antarctic winter.*

*The other evening we had a lecture from Titus. Everybody was greatly amused at the prospect of Titus delivering some erudite and worthy discourse. But, he informed and delighted us with his lecture on horse management. Everybody respected the straightforward manner in which he presented his material, and his advice and many tips will come in very useful to those of us who will be working with the ponies and leading them on the southern journey. He finished with an anecdote: a young lady arrived late and very flustered at the ball with the explanation that she had been delayed by the horse pulling the carriage which kept refusing to pull.*

*'Ah,' said her hostess, 'that would have been a Cobb. They can be quite difficult.'*

*'No,' replied the young lady, 'it was a Bugger. I heard the cabby call him so several times.'*

*Captain Scott used the last lecture to set out his final plans for the Pole. We will leave the hut on the 1ˢᵗ November, any earlier would be too cold for the ponies. The first part of the journey is over the sea ice to the old Discovery hut at Hut Point. From there we pick up last season's trail out onto the Barrier. We go past One Ton Depot and push on into the Barrier. Few of us have gone further than this but we will be following the same route that Captain Scott and Bill covered in the Discovery expedition's Farthest South attempt. It is also the same route used by Shackleton and the Nimrod men. We will go past Bill's Farthest South until we reach the mountains that only Shackleton and his party have seen. How quickly and effectively we can do all this will depend on the success of the supporting men, animals and machines. Captain Scott hopes that the two remaining engines will take us as far as possible onto the Barrier. The ponies and dogs will play their part in getting us to the base of the mountains but from there our ways part. The dogs will go back for use later in the season and next year. The remaining ponies will be shot and stored for food for the men returning from the Pole. Men, alone with their sledges, will carry on from here. We will follow Shackleton's route up the Beardmore Glacier and then out on to the plateau. There will then be a journey of some three hundred miles to the Pole.*

*How far will I go? We all try not to speculate too far but I know that I am in with a chance. If we make it that far, I really do hope that I will be with the men chosen for the plateau. That, in itself, would be a tremendous honour. Is it wrong in me to hope for more? Only one party of four will go all the way to the Pole. Captain Scott and Bill are the only two definites and I think that after the winter journey, Birdie stands a good chance. Could I be the fourth? When I look around at the many splendid sledging men such a wish seems fanciful. Teddy would be most terribly put out not to be chosen and even old Titus has a good chance. Then there are the men like Evans, Crean and Lashly who are all as hard as nails. But these expeditions call for more than sheer strength. When it comes to it, officers have a mental strength that can help carry them through. It is going to be a hard call for Captain Scott. One thing is sure and that is that I will put my best foot forward and give it my best shot. I found things difficult on the winter journey but I came through and I didn't let the darkness take me. There is still that chance that I can work my way through and into the light. Then home to Lamer and all of you, a good job done, a race won and a lifetime ahead of me.*

*I look back on the last letter I sent you and worry that it was all too negative, but it is sealed now and I will not open it because it is true to how I felt at the time of writing. I don't want my old weakness to get me down and am determined to make the most of my time here and if at all possible to be with Bill and Birdie on the summit.*

*Since my last letter things have become a lot trickier in the hut. The truth of the matter is that we are all itching to get away and get on with our bid for the Pole before the Norskies get too far ahead. You see they can start earlier than us as they will be using dogs which cope with the low temperatures. Captain Scott and Bill are convinced that dogs will not work out in the long haul and I have to say from what I have seen of them so far I share their doubts. Our ponies have struggled through the winter reasonably well and they are in not too bad shape. Old Titus has done a simply splendid job. When they are ready to go they will pull a lot more than the dogs. We still have the two motor sledges and, all being well, they will take heavy loads forward and put us all in a strong position. Still it's galling that we are waiting here and the Norskies have probably started already.*

*<u>September 5</u>*

*Captain Scott has confirmed the outline plan. He intends to take three parties of four men on to the summit. From there the third and then the second parties will return, leaving just four men to go on. Would you believe it, I am selected to be in the summit twelve? What do you make of that? There will be four seamen: Crean, Evans, Keohone and Lashly. Four naval officers: Captain Scott, Teddy, Birdie and Aitch. Two scientists: Bill and Silas. This leaves* two 'gentlemen landowners', namely Titus and me. I am pleased as Punch. It puts me in mind of making the cut for the House eight.

Teddy is full of it and determined that he will be in the last four but it's too close to call at this stage. Captain Scott has to be there and where he goes Uncle Bill will follow. But as regards the other two it's anybody's guess because there are so many good chaps. My eyesight and difficulties with goggles will work against me but I am going to make myself as fit and ready as I can. Birdie has been stepping up the lessons on navigation and I have been making progress with the dogs. I don't know if these skills will be of any use but it's better than hanging around. Do you remember when Bevis selected his gang? It's a bit like that. The leader doesn't always choose the biggest and brawniest. Little Charlie has a vital part to play in it all. So, you never know, I may be chosen for the final four yet.

I had a long chat about it all with Uncle Bill. He was worried that our bird-nesting expedition might have put me off but I assured him I was up for it. He thinks that he will go all the way but is quite prepared to stand down if he doesn't feel fit enough at the end point. He thinks that it is really important the final team is selected on the day and much will depend on how the twelve of us shape up over the distance. He showed me the sledging flag which the Master's wife at Caius gave him to put on the pole. He asked me if I would take it on in the event of my being picked instead of him.

September 17, 1911

We have been able to undertake a number of minor sledging expeditions which will help prepare both men and animals for the big journey. Parties have gone out to Shackleton's old hut at Cape Royds, to Hut Point and even as far as Safety Camp. These have been of general use to assist provisioning but also to get us fit for later in the month when we plan to set out for the big push to the Pole. I am fit and ready for the off.

Deb has been working on his fitness as well. He will not be in the great southern journey but is leading a team of four as part of a Western Geological party. He is very excited at the prospect of what he will find there and ribs those of us who are going on the southern journey for not engaging with real science.

My mind often drifts north and homeward to you. Lamer and you are constantly with me. I expect our trees will be in their radiant autumnal colours. I find myself thinking of Old Hobbs and his garden room. I see him sitting by his old stove while above him the swallows gather ready for their great journey south. Your autumn is in full spate but here it's spring and the dawning of the greatest challenge yet.

October, 16

The third volume of the South Polar Times has come out and you *will be delighted to hear has been very well received. Captain Scott was particularly congratulatory and I have to admit to feeling very pleased with myself, although it would have been nothing without contributions from people like Bill. I must share just one example because I have been thinking about it ever since I read it. It was submitted anonymously but we all know that it was by Uncle Bill:*

### The Barrier Silence

*The Silence was deep with a breath like sleep*
*As our sledge runners slid on the snow,*
*And the fateful fall of our fur-clad feet*
*Struck mute like a silent blow*
*On a questioning 'hush,' as the settling crust*
*Shrank shivering over the floe,*
*And the sledge in its track sent a whisper back*
*Which was lost in a white fog-bow*
*And this was the thought that the silence wrought*
*As it scorched and froze us through,*
*Though secrets hidden are all forbidden*
*Till God means man to know*
*We might be the men God meant should know*
*The Heart of the Barrier snow,*
*In the heat of the sun, and the glow*
*And the glare from the glistening floe,*
*As it scorched and froze us through*
*With the bite of the drifting snow.*

*We know it must be by Bill because it is beautifully illustrated with five figures on skis who are pulling a sledge. I wonder why he put five figures in. We never have more than four men in a sledge party.*

<u>October, 24</u>

*So, our great adventure begins in earnest, the two motor sledges have led off the start of our assault on the Pole. We gave them a great cheer to start them in good heart. Much depends on their success*

*I can't wait to be started but Captain Scott wants to give the motors a head start.*

<u>October, 26</u>

*Reports on the success of the motors vary. We keep tabs on their progress through a combination of contacts: through our field glasses, reports from the dog teams and from the telephone in the Discovery hut. There have been a number of problems cropping up and their progress is intermittent. I strain at the leash to be off with the main pony party.*

<u>October, 30</u>

*Captain Scott will set two of the weaker ponies off tomorrow with Aitch and Keohone. The main body of us start tomorrow. I can hardly bear the tension, it reminds me of starting off on the bumps in Oxford and waiting for the starting gun. All that seems very long ago and yet writing to you brings it nearer. It is as though you are here with me, running beside me in another of our adventures. I will seal it now and leave it in the postbag.*

*Give my love to the old places and tell them I will be back just as soon as I can, after I have finished this great task*

*Love,*
*Apsley*

### Summer 1958

Spring gave way to summer. The dark walls of Old John's felt it and responded. Summer brought a new end-of-year atmosphere and new freedoms. The school's order was breaking down. Time was running out, high summer slipped by and the nights started to draw in, something was pulling them into a slightly darker world.

This was last school term for Tom, Keith, Ivan and Laurie. Their futures were decided and the school lost interest in them. They were given useful jobs to do and allowed greater freedom. Jack and Pip carried on in the same old ways but the next school year would be different, they would be left behind in Old John's while the older boys ventured on.

'No more school, no more stick,

no more stinkin' old 'rifmetic.

No more Latin, no more French,

no more sittin' on the old school bench.'

They shouted as they erupted from the school in an empowerment of joy.

The boys were entitled to ride their own bicycles to school. Mum insisted that in the interests of safety they had to make their way across the common paths and not along the road. At the end of the school day, they would mumble a prayer, pile their chairs onto their desks and then a break for the bike sheds. All of them were intent on escaping from school and heading home.

The final afternoon of school was like other Friday afternoons but the older boys knew that they did these things for the final time. They cycled past the great, grim church and down into Earlswood. On entering Earlswood, the Whitebushes contingent swung away down the steep lane which ran through the middle of the golf course. They fastened the top buttons of their capes around their necks so that the yellow capes became the capes of Zorro and flew behind. They roared headlong down the lane, yelling and laughing. The route levelled out as they passed through the tunnel beneath the railway line and they pedalled respectfully round the fence that concealed the great house of Lamer. Past Lamer, there was another lane and another drop so that they sped downward again. Rushing past Hobbs's house and bumping over the White Bridge they caught sight of the Earlsbrook beneath them. The going was slower now as they approached

Whitebushes Common and had to negotiate the tethered animals that often meandered onto the path. Pip brought up the rear because the wheels on his bike were smaller than the other. The journey ended at Ma Batton's shop where what remained of the pocket money went on aniseed balls or gob stoppers or farthing chews if finances failed.

The long summer term seeped seamlessly into the long summer holiday and weeks of freedom rolled in front of them. During holiday times the gang met most days but never on a Sunday. Time was theirs but their sense of purpose was less. They dug defensive trenches by the concrete pill box at the head of the Magic Pathway but incurred the wrath of the cottagers and had to fill them in. They played Tin Can Tommy in the garden, hiding behind the hydrangeas and leaping from the laurel bushes. On really hot days Granny would spray them with the garden hose and they ripped off their clothes and roared about the flying water. When the evening light suspended time, the boys would dare each other to go part way down the Magic Pathway and stand very quietly so as to hear the nightingale sing, long-drawn-out notes of sadness that were filled with the deeply-old and far flung south where it was always warm and luxuriant.

If it was raining, they would hang around the house and crowd round the one-channel, twelve-inch television set in the lounge. The small screen was dominated by the American Wild West and all its heroes. The Range Rider with Dick West, the 'All American Boy' was hugely enjoyed. The Lone Ranger, assisted by the improbably devoted Tonto, blasted away with silver bullets and inspired them to cheer and wrestle alternately. English programmes were slow and lacked action. Muffin the mule playing the fool and Billy Bean with his infernal machine were beneath them.

The summer hummed on with the pace and grassy sweetness of the gardener's lawn mower. Mum bottled fruit and made jam. She pickled eggs in brown liquid, stored in large jars. She was endlessly busy and to rationalise responsibilities had made the garden over to Granny. Granny's stumpy frame in frock, boots, straw hat and gloves, was a familiar figure in the garden during the better weather. She found work for the boys: a bob for weeding, a tanner for picking a cauldron of blackcurrants. The boys pedalled away to spend their earnings on hooks and floats, stink bombs and sherbet. Miriam who was older ignored them and tended the little fat Welsh Mountain pony which nipped and bucked and fought its way round the paddock, or she pedalled off to meet with unknown people.

Pip revelled in the freedom of a full-blown English summer. He caught sticklebacks and leeches and kept them in an aquarium. He went for miles with his butterfly net and added to his collection: speckled wood, wall, tortoise shell, red admiral, orange tip and large white. In an old satchel he kept a rattle of pots and potions, he ran so wild that Mum began to worry about him. He found hedgehogs and fed them on bread and milk, sometimes enriched with hens' eggs. He caught a new slow worm and kept it in a tank and when it gave birth to a dozen or more miniature slowworms he fed them on chopped, white slugs. The season was over for birds' nests but he hoarded the few he collected in the spring, setting them carefully in cotton wool.

Members of the gang came regularly to Sunflower Cottage but days on end would limp past with little happening. Sometimes they went off on their bicycles and swam in the dark, weed-entangled waters of Earlswood Lakes. There was a floating platform and diving board in the middle of the lake. The boys swam out to the platform and dived into the thick water. They needed pluck to climb to the high board but from there they could see all round the lake, the people sitting on blankets on the grass bank at one end and the men and boys fishing at the other. They leapt from the high board, as high and far as they could, to relish the whirl and flash of flying before crashing into the water and sinking low into the opaque, silent depths. When their feet hit the mud they pushed off and flew like corks into the sunlight.

The gang fished for roach and gudgeon. They used bamboo rods, reels and heavy lines. They baited their hooks with red worms from the compost heap and sometimes caught perch. Perch lived by more ferocious rules, and snatched the bait, arching their hard scales and thorny fins in anger when caught. There were also carp, powerful and uncatchable fish which came from ancient worlds of sunken monasteries and fathomless depths, that drifted mysteriously and silently around the lake. Carp distained the boys' bait but sometimes in the summer months they would rise to the surface and glide around the surface, thrusting their dark backs above the water line to taunt the boys and display their immensity. Keith said there were pike in the lake, pike had teeth and could bite through your line if you hooked them but they never encountered any pike.

The brothers dug a pond so that they could replicate the pools where they fished. The rest of the gang sometimes helped but their enthusiasm waned when they realised that they were digging a pond and not a trench for combat. The pond grew into a kidney-shaped depression in the clay which was filled with water from the garden hose. They planted weed and went fishing to stock it. When this project was complete they wondered what to do next.

'Let's go to Lamer House,' said Keith. 'It's been deserted for ages and we might be able to find a way in and see if they have left anything behind.'

'What about the dogs?' asked Laurie.

He had a fair point. Fear of the guard dogs, more than the uniformed security man, had deterred all previous plans.

'My Grandad used to work up there when it was a great house,' said Ivan. 'He had this story which he heard from his Grandad about the Old People. The Old People came first, before anybody else, to Whitebushes. There were no roads then, everywhere was dark bushes, they followed the Earlsbrook until they came to the place which we know as the White Bridge. They left the brook and came to live here.'

Tom found it difficult to conceal his irritation. They had heard Ivan's story about the Old People several times before. It went down well late at night around a camp fire, when the naked fire and the primitive backdrop of dark bushes could put the wind up even the stoutest-hearted boy, but now it had no relevance.

'That's all very well,' he said, 'but how do they help us prepare an attack on Lamer?'

'We could enter the stream by my Grandad's old house, by the White Bridge, and follow it round behind Lamer. Just like the Old People did - but the other way round.'

'Brilliant!' said Jack. 'I saw this film at the cinema where they set tracker dogs after this man, but he got in the water and the dogs couldn't follow the scent.'

'Exactly!' said Ivan who hadn't thought of this but was pleased to claim the credit.

Tom laid down the battle plan and ten minutes later the gang marched down to the common. They called in at Ivan's house because Ivan wanted some supplies. While they waited for him, Grandpa Hobbs was in the garden and looked up at them. There was something in that look that made them feel uneasy, as if he knew where they were going and something about what they would find there. They carried on up the lane to the White Bridge. There was a good deal more crashing and splashing about entering the stream than they had anticipated but once in the water they tried to emulate something between commandoes and Old People and moved as quietly as they could. Pip's wellies were soon completely full of water and he was accused of squelching too much. The journey along the stream was more laborious and slow than they had anticipated. It was difficult to see exactly where they were heading because the banks were high and covered in vegetation. Every now and again they stopped while Tom climbed up a bank to peer through and fix their position. At last Tom decided that the place was right and they all scrambled up the bank to lie on their bellies and peer through the stinging nettles. There was an old brick building in front to them and around it were a number of standing stones. Tom motioned them forward and they crept forward on their hands and knees.

'It's the chapel,' whispered Ivan.

The graveyard was overgrown but the headstones were visible. The boys made their way to the front of the building. It was smaller than any church they had known, only a fraction of the size of St John's. The big house was clearly visible down a yew avenue. Over chapel and house alike, there was an air of desolation and decay. Tom pushed at the old door of the chapel and to their surprise it creaked open. The building had little enough to interest. The wooden pews had been stripped out and the glass taken from the high windows, leaving behind empty sockets. The walls were pock-marked with holes where things had been removed. One great stone slab still hung on a wall and on it in black letters was the following inscription:

*In memory of Major General Apsley Cherry-Garrard, 1833-1907*
*A great soldier and gentleman.*
*A beloved husband and father.*
*'Shout while you journey home!'*

'He was the old gentleman who lived here at the same time as my Grandad and his Grandad too,' said Ivan. The fact that he was a general, and that Ivan in some way had contact with such a wondrous character, was impressive. Pip wondered if the old gentleman he had met at the Natural History Museum could be the son of Major General Cherry-Garrard. There was also a box-like structure, which Ivan said held the bones of some of the Old People. On it they could make out some writing.

*Sum Quod Eris*, read the letters on the box but none of them knew what it meant.

They headed out of the chapel. The outhouses were not secured and they could wander freely through them. They came to an empty room with a cold fireplace in the corner. High above it were beams and they could see a number of swallow nests perched on the beams. Birds flew in through the open door and flitted through the beams before whisking back through the open door.

'Too late for nesting,' said Keith, 'they're getting ready for the winter journey south. Come autumn they'll go all the way to Africa.'

'My Grandad used to visit this room,' said Ivan. 'His Grandad used to have the stove going and kept things for the garden in here. The General's son used to come and talk to him.'

Pip watched the swallows, mesmerised by their garrulous comings and goings. If they went all the way to Africa how would they find their way back? He looked round the remains of the room. In one corner there was a small gap and when he looked down he could see that there was a room beyond. He speculated as to whether or not he would be able to crawl through, if he made himself really small.

'That's the coal chute,' said Tom. 'The coal was tipped down there to supply the kitchen. I don't think we could get in that way.'

The main house was secured against intruders and walking around the outside offered little of interest. They were not sufficiently bold to chuck stones at the windows and the attack drifted into little more than a bit of wandering and gawping at the great dead shell of the house. Pip looked through a window and saw the empty kitchen. He caught sight of the far corner and worked out that the coal from the chute would have come in there. The others wanted to move on and urged him to keep up.

They strolled back down the old Southern Avenue, past the wooden hut of the watchman and his infamous dog, pleased that there was nobody on duty. At the end of the avenue there were two trees. One was an old apple and they could see fruit forming. Some of the boys climbed up and tested them but they were not ready for scrumping. They plucked the odd green fruit and flung them at the heads of the boys in the other tree.

Those who climbed into the other tree were more fortunate. Their tree was covered in a dark, purple fruit somewhat resembling a blackberry. Although this fruit ran with juice there was none of the sweetness of blackberry. The fruit was sharper in flavour and the taste quite different. It also proved to be too soft to be an effective missile. The juice left their hands streaming as though covered in blood. Soon the boys were all duly blooded. Tom felt that enough was enough and called them to order. They formed up and marched down the lane and on to the White Bridge. Somebody added to the bloody triumph of the occasion by singing out:

*'itler, he only 'ad one ball!*
*The uver, was two but very small…*

They marched and sang, over the White Bridge and down into Whitebushes. There was something comforting about great wars that had been, as comforting as the smoke from Grandpa Hobbs's pipe or Mr Hobbs's woodbines. The march of the Canadians down the old Canadian Road swung through Pip's imagination. They were ever loyal, ever tough, good men for a tight corner. Due to men such as the Canadians, Britain and her Empire had won and the malice and power of the enemy only served to make that victory the sweeter. Thus it always was but would it always be? The past was a safe place where Hitler was always vanquished and would never be able to raise a threat to their security. The boys could base their play on the war and relish the story the comics told:

'Surrender or die British pig dog.'

'Not likely Fritz!' yelled back Hurricane Jones. 'You come and get us, Gerry!'

Hurricane Jones and Digby, his loyal Sergeant, lay back in the trench, grinning at adversity. Overhead a British spitfire spotted the comrades, ready to make their last stand and dived down into the oncoming Germans. Bang, crash, rattatt att.

'Ahhhh…' yelled the Germans as the explosions burst around them and flung them into the air.

'By golly,' grinned Hurricane. 'That was in the nick of time. For a minute there I thought we might be in a bit of bother.'

But the adult world was not secure and permanent. The talk was of a Cold War, because the Russians came from the cold. They had surrounded the Germans in the bitter cold of Stalingrad and then set about to murder the lot. The Cold War was not a hot war. There would be no deserts and men in shorts fighting 'Wommel', no Lawrence with his Arab headgear teaching Arabs to kill Turks, no guarantee of inevitable victory. The Ruskies could launch rockets into space and they had an 'H' bomb that was pointed at London. This bomb was so powerful that, if launched, everybody in Surrey would be burnt to ashes.

'We've got a bomb too,' said Ivan. 'If the Ruskies attacked us, we would attack them right back.'

'Yes,' said Keith, 'but where would we strike? Russia goes on forever.

You could kill a million and they wouldn't care or miss them.'

There were other matters concerning the Russians and their fellow conspirators, the Chinese, that threatened and disturbed the natural order of things. The teachers at school, and most adults, thought the Russians were cruel and horrible people who wanted to force on the British a terrible way of life. Dad and some other adults said this was all rot and everybody in Russia was happy and wanted to be friends. Tom, Jack and Pip were confused by all this talk but most boys kept the Russians under suspicion and the general opinion was that the Ruskies were not to be trusted. In the gang's judgement of such matters, one of their particularly damnable crimes was that they made their women fight as soldiers.

'It isn't natural,' said Keith. During the war his mum had driven a lorry and could swear and row along with the best of them, but fighting was something else. 'You can't fight a woman,' he went on, 'but with the Ruskies they all look the same and you don't know who you're killing. So you hesitate, but then they're ready for you and cut your throat.'

Pupils, teachers, doctors, postmen, soldiers were all male. Once, a female teacher arrived at school and although probably no more than twenty-eight had acquired the sobriquet 'Old Ma Harvey'. Her stay was short-lived and her departure hastened by rumours of a liaison with a certain Mr Darkwood. They had been seen kissing! That anyone should want to kiss Old Ma Harvey and that she should submit to the embraces of the beetle-browed flogger of the B stream, so disturbed Pip's sense of the order of thing that he chose not to believe it.

Sometimes they talked of girls but their knowledge of them was scant.

'What about Sheila Kitby then?'

'What about her? I never see her.'

'Yes, you do, she goes round to your house to see your sister and you done 'er in the rabbit hutch.'

What could it mean? How was she 'done' in the rabbit hutch and what was done?

In the boys' world view, girls should ape their mothers. They wore print frocks with flowers on them and tied their hair back. They wore ankle socks and sandals and usually carried dolls. They did baking with Mother and learned the arts of housekeeping and womanhood. They were bewildering and held a strange power, to be adored in secret.

Other female images only perplexed and confused the boys. At the cinema, blonde and gleaming in make-up, female figures, unlike either mother or sister, flashed across the Atlantic Ocean and deep into the boys' imaginations. As far as the boys were concerned, women had to be either guarded and guided or ogled obscurely. Meanwhile the mums cleaned the linoleum, went by bus to the shops and had their hair permed.

The idea of females fighting disturbed the natural order of such things, but the menace, in the form of Nicky Clough, was unavoidable. She was at the secondary modern and just that little bit older than the boys in the gang. She showed evidence of physical maturity and had swelled to monstrous proportions through a compound of national health orange juice, free school milk and unrationed sweets.

Nicky Clough lurked about the railway arches and the road that led to the safety of the common. It was as though she inhabited some unseen cavern in the arches, a Grendel-like figure, appearing from nowhere to torment them. She daubed insults on the walls of the arches and her raucous voice pursued them in echoing tones when they rattled through on their pedal bikes. She thought herself as good as them, as tough as them, she wore trousers and cropped her hair and was that strangest of creatures, a tom boy.

From humble beginnings her power grew. Her insults became more challenging and she acquired a small female following. Ivan was first to voice the unthinkable.

'My sister says Nicky Clough wants to be leader of our gang.'

'Can't,' said Tom. 'She's a girl, I can't fight girls.'

Tom was the warrior-leader of the tribe, there could be other warriors but there could be only one leader. It was the ancient lore that the leader could be challenged in his right to leadership through his skill in wrestling. There were token challenges, made more in fun and foolhardiness, but only Keith ran any chance of really challenging Tom. They would come together and then grip and hold. One boy had to force the other to the ground and then pin him down by sitting on his chest. This point marked the end of the combat. Keith could run Tom close but Tom always pulled it off, it was a mind thing as much as a corporeal one and in the end perhaps it was the way that Keith wanted it.

But the matter of Nicky Clough did not end there.

A message was daubed on the walls of the arches for all to see, a challenge that could not easily be ignored.

'TOM IS AFRAID TO FIGHT. NC'

It was scrubbed off but once stated it could not be forgotten. From time to time the motley crew of girls would turn up near Sunflower Cottage repeating their taunts, being disagreeable, swinging on the gate and generally calling attention to themselves.

Tom adopted the only possible stratagem, which was to ignore them and hope that they would go away, but they didn't.

Then on one dreadful day it happened. The gang had just set off on one of its route marches, marching to defend their territory against the new threat from the ever-present but invisible enemy. They marched determinedly out of the gates with the intention of heading down the Magic Pathway in quest of adventure. As they drew near to the Pill Box and the entrance to the pathway, the lane became narrower and bushes grew on one side and on the other there was a wide tangle of dock and nettle, couch and briar. Nicky Clough and her motley company must have been hiding somewhere because they appeared, bold faced and sneering, to block the passage of the passing army.

Tom, at the head, was dumbfounded. He could not get round her and he couldn't bundle her out of the way for fear of touching her. He had to stop. The unthinkable happened. Nicky Clough went up to Tom, far too close for comfort. She looked him straight in the face and said:

'Ere you, Tom, or whatever your name is, I challenge you for leadership of the gang.'

Tom hesitated, 'I can't fight you,' he responded, almost apologetically, ''Coz you're a girl.'

This had the effect of infuriating Nicky Clough further, 'You have to!' she screamed, 'It's the rules!'

It was the rules, they all knew it. Ancient lore had been evoked, the Achilles heel of the constitution probed and the unforeseen circumstances, which threatened to destroy not just the gang but the very balance of empire and all, exposed. Still Tom hesitated. To fight a girl was wrong, even if she wasn't a real girl. Not to fight would lead to further cries of cowardice. To fight and lose was a real and most dread prospect. The boys struggled with these thoughts and for all their defiant words they knew that the great spotty body of their common adversary was capable of hidden, terrible powers.

Yet in these dark moments, the conviction seemed to transmit itself between the boys that there was no other alternative but for Tom to chance it all in single combat.

Nicky Clough's unrelenting flood of verbal abuse gave way to physical action and she started to push Tom in short, two-handed thrusts, goading him into fight. With each thrust, he was pushed back, his face white and drawn as the emotion and the anger grew in him.

'All right, then let's fight.'

She threw herself at him, grabbing at his head in an attempt to envelop him and to use her great weight to force him to the ground. He staggered under the weight of the assault and for a moment they were locked, pitted in contention, while the world stopped and held its breath. But then he summoned all his strength and thrust her to one side while kicking her legs from under her. The effect was devastating and she was flung to the side of the lane and sprawled in the stinging nettles. She lay in abject defeat, stung and humiliated, wailing her protests and choking over her outrage.

Victory seemed total and they marched down the lane, with banners flying high and their unbroken voices raised in a carol of triumph. But for that small column of boys that encounter was the herald of many challenges to their values in the world ahead. As they passed the concrete pill box and filed down the Magic Pathway, doubt hobbled behind them and stayed a close companion on that journey and all that followed.

# CHAPTER TWELVE

## *ANTARCTIC LETTER SIX*

*Discovery Hut, November 2 1911*

*Dear Ida*
*We are on our way! My pony is called Michael and he and I work*
*well enough together, he is one of the better of the bunch. Birdie has*
*a more difficult charge in Victor, and Bill makes a good fist of old*
*Nobby, who survived the rigours of the depot journey. The worst of*
*the bunch is Christopher but Titus keeps him to himself and somehow*
*or other manages the little beast. In all there are nine ponies of*
*varying quality. We shall see how they perform out on the Barrier.*
*Camp One, November 3*
*Old Ponting and those that remain at the Discovery hut waved us*
*off yesterday. We've been filmed for the last time and we are now truly*
*alone. Ponies going well enough although the keen wind troubles*
*them, and old Nobby and Christopher can be handfuls.*
*Corner Camp, November 5*
*We have come across Day's motor abandoned. This is a great*
*disappointment. Teddy and Lashly are pushing on with the one motor*
*and man-hauling where necessary.*
*Strange to think that the bonfires are burning in England.*
*November 6*
*The surfaces have been wretched and now we are delayed by a*
*blizzard. We keep our spirits up as best we may but we are behind*
*schedule and in need of some positive news.*
*November 9*
*We are back on the march but have come across the second motor.*
*We all knew that this was inevitable but somehow hoped that it would*
*last for longer than this. Teddy left a note to let us know that, he,*
*Lashly, Day and Hooper are pushing on manhauling and will keep it*
*up until we catch up with them. We have all given so much to these*
*machines and invested so much hope in them but now we must depend*
*on blood and sinew alone. At least the surfaces are not too bad and*
*the ponies are making progress.*
*One Ton Camp, November 15*
*Captain Scott says that we must rest the ponies here for one day.*
*In general he is pleased with their progress but he has decided not*
*to attempt to take them up the glacier, which is good news indeed.*
*It is the success of the dog teams that has surprised us all. Maybe*
*Amundsen was right to take so many? On the other hand they need*
*the skilled driving of Meares and Dimitri and can only take a limited*

*quantity of gear forward.*

*November 21*

*We have caught up with the motor party who worked splendidly since the failure of the second motor. They all look done in by the effort. Maybe Teddy has overstretched himself and in so doing has reduced his chances of being selected for the final Pole party?*

*We have been over some pretty bad surfaces and the ponies are suffering.*

*Middle Barrier Depot, November 22*

*Day and Hooper have been sent back. It will be hard on them as a two man team is vulnerable on the Barrier, but the return route should be familiar and shouldn't give them too much trouble.*

*Poor old Jehu was shot and fed to the hungry dogs. He was failing fast and the dogs need the meat. Polar exploration is a rough business.*

*November 29*

*It has been heavy going and the surfaces have been unspeakable. Chinaman has been shot and we have had pony meat in our hoosh to raise morale. We are now beyond Captain Scott and Bill's previous furthest south record which is something of an achievement.*

*Best of all we have had a glimpse of the mountains away to our west. Maybe we'll make it after all and get there ahead of Amundsen?*

*December 7*

*Our luck with the weather has been preposterous and we have been held up here for days by gales and foul weather. Christopher and Victor have both been shot and either put in a depot for meat or fed to the dogs. I have also lost my little pony, Michael. It grieved me to lead him to his slaughter and although I knew it would always be thus, when the time came, it seemed an act of callous treachery. Bill was kind enough to speak to me about it because he knew how I felt and I do understand that animals must give place to men*

*We have called this camp 'Shambles Camp' and it lives up to its name. If the weather doesn't break soon all our hopes and plans will join Michael in the ice.*

*December 10*

*The weather has broken and we have made it here just in time. The gateway up the glacier is in front of us and all is now in place for this stage of the push. The remaining ponies have been shot and will await the hungry returners. Meares and Dimitri are sent back with the dogs and twelve of us remain for the ascent of the glacier with only our resolve, courage and courtesy to carry us through.*

*I have been moved into the tent with Captain Scott, Bill and Keohone. I trust that this is a good sign and I may yet make the final cut. Birdie, Evans, Titus and Crean share a tent and Teddy, Aitch, Wright and Lashly are in the other.*

*Upper Glacier Depot, December 21 1911*
   *It is not easy to write but I want to record it, in some small part, just as I am now.*

   *We had a rough time getting here but we have made it up through Shackleton's route and are here on the plateau, all twelve of us. It has been a challenge for all of us but nothing compared to our trip to Cape Crozier.*

   *Bill came to see me today to give me the final verdict on what happens from here. Our party of four, with Aitch in command, goes back tomorrow. We are the first supporting party. Two parties of four press on, a final supporting party and the Pole party. Captain Scott, Bill, Titus and Taff Evans will be in the lead party and Teddy Evans, Crean, Birdie and Lashly in the second. It still has to be decided but it looks as though the four in Captain Scott's team will be chosen for the final push to the Pole. Teddy has taken it badly and rails against Evans's inclusion but, for the most part, the rest of us are philosophical and accept the decision. I am pleased for Bill but wish that Birdie could have been included. I would choose Birdie every time. Captain Scott, Bill, Birdie and Lashly, or Crean, would be my final choice for the Pole party. Aitch thinks that the teams should have been thoroughly medically inspected before coming to any decisions but Captain Scott is adamant that he alone will make the final decision on who goes forward and who back.*

   *I have to admit to being pretty down about it all but I have tried not to show it to the other chaps as it would be bad form. Here is a really strange thing, I have had two people come and talk to me about it at some length. The first to come was dear old Bill because he was concerned in case I was upset, which was really decent of him. He knows me better than any man living, especially after our bird-nesting trip. He wanted me to understand that he thought me capable of the last leg but that somebody had to give way. He was more composed than I have ever seen him before and wanted me to understand that he thought that they would make it but if not I was to take the penguin eggs to the Natural History Museum on my return. I am to do nothing rash, I had to promise him on that. I can't quite think what he had in mind but Bill is like that sometimes. He added something really strange about being chosen to go on the last leg. Apparently he was very ill as a young man with tuberculosis and had to leave his work in Battersea to take alpine air treatment. He wasn't at all sure that Captain Scott was well advised to take a man with his medical background at all as there would be damage to his lungs and system which would leave him less than perfectly fit for the greatest physical challenge of all. He looked so strange, and momentarily unlike our dear old Uncle Bill, that I felt moved to reassure him. I have leant him old Saltmarshe's copy of The Odyssey, which Father gave to me*

*before he died and I want Bill to take it with him. I hope that it will
be a talisman of good fortune. He seemed pleased and touched to
borrow it and he looks forward to returning it to me after their march
and when we meet again.*

*My other visitor was Old Titus. He came into our tent when there
was nobody about and just sat down in silence for some time. When
he did get round to talking it was as though he found the words quite
difficult and he seemed unusually emotional for an old soldier. When
he did speak he came straight to the point. I will recreate his speech,
word for word, as best I can.*

*'It was always going to be you or me in the last push to the Pole.
I suppose you know that,' he said. 'Not that I am saying Scott would
only take one of us because we paid into the trip. I wouldn't say that.
But Scott has a reverence for the landed classes and, what's more to
the point, you proved yourself on that daft bird-nesting trip. But one
of us was bound to be picked. In some ways I'm sorry that it's me and
not you. I still have a spot of leg trouble that the Boers were so kind
as to give me, you're younger and more eager. Cherry, it's because
you are younger and have so much of your life ahead of you that I go
and not you. This is a damned bloody business and such a muddle
that anyone leaving now will be lucky to get out of it alive, but those
going further are going to need all the luck in the world. You go back
young Cherry, go back to the hut and go back to our world and life
itself. Go back to your Lamer and the deep lanes of England. Go
back to fish again on the old lake.' He stopped as suddenly as he
had begun and made his way out of the tent. I'm not sure what it all
meant but I am sure that he meant it kindly.*

*I have given away as much as I can in support of those going
forward: Finnesko to Birdie, pyjama trousers to Bill, a bag of
baccy for Bill to give to Captain Scott on Christmas Day, some
baccy to Titus, jaeger socks and half my scarf to Crean, and a bit of
handkerchief to Birdie. When I recall what Birdie gave me on our
winter journey, everything I have in the world would not be enough.*

*So, back tomorrow. This is my summit.*

*Ever love,*

*Apsley*

## Early Autumn 1958

There was a sense of change in England. Some of the old things clung on
but everywhere there was a sense of moving on. Angela and Cherry felt it in
Gloucester Place. Cherry was listless and showed less interest in going out
and about, although Angela was sure that this was good for him. She was
pleased on coming home one day from one of her now rare family visits to
find that he had been out for a wander to 'the Ramp' - he had been to the
Natural History Museum.

'I met a boy there,' he said, 'not a particularly remarkable boy but so full of enthusiasm and vitality, bit of a tonic to see a lad like that. He was there with his mother, they were much taken with the penguin eggs.'

'I hope that you were not more interested in the mother?' Angela liked a little tease.

'The strange thing is, they live near Whitebushes. Do you remember on the other side of the common, there was a scarlet fever isolation hospital?' Cherry thought of Elspeth, dancing at the ball, ever young, ever laughing, never to be seen again. Angela confessed to never having visited the place.

'Well,' he said, 'it's a special hospital for tropical illnesses. I wondered if we might not see them at Dorset House, tea or something like that. I gave them my card, hope you don't mind.'

Angela didn't mind, it was good news. Perhaps he would regain a little of his old self, be less inward looking and forget the fog of doubt and care that threatened to engulf him? It was she who took the initiative and rang the number that had been scribbled on the back of the Craven-A packet.

The first thing that grabbed Pip's attention was the emperor penguin. The great gold and black bird stared blankly from its glass dome on a side table in the entrance hall. Behind the penguin there was a picture of some men rowing a boat through a terrible sea to a place that looked ghoulish and frightening. Pip could scarcely take his eyes off it. Mum made one of her terrible, audible whispers,

'What a spooky old picture, they don't look very happy.'

In the sitting room, Mum admired the china. She caused consternation when she lifted up a full cup of tea and peered at the marks on the bottom. The tea slopped over the rim and ran down the patterned sides of the cup and into the saucer.

'I'm so pleased that you like the china,' said Angela. 'It's a bit grand for here but then it came from our old home, Lamer. Bit of a family heirloom one might say.'

'Oh, yes, Lamer,' said Mum, 'it must have been a wonderful house in its day.'

'Did you ever see a purple emperor?' asked Pip and he thought of the plate in Dad's butterfly book. The purple emperor, with its purple sheen, held a particular fascination.

Mum seemed quite put out by such an inappropriate remark but Cherry took it in his stride. 'I have seen one, once,' replied Cherry. 'I was with my sister but that was a very long time ago.'

'Did you catch it?'

'No, it was just too fast and they fly so high, but I have one in my collection which was given to me. It was old Bill who killed and mounted it. Strange, don't you think, to catch and kill something so perfect and precious? We did those things then without a backward glance and there was always the justification of science. Remarkable how we justify so much absurdity in the name of good old science. Would you like to see it?' Cherry wandered out of the room and Pip followed him.

'Good heavens,' said Mum, 'whatever can they be talking about?'

'I believe that it's butterflies' said Angela. 'Cherry has a butterfly collection given to him by Mrs Wilson. It was part of her late husband's natural history collection. They were very close you know. Cherry never got over it all - you know, finding them like that. I'm so pleased that you and your son could come today. Young company does him good, he's been so ill you see and had to have lots of treatment - but over the last few months he has seemed so much more like his old self.'

'Of course,' said Mum, 'I suppose that it was all that cold.'

In his study, Cherry went to the glass-fronted, wooden cabinet and opened it with a key. Then with immense care and solemnity he drew back the top drawer to reveal a display of small butterflies, to Pip's intense delight. They were lined up in rows, impaled on rusted pins. Pip's eyes were dazzled by the azured splendour of the blues. He was charmed by the names: holly blue, chalk hill blue, mazarine blue and adonis blue. Then he noticed the brown ones, he studied the thin, scratched-nibbed writing and read their names. There were the sturdy little, moth-like ones with tough sounding names: chequered skipper, dingy skipper and grizzled skipper, and slightly larger ones: coppers and fritillaries and hairstreaks, all in shades of dappled amber.

Cherry slid open more drawers to reveal whites and yellows entombed beneath glass.

'You don't see the quantity of butterflies these days,' he said. 'When I was a boy, at certain times of the year, there were clouds of them.'

Pip imagined a myriad of brown and iridescent butterflies swirling and dancing over open fields that stretched away to the dark thorn bushes at the edge of the world.

'These were singled out to be caught and preserved in time,' said Cherry, 'a shame, I always feel, but Uncle Bill justified it in the name of science. At least they are still here for us to appreciate. You were asking about purple emperors.'

The next drawer was thicker than the others and Cherry pulled it back with deferential care. Here were the biggest and the most splendid of the collection. Pip recognised painted ladies and red admirals but the magnificent white admiral and Camberwell beauty he had only seen before in books. Then, there it was, a purple emperor. Pip feasted his eyes on the sturdy brown wings, splashed in imperial blue. The white patterns reminded him of light falling on a woodland glade.

'Look at the writing,' said Cherry.

'Caught by EW, Davos 1898,' Pip read out. 'What does Davos mean and who was EW?'

'EW stands for Edward Wilson but we knew him as Bill. Davos is a place in Switzerland. Uncle Bill went there as a young man to take the cure, because he was ill with tuberculosis. He was meant to sit on a veranda and breathe in alpine air but that was not Uncle Bill's way. He walked, climbed, caught butterflies and collected specimens. It was taking the cure in Switzerland and Norway that gave him the taste for snow and ice. It was the purity of it, you see, that appealed. Snow and ice has him now, preserved and held like his butterflies.'

Pip didn't understand but Cherry was not talking to him but somebody else. Yet he remembered Dad's stories and what the boys had said about that expedition at school. He knew that these men were heroes and that they had done something truly heroic.

'Wow,' he said, 'you knew somebody really famous.'

'Dear old Bill would have been quite cross to have been regarded as famous, he was far too personal a man for that. He was in his twenties when he collected these butterflies, long before I knew him. He was a young doctor then but he worked too long and hard in the back streets of London and became ill so had to give up his career. It didn't concern him because he was really a naturalist and artist. Would you like to see one of his drawings?'

He took down a folio and, with slightly shaking hands, opened it carefully. Pip saw a pencil drawing of baggy figures walking away into the distance. The pencil lines were soft and clearly the product of great effort, the paper yellowed and slightly crumpled.

'Mrs Wilson gave me this to keep,' he said. 'She has so much of Bill's work and he did this one when we were out on the Barrier. He had to take his glove off to sketch and could only work for a minute at a time. The detail is magnificent, it brings it all back much more than photographs. That's Bowers with his back to us, leading his pony. He's caught Birdie superbly, that's him all right. I've followed that shape and that hat many a time. I've even followed it in my dreams.'

'Why did you follow him?'

'Bird-nesting' said Cherry and chuckled. 'I followed him for the weirdest bird-nesting expedition ever known in the long history of bird watching and egg collecting. We were collecting emperor penguin's eggs like the ones you saw in the Natural History Museum. The only problem was that we had to set out in mid-winter in the Antarctic and live out in the darkest and rawest conditions for weeks'

He closed the folio and carefully put it back on the shelf.

'I have some birds' eggs if you would like to see them,' he said.

'Did you bring back an emperor penguin's egg for your collection?' asked Pip.

'We managed to get three complete eggs back,' said Cherry. 'I'm afraid many others were broken because we had the most terrible climb back to our camp and then a ghastly journey back through the Antarctic night. Science is only interested in the perfect specimens. I gave those to the Natural History Museum - though they were hardly gracious about accepting them'.

'You could have kept the shells for your own collection, even if they were a bit broken,' said Pip. 'I found a willow wren's nest in the long grass and I took one egg for my collection. When I tried to blow it the shell cracked.

I still have it, but I had to arrange it in cotton wool so that it looks whole.'

'My sister and I did much the same thing with a shrike's egg,' said Cherry. We found the nest high up in a hawthorn hedge and I had to scramble up to get it but it didn't blow well.'

'Where did you find the nest?' asked Pip.

'It was near Lamer where I once lived. I believe you know the house?'

Pip felt a pang of guilt as he remembered the gang's expedition and how they had gone in the chapel and how he had stared down the coal chute and into the kitchen. He was relieved to recall that Cherry couldn't know about it.

'There's a boy in our gang called Ivan Hobbs,' said Pip. 'His grandfather used to work up at Lamer. He says that there's an outdoor room that Mr Hobbs's father and grandfather used to look after and the swallows come back every year to nest high up on the beams.'

Cherry looked wistfully at the boy in front of him. He remembered when his family had first come to Lamer in the carriage. They had crossed The White Bridge, by Hobbs's house, and a boy had stared rudely into the carriage and looked straight at him. It was so long ago but at that moment it seemed near. Angela came quietly into the room to inform Pip that Mum was ready to leave to catch their train.

'Do come again, we'd love to see you both,' said Angela.

On the way home, Mum was curious to know what Pip made of it all. He was agog with interest for all the bugs and animal things but what did he make of the man?

'I think that he's been very unhappy,' said Pip 'and I can see why, he had to witness the death of some of his best pals ever, but I can't quite see why he has stayed so sad. If I had a fantastic collection like that I could never be sad. I would have kept those penguin eggs even if the shells were a bit broken.'

September came round again and the children had to return to school. The last sun of summer mocked the heavy school clothes of autumn and all smelt uncomfortable and out of place. The boys could still swim at Earlswood Lakes and butterflies still danced on the sedum but their time was short. People talked of an Indian summer and Pip wondered what it meant. He saw the Red Indians bare-chested, running through the red autumn leaves.

Tom now went to the great grey grammar school three miles away. He left on the first morning on his bicycle sporting a new cap complete with white swirls and wearing a heavy navy blazer, short trousers, and long navy socks tied below the knee with his old cub garters. Keith and Ivan and several of the other boys went to the nearer Earlswood Secondary School where they wore jackets and long grey trousers. Jack was in his last year at Big Johns and was the next in line for the eleven plus but Pip, bringing up the rear, was only in his second year at the Big Boys. He still yearned for the Infants and the long-legged and bewildering girls of his innocent years, but now he was an experienced and established denizen of the strange world of the Big Boys. Tom's early advice on how to fight a gang need no longer be practised on a regular basis.

Mum missed the summer and the rush of children about the house, the way the stairs rattled with their endless ups and downs, somebody running in the back door with a cut finger, the little tiffs and laughs, the sun and the rain and Pip with some wonder in a jam jar to show her. She would have held back the future if she could. She waited at home while the world in its seasons careered onward and the children grew older - until the time came for them to leave and start new homes of their own.

Imperceptibly the world was moving on. Television aerials sprouted on roofs and people were gripped by new delights. There were drama episodes with flapping scenery, cartoons with talking animals in human clothing and other hitherto unknown treats. Along with the children's programmes and the family entertainment jostled the News. Prime Minsters talked and khaki–clad soldiers, with heavy boots, stiff gaiters and berets like plates, stood smoking and waiting to be packed home from pink places on the map. Strange music sprang from radios and records could be bought with pocket money. Telephones rang, engines roared and domestic machinery whirled. Mr Hobbs bought a second hand car and the family went out on Sunday trips. Cars rolled up sewage hill and Charlie Port in his pony and trap shook his fist and swore at them, outraged that they didn't give him priority on the road. But his own boys had old motor bikes, which they tinkered together from the scrap yard and roared up sewage hill, spilling oil and spitting dark fumes, defiant to mutterings.

The children went back at school and Mum and Granny were alone in the house to get on with the endless round of chores. Granny resented that there were no servants and, puffing quietly, blamed Dad. The wonders of modern technology came to assist them in their labours, including a new twin-tub washing machine which early on caught a long trail of Mum's hair and dragged it and part of her scalp into the mechanised wringer. Granny called it a 'Damned new-fangled machine' and went on doing her 'workings' the same as before.

The season was long past for the nightingale to sing in the Magic Pathway and the swallows gathered on the wires to chatter of journeys far down south in readiness to escape from the bitter cold English winter. Autumn came to Whitebushes and the first cobwebs hung on the turning leaves and with autumn came flocks of fieldfare and redwing to feast on the harvest of berries.

England and Whitebushes looked forward but could not always resist the desire to glance back and wonder if something was lost and left behind in the bushes.

# CHAPTER THIRTEEN

## *ANTARCTIC LETTER SEVEN*

*The Plateau, December 23 1911*

*Dear Ida*
*Yesterday they left us. We gave three hearty cheers to the forward eight as they pulled away. We watched on until they were no more than dots on the horizon. I couldn't be clear about Scott's sledge but the one behind stayed visible the longest. Finally, Birdie turned and waved his hand in full salute to us behind and we waved back and then they were gone. It's a strange thing but I felt that wave of the hand was for me in particular, the final gesture from the comrade of our terrible winter's journey. It also reminded me of you, waving at the quay in Cardiff and I thought of you all so far away. There is much in a wave of a hand.*

*We are all confident that they will make it. The final party only has to average seven miles a day to get to the Pole on full rations - it's practically a cert for them.*

*'Time to get back,' said Aitch.*
*'The sooner the better,' said Silas.*
*'The Tooter the sweeter,' added Keohone and we all laughed.*
*'Peaches and syrup,' I added for good measure and made them laugh the more.*

*We needed humour for the dispiriting task ahead, pulling away from our comrades and over ground recently travelled but as inhospitable and unyielding as before.*

*Tomorrow we begin the descent. I think of Vaughan as I sit here in the tent:*
*'Some men a forward motion love*
*But I by backward steps would move.'*
*December 24:*
*Christmas Eve! I am thinking of you all at Lamer. If I close my eyes tightly I can see it: tree decorated and aglow from the candles, the presents ready and waiting for the morning. Is a present there for me? I suppose Peggy is too grown up now for a stocking? Yes, of course, she is a young lady of sixteen. Time marches on as we march north. I will have missed so much, but there will be other Christmasses and we will share them more closely for having been parted.*
*December 25:*
*You will be pleased to know that we marked the occasion with a good feed of hoosh and plum pudding to follow. We even managed to sing a carol or two. 'In the bleak mid-winter' was a little too close to the mark but 'God Rest ye merry gentlemen' went down*

*well, although our voices had to battle against the din of the wind and flapping from the tent walls. There was a sense of being bound together in one great winter that spread from Antarctica to Lamer, it made me think of our chapel and the times we went as a family with Father. God bless you all on this blessed night and all the people we love.*

*December 28.*

*Struggling down is exhausting work, although we are keeping up a good rate. You have to keep your wits about you as crevasses are a real problem and for some reason poor old Keohone has had more tumbles than anybody else. We have to keep hauling him out. We can't wait to get back onto the Barrier and to a good feed on pony meat that waits for us there.*

*December 31 1911:*

*The last day of 1911! What a year it has been and what will 1912 bring? I think I am needed here and may stay another year. We will know more when Captain Scott returns and I need to talk to Bill about it. Birdie intends to stay, but if he is back in time to get the ship I am sure that Captain Scott will want to return in order to bring the news to the world and to assist in the final payments of the expedition. If he goes then Bill will surely go with him. Let's just hope that it all ties up and that the ship returns as planned and that the polar party gets back in good time.*

*January 2 1912:*

*Today I am 26 years old. We had an extra biscuit to mark the occasion. This is cold hard work but I am sticking to it. We are only a few marches from One Ton, which is as good as home.*

*January 5:*

*God be thanked, we are here at good old One Ton. We have had some decent hooshes well fortified with all manner of things. Now for the final push on to the Discovery hut.*

*Discovery Hut, January 26:*

*Hut Point at last - after 1,100 miles of hard sledging. I take some pride in this. Bill, Scott and Shackleton only covered 700 miles in their Farthest South expedition. It makes me into the real explorer that I promised you I would prove to be.*

*The Hut, Cape Evans February 1:*

*Imagine me now, if you can. I am at Cape Evans, in the very lap of luxury, with the sun on my face. All is so restful and cheerful after the drear silence and monotony of labour on the Barrier. There are the cheering sounds of life: barking dogs, screaming skuas, talking and laughing men. These everyday sounds comfort and remind me that we are part of a living world. At times, recently, I have felt as though I was walking in a dream, but now I am waking up again.*

*We keep a sharp look out for the old Terra Nova. The other day there was a bit of a hullaballoo as one of the men thought that he could see her but it proved to be a false dawn. What news will she bring of Lamer and that great world so far away but still so close to my heart? The anticipation is almost unbearable.*

*February 5:*

*The ship has returned!*

*It's wonderful to see Pennell, the old tub's skipper, and all those familiar faces again. Strange to think they have been back to that other world, which is your world, and so far away from here. They have brought us all piles of letters and news. Every man has his own private stock of delights and grabs as much time as possible to pore over his correspondence. There are letters for those still out on the Barrier which will await their return.*

*I can't believe what I hear and what is said in my letters and what is being done by those terrible Liberals. The country seems to have gone mad in our absence and the rendering of the Upper House into little more than a talking shop is just one symptom of it! Our world down here may have its limitations and denials and it may be charged with constant danger but it is a sane world fit for men who really matter.*

*But no more of this. What do you tell me about George Shorting? Are you really promised to be Mrs Shorting and no longer my Lassie of old? You will forgive me if I seem a little surprised by the news. Here in our isolation we all tend to assume that the world remains as we have left it and don't make sufficient allowance for life back in England moving on. You are a wonderful and dear person and it's right that your life should move on and allow you to find your true destiny. Shorting is a good fellow and has been a dear friend to the family and I am quite sure that you have made a good choice and will be deservedly happy. I hope that the dear Reverend knows what he is taking on and that he is ready for adventures and bird-nesting trips and a whole host of adventures. Shorting is a most fortunate fellow to have found both an excellent prospective wife and a peerless mother for his two children.*

*I will write a separate letter to you both.*

*February 10:*

*We have all been hard at work unloading the ship. This is much trickier and harder work than it sounds. We have been unloading seven mules and fourteen dogs which have been sent to us in case there has to be a second attempt on the Pole. It seems unlikely but they should come in handy in any case.*

*The mules are beautiful animals and their appearance and exotic names speak of India, far from here and so different to all the ice and cold of this place. Titus is responsible for their being here as he persuaded Captain Scott to write to Sir Douglas Haig and request them. He is convinced that they will be more serviceable than ponies.*

*We will have to see if his judgement is right. The dogs seem fit and hardy enough but it will be some time before they can be brought into full service.*

*We must now wait for the other two parties to get in.*

*February 11:*

*The job is done and weary work it was at that, pulling heavy loads twenty miles per day over the sea ice. I'm sorry that there has not been time to write more in this letter. The ship has left temporarily to go and pick up Deb and the Western Party. Pennell will also pick up Campbell and the Northern group. They overwintered in their own hut, near Cape Adare, but Pennell relocated them on his return from New Zealand in Evans Cove, which is 200 miles northwest of here. They have six weeks' provisions, which is more than adequate at this time of year. All being well, the ship will come back with both parties and await Captain Scott's return. So, I have not sealed up and posted this letter just yet.*

*February 16:*

*The ship is back. She has brought back Deb and the Western Geological Party but is having trouble in picking up Campbell and his men in the north. All here continues to be frantic activity, getting rations out on to the Barrier, with no time to write.*

*February 23.*

*Extraordinary news! A dog team has arrived from Hut Point, carrying a very sick Teddy Evans. Crean and Dimitri are with him and they have the most incredible story to tell. After we left them Scott decided, at the last minute, to divide up the eight men into two parties of five and three: Taff Evans, Birdie, Titus and Bill with him, Crean and Lashly with Teddy. God knows what possessed Scott to do such a thing as the tents and gear are all set up for parties of four. It meant that Birdie had a hell of a job to divide everything out appropriately, let's hope he got it right. As a consequence there have been a number of problems for the Final Supporting Party and they have had a terrible time of it.*

*Dimitri has the bare bones of the story. Apparently, Teddy struggled on with scurvy but eventually could go no further. They managed to get beyond One Ton and within thirty miles of the Discovery hut before being held up by storms. Lashly and Crean had a bit of a confab and decided that the only hope was for Crean to go off on his own, with no more than some chocolate in his pockets, and to try to make it to the Discovery hut. They hoped and prayed that there would be somebody there to assist. There was a break in the weather and Crean set off. The chances of him making it were very slim but somehow he did and by greatest fortune Aitch and Dimitri were there with the dogs. Storms kept them in the hut for another day and a half. Eventually Aitch got away and by good luck found both fellows alive. Teddy was very near dead and they say that he would have died if he had had to spend another day on the Barrier. He looks pretty terrible now and is not out of danger. It's clear that he will have to return to New Zealand with the ship.*

*Dimitri had a note from Aitch to tell me and Silas to go with the dogs to Hut Point. Aitch wants one of us to go out onto the Barrier and take supplies. It may well be me as Silas is more useful for scientific work. It would make more sense for Meares to go but his contracted time is up and he plans to go back on the ship.*

*I write in haste as I must finish this letter and see that it is left for the ship, along with the others in this bundle. I will stay another season, as planned, and do not suppose that I will get back to Cape Evans before the ship leaves to make one more attempt to pick up Campbell and the Northern Party before returning to England. So, this may we well be the last letter for the time being.*

*God bless you all and remember us in your prayers.*
*Your own brother,*
*Apsley*

### Late Autumn 1958

Mum and Pip went several times to see Cherry and Angela in Gloucester Place. Angela noted that Cherry was much taken with Pip's enthusiasm for fishing and that he and the boy were increasingly easy in each others' company. When Angela asked to 'borrow' Pip for a day Mum was pleased to consent.

In early October a hire car, complete with uniformed driver, turned up at the house to collect Pip and to take him on a fishing expedition. Pip was instructed to wear old clothes because he would be boating and fishing on the lake at Barn House. The lake and house were owned by the Oates family, who allowed Cherry and Deb to fish there when the family was away.

'We'll have a wonderful time,' Angela confided to Mum through the open window of the Bentley. 'The Oates family befriended Cherry after it all happened. Now that Lamer has gone he misses fishing and that sort of thing. Deb will be there to keep us all company and he has promised to show me over the house.'

The three of them sank into the seats of the Bentley which purred down the drive and away on their journey. Cherry remained aloof and impassive in the corner of the car but Angela kept up a steady stream of chatter, now noting this house, that village, even the vehicles they passed. Pip was most impressed when an AA man on a bright yellow motorcycle and combination approached from the other direction and saluted them as he passed. He hoped their journey would also deliver up an RAC man because they looked even more splendid in blue. It was surely worth belonging to both organisations if only to be saluted by the passing patrol men?

But before this could happen, Pip's worst fears were realised. Slunk low in the purring Bentley, with things flashing by and the unfamiliar smell of leather upholstery, he went from grey to ashen. Angela's voice became remote. The journey became interminable and intolerable in a dulled swirling world that left Pip mute and indifferent to all that life had to offer. Angela recognised the symptoms before the inevitable consequence. She ordered the car to stop and bustled him out. They walked up and down together. At first he felt too groggy to even stand properly but slowly, wonderfully, the misery passed out of his body and he returned to his normal self. For the rest of the journey he sat in the front of the car, next to the driver. He didn't know whether to be pleased by this development or embarrassed by his own frailty. Cherry's silence did little to alleviate his sense of inadequacy but Angela kept very positive, tapping on the glass and smiling reassuringly or pushing back the glass panel to thrust through some sweets. Pip was relieved when it became apparent that the journey was coming to an end,

They swept past the lodge cottage and Pip caught a glimpse of a man with two black dogs. Then the car drove on down a rhododendron-lined driveway. The first sight of the house caused a rush of excitement inside the car. It sat low against the fall of the land and the Bentley seemed to cruise at roof height. Pip saw the red, slanting roof and as the Bentley drew nearer the black beams and white plaster work of the great house appeared. Best of all, behind the house and away into the distance, he caught sight of the lake, mystical, majestic and alluring in its isolation.

A cheerful man in man tweed plus fours came up the grey stone steps and ripped open the door on Angela's side.

'Bravo and welcome, one and all, to Barn House,' said Deb. 'Simply marvellous to all be here together at Titus's old place! Cherry, you and Angela must take a glass of something before I show you round.'

'I would rather have peaches in syrup if you have any,' Cherry remarked. 'Pip and I are here to fish not to mess about with houses. You can show Angela the blooming old house, much more her thing.'

'Typical Cherry,' Deb chuckled, giving Angela a gentlemanly arm for the flight of steps, 'typical Cherry.'

'You see, Deb. He's much more like his old self,' said Angela.

'So it would seem. Very well then, Cherry - you know your way to the boathouse. We'll see you at about 12.30 for a noggin before lunch.'

The driver helped Cherry and Pip with the various boxes and nets and other things that constituted Cherry's fishing gear. Cherry had brought kit for Pip. Pip's own gear was only boys' stuff, a thick bamboo rod and an ancient reel that he had found somewhere, twenty five yards of heavy duty nylon and a large float made from what was allegedly a porcupine quill. The two rods in cloth bags, which the driver handed to Cherry, promised something much more professional and exciting.

They took the kit down the stone steps and past the timbered sides of the house. The lake swung into view, to Pip, used to the small pools and ponds around his home, it seemed a vast stretch of water. It was probably no larger than Earlswood lakes, but it was unknown and most significantly it was theirs alone.

'Gosh, it's even bigger than Earlswood lakes!'

'Well, now, we must not be too dismissive of Earlswood Lakes,' said Cherry, 'after all, my father had them dredged. They were called Lamer Lakes in those days, I learnt to swim there.'

Cherry saw the Old General, in his mind's eye, watching from the bank and smoking a cigar, and then the figure transformed into Uncle Bill eating a biscuit.

'I learnt to swim there too,' said Pip.

'I think that I'm right in saying that old Titus learned to swim in this lake here,' said Cherry. He paused and then spoke as though reciting something: 'Go back to Lamer and the deep lanes of England. Go back to fish again on the old lake.'

'I love lakes, they're just wonderful,' said Pip. 'Is it true about the Old People who used to live by the lake and in Whitebushes before the New People arrived to push them out?'

'The Old People, now who on earth told you about the Old People?'

'Ivan Hobbs, who's in our gang, often talks about them.'

Cherry laughed: 'You will be surprised to know that I was told the same story, a very long time ago, by another Hobbs. It's funny how many things in the past bind us in a common history.'

They quickened pace as they neared the water. Man and boy felt the excitement and the need to be on the water. They walked along the edge to a low-lying boat house with a corrugated iron roof.

'We'll tackle-up here,' said Cherry. 'Best to fix up the rods on land, where we have the space, before we get into the boat. You know what to do?'

Pip wasn't sure he did. Cherry handed him a bagged rod and Pip undid the bow to release it. What he saw left him speechless - a gleaming, varnished, three-piece, split-cane rod, the closeness of the whippings caught his eye.

'It was my father's,' said Cherry. 'The General didn't fish often but when he did he had to have the very best.'

'Your father was a general?'

'He was at the end of his career.'

'Were you ever a soldier?'

'I was once but not a very good one. I never went beyond the rank of Lieutenant Commander and even that was more honorary than real.'

This sounded pretty good although not as good as General. Pip followed Cherry's example and threaded the nylon line through the eyes of the rod. When he came to the next stage, he was surprised to note that there was no float, no split shot, not even a hook. Cherry took a dangling silver spinner with a great treble hook and tied it to the end of his line.

'Which war were you in?' Pip asked.

'I was in what they called the Great War. It was meant to be the war to end all wars, but some things are not as they should be. One man's great adventure is another's living hell. That could be said of Teddy. The Antarctic was a spawning ground for his reputation and the war enabled him to grow his reputation further. What is he now, an admiral or a baron or some such rot? We knew him in Antarctica for what he really was. You can't hide anything down there. Antarctica will discover you, strip you of all sham and conceit and expose your very soul.'

Pip didn't really follow this but he understood the gist. He was absorbed in tying a knot to join his line to the spinner. He was not accustomed to fishing for big fish and his improvised knot involved a mass of unders and overs. It finished with a flourish to form the arch granny of all granny knots.

Cherry laughed. 'Good God! If Bowers saw that thing he would put you in jankers for a week! Have you never tied a blood knot? Look here - this is the way.'

Cherry cut the line and started again and Pip watched with the intensity of a convert. He would never forget that knot nor the kindness with which it was shown to him.

The door of the boat house echoed open and there on the dark water floated an old but perfectly serviceable boat. The paint had flaked and the blue and white lines had lost their lustre, but the name *Terra Nova* was still just visible. Cherry slid the oars from the roof of the boathouse and told Pip to take the rowing position. Pip's role as the oarsman had been established in deference to Cherry's infirmities and in acknowledgement of Pip's training on Earlswood Lakes where many a time he had hired a rowing boat for thruppence. Cherry untied the boat and lowered himself into the stern and they slid out of the boat house and onto the open water.

'The most difficult point of any expedition,' said Cherry, 'is leaving port. I have Captain Scott's word on it and he borrowed the notion from Nansen. Make of that what you will.' He laughed and so did Pip, although he could not quite see why. It was good to be on the lake and to feel the pull of the oars and to share in it all.

Cherry had been sceptical of Pip's capacity to row the boat but Pip worked the oars reasonably well. The boat made its way out onto the lake with minimal advice and guidance. Pip's thoughts and energies were concentrated on rowing and Cherry felt confident to sit back and let his mind drift to his days on the Isis in the college boat. He remembered the great race and the bump, which had been such a triumph at the time. Next he was pulling on the oars of the skiff with Bill, looking out anxiously for somewhere safe to land on Cape Crozier. 'If only they had found a safe landing place would things have turned out differently?' Cherry thought to himself.

*Courage! he said, and pointed toward the land,*
*This mounting wave will roll us shore-ward soon.*

Cherry chuckled and shook his head.

Pip was taken by surprise at this sudden outburst, but he said nothing and rowed on. They came to the middle of the lake and threw out an anchor by a crust of lily pads.

'This lake has them all,' said Cherry. 'great green tench, lurking in the depths, and somewhere near them are carp. Nearer the surface are roach and bream and swimming clean to the top of the water are rudd. You name them and they're here. Today it's the hunters we want, we're the hunters of the hunters. We're after the perch and the pike that come to feed on the small fry. That's where our spinners come in you see, the hunters think the flash of silver is a small fish and when they strike so do we. Now watch and follow my example.'

He slipped back the catch of his reel, securing the free line with a finger. With a flick of the wrist, the spinner flew out across the lake to land in a little splash of sunlight. He waited a few minutes and began to reel in.

'First, let the bait sink. Then retrieve and as the spinner comes through the water it flashes and sparkles and creates the impression of a swimming fish.'

Pip was delighted with what he saw and only too eager to follow suit.

Back in the house, Deb had shown Angela around and the tour had ended in the sitting room. Above the mantelpiece was a boxed pike. Brown and dappled he flicked through the painted reeds, his teeth bared and ready to strike.

'How do you find Cherry?' she asked.

'Same old misery, God knows why you put up with him.'

'No, seriously, I think his progress has halted and he has started to go back. Deb, you see him today with the boy and about to go on the lake and he's at his best, quite the old fellow that you and I know and love. But the blackness is always near him and he feels that it will finally take control and engulf him. He dreams of Antarctica at night and even in the day. Sometimes he doesn't know which world he's really in. The other night I woke and found him fussing round the apartment. Do, you know what he was doing? He was trying to find his kit ready to go off on that terrible winter's expedition of theirs and all the time he was talking to Uncle Bill. It took me ages to talk him out of it. He was really upset about not being able to find the right equipment.'

Deb touched her arm. 'Just a bad dream, I suppose. I'm afraid all we old Antarcticians are prone to it. I get them all the time but I keep schtum about it.'

'No, Deb, it was more than a dream. It was really real to him. He was there in the hut and desperate to find particular bits of kit that he felt would get them through.'

'Well Cherry always took it badly and I know you've had all sorts of worries with him, but I thought things had pulled round.'

'That was the ECT,' said Angela. 'It was wonderful at first and gave him back to us but now I just don't know.'

'We'll have to hope those quacks come up with something else. Don't lose heart old girl.'

Out on the lake Cherry fussed with a bag in the bottom of the boat and Pip was absorbed in fishing. He had felt something heavy on his line and had struck but, whatever it was, the hooks pulled free. The experience had fuelled his imagination and he fished with intensity. Cherry found what he was looking for, an old thermos and two mugs. He poured two mugs of tea and handed one to Pip.

'Here, stop for a quick slurp of hoosh. If you keep fishing so hard you'll wear yourself out - and the fish for that matter. Take it steady, lad.'

Pip took the cup of tea and sat down in the boat.

'Will we catch any today?' he asked.

'Can't guarantee it. You can't be sure what you'll find when you go on an expedition. Yes, I think so.' There was a long pause as if he was thinking about something else entirely, something a long way away from the boat and the lake. 'It's all an expedition really, a journey. We journey from childhood to manhood and then old age.'

Cherry looked across the lake towards the Barn House and Pip knew somehow that he was thinking deeply about the past and looking into a place that only he could see.

'I loved my childhood,' said Cherry, 'the golden days at Lamer when the world was young and secure and the General was there to ensure that all was safe and sound. When he died, my direction was lost. The way seemed less obvious and all was clouded, but then I found Uncle Bill and Bill knew how to balance life and death and to find a way up a glacier with your head full of fear and your heart full of joy. He needed no map, no compass, he was guided by instinct and something almost divine. You could follow a man like that to the very ends of the earth. Only once he needed me - to help him find the way - but I failed him. I tried to find him as best I could but I let him down and in so doing I lost myself.'

Pip was unsure as to what he should do but he wanted to fish and so without another word he cast a good length of line and the spinner dropped just short of a patch of lilies. He let it sink. He started to reel in slowly, working the spinner in short, jerky movements as though it was a fish that was ailing and struggling through the water. His heart leapt. Something held the spinner firm. Weed? No! He struck at a sideways angle. An unmistakable force drove the line away and his rod bent under the pressure. This was no roach or gudgeon to be simply reeled in but a great fish. He stood up, confused as to what to do next.

'Reel back!' said Cherry, 'Play him!'

Pip reeled back and the pressure on the rod and line was less. The great fish ploughed forward in a straight line across the lake.

'Not too fast,' said Cherry. 'You have to make him work for every inch of line. That way you'll tire him.'

By now the fish was twenty yards from the boat and, fortunately for Pip, in open water.

'Bring him in,' said Cherry. His voice was steady and calm while Pip's heart beat furiously. 'Pump the rod up slightly and then wind in the slacker line as you drop it down.'

Pip followed the advice and sure enough - foot by foot - the thing was drawn nearer to the boat. When the fish was twelve feet away from the boat it changed tack and powered to the side. Pip had to swing his rod round in a great arc to follow the new direction. Cherry, in the stern, ducked under the taut line. Pip saw the fish briefly as it swam close to the surface, a dark shadowy shape, the size of which Pip had never seen before in his life. Cherry placed a large landing net into the water.

'He's ready. Bring him towards me and into the net.'

Pip's knees shook in the excitement, he reeled steadily towards the boat and the fish followed.

There was a swiping motion and Cherry lifted aloft, in the net, a great silver, shining fish. Water from the net sprayed and danced as the pike dangled momentarily in the air before being deposited in the bottom of the boat.

'Good show!' Cherry saw Pip's white face staring with amazement at the great fish, tangled in the net on the floor of the boat. He laughed with sheer pleasure, a thin but genuine laugh of pure delight. 'Good show, indeed,' he said and held out his hand. 'The Old People would be proud of their fellow hunter.'

The pike was deftly killed by Cherry and brought back to Barn House with much trumpeting. Deb insisted on shaking Pip by the hand and there was a ceremonial weighing and it was decreed that the pike weighed six pounds. Pip loved the moment and the excitement, but deep down he felt sorry for the dead fish. He wished that it could have been mounted in a box, like the one he had seen in the sitting room. He would have liked to have held the moment tight and to have preserved the fish.

Angela produced a basket to hold it and armed with his trophy Pip enjoyed the journey back. He showed it to everybody and presented it to Mum, who, unabashed by the challenge, looked in *Mrs Beeton's Household Management* for a suitable recipe.

Angela was happy too. She had Cherry back. She had seen his face when he had returned from the lake with Pip and had heard him laugh. It was a moment for her to treasure as well.

# CHAPTER FOURTEEN
## *ANTARCTIC LETTER NUMBER EIGHT*

*Hut Point February 23*

*Dear Ida*

*I start a new bundle of letters  under strained circumstances, I'm not sure that I will have much time to write over the next few days. Aitch and I have discussed the situation and it has been decided that I will take one dog team and Dimitri the other. The plan is to go to One Ton Depot, some 140 miles, and see if we can help the Pole party home more quickly. Captain Scott needs to be back in time to join the Terra Nova for her return journey to England. Let's hope that he carries news of a British triumph that he can report to the waiting world.*

*The Barrier February 26*

*My team is difficult and I struggle to see in this light and conditions. Dimitri's team takes the lead. Progress difficult.*

*February 27*

*Better progress. 18 miles on good surfaces. Dogs pulling very fit and not done up. We came to an old motor, rusting in the snow. I thought of the other motor at the bottom of the sea and it made me think of fossils, old and obsolete and viewed thousands of years later by new people in a new time. It was a strange feeling, but at least the presence of the motor showed us that we were on the right course and there was comfort in this.*

*Bluff Depot February 29*

*I had a bad fall yesterday. My sledge capsized and as I was trying to right it the dogs took off after Dimitri. I missed the driving stick but got on to the sledge with no hope of stopping them and I was carried a mile south leaving most of my gear behind. We managed to get them under control but then had to go back to collect the missing gear. In spite of all this we made 17 miles yesterday.*

*Good progress again today with no major incidents. It's a leap year. Let's hope it's a good omen. Dogs tiring.*

*One Ton Depot, March 3*

*Temperature minus 24.*

*We have made it to One Ton but no sign of our comrades, so they must still be out there on the Barrier. At least we did not miss them on the way out here which would have been all too easy in these conditions and they will have the extra stores we bring.*

*There seems to be a problem with the stores we left here last season. Some paraffin has escaped from the containers and contaminated the stores. This is very strange as the seals are secure*

and there are no obvious signs of leakage. There is enough here that
is sound but I hope that the same problem has not affected the stores
we left along the route to the Pole and upon which Bill, Birdie and the
others will be relying.

We will wait here for the time being.

One Ton, March 4

Temperature minus 28.

Weather a lot worse and a strong wind blowing south. The wind
helped us on the journey out here but will work against us on the
journey home.

Dimitri complains of stomach pains. He is not an easy tent
companion. I envy Captain Scott the company of Bill, Birdie and dear
old Titus.

We are low on dog food as somehow or other it has not been
remembered to depot extra dog food. We will not be able to stay here
too long

March 5

Temperature minus 10.

Today is the first really good one we have had, there is even some
sunshine. We have shifted the tent, dried our bags and gear a lot and
been pottering all day.

The better weather should help the Pole party push north. I wonder
where they are now? If this weather holds we could run south for
twenty miles and if we hold closely to the route out we just might find
them.

I worry about the dogs and Dimitri. The dogs are in poor condition
and need good food and rest but we are short on dog food and must
make sure that we have enough to get us back.

Dimitri is very low and against going anywhere. He seems to have
changed character entirely and I can't see anything of the man who
danced that wild Cossack dance with Titus at the mid-winter feast.
Where is his character and where his steadfastness?

March 6

Temperature Minus 15.

Weather not as good but holding. Discussed with Dimitri the
possibility of a run south but he is in a very poor way. He complains
of pains in his right arm and down his right side. I could leave him
here with his dog team and go south with my team but if the weather
gets worse I might lose my way entirely. If only I could see properly!
Out here is like nothing you can imagine. You could pass a marker
or a sledge within thirty yards and miss them entirely. It could make
matters worse. We are best to wait here for a few days more and hope
that they find us by then. At least everyone knows where One Ton is
and we can't miss them here.

*March 7*
*Temperature Minus 34*
*Strong winds.*
*Thank goodness I decided not to push south yesterday!*
*Dimitri more or less incapable. He is not the calibre of an English gentleman. I will try to live up to Father's expectations. I so wish Aitch was here.*
*The dogs howl piteously to go north.*
*Let's hope the weather picks up tomorrow.*
*March 8*
*Temperature Minus 37.*
*We are in a poor way. We have no option but to head back north as soon as the weather improves. This is a terrible situation made worse by the want of real company. On our winter journey things were worse than this but then I had the company of Bill and Birdie to help me through. Now all the responsibility is mine.*
*March 9*
*Temperature Minus 33.*
*Weather slightly better. We are so low on dog food that we will only just have enough to get us back to the Discovery hut.*
*I must preserve the dogs as Captain Scott will want them fit and well for next season.*
*We leave tomorrow come what may.*
*March 10*
*We are heading north for Hut Point*
*The dogs went mad - stark, staring mad. Dimitri's team wrecked my sledge-meter and I had to leave it on the ground a mile from One Ton. All we could do was to hang onto the sledge and let them go, there wasn't a chance to turn them or steer them. Dimitri broke his driving-stick and my team fought as they went. It went on for six or seven miles before they steadied.*
*March 12*
*Difficult to write. We're struggling to find our way. Dimitri is in a bad state and I'm dependent on him for his eyesight so we have to work together to navigate. At one point we thought that we saw a flag by an old motor but it turned out to be a mirage. We're still going at a good pace but I am sure that the dogs are taking us too far westward.*
*Must sleep now. God help us!*
*Corner Camp, March 14*
*We have been in a tight place but are now finding our way. We know that we have been crossing big crevasses by the hollow sound the sledges make - so far our luck has held.*
*The weather cleared enough for us to see Erebus, puffing out a smoke signal of safety. Dear old Erebus not so much an entry to the underworld as the entrance to new hope and life.*
*We've found Corner Camp more by luck than judgement.*

*March 15*
*Delayed by blizzards but eventually ran into Aitch on the sea ice. A short run tomorrow to Hut Point and a good feed for men and dogs! At least I have delivered the supplies and got both men and animals back alive.*

*Discovery Hut March 16*
*There are four of us at Hut Point: Atkinson, Keohone, Dimitri and myself. Aitch gave us the news that the ship has gone. Gone with it are many dear friends and those of us left behind for another season must continue the waiting and the hoping.*

*One of the many worries is that the ship was not able to get through the ice to pick up Campbell and his party. So, there are two parties of men out there: The Pole party somewhere out on the Barrier and Campbell and his men somewhere in the north. Campbell could dig a cave and build up supplies of seal and penguin to overwinter but the Pole party has no such option and must make it through before winter sets in.*

*Now we sit and wait. Given the position of the Pole party when the final supporting party left them and their average daily travel rate, taking into account loss of time through blizzards and the like, they should make it fine. Captain Scott will be disappointed not to have made it in time to return with the ship but that was always going to be a long shot.*

*March 20*
*There is still time, time for all to be well again. How I long to see Bill and Birdie and dear old Titus. Time passes heavily. Dimitri is restored to health and will return to Cape Evans but now my health seems to be going down and I must stay here in the old Discovery hut. Everything has become such a great effort and I am very tired. Aitch has diagnosed exhaustion.*

*Aitch is planning a rescue attempt but he refuses to take me with him because he says I'm too exhausted. I must wait here. I will stay here with Dimitri, who appears to have rallied completely while I am knocked up by it all and fit for nothing. Aitch will take Keohone with him. Keohone is a good man but they can only man-haul because it is all so late and it will be unbearably cold with just two in a tent.*

*These are desperate days. Oh, God how I pray they find them.*

*March 22*
*The dogs 'sang' - a weird primeval cry. My heart leapt for joy in the hope they saw something. Let it be them. Oh God, let it be them. I ran to the door and burst outside calling and yelling but there was nothing there, nothing. Aitch pulled me back inside. He thought he heard it too but it could have been anything - a seal, the wind beating on the walls, even a fall of ice. God knows.*

*March 25*
*Something knocked on the hut door and rattled the windows.*
*At first I was terrified but then I thought that it had to be them. I*
*imagined Birdie rapping on the windows to make us all laugh. That*
*would be just like Birdie. But it wasn't. Aitch and Keohone heard*
*nothing. They say my nerves are shot.*

*March 27*
*Aitch and Keohone have left. I must keep a hold on things. It may*
*yet turn out well.*

*March 30*
*I grow more and more irritable with Dimitri. Now that he's safe*
*he seems to have not a care in the world. How easy for those with no*
*sensitivity of disposition! This hut is a cruel, cold place and has none*
*of the warmth and comfort of Cape Evans.*

*I pray for Aitch and Keohone. May they find them, may they find*
*them.*

*April 1*
*Aitch and Keohone are back and in a bad way. There was no sign*
*of the Pole party.*

*Aitch spoke to me at length. We assume the worst.*

*April 9*
*Aitch must get back to Cape Evans. If the Pole party is lost, and as*
*Teddy has been invalided home, Aitch is now the senior officer and*
*must take charge. We need fresh supplies and fresh men. He asked me*
*if I could manage here on my own. He wants somebody to stay on the*
*outside chance that the Pole party make it.*

*If the sea ice is good he will take Keohone and Dimitri with him*
*and leave me here with some dogs. I assured him that this will be fine.*

*April 12*
*I am utterly alone and so weak that I crawl on my hands and knees.*
*I can do no more than feed blubber into the stove and lie in my bag.*
*The dogs run wild. I don't have the energy to whip them. The effort of*
*writing exhausts me, but I must write to you, dearest Ida. You keep me*
*sane. I think of Lamer and all of you. We must keep it safe!*

*Am I running mad?*

*April 14*
*I must write. Writing is normal. I note time passing and keep the*
*dates. Faces stare at me from dark corners. I see Father sometimes*
*but that boy is also here, watching and mocking. Do you remember*
*the boy from Hobbs's house, whom I first saw when I came to Lamer?*
*He was there when we first went over the White Bridge and he was*
*there when we failed to wade up the stream like the Old People. He*
*has come to find me out again and mock me. I am not afraid of him*
*and shout at his shadow to go away.*

*April 16*

*Aitch is back with Silas, Keohone and Williams. They will have a go to find Campbell and his men tomorrow.*

*Gran and Dimitri will stay with me. The Hobbs's boy has gone. Is he with you at Lamer?*

*April 23*

*Aitch is back. The mission was a failure. The sun has gone for the last time. Campbell's party may well be able to overwinter. There will be no more rescue attempts. We will all go back to Cape Evans for the winter just as soon as we are able.*

*April 30*

*Last night I had the most terrible dream: I heard the dogs singing, that high-pitched, primeval cry from another world and my heart leaped for joy in anticipation of the one thing in all the world that would bring back the light of life. We stood transfixed and staring at the door. I stood by Debenham and Deb's face was white. 'My God!' muttered Deb, 'it's them'. There was dread in his voice as though he feared the arrival of the five missing men who by now can be no more than emaciated and frozen spectres.*

*I saw the door push open and Scott came through knocking the ice from his body with his mittens and looked straight into my eyes as though he knew everything. Then came Bill, who could never change no matter what, and his blue eyes danced to see us there and he allowed himself a smile of recognition. Then finally Birdie entered, still wearing that ridiculous green hat and he just shook with laughter. All this time I couldn't move. I desperately wanted to rush forward and touch them, to feel their life, but I couldn't move. I counted three. For some reason Taff and Titus were not there. It seemed so real and brought such intense happiness but the moment passed and the door closed and the darkness and the cold returned to claim its own.*

*Will I remain suspended in the thrall of the ice for all time?*

*These are light-denied days. We return to Cape Evans tomorrow. The swallows will be with you now. What do they tell you?*

*I seal this letter now and will write again when we are in the hut. Pray for us Ida.*

*Love*

*Apsley*

## Early Winter 1958

The cold in Sunflower Cottage found its way through the thin walls. The boys tried to light a fire in the grate with newspaper but it flared up and threw smoke into their eyes. The gang still met on Saturdays but some of the magic had gone with separation into different schools. The number in the gang fluctuated. Keith and Ivan still came round reasonably often on a Saturday morning, propping their bikes against the wall, but their attendance was less predictable. Laurie and some of the others also came from time to time. At the grammar school, Tom discovered new challenges including the wonders of rugby football. He thrived on the physical nature of the game and there was talk of Saturday fixtures taking place in the new term. The gang held together but time was against them and the dwindling light and colder days seemed to emphasise that the warmth of childhood was fading fast. If Tom was present then things went on much as before but in his absence, leadership fell by default to Jack, who hesitated to seize command. The boys lounged in the old chairs and read their comics. Their planning was indecisive, they had lost the instinct for marching and their projects were less imaginative. Other schools and other concerns stole their thoughts as the values of primary school were eroded. Pip was keenest, he was desperate to keep the gang together. He missed the easy confidence of it all: the long marches to nowhere, the mock battles and the wonders of discovery. But, in his heart he knew that it wouldn't hold.

Grandpa Hobbs died. The old order of men was giving way and a new order emerging. He was buried in St John's Church, beside his father and grandfather and in sight of General Cherry-Garrard's tomb. Although the boys didn't know Grandpa Hobbs well it was their first encounter with death and they were sorry for Ivan and his family. A link with the past had been broken and something special had slipped away. Ivan's father had no interest in the old times at Lamer and Ivan's knowledge was sketchy. He remembered some things his Grandpa had told him and he could still whistle Grandpa Hobbs's tune.

A film was going to be shown to the younger boys at Old John's. The news flooded through the form creating excitement and anticipation. They said that the film was called *Scott of the Antarctic*. Pip could scarcely believe his luck. He had seen films at the local cinema. Robin Hood with a neat moustache and a jaunty little hat defied all men, leaping onto the drawbridge and laughing at dangers. Captain Ahab had beckoned to him time and again in his dreams but how could a film take place at school? How could it happen outside the dark mystery of the cinema? It was too incredible to be believed and the fact that it was about Scott made the whole thing implausible. Yet he wanted it, most devoutly, to be true.

One morning they were summoned to the playground and lined up. The difference to the normal routine raised the level of anticipation. Mr Rose then led them off on the all too familiar route down the footpath and to the 'Pokey Old Hall', where school dinners were served. They filed into the hall which had been prepared for their coming. The tables had been shifted to the sides and the benches were lined up in front of a metal projector with a huge wheel. The smell of severely boiled cabbage and steam lingered and mixed with the wet scent of somewhat unclean boys. Mr Rose fussed while the boys rushed to sit where they would on the benches. They found that they could slide along them and crash into each other in joyous, chaotic abandon. Mr Rose walked to the front and stood with his back to the screen.

'The film you are about to see...' but the noise and excitement prevented him from being heard. He shouted at them to be quiet and began again.

'The film you are about to see is a classic and should act as a lesson as to how you should behave. Captain Scott was a really great Englishman whose courage and gallantry should inspire you all. He gave his life in the pursuit of a noble and great objective, namely to be the first to the South Pole. Although the Norwegian party, under their leader Amundsen, won the race, the achievement of Scott and his companions was none the less remarkable, particularly as it was achieved by man-hauling and did not require cruelty to dogs. I want you boys to watch carefully and to learn. There are lessons here that will stand the test of time. You boys may one day be called on to meet a great test of national character. You must be ready and prepared to meet the challenge with the manly courage and sense of duty of Captain Scott and his companions.'

Mr Rose waved his hand to the master who stood by the projector. Boys were sent to turn off the lights and the great machine clunked into life. Through the dark a beam of light struck the screen and images and words flickered, music swelled in the hall. The boys fell silent, caught like rabbits in the headlights of the unfolding drama. Wailing, high-pitched and fearful music broke onto terrible white images. There were eerie whistling sounds and vast chunks of insurmountable ice rose in front of the boys' eyes. Then came Captain Scott, strong, determined and re-assuring in his naval uniform. Kathleen stood firmly behind her man and softened the tone.

Pip warmed to the scene with Bill Wilson and his wife. Bill seemed all that he should be, in an idyllic cottage, charmed by birdsong in a British spring, and at one with the minutiae of nature. A bang from Scott's car heralded the intervention of the world of men. Bill must go with Scott, how could a man resist?

'An Englishman should get there first.' Bill's wife clung to him and wept but she knew that he must do right.

Scott needed some luck. A school girl had raised enough money for a dog. Oates stood in the rain waiting for Scott. 'You're on the string,' said Scott. Their luck had changed. Even Nansen with his gloomy Norwegian mutterings about dogs and more dogs couldn't prevent it and when the muscular Birdie walked into the office their destiny was secured. Scott scored the chart with the line of success. 'Well, I'll take you. What do you think of that!'

'Thank you, sir!' said an overwhelmed Birdie.

The quayside was crowded with people cheering; the wives wept and the men cast off into the unknown. A body-blow from Amundsen was delivered to the happy ship: 'Going South!'

English images drifted behind. Penguins, seals and whales replaced them. They were sporting in icy waters; the ship headed south. The ship arrived at Ross Island where they found a place to land, unloaded their stores and built the hut. The hut was a wonderful place that made Pip think of Sunflower

Cottage. Scott's lecture was clear, there were three phases to the journey: Barrier, Glacier and finally the Plateau. On the final push he planned to take four men, but which four was it to be?

The dark winter was bleak but they were together. Puppies were born. Oates and Meares smoked their pipes over the boiler and tended the horses.

'How are they shaping up, Soldier?'

'Not too dusty.'

Pip looked hard for Cherry in the hut, but the glimpse was fleeting and he couldn't be sure. Best of all was the midwinter feast with all the flags at the great table and Scott at the head, Birdie's crazy Christmas tree in the background and the hut echoing to a familiar carol sung in the crusty voices of trusty men, then Titus danced a crazy Russian dance with Dimitri although the athletic little Russian out-danced him. Pip wanted it all to go on and not to change and for sad things not to happen.

Then the film broke, snapping the magic and sending the big wheel of the projector in demented circles. A roar went up from the boys and Mr Rose shouted for silence and the lights went on and they all sat quiet, blinking and confused. Pip wanted the film back, he wanted to see more. Mr Rose conferred with the teacher who was ministering to the projector. The film resumed but wound on to the return of the sun and the departure of the southern party. First the motors departed and then the ponies - with sixteen men all told. The motors failed only four days out and Scott thought of Nansen's prophetic words:

'They are no more than a heap of metal in the snow.'

They had to man-haul. The stove was lit in the tent. The men were bonded in their enterprise their faces blacker but their spirits undaunted. The ponies would not come back. They floundered in the snow, battling against the dramatic scenery, even Oates showed emotion. Then the terrible scene when they shot the ponies. The men touched the horses' faces and led them off to execution. Each shot was greeted by a howl from the dogs and the empty harnesses were cast in a heap in the snow.

'Look!'

The glacier was in sight. They had achieved this first part of their journey.

'I thank you, Titus,' said Scott.

Meares and the dogs went back with the mail. Twelve men - three sledges, man-hauling - Cherry was still with them. They had to toil up the glacier through a stunning panorama of white. Lashly fell down a crevasse but his friends pulled him out. They were together, united in their labours. They shared Christmas in the tent, not the wild Christmas of the previous year, but full of life and joy. Titus joked about brandy and they laughed.

Nine thousand feet up on the plateau, the third and final phase. They pushed on towards their goal but Atkinson and one party of four had to go back. Pip saw Cherry. He stood before Titus knowing his fate.

'I'm sorry, Cherry,' said Titus. 'It was between you and me to go on.'

Cherry took it well but then he would.

Two sledges of four each pushed on. Scott marched against the wind, weighing up the hardest decision of all: 'Who were the best four?'

Birdie's cheery face beamed into the camera as he marched past. Scott was about to make his final decision.

'The last letters go home tomorrow.'

Each of the eight men hoped fervently that they would be included in the final party of five who would be privileged to die. Scott told them his decision. Lashly and Crean had done splendidly but they would go back.

'Lucky devil, Taff,' they muttered.

When it came to Teddy's turn, he responded with dignity but expressed amazement that Scott was taking on five. Pip knew five was wrong. The film didn't state it but he knew it. Five was a mistake. The balance was wrong and Scott had selected the wrong men. He should have taken Wilson and Bowers, not Taff Evans and Titus. The returning three stood on the ice and watched while the lucky five pushed on into the distance, their figures shrinking smaller and smaller until they vanished entirely.

The surfaces were horrible and the worry showed on snow-encrusted faces.

'I 'eals easy,' grinned Evans with regard to his cut hand but nothing was easy. They saw an object and the music confirmed that this was the Norwegian flag.

'Amundsen!'

They assembled for that last, dramatic photo, five men staring into the abyss of failure while a shutter was tugged.

'Great God this is a terrible place!'

January the 18th 1912 and every inch of the journey out had to be re-traced on foot. The Union Jack flew behind the sledge.

'Only 900 miles to go,' said Scott, brightly.

The sledge meter carved the distances but everything was against them. The wind played tricks, Bill wasted time gathering fossils, Oates and Evans were frost bitten. Evans's hand was a blackened claw with rags tied round it. They descended, casting about and looking for food depots. Evans grinned but his face was ghastly and he undid his skis with his terrible hands. He fell in the snow.

'It's a terrible thing to lose a companion in this way.'

A cross confirmed his death. Four men scrambled onto the barrier. The plateau and the glacier were now behind them but they were not going strong and Titus's foot was bad. The light from the primus caught their faces in an eerie glow. They needed fuel but there were eight and a half miles to the next depot.

'Bill, what chance have I got?' asked Titus.

'A very good one,' said Bill. They all knew it was a lie. Titus choked slightly and gulped on the brandy.

When they reached the depot their fuel was nearly gone. Pip wondered how on earth it could have escaped from a perfectly secure can. The tent flapped violently in the raging wind. Inside it, Scott wrote:

'Poor Soldier at the end of his tether.'

'I hope I don't wake up tomorrow, Bill,' said Titus. There was no end to the dreadful flapping of the tent and the wretched faces stayed awake, denied the still of nothingness.

'I'm just going outside. I may be away some time.'

Birdie moved to restrain him but Scott intervened. Titus stumbled into the blizzard, then blankness.

Three men battled on. Bill tried to jettison the fossils but Scott put them back on the sledge. Twenty-nine miles to One Ton where there would be food and oil in plenty. The distances were scrawled on a piece of paper: eight miles, five-and-a-half miles, and four-and-a-half miles. There were eleven miles to go, eleven miles echoed round the whistling tent and their haggard, blackened faces. Pip wondered where Cherry was at that point in time. What was he doing then and what was he thinking? Oriana Wilson floated in a dream across Bill's imagination and Scott recalled a time strolling with Kathleen on a beach. They wrote to the women they loved.

Scott wrote his last words:

'Had we lived, I should have had a tale to tell of the hardihood, endurance and courage of my companions which would have stirred the heart of every Englishman.'

Pip was gripped by these words. He wanted to shout out that some of them *did* live and lived on still - Cherry had lived! The last flame of the primus flickered and then went out. The screen was blank.

The return of the sun came eventually and sledges and dogs went searching for survivors. Pip knew that Cherry was among the searchers. The searchers found a mound of snow and scraped it away to reveal the top of a tent. They found Scott's diary. The film ended with the cross and the words:

'To strive and not to yield.'

The boys filed out of the parochial hall their heads swimming with the wonder of it all but Pip was buzzing, he wanted to know more. Three of the explorers, at least, could have lived if only Scott had made better choices: if he had selected his final team more wisely, if he had chosen four and not five, if they had not wasted time gathering fossils and then transported the fossils on the sledge, if somebody had come out to help them for the last eleven miles. Eleven miles or two good marches would have done it comfortably. Only eleven miles.

# CHAPTER FIFTEEN

## *ANTARCTIC LETTER NUMBER NINE*

*The Hut, Cape Evans, 24ᵗʰ May 1912*

*Dear Ida*

*I have not written for some time as I have been low in mind and body but today is the 24ᵗʰ May and I have to write to you as you will remember that Empire day we celebrated at Lamer not so long ago. It was all so perfect and just as I wanted it to be and Father was so happy. I can see him now on the steps:*

*'Where is the heart of this empire?' he asked the assembled villagers.*

*For him it was in rural England, in Lamer itself, for me it was here in Antarctica with those splendid fellows. Now they are gone it is as though the heart of the Empire, its very best and truest qualities, have been ripped out.*

*I was telling Deb about our Empire Day. He was very amused. He clearly regards the English as eccentric, but we must still hold on to Lamer and its true values. These terrible experiences have taught me that.*

*June 1*

*All hope is gone and we must live out the winter as best we can. This expedition has turned from a joyful journey to misery. We have been tested and we have failed. The bodies of those five great spirits are out there somewhere, no more than frozen corpses. Campbell and his people may still be alive but there is nothing we can do to help them.*

*Aitch, Deb and Silas have all been true and I don't know what I would have done without them. If only I could have been more like them - more of a man. I try to pass the time as best I can. They have encouraged me to work on The South Polar Times and sometimes I can be engrossed in my work and my mind protected, but then I see Birdie's empty bunk, and the pain comes back, dreadful black pain that lies in wait to catch me in an unguarded moment and sweep away any glimpse of light.*

*All is familiar and yet different. I think of Erebus outside the hut, puffing out his clouds of smoke into the darkness. What once was familiar and kindly, that we used as a landmark to welcome us back, has become a thing of darkness. I am Odysseus as he enters the Underworld. How dark a place it is. I draw my bright sword and make a mark in the sand so that it forms a trench and if I have served all the rites and done all things as they should be done, they will come to me from the darkness. First comes poor Bonner and I know it's him because he grips the weather vane he clutched in his descent from the Discovery's crow's nest and he waves to me as he waved to the shore before his fall. Next comes Vince, wailing that the rites have not been done to his body although his cross is still here. His body lies deep in a crevasse, frozen, as perfect as the day he fell. We must honour his cross so that his body may rest in peace. From the shades comes Father. I know* him for his frame and the set of his body but when I try to go towards him he flickers back into the dark. I call to him but he doesn't seem to hear me. He shakes his head at me as though he disapproves of my presence here and withdraws back into the darkness and my soul aches to call him back. Then from the depths of the darkness there is the swish of a drawn sledge and they come resolutely out, dragging a sledge with them. First there is Taff, once so big and strong and sure now broken to a thin shade. Taff wails that he is dead and wants his life back. Old Titus hobbles out of the dark. He stares, says nothing and seems composed. There is just the faintest suggestion of a smile in his face and yet there is sadness about him that is hard to take. Scott stares hard at me and begins to speak but then gives one shake of his head and slides away. Birdie steps forward and he gives me his old, familiar smile as if to say, 'All's well' but starts to fade. I call out to him. He pauses and points to the figure behind whom I know is Bill. He will speak with me and looks squarely into my face. His eyes are shining, but when he starts to speak it all spins away and I am left here with the empty bunks and the sound of coughing from a nearby figure and the hiss of a lamp.

Will I be with them soon, in some twilight zone, dwelling for ever with the shades of Bill, Birdie and Titus? Is Father there too? Oh, Ida, what will they say to me when the time comes? I told Deb about it all. He says that I must go forward and that Bill, Birdie and Titus would have wanted that. It's like falling in a crevasse and hanging on a rope. I must look up and aim for the light. If I look down into the dark I will lose my head.

*June 10*

June is the perfect month in England. What are you doing in England? I see you all in the sunshine. The swallows are with you and have built again in Hobbs's old room. I see them swooping down to enter and feed their brood of calling youngsters. Another week passes and the young birds are out of the nest but calling to be fed and then taking their first flights through the open door. Another week passes and they are flying free and well, building body weight and muscle and feeding freely on the abundant insect life. They will need to be strong to fly south when the time comes.

*June 23*

Last night we held our midwinter feast. Deb and Silas rose to the occasion and sang a number of amusing duets. I announced the latest edition of *The South Polar Times*. It has been well received and Aitch was most complimentary. He says that we will resume the regular lectures of last year.

*July 4*

There are squares of wood boarding above my bunk, on the ceiling of the hut. I have allocated them blocks of time so that I can score in my mind the passing of time. This is a troglodyte world. I can't stop thinking about those strange stories that people from Whitebushes told, stories of an old people left behind and hidden as troglodytes. Did you believe old Hobbs when he told us those stories? I look at those squares and I think of England.

*July 13*

*I can talk to you in these letters because I know you will understand. Deb has something of your understanding and I have talked to him about Father and you and the Underworld and a great many things beside and he doesn't judge me. I never realised before his great strength. Aitch and Silas look for words to explain it all and come up with such vague notions as 'exhaustion' or 'mental fatigue' as though my condition can be diagnosed and cured, but Deb accepts me as I am.*

*They want me to focus on the spring and what we should do and there are long debates about it. It makes sense to see if we can find Campbell's party, who could be alive, and see what support we can give them. But it will be like looking for a needle in a haystack and, if they are alive, it is reasonable to assume that they can get back to us anyway. On the other hand we know the exact route of the Pole party and can retrace our steps until we find them. I can't but doubt that we ever will. It would seem most likely that they have fallen down a crevasse. I pray that God granted them a swift death and that they did not have to face the pain of dying.*

*It's almost a contradiction, but I think we should prioritise Campbell because we know that Bill, Birdie and the others are dead whereas Campbell's team could still be alive, if they have found or made a decent shelter on the coast and have stored enough meat for the winter. However, the majority view will probably be to find out what happened to the Pole party. If this is what is decided I will do my best to assist.*

*August 15*

*I have seen the light. It was brief and distant but I have it and it's coming. God, how welcome is the light! Sometimes I stand and look up into the heavens. Is it His light or the light of life, or both? Any more darkness and I would have run mad.*

*Aitch encourages me to get out and about and plans are in hand for sledging parties hither and thither but I am as weak as water and not up to sledging at the moment. Deb has taken me for some walks. He says that he is going to train me to the peak of physical fitness ready for rowing in Cambridge. He plans an academic career in Cambridge and I must motor over from Lamer so that we can row together.*

*Rowing and England are a million miles away and so far in the past.*

*We have been up to the old Ramp together. I was pretty blown when we came in but I managed it. Aitch is off tomorrow with a sledging party over to Shackleton's old hut. He has left me some pretty clear instructions on the training regime I must follow. They have promised that, if I can get fit, I can be on the search party when they go out to hunt for the Pole party.*

*September 5*

*The chimney caught fire and it took all our efforts to contain it and put it out. If it had taken more of a grip the hut could have gone up like a torch and I would have been with Father sooner than expected. I do not want to be like poor Elpenor - to go on a great expedition and then to die in a silly accident.*

*How fine is the line between the glorious and the absurd!*
    <u>September 12</u>
    *Deb's encouragement, and our walks up the Ramp, are working and I am regaining the will to live. I have put myself on a rigorous course of fitness work. I will make Bill and Birdie proud of me yet.*
    *We have survived the terrible winter. I am ready for what the spring will bring and so seal up this letter to join the others in the mail sack.*
    *Love*
    *Apsley*

### January/February 1959

Christmas was over and a new year dawned for Cherry and Angela. They had spent Christmas day with Ida and her family. The Reverend Shorting, now very old, had retired from the church and his two children had long gone their ways so it was quiet for the four of them. Angela was very fond of Ida and was particularly grateful to her for never reproaching Cherry for the loss of Lamer, although Angela knew that she felt it deeply. Angela was aware of the special bond between Cherry and his sister, and knew that in many ways Ida was grateful to her for taking on the worry of Cherry. The women understood each other, although they never discussed the matter.

The dark days lengthened slightly into the cold of January. Angela welcomed the occasional, thin, wintry light. It brought the drab old building to life. Dorset House was convenient, warm and sensible but she missed the space and the fields nearly as much as Lamer itself. She knew that they had no alternative but to sell Lamer. In the end the old place was too infused with the past, Cherry couldn't escape it there. The doctors had explained that he needed to cut himself off from the past and live in the present. It was an essential ingredient of his treatment. The move to London, combined with his treatment, had worked for a time. In the spring, summer and early autumn, Angela had been delighted to see Cherry more active and happy. He could go off by himself, potter around London, call in at his club, frequent museums or libraries. Losing Lamer was a small price to pay. Pip had played an important part in Cherry's rehabilitation, but since the fishing trip his visits had been much less frequent. He had been up to visit a couple of times and he and Cherry had gone to London zoo and various aquarium places, but Cherry looked worn out on his return from these trips. A darker mood seemed to hold him with the dark nights and the starkness of winter. Something about the winter was all too reminiscent of that last winter he had spent in Antarctica.

'It's just that he doesn't like these dark nights,' Angela said to the emperor penguin in his glass case, as she pottered round the flat, dusting and tidying. She knew enough of Cherry and his illness to know that getting out and about was essential to his well being and decided that she would make sure that he kept his monthly meeting with Deb at the club.

Deb was one of the few remaining Antarcticians with whom Cherry maintained regular contact. Deb with his easy manner and relaxed view of the world was definitely good for Cherry and they could talk about the old days in a way that was not meaningful to Angela, who had never experienced any of it. Talking about the past was one of the things that the doctors had recommended.

'Articulation is the key to rehabilitation,' stated Dr Renwick and it had been Renwick who had first started to unlock the dark cupboards in Cherry's mind which had such a strong bearing on his physical state. After his treatment, the bad dreams had virtually left him. The autumn brought their return and one night in January the dreams trawled new depths. Cherry tossed and turned as though something was burning up his mind. At about two in the morning, he sat up in bed and shouted, 'Had they lived! Had they lived!' His whole body shook and he was sweating. Angela did her best to try to calm and reassure him and when he was calm enough he insisted on sleeping in the spare room. He left her alone and fretful and more awake than asleep until morning.

In the morning she had fussed about Cherry to his mild irritation. There was talk of cancelling his meeting with Deb, but she decided to go with him in the taxi, as far as the entrance to the club anyway. She made some excuse about the need for a particular visit to a particular shop and the saving on a shared taxi but Cherry suspected the real motive. The taxi rumbled its way through the London streets with Cherry and Angela safely ensconced inside. She wore a hat and gloves and he was bundled into an overcoat and muffler against the winter chill. They had made that journey many times through differing circumstances, a grey-faced couple looking out from their taxi window at grime-blackened London. The view out was gradually changing as London put behind it the austerity of the post-war years. A few bomb-devastated locations remained: gaping sockets where there had once been eyes. London was leaving behind the war years. The streets were brighter and more colourful; there were more shops, more movement and more people. Angela looked across to where Cherry sat while he stared steadfastly and inscrutably out of the taxi window. She had known that face for some twenty years. He had never been young in all the years she had known him, but the troubles and worries of his life had weighed down on him physically and he was old before his time.

'Young Cherry was a tower of strength and never happier than when hard at work,' Scott had written of him, dubbing him 'Cheery Cherry'. She had noted the comments in the back of her diary. Cherry was the youngest man on the expedition and they had all admired him. She wished she had known him then, to share his triumphs and tribulations. Perhaps she could have helped him more if she could have understood the nature of his experiences? He didn't like to be asked about them. Sometimes he would speak of them but in the form of reminiscences of the small incidents, the domestic and ordinary, the silly and the comic. He did little to aid her understanding. Why should this man whom she loved now suffer for something that had been over and past for nearly half a century?

Cherry saw the altered people on the London streets. He marvelled that there should be so many of them and all so different and none of them knew him and he knew none of them. At school, at college, in the Antarctic, even at Lamer there had been people but they were his people, people who knew his likes and dislikes his strengths and weaknesses. He mattered to those people and they mattered to him. London was impersonal, a place to hide and be hidden. He was irritated by the sight of them, their strange clothes and strange confidence. A group of youths huddled by a lamp post at the corner of the street, their hair had been slicked back with grease, they wore long jackets and bootlace ties. They smoked cigarettes and shouted and gesticulated as people passed. One of them pointed at the taxi and shouted something but the taxi went past, heading on to its destination. Cherry was unsettled. Who were those youths and what right had they to shout at him?

'They're having fun,' said Angela.

He struggled to understand, the arrogant, self-confident and threatening 'they' who sneered and mocked his world and reached out to some strange, phoney American culture. 'They' thought only of themselves and paraded their sexuality through jazz and jive. 'There's no place like the Antarctic for discovering a man's true nature.' His own words came back to him. 'Be you ever so sure and confident and filled with your own self-importance, the Antarctic will catch you out.'

'They wouldn't last long down south,' he muttered to Angela.

'I don't suppose that they would want to go,' she said, without thinking.

The taxi dropped him off outside the club and a uniformed doorman opened the door. Angela waved through the window. He didn't see her wave. He was intent on his own, shambling progress into the club. Deb was ahead of him and waiting. He climbed out of his armchair and shook hands with his old companion. Deb ordered coffee and they sat down together to catch up with each other's news.

'You look a bit peaky, old chap,' said Deb, 'are you getting enough peaches in syrup ?'

'Sorry, Deb. I'm not quite your normal cheery Cherry. I had a rough night - that same old dream.'

'A down-south dream?'

'I've had the same dream for nearly fifty years but last night it was so intense, so real. We are in the hut, you me, Aitch the whole hut party, and we are waiting, waiting, waiting. The door of the hut is flung open and there they are. Birdie comes in first knocking the snow and ice from him, just as if he's been for a bit of a stroll round. Then in comes Uncle Bill and my heart leaps for joy. He catches my eye and smiles in that way he had of making a fellow seem special. Last comes Scott looking thin and worn but still in reasonable shape when you recall what they'd been through. He looks at me and I know what he's thinking.'

'Well, what do you imagine he's thinking?' asked Deb.

'He thinks I let down the three of them down and that I could have rescued them.'

'Oh, for God's sake, Cherry!'

'Then I have to wake. I don't want to but I have to. I'm like Caliban who weeps to dream some more but can't.'

Deb caught Cherry's arm so that he could feel the reassurance of human presence. 'Cherry, that's enough. Let's get rid of this damned coffee and get a stiff drink before lunch.'

'I could have made it through,' said Cherry, 'if I had gone on from One Ton Camp, killing dogs until I found them.'

Deb cut him short. 'We've been through all this before. You *couldn't* have gone on from One Ton Camp and you know it. There was never any suggestion that you should. Your orders from Aitch were quite explicit. You were to go as far as One Ton Camp and then return.'

'But they were *there*, little more than eleven miles on, emaciated, exhausted and full of scurvy but alive and battling on and I let them down. I had the dogs and the essential stores all around me and I did nothing. Eleven miles, for the love of God!'

'It was a damned sight more than eleven miles and you did all that you could have been done. You had that light-weight Russian with you, he couldn't have gone on. What would you have done with him? Even if, for some insane reason, you'd headed south would you have ever found them? For God's sake man, in those conditions you can pass within a few feet of somebody else and never know that they're there. The more likely outcome would have been to kill off Dimitri and yourself, for no gain.'

Cherry had heard it all before. It was just words, nothing but words. 'They could have lived and if they had lived so much would have been different. That's what Scott wrote: 'Had we lived.' He wrote a reprimand for me. They should have lived and not me.'

Deb nearly knocked the coffee over and looked straight into Cherry's face. 'For God's sake Cherry, chuck it!' he almost yelled, Cherry thought of Bill shouting into his face on the winter's journey, when the gale had blown away their tent, and begging him not to get out of his bag. 'If anybody was to blame it was Scott and certainly not you. Even up to the point when you left them on the Plateau, and despite everything, they could and should have made it home. Bad team selection – five rather than four – wasting time burying Evans, gathering and dragging those bloody stones did for them, not you.'

'Scott had to wrest something from defeat,' said Cherry. 'They'd lost the Pole and wanted to score a point for science.'

Deb sensed that there was anxiety in the club as to what was going on.

'I know, we scientists are to blame. At least I put up with your dotty dreams and even dottier notions. Poor Angela, the girl's an absolute saint to put up with you.'

Even Cherry had to smile. 'Yes, I am fortunate to have found Angela.'

'Fortunate? It's a bloody miracle that a young woman like that should hitch her wagon to an old crock like you. There's no understanding the ladies. Now, let's think about lunch. I wonder if they can offer peaches in syrup.'

February brought a lighter touch to the days despite winter being in full control of the world around. Occasionally, a weak winter sun dared to catch and light a moment, like a candle in a dark place. Angela was still young enough to want the sun and to relish the way that it busied itself into every room, Cherry was seated comfortably in a favourite chair that enabled him to look out on the stone-faced buildings below. He testily refused when Angela had attempted to fuss the blanket around his knees, an unkindness for which he felt guilty.

'Bill would never have behaved like that,' he thought. 'He wouldn't have shown that degree of selfishness and allowed his irritation to be visible.'

'I really don't require a blanket,' he said, 'but thank you for your consideration. In fact, I may go out and take some air. We must enjoy the promise of the light to come.'

'Don't go far,' said Angela. Then, because she didn't want to fuss and was secretly pleased that he wanted to go out, she added playfully, 'no expeditions.'

He was warmed by the sun and pleased by her humour. 'Come with me. We could take a turn round the park.'

They walked side by side. She took his arm and held it tight.

'Why does she care?' He thought to himself, 'This slight, younger woman with all her world untouched and untarnished.' He remembered what Deb had said about her and he knew he was absolutely right, 'Why should she care?'

She thought of what he had been through and what he had done. It wasn't his achievements that impressed her, although he would never understand that. It was his weakness, not his strength, she admired, his courage to overcome the obstacles of his life. Deb would say things like: 'Angela, poor, kind, dear Angela, a tower of strength to old Cherry.' He didn't realise that Angela found her strength *from* Cherry.

The mallards rocked with laughter from across the park. The old winter was sharp and cold but the spring was not so far off and then the prospect of another summer. Angela knew that these days were particularly difficult and that she needed to do something sooner rather than later. Maybe he needed fresh diversion? Maybe he needed to think more about the boy in him and less about the man? Deb had told her something about his last meeting with Cherry at the club. It was not like Deb to fret about Cherry. Deb was always so positive and reassuring. She rang Deb and they agreed to meet up for a little chat. They met in Lyons Corner house like a couple of conspirators. Deb was ill-at-ease, perched on a high stool and trying to take an interest in a plate of fancies, Angela was anxious and clutched her handbag.

'Do you think that we will lose him this time?' she said.

He took his time in replying.

'Now look, Cherry's tougher than you think. He's been crook recently but this isn't the first time he's gone down. He'll get back I reckon - don't you go fretting now.'

Angela relaxed slightly. She was aware that Deb had tried to lighten the conversation by the use of the word 'crook' but she was still wrapped in anxiety.

'The thing is,' she said, 'it isn't just physical with Cherry. There's something else, something that he never confides – not even to me. Deb, please tell me what it is.'

The conversation was taking a turn even less to Deb's liking. He had given up on the fancies entirely and rummaged in his jacket for his briar and tobacco.

'Cherry's just one of those sensitive fellows. He took it all pretty well physically but it was hard, you know, that last winter. He went down a long way and has had to climb back. Every now and then things become more difficult. You must remember that he's tougher than he looks.'

Deb fenced as he started to work the flake tobacco in his hands. Angela saw her opening and wasn't going to let it go.

'What happened down there in that last winter? Something happened, I know, but none of you will tell me. You close ranks. Please tell me.'

Deb stopped working the tobacco and any way it was over rubbed now. He was caught between a desire to protect and a need to keep confidence.

'You know what happened. Scott, Bill and Birdie died and, in the end, that was all that there was to it. We had to wait and see the winter through and finish the scientific work. We knew they were dead and that was a rum 'un. Cherry's sensitive and he cared one hell of a lot for both Bill and Birdie, them having come through with him in their penguin eggs expedition, so the winter was worse for him. That's all.'

'But that's not all is it?' said Angela. 'Something else happened that you are not telling me.'

Deb shrugged his shoulders with the air of a man who has said enough. He fell to filling his pipe. Angela felt close to something that had eluded her for decades and she wasn't to be put off.

'It's revealing,' she said, 'that you all talk about the three that died in the tent and nobody has much to say about Evans and Titus. Why's that do you think?'

'Titus and Evans couldn't have been saved; they died a long way back.'

'Exactly, nobody could have saved them, but the three in the tent were close enough to One Ton Camp to have been saved and Cherry was the one who you chose for the rescue attempt. Why did you choose Cherry, who was the youngest, couldn't see a thing in his glasses and was the least experienced? Why him?'

Deb was on his guard now and realised that the little he had said was too much.

'No, you've gone down the wrong track there,' he said. 'There's no great conspiracy. Cherry was keen as hell to go and we didn't think at the time that they needed rescuing. It was more of a go-look-see. Cherry was young and very fit and he'd worked hard to master essential skills such as dog handling and navigation and he had young Dimitri with him as a dog specialist. We were also short staffed with so many going back on the ship - particularly Meares. The only other realistic candidate was Silas but Silas was needed for the scientific work and, as I have said, nobody suspected that anything was wrong.'

'But you must have guessed there could have been something wrong? From the moment that Crean came back with news of Teddy's near death out on the Barrier, it must have crossed your minds that something could be wrong with the Pole party?'

'All right,' said Deb, 'we were surprised that Scott had split them into two teams of three and five. Looking back that was clearly a mistake. But we honestly thought that the worst affected would be the team of three, because they were one short of a full team. Scott had the strong team of five and he was brilliant on the ice. The Pole party should have been fine.'

'But it wasn't!' snapped Angela. 'Five were too many for a four man tent and he should never have chosen either Taff Evans or Titus. Cherry told me that Titus had a wound from the Boer War and didn't even want to go on. It was all so ill judged!'

Deb saw that her brief show of anger had run its course. He thought her ready to bring back to the boat.

'Believe me, Angela,' said Deb, quietly, 'we did the best we could at the time. Let's leave it at that for the time being. Your tea is getting cold and we mustn't forget these jolly little cakes.' He fussed with the hot-water jug and poured Angela more tea. 'Tell you what. You want to give Cherry a bit of a pick-me-up, why not bring him down to Cambridge? We could have a look over Caius and go on the river. You know, bite to eat and all that. What do you say?'

'I say,' said Angela, 'you're an old fox but a dear old fox for all that. Cherry would love to go to Caius and see Bill's old college again. But don't think that I have given up on my questions. I know there's something else and sometime I'm going to find out what because it's the key to unlock this mystery and make Cherry better.'

Deb laughed, pleased that the conversation had shifted. 'You're irrepressible,' he said. 'Cambridge it is.'

Angela was right. Cherry liked the idea of a visit to 'the other place,' as he called Cambridge. The appeal was of something old and familiar, with echoes of a deep past, combined with a lacing of the most recent. He knew Cambridge from motoring trips over from Lamer to see Deb at the Scott Polar Research Institute, not that he wanted to visit the institute now. It was too full of memories, too close to what had happened and too associated with his years at Lamer for comfort.

Deb met them at the station and they took a taxi to the University Arms Hotel. The undergraduates were back in force, the roads full of young men, sometimes two or three abreast, laughing and chattering on their bicycles. They wore coloured scarves over jackets to proclaim their different colleges. Some of the cyclists were young women, wearing skirts and pedalling carefully on bikes with no cross bars. Cherry noted that the percentage of young women had increased since his university days. There was something about them that exuded confidence. He remembered that last ball at the House, 'What do you think about votes for women?' Elspeth had asked all those years ago and he remembered that he had never replied.

'I always wonder where they are all rushing to,' said Angela, buoyed by the sight of optimistic youth.

'You can tell that by the way they're pedalling,' said Deb, 'if they're pedalling slow they are going to lectures, if they're pedalling fast they're off on a spree.'

Cherry allowed himself a smile. He liked the feeling too, the surge of young life, the easy camaraderie of the young people swinging dominantly down the narrow roads, the brief joy of young worlds.

Lunch was a cheerful affair. Angela allowed herself a dry sherry and a glass of white wine with her meal. Deb ate and drank plentifully and even Cherry warmed to the occasion taking a gin and tonic before lunch and two glasses of red with his beef.

'Do you remember those midwinter feasts we used to have down south?' said Deb, 'roast penguin and seal livers and all that port!'

'Oh, how disgusting,' said Angela.

'I remember the after dinner entertainments,' said Cherry, entering into the mood of it all, 'and Old Titus performing, or trying to perform some kind of Cossack dance along with young Dimitri. I can see him, his eyes rolling, flinging himself around the place. It was more whirling-dervish than Cossack.'

'Not that we cared one jot about the difference,' said Deb, 'I remember those crazy wardroom games we played after dinner, at least I think I can.'

'It was a wonder nobody broke their neck, we were so young and daft and oiled with wine, we thought we were indestructible.'

'Really,' snorted Angela who was revelling in this conversation, 'I don't think you men grow out of being boys.'

'Maybe we do all too soon,' said Deb. Cherry nodded.

After lunch they went for a stroll through the colleges and down the Backs. Deb acted as their guide and instructor and showed a remarkable knowledge of each of the colleges. They admired King's Chapel. Angela was quite delighted with it all and Cherry seemed to be enjoying himself. They entered Caius through the Gate of Honour and Deb had arranged with the occupant to show them Bill's old rooms high above the Gate of Virtue. Carved in the stone below the mantelshelf the inscription read:

*EDWARD ADRIAN WILSON WHO REACHED THE SOUTH POLE WITH CAPTAIN SCOTT IN 1912 LIVED IN THESE ROOMS FROM 1892*

*TO 1895*

'He loved this place,' said Cherry, almost as if to himself, 'he used to reminisce about rowing, playing rugby, and some of the larks they got up to. The story goes that he used to slip 'Gates' in the early mornings to fish on the river. Once he caught a particularly good trout and gave it to the kitchen staff to cook for the Master's dinner. He said that the old man was quite livid about it but ate the fish all the same.'

'Why on earth would the Master be cross?' asked Angela.

'Bill was out of College at three in the morning, so the Master sent him down for a week.'

The two men laughed but Angela couldn't see why the anecdote was amusing.

'It's almost as though we can feel his presence here,' said Cherry, 'he could be one of the undergraduates we see in the courts below, so full of confidence and life and optimism, so alive.'

'Shall we see the sledging flag?' Angela asked of Deb, 'the one the Master's wife made for him to take to the Pole?'

Cherry followed Deb and Angela across the open courts. He saw the men going to and fro with purpose, doing all the old familiar things, chatting, planning, laughing, and eternally young. He saw a cluster of undergraduates looking at the notice boards. He remembered the last days in Oxford when he had seen his name with a third marked against it and the pain it gave him. He remembered flinging the swallow out of the window and watching it catch flight. How little it all mattered now. Colleges regenerated, men grew old and died but the ancient walls recycled the optimism and the restless joy of eternal youth. The undergraduates laughed, loved, worried, and dreamed for three glorious years together and then passed through the gates and out to the uncertainty of life. What would they face? Not the Antarctic - other challenges and other wars loomed to rip away youth from the man.

They crossed the courtyard and went up a short flight of steps to the hall. Cherry felt the presence of Bill strongly in the panelled room and imagined him at the freshman's dinner. Deb went up on the dais of high table and pointed at a small curtained area. He drew back the curtain to reveal a case, inside the case was a light blue pennant bearing the college crest.

'We normally only draw back the curtains for special occasions, dinners and the like. What do you think?'

They stared at the intense blue cloth with the carefully worked insignia. Cherry remembered finding it and the blue put him in mind of a Dunnock's egg

'He asked me to take it on to the Pole in the event of my being selected and him being unfit. Can you credit that?' said Cherry.

'But it did go the Pole,' remarked Deb.

'It was also there in the tent with their frozen bodies.' Cherry saw them again, lying in their bags in the tent. He was searching Bill's body and found that tatty old book of Saltmarshe's. 'I wish it had been the other way round and I hadn't been the one chosen to live,' he said.

Angela took his arm. 'That's enough of that. It's time for tea,' she whispered.

There were tears on his cheeks as they hurried back through the courts.

Deb was very sweet and never made any reference to those tears. Yet it was shocking to see how quickly and unexpectedly Cherry's mood could swing back to the dark side. Angela brought him home exhausted to Dorset House. He was so weak that she had to help him undress and get into bed.

'Thank you for all you have done for me. I don't know what I would have done without you,' he said.

'Stuff and nonsense, you would have done very well.'

'No, you pulled me out of a chasm and have made the last twenty years bearable and at times very happy. You have made it all possible and I owe you everything.'

He fell asleep holding her hand.

# CHAPTER SIXTEEN

## *ANTARCTIC LETTER TEN*

*The Hut Cape Evans, October 1, 1912*

*Dear Ida*
*Aitch has had a good look at me and conducted a thorough medical. He declares me fit for active service. I am to go on the search journey after all. Not so the news for Deb. Aitch is not satisfied that his knee is mended, the poor old chap will have to stay at Cape Evans and continue his scientific work. He takes it well. He is a real gentleman to help me all this time and yet not go out himself._*

*October 11*
*Aitch, Dimitri and I are to run two sledges to Hut Point. Let's hope I can justify Aitch's confidence.*

*October 14*
*Hut Point again but now with Aitch and Dimitri. Silas and the mules will follow on and join us. In the meantime we are to run out some depots.*

*The light grows better and Hut Point is no longer so desperate a place. I enjoy watching the seals. They are birthing and calling to their young. It strikes me as a strange contradiction that their lives regenerate in a frozen world.*

*October 29*
*Silas and the mules have arrived. They will set off tomorrow for the Barrier. We will let them have a couple of days' head start before we follow up with the dogs.*

*November 3*
*We are at Corner Camp. There is a note from Silas. Mules are going well. All well.*

*November 5*
*Weather poor. We followed the mule tracks and have now caught up with them.*

*Bonfire night in England. No doubt there is one at The Grange tonight. I remember when the older boys built it and it seemed so high. It all seems a thousand years ago.*

*November 6*
*Twelve miles covered today. Erebus is beginning to look small but we saw an unusually big smoke from the crater all day. We footwallop on in soft snow.*

*November 8*
*Bluff Depot. We had to battle to get here. The surfaces are poor. Yesterday, Aitch thought he saw a tent. My heart stopped and I couldn't help but pray that it wasn't them. If they had come this far I could have saved them. False alarm.*

_November 10_

We are at One Ton Camp and there is no sign of them. I am full of foreboding. At one point I thought that I saw their tent but it was just my imagination.

I have found a note that I left for the Pole party. I have it in my hand. I think of when I wrote it and still had hope.

There are grim discoveries. The provisions we left are soaked in paraffin and ruined. Had they come this far they would have had to make do with little fuel and reduced rations. How could this happen? The seals are secure and yet the paraffin has leaked. What devil's hand is in this?

_11 to 12 miles south of One Ton, November 12_

We have found them! Oh God, we have found them. I cannot write about it in my diary as it is the property of the expedition, but a private letter will never be seen by anybody else. I shall write it down for you now because I can never speak it and I must tell you.

Silas saw the tent first and we thought it was no more than a cairn but, when I looked again, I knew it was them. We cleared away the snow and there it was. The tent had been so well pitched that it had survived an Antarctic winter. Aitch said, 'Shall you and I go in first, Cherry?' He meant it kindly, to give me a chance to face down the thing I most dreaded.

We scraped our way through the snow and when we came to the centre of the tent we saw three bodies, still in their bags. Scott lay in the centre, Bill on his left with his hand toward the door and Birdie on his right with his feet towards the door. My mind was numb with horror, almost blank, as though my feelings had frozen with their bodies. My eyes saw but my soul could not feel.

The faces were not their faces but pinched, blanched, lifeless masks. I knew who each one was but there was little enough in those masks to remember them by. I thought of insects which had been impaled and stored in a collection, or specimens preserved in some clear fluid. There was nothing to tell how they had died, whether in pain or not and what they had thought at the end. I think there was just a nothingness, a giving way to the inevitable and an acceptance of the end. The pain and suffering had all come before. In death there was just oblivion - the emptiness of a great, endless sheet of white. I knew Scott died last as his arm reached out to touch Bill. It seemed so right. Anyone would reach out to touch Bill in the last moments, because his great soul would lead them forward into the unknown and they would be comforted and stronger for it.

They have stuck to everything. There were geological specimens, dragged all this way along with all their kit. These dead stones must weigh nearly forty pounds and would have weighed down the sledge and made pulling on poor surfaces even harder. I felt such a rage *of pity when I saw those damned rocks, if they had not wasted time collecting them and man-hauling them all this way, surely to God they would have covered those eleven miles. No matter what else, those damned rocks killed them and all in the name of science.*

*Aitch suggested we moved Scott's arm so that we could prepare his body but when he tried it snapped off in his hands, like a rotten branch. It sounded, and felt, like a pistol shot into my head. I was there, with Father in the veldt, looking over the body of Saltmarshe. That terrible moment nearly broke my spirit but Aitch steadied me and asked if I was all right to carry on and I agreed. Aitch elected to check Scott's effects and I checked Bill's. In the wallet by Bill's side I found a sketch pad which opened with a picture of old Birdie leading his pony. There was the Caius sledging flag, folded inside a union jack. It seemed so blue. There was also: an old briar, tobacco and some letters, including one to Oriana. Then I had to check his body. It was as though I was watching myself, I saw myself checking his pockets, like an old nanny. I knew what I would find, something which was all too familiar me - that old book of Saltmarshe's, which I had leant to him. Bill must have trusted that I would return for them and he had kept the book to the very end to give back to me! I saw that book as a silent reprimand. The magnitude of my failings came to me. When Dimitri and I had been messing around at One Ton they were only just to our north, possibly within one good day's run for the dogs. If we had gone on, killing dogs for food, we could have found the three of them alive and waiting for us.*

*God forgive me for failing the men I loved the most.*

*Aitch has read to us from Scott's diary and we now know the truth. They made it to the Pole but were beaten by Amundsen. Evans went down first and then dear old Titus. Scott writes wonderfully: there are no recriminations, no blame. They played the game out to the bitter end. Scott's line in his last message to the public plays on my mind:*

*'Had we lived, I should have had a tale to tell of the hardihood, endurance, and courage of my companions which would have stirred the heart of every Englishman.'*

*The phrase, 'had we lived' haunts me. Had they lived they would have returned to those who loved them and to a grateful nation who would have prized the true qualities of the very best of men. They would have lived in peace and security and in a world made better by their noble endeavours. They would have been living proof of the value of an English gentleman, true inheritors of Father's world.*

*But they didn't live. They died and I live on. I must finish the journey without them, dragging with me the guilt of having failed the men I admired and loved best.*

*November 14*

*We have followed their route south to see if we can find Titus* where he left the tent and went to his death. We have found his bag. Inside the bag were the theodolite and his finnesko and socks. One of the finneskos was slit down the front as far as the leather beckets, evidently to get his swollen foot in. Strangely there is no trace of the man himself. His body can't simply have vanished but I must accept that it has. It strikes me that I am now the sole landowner in the party. I am the last survivor of an ancient breed of men. I hope his spirit is now out on the lake back in England that he loved so well.

We have built a cairn to mark the spot near which Titus walked out to his death and placed a cross on it. We record him as: 'A very gallant gentleman,' which is what he was - and always will be to me.

There is no point in looking for Evans's body. We would prefer not to have any more discoveries and will return tomorrow to the hut.

<u>November 25</u>

Campbell and his men have returned, safe and well. There is some comfort in this remarkable turn of events.

They are totally unrecognisable as the men we knew but it is them sure enough. Now they have food in plenty and rest and will begin to recover. Everybody is delighted to see them back, alive and well. I too am very pleased and relieved but there can be no compensation here for my personal guilt in abandoning my friends. In the long run no man can escape himself.

For all that we have recovered the northern party, we have failed as Archaens, and my part in this journey is ended. I am reminded of that old picture of Father's, which hangs in the hall at Lamer. Odysseus so confident, heroic, and pleased with himself at that point is about to lose all. All those men in the boat, who depend and look upon him as a hero, are doomed. They are doomed to death by Odysseus's failings and he will be left alone to travel on by himself. I will share the same fate as Odysseus, to wander alone in the world with an oar over my shoulder, a stranger to home and an outcast from the world of men. Finally, I will meet a fellow traveller in a new and strange land, a land which does not have the same values as we do. The traveller will mistake the burden I am carrying and think it no great burden. He will think it a thing of beauty. Tiresias, the prophet of the underworld, tells me, in Saltmarshe's old book, that after I have met the traveller death will take me gently and unite me with the things I love most.

'As for your own end, Death will come to you far away from the sea, a gentle Death. When he takes you, you will die peacefully of old age, surrounded by a prosperous people. This is the truth I have told you.'

We are to set a memorial to them at Cape Evans. There was some discussion about the words we should use but I was insistent that

*there could only be these words:*
  *'To strive, to seek, to find and not to yield.'*
  <u>*January 18, 1913*</u>
  *THE SHIP HAS RETURNED. Somebody called through a*
*megaphone on the bridge, 'Are you all well?'*
  *Will anything ever be all well ever again?*
  *I will post these last letters from the Cape, and then it is done. Let*
*nobody but yourself see these letters. Once read commit them to the*
*underworld. I will follow after to meet you at Lamer. As for that old*
*book of Saltmarshe's, I want no more of it and it too can go to the*
*underworld. Let them stay in the underworld until they are found by*
*the traveller.*
  *It seems a pity, but I do not think I can write more.*
  *Ever,*
  *Apsley*

## March 1959

'The Nobs have challenged us to battle,' said Tom in such a way as to suggest that there was more here than he liked.

'When would it be? How would it be? Where? Could they use bows and arrows?'asked various members of the gang, all at once.

Tom motioned them silent.

'They have challenged us for two Saturdays away, in Petridge Wood. We carry our own flag and the winner will be the army that takes the other's flag and carries it off to their base. Do we accept or not?'

There was no real debate on the ethics. War was their thing. Had they not prepared for it always? Of course they would accept and preparations should start immediately. Could there be any other response to such a challenge?

Their preparations for the great battle were meticulous: the building of an impregnable keep in Petridge Wood, the stock piling of clay balls for 'pugging' with hazel wands and the cutting of arrows. Their enemies were clever and their strength unknown but the gang had guile and cunning and they were prepared and ready.

It was a bleak March day, the fag-end of a cold winter, when the grim—faced warriors marched out under their flag, stepping with their forebears over the muddy fields of England. Their helmets clanked, wellingtons squelched and their equipment rattled and bounced against their bodies. They sang to keep their spirits up and in readiness for the battle ahead:

'It's a long way to Tip a Hairy: it's a long way to go.'

Over the great fence (don't forget to roll).

'Onward Christian So...o...o. oldiers,

Marchin' as to war.'

Onward into battle, they heard the nations sing, and they did sing until they tired of singing. They pushed on in a straight line through hedge and field, across the railway line and deep into foreign territory, the foreign lands of Salfords.

Battle had been called; battle must be joined.

They arrived later than planned - the Nobs were there before them. The meeting and parley had to be quicker than intended. The gang did not like what they found. The Nobs had the same number (that was fair) but several of the boys were older and had not been at Old John's and were established in the manly world of the secondary modern (that wasn't fair).

'Never said anything about them all having come from Old John's,' said Butcher with yellow-toothed cunning.

'Didn't have to, it's flippin' obvious,' said Tom.

What to do next? The challenge had been made, the place of battle agreed, the battle lines drawn and the two armies ready to join battle. The preparations for war had been made, the armies mobilised. There could be no going back with honour.

'We'll show them yet,' said Keith and Jack agreed. 'They'll never find our base and we'll outflank them.'

The gang gathered around Tom for final instructions. Jack, Ivan, Johnnie, Laurie and Pip would defend the base. Tom, Keith, Chris and Dick would form the raiding party to triumphantly carry off the Nobs' Flag.

'Count to one hundred and the battle starts,' said Tom.

They sped off to their respective positions.

One hundred.

The old, cold wood was silent.

The defenders spread themselves around their base. Each man fixed a pug to his hazel and waited. Silence aided concealment. To their left they heard noises and boys' voices and they knew that the raiding party had engaged the enemy.

A crackle of wood. Ivan launched his pug at the place where it came from and quickly reloaded.

'Hold your fire,' whispered Jack

It was too late. The sound gave them away and they heard the crunch of broken twigs. The Nobs charged in a rush, leaping through the undergrowth and yelling like banshees. The defenders gave voice back and launched their pugs which whizzed around the attackers but to little effect. Against all the conventions of such battle there was no circling and harmless posturing, just a focussed rush at the base. The defenders engaged the enemy in hand-to-hand fighting; some of the Nobs were brought down to be wrestled on the ground. But Butcher and another broke through, ransacked the base, grabbed the flag and sped away down the hill with the fluttering trophy.

The line was broken, the flag was taken and the day was lost.

A broken troupe trailed back to Sunflower Cottage. They had lost their flag, their cause and their self-belief. The sun would shine again but it would never shine so brightly.

Pip and Mum went to tea with Cherry. The emperor penguin was still in its glass case but other things had changed at Gloucester Place. The curtains were drawn and a sombre air hung over the place. Angela fussed about them, much as before, but she was upset about something,

'I'm afraid you'll find Mr Cherry not quite himself,' she said. 'This winter has been very difficult for him, and well he's gone down a bit. But he'll soon rally, just you wait and see. We just need spring to get going.'

'Of course, of course,' said Mum. 'Winter seems to go on and on when you're not feeling too perky.'

The ladies and Pip took tea in the sitting room. Then Angela took Pip to Cherry's bedroom.

'I'm sure that a little chat about fishing and birds and things are just what you two need,' she said.

Pip stared into the gloomy room. It was some time before he recognised that Cherry was in bed. Angela put on the side light so that he could see clearly. Cherry, looking thinner and older than before, was sitting up in bed. He wore a lumpy, patterned jacket and gave no indication that he was aware of Pip's presence. Pip noticed his hands which had become thin, the veins prominent with patches on the skin.

Angela plumped the pillows under Cherry's head and motioned Pip to sit on the chair by the bedside.

'There, I leave you two for a nice little chat,' she said.

Pip sat and Angela closed the door behind her. At last Cherry spoke, in a rather querulous voice, 'Don't suppose as you want a 'nice little chat' with some old relic.'

Pip had been told to chat nicely so he felt he ought to.

'Are you really very ill?' he said.

'Bad enough.'

Pip didn't feel awkward sitting in the gloom with the strange old man. Cherry spoke again but with a lighter tone.

'Remind me, what happened to the willow-wren's egg.'

'It's fine. It looks quite good really and you can't really see that it's broken at all, least ways not just by looking at it. If you were to take it out of its box and examine it you would see all right but not otherwise.'

'Then don't take it out of its box.'

There was further silence.

'We had a battle, my brothers and I,' said Pip, 'but we lost. The Nobs were too big for us and we didn't stand a chance.'

Cherry thought of Bevis and his battle and remembered how he had loved to read of Bevis's adventures in the General's book. He had a picture in his mind of Lamer and the summer's sun beating down on him. He was there on the bank, with his net and butterfly book and all was well.

'How did you lose?' he asked.

'Well, the rules were that we each had flag in our base and the winning army would be the one that took the others' flag back to their base.'

'Ah - perhaps all men's wars should be like that?'

'But they cheated. They had much older boys than us and they charged our defences and took our flag.' Pip knew that he sounded peevish, but he couldn't help it.

'Beware of the cheat in our games,' said Cherry. 'They said that Amundsen won by cheating but in the end it was enough that he won. There are bigger issues than winning or losing.'

'Did you lose because you didn't have enough dogs?' Pip asked. He recalled the film vividly.

Cherry shifted on the bed. Pip saw the sick face of an old man - but the eyes were clear and strong as of a man who sees well.

'Everybody says that about the dogs,' said Cherry, but even if we had taken two hundred dogs Amundsen would have reached the Pole first. The Norwegians were specialists in dog handling. They were a crack team and they went south for one purpose only and that was to get to the Pole first. Our expedition had several objectives and only one of them was to see if we could reach the Pole.'

'Did Amundsen's telegram really make a difference?'

'Yes, I'm afraid it did. It didn't cause us to jettison our scientific work but it inclined us to give too much emphasis to one element of our total plans. We didn't give up entirely on our wider plans but the Pole became our predominant interest. It felt like a challenge to our Britishness, our values and our world. But, if our world was truly better than the others, we should have been above all that. Bill saw it but I don't think that the rest of us did.'

'Do you think that Captain Scott might have turned back sooner if it had not been for the rivalry with the Norwegians?'

'Possibly.' said Cherry. 'There are so many 'maybes' in life. In the end we just did our best and ran the race as best we could.'

'The gang's very low about losing the battle and nobody knows what to do,' said Pip. 'Sometimes the others come round and we just sit in Sunflower Cottage. Nobody wants to do the old things now and Tom has gone to the grammar school and he plays rugby on a Saturday morning and everything has changed.'

'You must move on in your journey and find new challenges and opportunities.'

'I mind more than all the others. It's like the end of things. I still want to belong but there isn't anything to belong to.'

'You want your world back?' asked Cherry.

'I do. It seems sad that all must change when it had been so good. I miss them all and the good times and the adventures. Spring will come again and Sunflower Cottage will be there and Skellum too, but it will all be empty and dead.'

'This may seem strange to you,' said Cherry, 'but I know how you feel. Back there in the hut, during that last winter, we felt that we had lost something so dear that it could never be replaced. So much was lost that we felt that we couldn't go on. Even Deb, usually so strong, so sure, felt the same way. I felt as though the light had gone out in the Antarctic night.

All our fuel had run out and I could see nothing but blackness. I could call out to the others across the hut but the darkness would take my voice away. In the end, I would be left standing alone in the perpetual and utter darkness.'

Pip listened in absolute silence. If he had tried to speak nothing would have come out. Cherry seem to know that he was there because, after a while, he continued.

'There was a time when I believed that I could turn and fight. I would be like Ulysses, setting out for one last adventure, which would take him to the very ends of the earth. 'What use an idle life?' Tennyson asks us in the voice of Ulysses and the answer is 'none.' I have been too idle and now it's too late. Maybe the last adventure is now. You must travel on now Pip. Remember - always look into the light and maybe you will find more than you are looking for.'

Pip was aware that he and Cherry were no longer alone. Angela had come in quietly and was listening. Pip wondered if she was crying and her presence roused Cherry.

'I'm sorry,' Cherry muttered. It was unclear as to whom the apology was directed. 'I've been a rotten host. Pip, I want you to have something to take home that I am sure you will treasure.'

Angela gave up all pretence of not being in the room. She stepped forward and bustled over Cherry. Cherry said something and she fetched down a neat wooden box with a hinged lid.

'Go on, open it,' said Cherry.

Pip lifted the lid carefully and there to his astonishment were several large eggs, each with a perfect, circular hole in its side.

'You will find there one each of Adelaide penguin and skua eggs,' said Cherry. 'But what do you think of the one on the end?'

Pip's eyes feasted on the treasure but when he looked at the end specimen it was little more than a fragment of shell.

'Gosh, it's an emperor! It's beautiful.'

'It was left in my mitten after I took it from the emperor colony. You recall how I fell and it smashed. It's just a broken shell but there is still some magic there. I've kept it all this time and you'll be pleased to note that I took your advice and have set it as best I can in cotton wool.'

'It's very kind of you, thank you very much,' said Pip. 'Won't you miss them if you give them to me?'

'No, I take pleasure from your pleasure. I don't need to remember now because I can forget, but you must keep them, my boy. Take them with you on your journey. It will please me to know that you treasure them. Your journey is just starting and I'm sure that it will be a remarkable adventure.'

Pip didn't make any sense of Cherry's final remarks but he did indeed treasure the eggs. He had only to lift the lid of the box and there were the best eggs in the world. The best of them all was no more than a fragment and yet the fragment of shell held a world of promise.

Mr Cherry would become 'too ill' to see him again and he and Angela would go back into their private world. They were lost to Pip: a few strange memories trapped in a drawer of the specimen case of childhood, but to be viewed again through the glass of memory.

*It was during that terrible second winter, when every hour and every day seemed to be the same and the longing was part of the darkness that never seemed to go away, as though Cherry had been plunged into perpetual blankness and the world was intensely cold and bleak and all that really mattered was dead. Then they heard the dogs 'singing', a high-pitched, primeval cry from another world and Cherry's heart leaped for joy in anticipation of the one thing in all the world that would bring back the light of life. They were transfixed and staring at the door. Cherry stood by Debenham and Deb's face was ghastly white. 'My God!' muttered Deb. 'It's them.' There was dread in his voice as though he feared the arrival of the five missing men, who by now could be no more than emaciated and frozen spectres.*

*Cherry saw the door push open and Scott came through, knocking the ice from his body with his mittens and he looked straight into Cherry's eyes just as if he knew everything. Then came Bill, Bill who could never change no matter what and his blue eyes danced to see them all and he allowed himself a smile of recognition. Then finally Birdie came in, still wearing that ridiculous green hat and he just shook with laughter. Cherry couldn't move. He desperately wanted to rush forward and touch them to feel their life but he couldn't move. But the moment didn't go. It seemed to pause and hold on and hope began to swell and the thought came strongly, 'They had lived after all!'*

*He counted three, two were missing, but then the door burst wide open and the light came flooding through and there framed in the doorway were Titus and Taff Evans. Then Cherry felt the life and power come back into his body, as though the blood flowed again through frozen limbs and he rushed forward into the light.*

# AFTER DEATH (AD)

The gang's days were over. Tom was well established as a grammar-school boy and was not available to give a lead. Most of the gang had gone to the secondary modern in Earlswood and a barrier had fallen between the gang and its leader. Two other mainstays of the membership hastened the end by getting jobs: Ivan at the local pig farm, earning himself ten bob for his troubles, Keith with occasional seasonal work. Jack's world was changing too. Only Pip kept the myth alive. He hoarded the old shields and staves and treasured the store of old stories.

The cold held fast in Sunflower Cottage and there was nothing to do. Mum had plans to refurbish it and make it into guest quarters for the increasing number of people who came to stay. There was talk of painting it all up and she had already imported two more heavy iron bed frames in readiness for the impending transformation. Not that the guests would be expected to stay in it, in all but a very few cases it was far more likely that the brothers would be expelled from their rooms to make way for them.

One Saturday morning in early November, Pip was alone in Sunflower Cottage when he heard the familiar sound of a bicycle coming up the drive and the familiar, cheery figure of Keith dismounted to prop his bike, in its usual place, up against the wall of the cottage. His Saturday job had been cancelled so he had come up to see what was what.

'Hello Pipsqueak,' he muttered in his usual friendly way and flung himself into one of the remaining chairs that Mum had not as yet got round to jettisoning. 'What's on the go?'

'Oh this and that. I suppose we can't fish?'

Pip sat on the edge of a bed and swung his feet. He hoped that something could be found to do so that the opportunity wouldn't be lost.

'No, it's too cold,' Keith answered.

Jack had heard the sound of the bicycle and came in to the cottage to see what was going on. Now they were three and three was better that two, and a lot better than one and it was Saturday morning with nothing to be done till lunchtime and the gang had never officially stopped being the gang. All that was required was a plan. It was Keith who came up with one.

'Let's go to Lamer and get in the house and see what's what. The builders have left off and there's only the one security man and he's off most Saturdays so there'll be nobody to stop us. They say that the whole house and gardens are to be bulldozed any time now so this will be our last chance.'

It was typical of Keith to come up with something that was going too far and only Tom would have had the authority to rein him in. Jack was impressed by the audacity of it and Pip held his breath. He wanted more than anything to be with the gang and this was exciting. Jack muttered something about 'trespass'.

'Trespassers will be persecuted?' said Keith. 'Who's to know and who in the end cares? There's nothing to pinch and nobody to be troubled. We just go in, have a look round and get out.'

Jack knew that to refuse this plan would show a lack of pluck that was not commensurate with a leader.

'All right,' he said', 'let's go now without saying anything to anybody.'

What seemed easy and audacious in Sunflower Cottage did not feel the same when they approached Lamer. They decided not to march in boldly and went down their secret stream route. They waded down the stream and scrambled out by the old chapel. They were careful to keep a low profile and scurried from hedge to bush. The raid developed into a commando adventure of a heart-stopping nature. The three of them lay beneath an old laurel bush and stared across what had once been lawn to the back walls of the house. The last twenty yards required a dash but then there was going to be the problem of access to the house. All the windows were boarded up and to pull away the boarding would require time and tools and leave them fully visible.

Pip remembered the old coal chute which he had seen in what had been Hobbs's garden room. It had been used to feed the kitchen fire and therefore gave access to the kitchen. Were he to crawl down the chute he would be in the kitchen and might be able to open the kitchen door from the inside.

'Only do it if you're sure you can get through OK and back the same way, if necessary,' Keith whispered. 'Once inside, see if you can open up anything to let us in. If so, give us an owl-hoot to let us know where to come across. We'll give two owl hoots to let you know if anybody comes along.'

'In which case,' said Jack, 'we'll leg it back to Sunflower as fast as we can and don't stop for anybody or anything. Got it, Pip?'

Pip nodded.

'Ok, off you go.'

Running as low as possible and keeping cover, Pip made it to Hobbs's old room. It was quiet and empty. He looked up for the swallows but they were not there. All he could see were the empty nests of previous seasons. He studied the chute. The aperture was small but it was just possible that a nine year old boy, if he made himself small enough, could wriggle his way down it and into the house. His smallness, compared to the other boys, was a positive for once. The entrance to the chute was a small metal frame with a downward-sliding piece of metal that had become rusted and jammed open. The coal or coke had long gone. He pushed his head through and saw that there was about six feet of a metal chute and light beyond. His shoulders were a problem but he angled them sideways and pushed hard with his feet so that his whole body was squeezed through the opening. He rolled down the chute and out on to the stone floor of the kitchen.

Enough light filtered through the shuttered windows to see in the gloom. There was the old range, rusted and cold from lack of use. Pip inspected the windows but they were well above the reach of a small boy and nailed firmly shut. Light came from the back door so he followed the light to inspect it. There was a massive lock on the door but either the great key had been lost or it had proved too heavy to turn. The door had not been locked because the key's bolt hadn't been drawn across - although the door was perfectly secure from the outside, being bolted top and bottom. Using both hands and with a lot of wiggling, Pip slid the top bolt across. He did the same with the lower bolt. The door was stiff and didn't want to open, but he put his shoulder behind it.

Keith and Jack waited. They were debating whether or not to go over and see if Pip was all right when they saw the back door edge open. Pip's owl-hoot was not his best effort because his hands were trembling so much that he couldn't make the right sort of cup in his hands and the sound came out all airy and funny. It was unnecessary anyway, because Keith and Jack saw the door open and ran across the lawn to join him.

'Well done, Pipsqueak,' said Keith.

From the kitchen the boys worked quietly through the lower part of the house. The great living rooms, the dining room and the sitting room were all bare. They were enormous and the boys couldn't imagine anybody sitting there or ever feeling at home. They went from room to room in silence, not knowing what to do next. The great stairs led them past more blank walls to the second storey of the house. Here they felt more secure.

'We'll split up and thoroughly search each bedroom,' said Jack. 'They may have left something behind.'

Jack and Keith headed towards the main bedrooms and Pip was left to wander down a corridor towards a series of smaller rooms. The first room was bare and bereft of all signs of former occupancy but the second retained vestiges of life. The walls were a very light shade of pink and the room had something feminine about it even now. Pip saw something written on a wall in a child's hand writing. The writing was low down, just above the carpet, and it had been covered by something which had been removed and now left it visible. He went closer and a board creaked. The writing on the wall read:

*LADDIE AND LASSIE. THE UNDERWORLD*

He had a creaking floor board at home which he had learned to lift up so that it made a hiding place. It was where he kept he kept his special treasures: several bun pennies, some foreign coins in a little tartan bag, one of Dad's running medals and a lucky four-leaf clover in a snuff box. He tested the creaking board before him and found that it was loose. He took his penknife, slid the blade to the side of the board and prized it up. Below was dark with a faintly musty, mousey smell and he saw something white. He put his hand down and pulled out a big bundle of letters, tied together in a pink ribbon. There was something else tucked deeper in the hiding place. He pushed his hand in further and pulled out an old and worn book. On the front cover there were words in a strange script. It crept into his mind that they were Greek words.

Pip was wondering who had hidden the letters and the book when he heard men talking below. He stayed motionless and listened attentively. The men were talking normally which gave him heart. He stuffed the bundle of letters into one coat pocket and the book into the other, closed his knife and put it back in a trouser pocket then slid the board very quietly back into place. The voices below carried on talking. Pip was kneeling over the loose floorboard when Jack put his head round the door.

'Come on, Pip, let's leg it as fast as we can.' Keith stood behind him, they were ashen-faced.

Keith went ahead, moving quickly and silently. Jack followed carefully so that Pip could keep up. At the top of the stairs, they abandoned all pretence at silence and hurtled pell-mell downwards in spectacular bounds and leaps. There were two men in the hall. They saw the boys' wild descent but were too surprised to take any action.

'Oi!' shouted one of them.

The boys dashed past, back the way they came, out through the open kitchen door. If the men had gathered their wits and really wanted to they could have cut them off in the garden but they didn't try. The boys shot across the lawns, running like colts. They left the house and the old apple and mulberry trees behind them and raced down the white lane, heading for Hobbs's House and the White Bridge and the safety of Whitebushes. When they hit the White Bridge they knew that they had made it and Jack laughed and Keith let out a triumphal hoot. Pip was only a step or two behind the others. He ran easily and he could keep up. There was something else, something he didn't understand and never told anybody about because it was just a feeling. While he ran he sensed somebody running beside him. There were four of them, not three, who ran down the footpath and clattered over the White Bridge - and the fourth was a girl.

When he thought about it later, he supposed that the feeling came because of the letters in his pocket. It might also have been to do with the fact that they were running away from Lamer and old things, back into the modern world. There was something else strange. When they reached Sunflower Cottage the bundle of letters was wedged safely in his pocket but the old book was gone. He assumed that it had dropped out of his pocket and into the stream as they ran over the White Bridge. He didn't mind about losing the old book because it was old and tatty, but the two incidents, losing the book and imagining the girl, always intrigued him.

**The End**

## Acknowledgements

*This novel is a work of fiction. I trust that the facts surrounding Captain Scott's last expedition are essentially true but the interpretation of the characters of the members of the expedition is mine. All the characters in the 1950s section of the novel are fictitious.*

*I am grateful to The Scott Polar Research Institute for allowing me access to primary sources.*

*In writing this novel I have drawn from a number of secondary sources, which include the following:*

*Homer: The Odyssey, translated by E.V.Rieu, Penguin Classics, 2003*

*Apsley Cherry-Garrard, The Worst Journey in the World, Picador, 1994*

*Captain Scott's last Expedition, The personal Journals of Captain RF Scott, Universal – Tandem Publishing Co. Ltd, 1973*

*Edward Wilson, Diary of the Terra Nova Expedition to the Antarctic 1910-1912, Blandford Press, 1972*

*D.M. Wilson & D.B. Elder, Cheltenham in Antarctica: The Life of Edward Wilson, Stoate and Bishop Ltd, 2000*

*The Journal of Lt-Colonel John Scott, South African Military History Society, Vol 1 No 5*

*Frank Debenham, In The Antarctic: Stories of Scott's Last Expedition, The Erskine Press 1998*

*George Seaver, Edward Wilson of the Antarctic: Naturalist and Friend, John Murray, 1943*

*Sue Limb and Patrick Cordingley, Captain Oates: Soldier and Explorer, The Anchor Press Ltd, 1983*

*I am significantly indebted to Sara Wheeler for her excellent biography, Cherry: A Life of Apsley Cherry-Garrard, Jonathan Cape, 2001*

*D.M. Wilson and C.J. Wilson, Edward Wilson's Antarctic Notebook, Reardon Publishing, 2011 has inspired the back cover design of this book.*

*I am very grateful to Ann Daniels for the warmth of her encouragement and support. Bob Fowke and Steve Edwards of YouCaxton have offered advice and technical guidance and made the publication of the book a reality. I also want to acknowledge my gratitude to Charlotte, Mark, Pip and Edward for their enthusiastic encouragement. They have been strong allies throughout.*

*Christine has been wonderful throughout the long process of writing this novel and her help and support have been invaluable.*

*Richard Jopling*

Books are to be returned on or before
the last date below.

LIBREX-